I0562444

THE
SERPENT'S
SONG

by S. Robertson

CCB Publishing
British Columbia, Canada

The Serpent's Song

Copyright ©2015, 2019 by S. Robertson
ISBN-13   978-1-77143-232-0
First Edition, Revised

Library and Archives Canada Cataloguing in Publication
Robertson, S. (Sally), 1943-, author
The serpent's song / by Sally Robertson. -- First edition.
Issued in print and electronic formats.
ISBN 978-1-77143-232-0 (pbk.).--ISBN 978-1-77143-233-7 (pdf)
Additional cataloguing data available from Library and Archives Canada

Book cover designed by Megan Simpson, Victoria, British Columbia, Canada.
Megan Simpson may be contacted through her website: http://megansimpsondesigns.com

This work has been registered with the Canadian Intellectual Property Office:
Copyright Registration #1118714

Publisher: CCB Publishing
              British Columbia, Canada
              www.ccbpublishing.com

To Bill and Gregory

The most beautiful experience we can have is the mysterious. It is the fundamental emotion which stands at the cradle of true art and true science.

- Albert Einstein

PROLOGUE

The Hill of Tara, Ireland

At dawn, a group in yellow ponchos gathered on the Hill of Tara, each assuming a definite position in a drama which was about to unfold.

On cue, a woman stepped forward and placed her hand firmly on the Lia Fail standing stone. Looking around to be certain everyone was prepared, she proceeded with a forceful command to an unknown recipient; first in English and then in Irish Gaelic. Nothing happened.

A second command conjured up a menacing cloud out of a clear sky.

A third command brought forth lightning bolts from the cloud splitting the paving stones around the standing stone just inches from the woman's feet.

A fourth command brought drenching rain which dripped off the yellow raingear forming puddles around the participants' feet. The group stood motionless absorbing the onslaught. The hill was now engulfed in its own storm while the surrounding region was bathed in morning sunlight.

A fifth command stopped the rain and ushered in a warm breeze which encircled and dried the participants.

As the cloud evaporated a large metallic circle of a golden serpent with a cascading centre of flowing energy appeared hovering inches from the ground. Out of the circle stepped several tall individuals who were welcomed by the Hill of Tara participants.

A prophecy, shrouded in myth and legend, had finally been fulfilled. The Celtic Serpent Gate to another dimension, securely locked away by first century Druids, had reappeared at the command of a twenty-first century woman in possession of an ancient medallion.

Following a brief greeting, the new arrivals turned to accompany twelve of the Hill of Tara group back through the gate. Once the last ones entered, the gate evaporated. Without comment, the rest of the party retreated down the hill to board waiting buses.

Watching, a tall ghostly figure, silently reflected on the event, saying to himself, "The *'coming times'* has finally arrived, now the real work begins. That group of twelve will return in three months. What is three months after so many centuries? Their mission will awaken forgotten memories of the vibrational nature of this world and its connection to the soul of humanity. While we wait, I'll use the occasion to prepare my students for what lies ahead." Imergin, a Druid Seer, raised his hand to signal his students to gather at a distant oak tree. He watched as his seven gifted students, of different ages and rank, settled onto a well-worn, semi-circular bench. They were dressed identically except for their coloured sashes with the golden serpent emblem.

"Master, while we wait for their return, can we again discuss the medallion?" asked a senior student, anxious to understand their role in the evolving prophecy.

Imergin stood, as was his custom, to talk to his students saying, "Indeed, since our last discussion focused primarily on the time from the attack on our community by the Roman army in the first century and into the centuries thereafter, we shall now broaden our discussion. As you will recall, my sons, humanity goes through repeated cycles of learning and forgetting."

"True Master, but surely the technological advancement of this age is a positive sign?" asked an older student, pleased to be a witness to such change.

"Technology has certainly helped mankind, but in their rush they have lost sight of their true mission. For few know of the *Great Year* or its meaning," replied Imergin.

"But some must intuitively suspect there is more, after all, they are familiar with the cycles of days, months and years?" mused an older student. "Records must exist from ancient times."

"Yes, ancient cultures knew of the *Great Year*; the Egyptians used it to predict events long into the future."

"What about written records?" asked another student.

"There were plenty, information was chiseled onto statues, tombs, and buildings, and written into various types of documents, but, as I now see, many of these messages were destroyed by wars, misunderstood in translation or, relegated to mythology. It is no wonder today's scientists are frustrated in trying to explain ancient anomalies which keep turning up."

"So, how do they explain such anomalies?" asked an inquisitive student.

"Mankind, when faced with anything that does not comply with their current theories label such discoveries fakes, or dismiss them all together. The tragedy is that when the knowledge of the *Great Year* is forsaken, along with its cosmic connection, mankind becomes disoriented, lost in time and without hope."

"But surely, more intelligent minds would challenge such thinking?" argued an older student unwilling to believe the entire human race could reject such evidence.

"Perhaps, but those rare individuals keep such unorthodox opinions to themselves," replied Imergin. "But in fairness to humanity perhaps there is another point to consider. As humanity slipped into the Kali Yuga, the great world cultures disappeared, to be replaced by inferior ones. What humanity currently considers advanced, highly sophisticated ancient societies, are actually inferior examples of the true capabilities of their ancestors. This may be the greatest hurdle. The last time mankind was at an advanced stage of development, was at the time of the last descending Dwapara Yuga, from 3100 BCE to 700 BCE, which is out of the range of most of their historians."

"Was that when the medallion was created?" asked another student, anxious to get back to the medallion.

"Yes," replied Imergin, "The medallion is a piece of ancient Dwapara Yuga technology left on earth to survive the centuries for a time when mankind reached a level of enlightenment to comprehend such complexity."

"Wasn't that a bit risky?" came the skeptical reply of another student.

Imergin turned to look at one of his brightest students saying, "The ancient scientists knew that mankind's intelligence and consciousness changes as they move through the ages, decreasing in one twelve thousand year arc and ascending in another twelve thousand year arc. When humanity entered the ascending Dwapara Yuga around 1700 CE, there would be an increased number of receptive souls that might understand such technology. Today, as they emerge from three hundred years of transition from one Yuga to another, there are even more individuals."

"Master, I wonder if we might get back to the medallion?" asked the persistent student focused on the medallion. "Was the medallion created here in Ireland?"

Imergin smiled as he turned to respond, "As much as we'd like to claim ownership of this magnificent handiwork, we cannot. It was created in Egypt at the beginning of the descending Kali Yuga, by a group of priests advanced in the Sacred Science."

"Who possessed the medallion in Egypt, the Pharaoh?" asked another student.

"Because the medallion was so dangerous, it had to be controlled by a chosen High Priest, one in possession of a unique genetic makeup," replied Imergin.

"How did they determine who possessed such a genetic makeup?" came the immediate question from another student.

"Royal families, known for their strict marriage laws, kept meticulous records," was Imergin's reply.

Finding this incredulous, another student asked, "You mean every royal family member was a candidate for the medallion?"

"Not exactly," replied Imergin, "When strict marriage laws became linked to royalty, all the elite, and those anxious to become the elite, adopted a similar practice. But only a small group, referred to as the 'S*acred Gentry,*' really counted. They were always known to an inner circle."

"What would happen if the wrong person tried to wear the medallion?"

"The experience would be fatal. At first there would be a burning of the skin beneath the medallion which would be followed by an electrical shock programmed to kill the unqualified wearer."

"Then it is a miracle the medallion survived at all considering the wars and disasters over the centuries. Did the quality of ancient technology also deteriorate as the centuries passed?" asked a quiet student who had been mulling over the information.

Imergin noted the thoughtful question and replied, "In the early centuries I expect the wearer of the medallion was able to achieve amazing results, for legend has it that the medallion possesses layers of advanced technology. But as the Kali Yuga progressed the skills of the wearer would diminish. Now where was I in the medallion's journey?"

"We're still in Egypt," piped up a younger student totally absorbed in the story. "What happened next?"

"Ah yes," came Imergin's reply as he turned to the young student. "From Egypt, the medallion was passed on to Moses, and down the centuries through each chosen Israelite High Priest. In 585 BCE, Jeremiah, the prophet, at the time of the fall of Jerusalem to the Babylonians, brought the medallion to Ireland, where it was passed on through chosen Arch-Druids. The centuries passed with the medallion used openly by the Druids up until 60 CE, when the Roman army attacked the Celts in Britain with a directive to eliminate the Druids. At that time the gemstones in the medallion were removed and placed in the protective care of female Druids. For generations the gemstones were reinserted sparingly, because of the danger of such technology falling into the wrong hands. Finally, as I mentioned before, by the 1600s, when the situation in this part of the world grew untenable, the medallion and the gemstones were placed in the care of eight 'Sacred Gentry' couples, again mainly in the custody of women. Four of the couples were dispatched to America to wait the 'coming times,' which was prophesized to occur hundreds of years into the future. This is the capsulated version of the medallion's history. Are there any more questions?"

"But Master, the individual called Angi Talismann, who now wears the medallion, barely knows what to do with it. Without Sirona she might have found herself in serious trouble."

"True, but amazingly, she has sufficient genetic inheritance that the medallion did not kill her in the first place, and that alone is a miracle. I'm certain that Sirona and the others, who I know well, will be able to prepare Angi and the others for the challenges that lie ahead. But it will take time. In the meantime, we must wait and prepare for their return."

"I'm curious, Master, if we are spirits of a forgotten time, how long will we be permitted to stay on Earth?"

"A good question, my son," came Imergin's response, "Even I do not have the answer to that question. I only know that at specific points in the evolution of humanity certain spirits linger closer, to give guidance. We will know when it is time to leave."

As Imergin and his students continued their conversation, the players of a cosmic drama were assuming their places, some still unaware of the responsibilities and dangers which lay ahead.

Chapter 1

House of Learning, Angi's Suite

Dreaming, Angi found herself in a pitch black room determined to reach a dimly-lit dais in the distance. Stepping forward, a menacing presence with flaming eyes landed on her chest suffocating her and causing her to fall helplessly backwards into an open pit.

Bolting upright in bed, her reality stabilized as she recognized her surroundings. With sleep impossible, she threw off the bed cover and reached for the manual clock she had wisely tucked into her travel bag. "Three a.m........everyone is asleep .... I pray that wasn't a harbinger of what lies ahead. I'm not sure I'd like a rebroadcast. Perhaps some fresh air will clear my head," she thought to herself.

In her twenty-sixth year, Angela Talismann, whose friends called her Angi, had her life abruptly changed from an established health career in the western world, to a cosmic traveller. Much to her consternation, she was now in possession of an ancient medallion, possibly advanced technology from an unknown source, which presented not only a danger to her own life but had already attracted ruthless admirers. While stepping into another dimension may have appeared foolhardy, it seemed to present the only option for her to gain control of this magical device.

Born in New York, Angi had spent most of her life living with her maternal grandmother on Prince Edward Island, Canada's smallest province situated on the Atlantic coast. This was the world she knew and loved even though her studies had temporarily taken her into an adjacent province. When asked, she always referred to herself as an "Islander," it never occurred to her to say she was an American. But even these designations were slipping away as she tried to imagine what an entirely different world would mean to her life.

The coolness of the marble floor was comforting as she walked barefoot towards the balcony. Angi's graceful, coordinated cat-like strides had been groomed through childhood dancing classes and running competitions. She prided herself at being able to cover great distances faster than others.

"Why can't I have pleasant dreams like normal people?" she thought. "Maybe it is the medallion. I'd hate to think my subconscious is rebelling at my stupidity in stepping into another dimension for which I have no certainty of survival. That, of course, begs the question. What are we doing here? Why did twelve of us step through a gate into an unknown world? Were we all possessed? I could hardly fault someone thinking I must have lost my sanity. Whatever, I'm here now, best make the best of it."

Exiting her suite, she felt the tingle of the energy beam. "No doors or windows here. Air flows through these energy beams which block any unwanted guests, and, we've been told, make adjustments for climate change. Not sure how this works but what an invention. The climate seems Mediterranean. No rain so far. Good thing we brought manual calendars, our electronic devices need recalibration according to Sirona. It is likely the power source."

Angi liked her sparsely furnished spacious suite, especially the balcony with its large plants providing privacy and an intoxicating variety of subtle floral scents. "I'm no botanist, but I'm sure these plants do not exist on Earth," she thought as she examined the small white blossoms in one pot and clusters of yellow ones in another. Standing near the railing, she admired the reflection of two moons on a distant body of water. "Now that's a photo." But a photo would have to wait until their communication devices had been returned. Finding a comfortable bench, Angi sat down.

Thinking out loud she observed, "You know, except for the dual moons, one larger than the other, this could be anywhere in Italy or Greece. So far, from what we've seen, this world seems to have a blending of ancient and advanced architectural structures, a fascinating combination. But then again, we've been confined to this hill, a larger community exists in the distance near the water."

Turning to more practical issues she went on, "I expect travelers are much alike, their first priorities are the basics. I thought that thin amethyst mattress and pillow would be impossible for sleep, but, except for tonight, I've been impressed. The washroom took some adjusting. The shower is like stepping into a forest mist which cleans, dries and oils the skin in a matter of minutes. Vette and I are still trying to figure out how to manage our hair, the men have it easy. I think I will ask Sirona if I can try out their clothing while I'm here. Apparently, the fabric sensors adjust to environmental shifts, and the material can be easily cleaned in that device outside the shower. Might as well do some practical research while I'm here."

Angi was not your typical adventurer. She possessed a quiet personality, usually preferring time to assess people and situations before getting too involved. While this hesitancy persisted, rapidly changing circumstances were forcing her to react faster which increased her anxiety. She originally saw herself spending her entire life in the Maritimes of Canada close to her grandmother, but destiny had altered that scenario.

An hour passed as she slipped into meditation to shed the negative effects of her dream. "Maybe now I can get more shut-eye," she thought as she rose to leave. At that moment she was startled to hear a woman's voice.

"Well, Angi Talismann, how are you enjoying your new home?"

Angi looked around the balcony but could see no one. "Where are you?" she asked. "How did you get to the third floor of such a well-protected building?" Guarded, she thought, "Should I yell out for Vette in the next suite?" The calming voice of her intruder made her hesitate.

"Oh, I'm skilled at getting into strange places. I just wanted to chat with the wearer of this fascinating medallion."

"It sounds like a mature voice," thought Angi, "one unfamiliar with English." She moved about slowly, making her way to the suite entrance. There, to her amazement, sat her intruder, securely positioned on a low branch of a large potted tree. "I must be hallucinating," she said with a chuckle, "And you, my charming guest, must be lost." Before her sat a Snowy Owl, the cat-like eyes burrowing a hole into her psyche. What little she remembered seemed to fit. Her intruder, one of the largest owl species in North America, had yellow eyes, a black beak, a smooth rounded head and no ear tufts. Even in the moonlight, she could discern the feathers were mostly white with speckled brown markings.

"No, I'm not lost," came the gentle response, "I chose this disguise as one from your world to make you feel at home. What do you think?"

Angi could almost sense a smile behind the question, and replied, "Your thoughtfulness is indeed appreciated even though Snowy Owls exist much further north in Canada from where I grew up." Silence fell as she tried to comprehend the situation. Then she asked, "Does this mean you are a shape-shifter?" The thought popping into her head from a once read article.

The respondent hesitated as if trying to translate the word 'shape-shifter.'

Before she answered, Angi continued, "I read once that certain aboriginal shaman had the ability to change themselves into birds or animals. Is that what you are doing?"

"Oh, I see," came the reply, suddenly understanding the question, "Maybe that is the closest we will get to a description. For now, can you and I live with this arrangement while we get acquainted?"

"I guess so," replied Angi, "Weirdness has seeped into every facet of my life of late; holographic people, ghosts, and teleporting items I never thought possible. Why not add a talking Snowy Owl to the list. So, what can I do for you?" Whirling through her mind she tried to remember what little she had read about owls. Angi thought to herself, "Celtic tradition regarded the owl as a symbol of divinity and a messenger of the gods. They also thought birds represented freedom and transcendence; the human soul in flight. Other societies thought the owl a symbol of Mother Earth, a harbinger of wisdom and a protector. Similarly, Native Americans associated the owl with wisdom, foresight and a keeper of sacred knowledge. So, what does my special guest represent? Is she a messenger of the gods? What gods? Fascinating.......... For now I will count my blessings and see what transpires. This journey continues to offer an unending array of mysteries."

"Well, Angi, tell me briefly how you came into the possession of this wondrous medallion?" came the clear directive.

Angi, glad for the diversion and not wanting to analyze the situation further, began, "Briefly........well that may be difficult, but here goes. I can hardly believe it is just months since my life went into a tailspin. In my world, I had progressed in my profession to being a director of an emergency department of a large teaching hospital in a capital city of an eastern province in my country, Canada."

"Were you a healer or what your culture calls a physician?" asked her guest.

"A healer, yes, but not a physician. I studied to be a nurse, a role I preferred. My simplest explanation is that in our health system physicians diagnose and prescribe while nurses manage the care. It took four years at university to get my nursing degree." Angi waited, but when no questions appeared, she proceeded, "I had just been appointed to my position when I was diagnosed with a fatal disease and within days my grandmother was attacked by an international thief trying to steal a family heirloom. While she survived the attack it was too much for her weakened heart and she died." Remembering her grandmother, her voice faltered as she thought, "I've had little time to properly mourn my grandmother's death and that's not right. I must make time while I'm here."

A sympathetic response filled the temporary gap, "You must have loved your grandmother a great deal. I'm sorry for your loss. Where were your parents?"

"My father and mother were divorced in New York, United States, when I was a little girl and my mother and I returned to her home in Prince Edward Island, Canada. A few years later my mother died of an allergic reaction to a medication. I was brought up by my maternal grandmother." Angi could almost sense the recipient calibrating the geographical distance on an invisible map.

"How did the medallion come into your life?"

"The medallion, or family heirloom, had been in our family for generations, mainly in the care of women. I was negligent in knowing its history or value because I did not pay enough attention to my grandmother when she tried to instruct me on its importance. All I knew was that this was a revered family secret. To me it looked like an old piece of jewelry with missing gemstones. However, after my grandmother's death, and uncertain over my own future, I thought it prudent to share this well-kept family secret with a few trusted people as the responsibility for the secret had now fallen to me. At that point, the medallion was practically sidelined due to the mounting concerns over my safety when the international thief who attacked my grandmother was subsequently murdered while being incarcerated in the local jail. Friends insisted that I should have a bodyguard. This brought Vette Gallant, an off-duty police officer, into my life, and we have been together ever since."

"Vette is the young woman in the adjacent suite," came the quick reply.

Angi, searching for every clue, thought, "Why do I feel she already knows the layout of this place and details of our group. Play along, maybe I will learn more," and replied, "Yes," and proceeded. "My Grandmother's death blocked my normal response to the unfolding danger. But the death of the thief indicated others might be involved who knew far more about the medallion."

"What happened next?"

"After my grandmother's funeral, I decided to deliver the medallion to my grandmother's Boston contact, one of two women she corresponded with every Christmas. Vette and I travelled there where we met not only my grandmother's contact, but two other females; one from Australia and the other from New Zealand. There I learned that they, and myself, belonged to a group of specially chosen families from the 1600s committed to protecting this ancient treasure. Ironically, so much time had passed that much of the medallion's information existed in bits and pieces which, in some instances, made little sense. Yet, they were convinced that my grandmother's death marked the beginning of the '*coming times*,' a phrase which had little meaning to us. Anyway, I thought my role was simple; place the medallion into the hands of these women and return to my island to die."

"But that's not what happened?" came the reply of the stranger who was carefully following the story.

"No, events soon transpired that forced me onto another path. Oh, I forgot to mention. In Boston, I met Wolfram Stark, the grandson of my grandmother's American contact. While we were in Boston he took charge of matters, arranging our stay and keeping the killer at bay. He confirmed there was only one mastermind behind the attacks, and that this killer was closing in rapidly. But this gathering of four women was unique. For the first time since the 1600s, half of the medallion's gemstones were together in one place. Each family guarded one gemstone. So, Wolfram's grandfather invited a gemologist to authenticate the gemstones on the premise that if any were fake there was no reason to pursue the matter further. I was convinced that would be the outcome as so much could have happened in over three hundred years."

"What did the gemologist find?" The owl blinked her cat-like eyes and her feathers fluttered in the breeze.

"He confirmed the superb quality of the gemstones and added that in his opinion the gold workmanship and the selection of gemstones might have some connection to a legend of an ancient magical device from Atlantis or Egypt. Needless to say, most of us scoffed at this, but such doubts were soon challenged."

"Go on, what changed your mind?"

"Once the gemstones' quality had received a preliminary authentication, we faced the next problem. With no instructions, how were we to insert three gemstones into the open sockets of the medallion? Since I possessed the medallion itself, my gemstone had not been removed. Unsure, we laid the other three gemstones next to the medallion and waited. What happened next was the initiation into a magical world none of us could have envisioned. First the central blue stone came alive and, like some programmed computer, shot forth an arc of light, and one by one lifted each stone into the air and dropped it into its designated position. Yet, even with this miraculous display, I was still convinced that I would be heading home."

"But next came the question as to who should wear the medallion. When the other three women tried on the medallion they received a critical burning of the skin under the medallion. When it came my turn, it did not burn my skin, instead I collapsed onto the floor. In a faint I heard the voice of whom I would later identify as Sirona, someone from this world, who reassured me that everything was fine. When I came to, it was clear I not only was the one to wear the medallion but, from the bits and pieces of past information, taking it off before all gemstones were inserted could endanger my life. This was not an appealing proposition. I thought I might be permanently attached to this unstable piece of technology for the rest of my life. So, Vette, Wolfram and I headed to Ireland and Scotland to retrieve the remaining gemstones, a quest fraught with uncertainties. Eventually the stones were found thanks to Andrew Sinclair and Bryce Roberts whom we met in Scotland. As each gemstone was inserted Sirona's holographic image grew stronger and she was able to instruct me on how to handle the medallion's powers without inflicting harm on myself and others."

"What happened to the killer who was stalking you?"

"That had a bizarre twist. The predator was himself killed by another conniving individual who was arrested by the Scottish police. After that incident we were able to focus all our attention on getting to the Hill of Tara in Ireland and the Serpent's Gate. That's the story in a nutshell devoid of our emotional ups and downs in getting here. It has been an amazing, stressful few months."

"Ah yes. So that is the reason you are here? If so, why so many?"

"That's a good question," replied Angi, realizing others might ask the same question, and thinking out loud continued, "I expect we were all caught up in the initial quest and proceeded on that principle to see it to its conclusion. In the group of twelve there are actually two, maybe three, subgroups. There are myself, Vette, Wolfram, and Morgan Mandelthrope; I and Wolfram belong to the 'Sacred Families,' Vette became my friend and bodyguard and Morgan, a friend of Wolfram, is an archeologist/historian who knows a great deal about the Celtic world and was the one who initiated the research on one of the gemstones. Andrew and Bryce both belong to British gentry and have very important contacts in secret and not so secret societies. Without them, I'm sure we would not be here. The other six are under orders from Andrew to be our bodyguards while we're here. But then again, I expect you already knew most of this."

"You are very intuitive, Angi. Yes, I already knew most of it but felt this would be an easy starting point for us to begin our chats."

"Chats? So you expect there will be more. How many? What is the purpose of these chats? Will I ever meet you in person?" The questions bubbled forth as she scrambled for more information.

"Yes, there is a reason and, I expect, a few chats should suffice. In time we will meet in person, as you say," came the reply.

"By the way, what's your name?" asked Angi, realizing she needed to know who she was talking to.

"Yes, a name.............. I'm known as Adawee."

Angi repeated the name, "Adawee, that's a nice name." She sensed the name was somehow irrelevant and wondered, "Does she not need a name or is her real name too foreign for me to pronounce?"

Suddenly, Adawee shifted the conversation and said, "Angi, a word of caution. As you were careful in your world with the medallion, follow the same pattern here. Not everyone is pleased that you have this technology. Sirona and others will help you become more proficient in its use. You have many wonders ahead."

Angi sensed Adawee wanted to say more but hesitated. "Thanks for the warning, I will not let my guard down." Then with a smile she continued, "Wait till I tell my friends I've been talking to a Snowy Owl."

"Oh, I wonder if you might hold off telling them for now. I need some uninterrupted time with you. Can you do that?"

"Fine," came Angi's hesitant reply, "But I hate keeping secrets from my friends." At that moment the morning sun peeped over the horizon and Angi stared at her visitor. "Well, you've added another dimension to the Snowy Owl, your white feathers have a rainbow tint. It is beautiful!"

Not responding to her comment, Adawee said, "Is that your friend Vette on the other balcony?"

Angi turned thinking Vette, hearing voices, had come out onto her balcony to investigate. But Vette was not there. When she looked back Adawee had disappeared. "Now that's odd," she thought, "No flapping wings, not a sound. What do I really know about my Snowy Owl? Practically nothing except she's definitely mysterious. But why the disguise? Even if I wanted to tell my friends, I've little to report. If I told them I was talking to a Snowy Owl they would question my sanity. Silence for now. No time to think........Look at the time. I will need to scurry to get to breakfast." She raced into her suite unaware of the significance of the messages which had just been delivered in diverse ways.

The House of Learning, Dining Area

An inner patio near their sleeping quarters served as a dining room. As Angi arrived, she could hear students assembling in the lower courtyard for their morning calisthenics. Sunlight caressed the tip of the tiled roof, and tiny yellow birds flitted in and out joyously heralding a new day.

Greeting her colleagues, she proceeded to make selections from a buffet of fruits, vegetables, and other tantalizing delicacies. Aed, a tall, English speaking attendant, dressed in blue, provided assistance and answered questions. But after a couple of days the team had adapted to their unfamiliar diet, with few gastric complications.

The simple seating plan in their dining area consisted of two tables of six. Initially their bodyguards chose to sit together, but the team had already decided a more democratic arrangement would be introduced.

"Running late this morning are we?" asked Wolfram with a grin as Angi sat down. "Still wrestling with the shower system?" He knew the women in the group were grumbling about what to do about their hair. "I rather like your platinum curls."

Wolfram Stark was the child of the lost generation which became ensnared in the music industry's drug scene. His father died of a drug overdose somewhere in California and his mother spent her life in and out of drug addiction clinics. He grew up in Boston with his maternal grandparents who were in the lucrative antique business. Perhaps as a need to understand his parent's destroyed lives or to strike out on his own, he opted for a police career over the wishes of his grandparents. Restless, he soon branched out and began studying part-time for his law degree with a specialty in antique fraud. The week he graduated from law school, and in his last days as a police officer, he had a devastating car accident which left him disabled with a shattered left leg, and a white streak through his black hair, a lasting symbol of the ordeal. His entrance into the medallion quest was initiated when he asked his friend Morgan to look into a 1600s secret with roots in Scotland or Ireland connected to his family. His involvement increased when he discovered a killer was not only after his grandparents, but also anyone with a gemstone of this mysterious medallion. Having resigned himself to a life as a disabled, he was ecstatic when Angi healed him with the aid of her medallion. Rejuvenated, Wolfram became more outgoing with the occasional jovial comment to members of the team. His new found friends had restored his life and their quest had focused his energies.

Angi took his jibe in stride as she liked Wolfram's calm, in-charge manner. Smiling, she responded, "I suppose change is as good as a rest. We will either find a solution or settle on this new hairstyle. Actually, overall I rather like our hotel arrangements, my skin has never been so healthy. How about you, Vette?" her question directed at her friend sitting across the table.

Vette Gallant was born on Prince Edward Island into an Acadian family in Canada. The opposite of Angi, she was slightly built, with dark hair, piercing brown eyes and an extrovert personality. Her first career choice was the theatre until her only brother, the youngest of her three siblings, was killed while on duty as an RCMP officer. Devastated, she decided to honour the family tradition and enlisted herself, much to the disapproval of her father, a senior member of the police force. Trying to prove herself, she not only excelled in the training program but upon graduation volunteered to work undercover in the Atlantic coast drug enforcement squad. Recovering from a gunshot wound brought her into a temporary assignment with Angi. Enchanted by the medallion adventure, she took a leave of absence from the police force to accompany the group on their quest.

Nodding her head, Vette responded, "I agree. Whatever is in the mist it certainly has helped me. It is like stepping into a spa. I had no idea what to expect. So far, this seems to be working out quite well. By the way, Andrew, what have you learned about Tir na nOg?"

Being a descendant of an illustrious Scottish family, Andrew Sinclair in his late middle age had accumulated an impressive array of credentials as a competent statesman and businessman, at times being appointed to senior military and international positions for his country. He was comfortable commanding forces to achieve a mission especially in the political uncertainties of a foreign country. Such family and outside activities had given him a global network of contacts and plenty of private resources. Yet, he was known to live a disciplined life with commitments in many organizations, secret and otherwise. Widowed with three grown children, he longed to have one final adventure to add to his accomplishments and bring honour to his family and country. The opportunity arrived with Angi and the medallion. Through one of his secret societies he was made aware of an old legend that somewhere in Scotland and/or Ireland an ancient piece of technology had been protected for generations. A faded sketch confirmed that Angi's medallion was that item. Through Andrew, the team fully resourced and protected, managed to acquire the last four gemstones. His quick acceptance of a magical medallion and another dimension showed the adaptability of the man, the option of entering another dimension only whetting his appetite for adventure. Putting his affairs in order, he willingly stepped through the Gate of Tara, with the hope that this mission might give him continued purpose in life. Being the only Gaelic speaking member of the team, he was busy quizzing anyone who ventured into their quarters. Being older, the young students gave him respect and tried to answer his questions.

Responding to Vette, he said, "Not much. As you can see, we have been relegated to this educational centre on a hilltop above a city down near the shore. I expect they are holding us here until they are certain we will not contaminate their environment. After all, we could be harbouring some unwanted germs. This likely explains Sirona's frequent scanning of us since our arrival."

"I hope you are right," came Dylan's frustrated response from the other table. Dylan Gabriel, as head of the bodyguards was restive at being restrained, and openly questioned the length of their confinement. "We're losing valuable time just sitting around. Surely with their technology any major issue could have been resolved by now."

"Maybe so, Dylan, but let's not forget the devastation to the American Indians when the Europeans arrived. Millions died from diseases for which they had little resistance," came Morgan's thoughtful response.

Wolfram's red-haired friend, Morgan Mandelthrope, was an eccentric academic professor of Celtic studies at Boston University. His tussled red hair and previous matching beard gave him the unofficial distinction of being Boston's own leprechaun. Morgan's stultified academic life was torn apart when he agreed to investigate for Wolfram a lost secret of a seventeenth century medallion. To his horror, his inquiry led to the death of two people; his academic colleague in Ireland and Angi's grandmother in Canada. Morgan was terrified when the killer turned on him in his determination to get to the medallion. Naïve, and seeking an escape, Morgan's wife, Kari-Ann, not only became the killer's pawn to ensnare Morgan but lost her own life in the process. Morgan, struggling over the episode, shaved off his beard, joined the world of the 'ordinary' and took off to Scotland to accompany his friend in search of the medallion's gemstones. His love and fascination with all things Celtic proved a healthy diversion in his recovery. His entrance into what appeared to be the lost world of the Tuatha de Danann, the ancient Irish gods, not only captivated his academic interest but fueled his imagination.

Realizing the dangers of even minor diseases to a community with little resistance, Angi interjected, "I'm sure Sirona has her reasons. We can wait. But I'd love to know more about that flashing device she and the others use. Andrew, this highlights an important point. What do we have in place to prevent us returning to Earth with unwanted organisms?"

"Angi, once we make contact with our home team, I will get something set up," replied Andrew. "While I am aware our time is limited, it is best we walk gently at this point. So, for now, let's review what little we know." Bringing the whole group into the conversation he continued, "As you may or may not know, this area is the royal centre of their kingdom. The region has four cities: Gorias, Falias, Findias and Murias. We are in Murias. Morgan, can you recall anything about these four cities in your Celtic studies, especially Murias?"

"Vaguely. Let's see, isn't Murias supposed to have a cauldron with an endless supply of food and abundance? This magical cauldron was also supposed to be able to revive wounded warriors on the battlefield. It is associated with water, cleansing, healing, rebirth and resurrection. Whatever that means is hard to say. Sometimes legends get a bit scrambled over centuries. We will see."

"Thanks, Morgan," replied Andrew, "It is a start." He continued, "This building is called 'The House of Learning' or 'Teach na Foghlama' in Gaelic. As you will recall, when we arrived, to get to this building, we walked across a stone plaza from 'The House of Life' or 'Teach na Beatha,' the centre housing the intergalactic gate."

Excited, Morgan interjected, "Do you know that certain temples in the early centuries of Egypt were referred to as a House of Life? The temples were usually near a sacred enclosure and served as a place for the learning of medicine, astronomy, magic and alchemy. Some were famous for their libraries. Imagine having the chance to be in one that is still active."

"Interesting, Morgan, could we explore this later?"

Unperturbed, Morgan replied, "Sure, I am certain we will have much to chat about in the days ahead."

"From my brief observation, this House of Learning is a huge structure with many students. It has both resident and training facilities for the education of specially chosen members of their kingdom; male and female. I've asked about the colour coding in their uniforms. Similar to the Druids they use three basic colours: green, blue and white. Those in striped uniforms of blue, green and white are novices. If they follow the same pattern, then Green is the lowest rank. It is the colour of learning. The Druids called these the Ovate or Avydd, who were expected to know something about medicine, astronomy, poetry and music. The next highest Druidic rank wore sky-blue which represented harmony and truth. These were the Bards or Beirdd, who were expected to memorize thousands of verses of Druidic sacred poetry. They were sometimes depicted with an Irish harp and were said to be mentors for those entering the Druidic Mysteries. The top rank wore white, the Druids or Derwyddon, which was symbolic of purity and the colour for the sun. These individuals administered to the spiritual needs of the people and the training of their youth. While this information may help, there is no guarantee the two worlds are identical."

"The students go through a rigorous program taking years to reach even the lowest level. That flat-topped pyramid between these buildings is their testing centre. When students reach a certain point in their training, they go through a very stringent fasting and examination process. As best as I can understand, this testing consists of a series of computerized holographic programs, the tests graded in severity for each rank. Have you noticed, there are few students in this area in the higher ranks? Likely more advanced students are relegated to other sectors of the building. As I recall, Druidic testing could be so severe that some candidates died in the process."

"That's true," came Morgan's immediate reply. "But such extreme testing also occurred in some of the old mystery schools of Greece and Rome and in aboriginal societies on Earth. The *Spirit Quest* in North American Indian societies is said to tax the physical, mental and spiritual stamina of the candidate. I don't suppose they'd allow an outsider a look see?" asked Morgan, well aware of the answer.

"Not likely," replied Andrew. "This testing is secretive. Unless invited, we do not push our way into such spiritual or sensitive spaces nor expect an invite to meet Queen Dana na Gig, Sirona's mother. The Royal Court resides in that magnificent building at the top of the hill. By the way, I discovered that Sirona is next in line to the royal throne as this is a matriarchal society and Sirona is the only daughter."

Having the medallion, Angi was the first to encounter Sirona who appeared as a hologram in Angi's bedroom in Scotland, an image which gradually improved as they located the rest of the gemstones. Still in holographic form, Sirona proceeded to initiate Angi on how to handle the medallion's powers. While Angi considered herself tall for her world, Sirona stood at least five inches above her. Angi's later description to her colleagues was that Sirona had an oval face with dark emerald eyes and platinum hair which she wore in a long braid. Her slim athletic build was clothed in an off-white uniform of pants and tunic accompanied by few adornments; a circular serpent badge, a gold serpent ring and a flashing wrist device. She moved swiftly giving the overall impression of elegance, assurance and grace and someone familiar with being in charge. As an instructor, Angi found her firm with little leeway for frivolity. In their initial encounter they had come to terms with their unusual situation, Angi fully aware that this was her only path to survival in managing such unknown technology. Arriving in Tir na nOg they were getting to know Sirona in person, which differed slightly from her holographic image.

"Wow, that's a discovery. You mean that we have had the princess of this kingdom as our guide? Have you any idea when she might assume such royal duties?" asked Angi, who was hoping it wasn't imminent, as she needed to learn a great deal more about her medallion.

"If age is the factor, it is going to be difficult to determine," replied Andrew. "By our calculations, Sirona might be hundreds of years old in Earth time. But keep in mind, in this world Sirona may be no older than you or Vette. Time is measured differently here. One unknown question is, can the present queen abdicate or does she have to die before Sirona takes her place. If it is any help, Angi, there is no evidence this is imminent. By the way Sirona's full name is Sirona Anna Eriu. We should keep this in mind as this may be the name familiar to her subjects."

"Has Sirona any siblings?" asked Vette, interested in Sirona's family.

"The number is unclear. I think she has two older brothers who have all been assigned major centres to govern, none in this vicinity."

"What about her father?" asked Vette.

"He apparently died in a battle some time ago. His name was Nuada Dago and, as much as I have learned, he was well respected. One interesting point is that he was over eight feet tall and heavily built. One wonders if any of Sirona's brothers are like him. Sirona, although taller than any of us, seems average. Just look at the height of those students below. Her father commanded fleets of ships, likely space ships. When her husband was killed, Sirona's mother took command of the forces and pressed on to victory. Don't underestimate the women on this planet."

"Don't underestimate the women on our planet either," came Vette's clip response.

"Point taken," said Andrew with a chuckle, knowing Vette would react.

Bryce, the second senior member, was more interested in the royal court. "Andrew, as with most royal settings, have you learned anything of any contenders to the throne or of any court intrigues? I expect it is too soon and our charming attendants would be sworn to silence."

Bryce Roberts, also known as Lord Lywillan, in his seventies, on his first meeting with Angi back in Scotland was recovering from knee surgery and beginning to realize that his senior years lay ahead with many uncertainties. This surgery had been his only frailty after years of an active sports career, at times bordering on the professional. He maintained an ongoing interest in rugby and golf. Bryce looked back on a life of numerous business and academic achievements, culminating in his appointment as Vice Chancellor of Cardiff University, a position he still held. He had worked with and been friends with Andrew for decades, having met in various senior government positions and social organizations. They knew and trusted each other. Widowed for over a decade with no children, Bryce was relying more and more on his wide network of friends to fulfill his life. An adventure into another dimension had never crossed his mind, but when it occurred he was surprised at his enthusiasm. Crossing into another dimension had renewed his purpose in life and he was enjoying the energy of the younger members of the group.

"Much too soon," was Andrew's immediate reply, "and it may be impossible to assess anyway. As you know Bryce, such intrigues are likely there but cleverly camouflaged. As such, we must be careful that we do not stumble or get ensnared into someone's nasty court intrigues."

Bryce pressed on, "Have you any idea Andrew, about their politics? We're counting on your Gaelic to find out such details."

"Actually, Bryce, my Gaelic is somewhat antiquated. It is like the difference between old English and our modern lingo on earth, almost incompatible. They have phrases that, for me, are complex and unclear. So while I can translate certain words, I'm still struggling with their fast-paced responses. But from the little I've learned, there is a Council of Elders, possibly the heads of traditionally powerful groups in the region and the Queen has a small cadre of advisors. It appears that any major wars were centuries ago. There are squabbles in distant kingdoms but generally peace seems to prevail. Presently, their priorities seem to be on honesty in government and environmental stability. Opening the Serpent's Gate has relieved a great deal of anxiety by restoring some balance in their atmosphere. Again, the details are sketchy."

"By the way, Andrew, who runs the school?" asked Angi, interested in who administered the building they were housed in.

"Angi, remember that fellow in the welcoming party who would not shake hands with us?"

"Yes, the fellow with the sallow complexion, grey hair and piercing black eyes."

"That's him. His name is Zolar. It was fortunate I mentioned before we departed that shaking hands is not an accepted custom in all societies. His tradition may be one that shuns such contact as no one in the welcoming party seemed perturbed by his action."

"He seemed cold to me but perhaps that's unfair, I only met him once. I wonder how I'd react to meeting someone from another world," replied Angi thinking out loud.

"It is rumoured he is one of a number of possible suitors being considered for Sirona. Keep that in mind if we have anything to do with him. I'm not sure how complicated such arrangements may be here in Tir na nOg."

"Don't you just love the name?" replied Vette, as she repeated the name softly. "It is musical. Morgan do you know anything about the name?"

Morgan, always glad to share his information, responded, "Tir na nOg or the Land of Promise is one of the Irish names for the Otherworld. It is depicted as a supernatural realm of everlasting youth, beauty, health, abundance and joy. Its inhabitants, they say, are the Tuatha de Danann of mythical tales, a name we've discussed before. While other cultures talk about similar enchanting isles, this is the first time that I've had the exquisite delight in landing in one."

"Thanks Morgan, you are a treasure," replied Vette. "Now I'd like to return to Sirona. I suppose arranged marriages are the norm in royal families. I'd love to get her viewpoint on such matters, but I will stifle the impulse," she said as she winked at Angi.

Andrew, found an opening and pressed on. "Rumor has it that Sirona has rejected quite a few suitors. Apparently, she's not anxious to marry or to assume her queenly duties. She likes her freedom and enjoys unique projects like us. We are under her royal protection, a position which definitely works in our favour."

Suddenly unable to control his enthusiasm, Morgan commented, "By the way, have you tasted this fruit? It has the roundness and redness of an apple but tastes like a combination of a peach and pear. True ambrosia! There is an orchard just outside this House. I suppose taking a bag of these back to Earth would be prohibited. What a shame."

Wolfram, biting into what appeared to be a piece of ham asked, "Speaking of food, I was wondering, are we really eating meat or does it just look like meat? It has the oddest taste........it is fine, but definitely different."

At that moment Sirona appeared, and hearing Wolfram's question responded, "Actually, Wolfram, we don't eat meat. Myttrwn - *pronounced Mitron* - and I are creating your diet on our replicating equipment from what I learned from my visits to your planet and what we've observed on your Internet. We have plenty of fruits and vegetables, it is protein that is in question."

"Woops, media food presentations could produce surprises," came a reply from the other table.

Dylan spoke up, "Sirona, Joel Tomkins here is a trained cook, and perhaps he can help your guys with the food replication."

"That is a great idea. I will make the connection," replied Sirona.

"By the way, while you are creating," looking at Joel, "could you conjure up an occasional pizza, or maybe some tea and coffee?" asked Vette.

Joel nodded and quietly responded, "I will try, but no guarantees, Vette."

"At the same time, maybe we could try more of your dishes," interjected Angi as she looked at Sirona.

"I will discuss that with Myttrwn," replied Sirona, and continuing she added, "I'm no expert on food but I'm sure we would love to taste some of your food like this pizza just mentioned by Vette."

Sirona then flipped open a light satchel she was carrying. "I'm returning your communication devices. We've recalibrated them to our energy grid. You can communicate with each other but, because of the differences in our technology, you cannot link up with our equipment."

Each member of the team examined their phone, turning it on and checking certain functions. Contented, they seemed relieved that they could now communicate with each other even though most apps had been rendered useless.

"Great, I've got my calendar back," said Angi. "That makes life a little easier."

"Me too," came Wolfram's reply. "By the way Sirona, will these be reengineered before we return home?"

"Myttrwn has that worked out. We can make the adjustment the day before you leave. Note the serpent symbol on your devices. This is an emergency link to myself or Myttrwn. We're hoping it will never be needed. In addition, Myttrwn wondered if you would like a translation device to help you understand what is being said around you but it will do nothing to aid your response."

"That's fine by me," Angi piped up. "I now appreciate the difficulties faced by immigrants when they don't speak the local language."

"Actually, Sirona, I expect we would all like such help," came Andrew's reply. "My Gaelic is not quite up to scratch."

Receiving a positive response, Sirona brought out a box with twelve small compartments each containing a single device which looked like a hearing aid. Speaking as she passed out the items, she said, "Insert this in your ear. You will feel a slight movement as the device adjusts to your ear canal. The devices are inconspicuous and you do not have to remove them until you leave. Now let's test them." At that point Sirona switched to her own language requesting something from Aed.

Listening carefully, most of the group smiled. "I got it!" exclaimed Angi. "You asked Aed to bring you a glass of water. Right?" Others nodded.

"Does everyone agree? Good, Myttrwn will be pleased. By the way, we will be having our first session with him this afternoon. You are now cleared to move about. However, for your own safety I would ask that you travel with one of us for the first week or so until you know the area."

"Is there a reason for this?" asked Dylan, glancing at Andrew.

"Myttrwn will be covering that this afternoon," came Sirona's quick reply. "I've been asked to give you a quick overview of the House of Learning en route to the House of Life. We will be having lunch there today."

"Before leaving, I wonder if you might help us with another matter?" asked Wolfram. "Could you or someone in your group help us learn some basic words in your language, such as hello, goodbye, thank you, etc.? Andrew will be the fastest learner, but all of us would like some basic words of courtesy. Is that possible?"

"Certainly, I will join you for your first meal of the day and we can select one or more words each day. You can test them as you walk about. The students will be delighted to help you."

Getting their freedom and improved communications gave the team a feeling of normality, however strange their new setting. Ahead lay new challenges in preparation for their still unidentified future role.

The House of Life

The House of Life, a gleaming white edifice, was equal in grandeur to the House of Learning except larger. It rose six storeys above the stone plaza, three more than the House of Learning.

As they entered the lobby they encountered throngs of students, graduates and others scurrying about oblivious of their presence. The quietness of such a large group was remarkable. Light bounced off the vast ceiling, long window-like open spaces allowed fresh air to circulate, and a gigantic in-flight bird sculpture filled the lobby with grandeur.

As they followed Sirona through the foyer and along one of three corridors, she provided a brief overview of the building. "There are seven levels. The lowest, below ground, houses the intergalactic gate, the only restricted area. The six levels above consist of two each for learning, research and healing, with healing on the upper levels. The rooftop has the docking facility for those emergency moth-like flying vehicles which you see coming and going. These vehicles, are designed to maneuver in and out of confined spaces. Larger flying vehicles exist and are stored nearby."

Angi, fascinated by the petite glass-like vehicles, asked, Sirona, "So these are your emergency work horses?"

"I knew you'd be interested, Angi. Since the majority of our people are healthy, and there are few military activities in the region, the healing service mainly deals with accidents, or unexpected special health incidents. The House of Life is renowned for its light and vibrational healing, research and robotics. This is Myttrwn's domain where I received my first lessons in the Sacred Science. Myttrwn is my ancestor and mentor. It is a great honour to have him take time to personally instruct you."

Stopping, they entered a dimly lit room, the light improving on a command from Sirona. The stark room revealed fourteen separate arm chairs arranged in a circle, two larger than the others, obviously for Sirona and Myttrwn. "Take a seat while I summon Myttrwn," said Sirona as she left the room.

She had no sooner departed when Andrew commented, "I hope you took note; Myttrwn is her ancestor which means he must be very old indeed, and, he rarely takes time for individual group instructions. We are privileged." He ceased speaking the moment Sirona and Myttrwn appeared. In respect, the group stood.

All eyes were focused on Myttrwn, a tall slim man wearing a pearl colored vest over a white cotton suit. The only visible ornamentation was a royal purple badge with a golden serpent located on the left shoulder of his vest and a matching gold serpent ring on his left middle finger.

Angi tallied up her first impression in her thoughts, "Myttrwn definitely has presence. But what is it? Is it an aura of peace, intelligence, longevity or all of these and more? He is visibly six inches taller than Sirona, and I thought she was tall. He moves with the grace and speed of an athlete in total contradiction to his mysterious age. His face is mesmerizing; oval, clean shaven, chiseled with high cheek bones. His skin appears tanned or is it weathered? His gray eyes are almost invisible when he turns his head. Yet, he gives the impression he is taking in everything and everyone at one glance. His curly neck-length hair, mainly white with a red streak across his left eye, glistens in the light. Maybe he once had red hair. I don't believe I've ever met anyone so unique. This is definitely going to be a memorable encounter."

Sirona, in respect, took her seat beside Myttrwn and remained silent for the rest of the session, a change in behaviour noted by the group.

Myttrwn, with a crisp, lilting voice and a broad smile began talking as he took his seat. "Let's be seated, for we need time to get acquainted." He then took a few moments to register each member, spending a fraction longer on Angi. "It is a delight for me to again welcome the citizens of Gaia," his words conveying genuine warmth.

"Gaia," replied Dylan, in surprise. "But we're from Earth."

"Gaia is the name the Greeks called Earth," explained Morgan.

"Ah yes, not everyone may recognize that name. You will be known by that name here, as it is one I have often used. I hope it is acceptable," came Myttrwn's reply, unperturbed by the interruptions.

Carefully registering Myttrwn's choice of words, Andrew asked, "Have you had other visitors from Gaia over the centuries?"

"In time, you will learn we've had other earthly visitors in the past. But my comment is more personal. I spent a great deal of time on your planet and regretted leaving. But we are under strict orders to depart when a planet enters its Dark Ages or Kali Yuga."

"What is a Kali Yuga?" asked Wolfram.

"Ah, I'm getting ahead of myself.............. We will set aside your question for a moment, Wolfram, as I first would like to explore your reason for being here." This took the team by surprise.

Sensing the uneasiness, Angi was first to reply, "Well I'm here to get to know more about this medallion, an item I now know is ancient technology which I'm still scared to remove because it might kill me. I'm hoping that you and Sirona will instruct me on its capabilities and perhaps explain why I've been chosen to be its designated wearer. I'm still not comfortable with that honour."

Before replying, Myttrwn raised his right hand, and mumbled a few abrupt commands in a foreign language. Instantly, the clasp on Angi's medallion opened and the medallion flew across the circle, landing in Myttrwn's hand. It happened so fast Angi didn't have time to react.

Smiling, he responded. "There now, Angi, you can see that removing the medallion will not kill you because all the gemstones are in place which keeps the technology in balance." Then holding the medallion close to his face he examined it carefully and remarked, "Amazing...........it has hardly changed. It is magnificent! I was there when this spectacular piece was created." Then, as quickly, his next set of commands found the medallion back in the air, landing gently at Angi's neck, the clasp snapping shut. "In time, Angi, I will share the wonders of this medallion with you." The others sat in silence, trying to come to terms with Myttrwn's magical ease.

Surprised, Morgan reacted, "When did you create the medallion?"

"A long time ago, Morgan, around 680 BCE in your calendar. As the Kali Yuga was beginning, we decided to leave this and other signs in your world, so their discovery in the future would trigger memories of your glorious past."

"What is the Kali Yuga, and who are 'we'?" asked Morgan.

"All in good time, Morgan," replied Myttrwn. With no introductions he knew each one by name.

It was now Andrew's turn to ask, "If you existed at that time you must be hundreds of years old, a figure beyond our comprehension. Is there a reason that you have such longevity or is it common in this world?" Andrew suddenly realizing his elder status on earth would have little meaning against such numbers.

"At times a few individuals or spirits are given exceptional longevity when the cosmos is about to shift. I am one of them. But we shall discuss this more later. Perhaps we might return to my first question. Would anyone else like to comment?"

Andrew acquiesced, "I guess the rest of us tagged along because we were all involved in finding the gemstones and, speaking for myself, I wanted to know why this piece of ancient technology was so important to mankind. I have been a member of various societies in which ancient messages were supposedly handed down to mankind, but this was the first tangible piece of advanced technology that not only appeared but actually worked. Personally, at my age I would be delighted to discover a renewed purpose in life, one that would give mankind a helping hand at this rather critical stage in its history."

"Do the rest of you agree with Andrew?" asked Myttrwn. The nodding of heads confirmed their response.

"Good, your reasons are honest. But your destiny is far more complex. My task in the next few months will be to get you to understand your new role, at least the beginning of it." As he looked into their thoughts he sensed their anxiety and thought, "Whatever their motives, this is a courageous bunch. I didn't expect twelve, but that's a bonus. I must walk slowly so as not to overwhelm them on their first visit."

Responding to Myttrwn's comment, Angi asked, "You mean this team has some further role connected with the medallion?" She was still uneasy about her own role.

"Yes, Angi, each one of you here and those you left behind will all be involved," and glancing at Andrew and Bryce, he said, "and age will not be an issue. This will not be your only trip, just the first."

Hesitating, he chose his next words carefully. "While Sirona and I and our hand-picked circle are delighted to see you, I must caution you that this opinion may not be shared by everyone. For this reason, you will be free to move about but we insist that you have one of our members with you as much as possible." He let the words register.

Dylan, alert to trouble, reacted, "Can you be more specific?"

"In the 1300s of your calendar an event occurred which produced a calamity here on our planet. Perhaps it was due to some cosmic hiccup, we never found out. In the country you call France, at the time of the Pasteurella pestis or Black Plague epidemic, a man crawled into a cave unaware it housed an ancient intergalactic gate."

Interrupting, Morgan asked, "But I thought all the gates were sealed shut when the Druids disabled the Gate of Tara against the Romans?"

"That is what we thought, Morgan, but somehow this cosmic shift momentarily activated this gate. The diseased individual stumbled through our receiving station. Before anyone knew what happened, the disease had spread. As we did not know what we were dealing with, by the time we brought it under control hundreds had died. Many blamed the calamity on the Earth and rumors spread that anyone from your planet during its Kali Yuga phase had to be isolated or destroyed. You are the first earthlings to arrive since that calamity. We have made every effort to explain the situation and to stress that the Earth is now past its Kali Yuga, but that may be insufficient to quell the fears of everyone."

"What happened to the carrier of the disease?" asked Angi.

"He died shortly after his arrival. He never regained consciousness and I'm sure had no idea where he was."

Angi felt an urge to add, "Would it help to inform your people the Black Death in the fourteenth century killed thirty to sixty percent of Europe's population?"

"As you know, Angi, no rational explanation will suffice when an individual is determined on nursing old wounds."

Letting that information sit, Wolfram proceeded onto another topic, "I wonder Myttrwn if you could help us with another matter? Several women, also guardians of the medallion, kept insisting that the activation of the medallion was a sign of the '*coming times.*' After centuries most of the verbal messages handed down in families were garbled. What does this mean?"

"Wolfram, that's a perfect entrance to my next point," replied Myttrwn anxious to move on. Then looking around he asked, "What do you know of the Great Year on your planet? It may be known as the Perfect Cycle, the Long Cycle or the Frame of Time."

"Has it got something to do with the precession of the equinox?" asked Angi. "I read something about that years ago."

Morgan, thought for a moment and added, "In my research I read that ancient societies thought the Great Year, or whatever they called it, was the key to understanding the cosmos. Some wove it into their myths and legends. It is rarely mentioned in our modern academic world, and if whispered at all is assigned to primitive superstition."

"Very good, you have some acquaintance with the topic. As you know there are different cycles of time: birth, childhood, adulthood and old age, or day and night, the seasons, and some may even know of a fifty year cycle."

The fifty year cycle triggered Andrew to respond, "I believe the Israelites had a fifty year Jubilee Cycle when debts were forgiven. And the Mayans had a fifty-two year cycle which they called a Sacred Round or the '*binding of the years*'. They said it helped them understand the past and the future."

Myttrwn, pleased with their responses, continued, "As you may know, these smaller cycles all have an effect on the evolution of consciousness, but the greatest cycle, the precessional cycle, lasts twenty-four thousand years and has the most extreme effect on your world. It has often been referred to as one year in the life of humanity."

Andrew interjected, "But what causes this Great Year and why is it so important?"

With a smile Myttrwn thought, "Oh, how I've missed my Gaia family. They are quick, inquisitive, and ask questions.........so many questions." Responding he said, "Perhaps it would help to provide a visual image of our topic." Following another verbal command a circular holographic image of the Great Year appeared and hovered above the laps of each individual.

Startled, several members tried to touch the hologram, while others concentrated on the details of the image in front of them.

Myttrwn regarding this step as normal, continued, "As you can see, the Great Year of twenty-four thousand years has two arcs; twelve thousand years descending and twelve thousand years ascending. Within each twelve thousand year arc there are four distinct ages, each with a specific number of years, the Golden Age being the longest. Terminology for these ages differ. For example, in India they are Yugas, while the Hebrews call them 'seasons', and the Greeks and Celts used metals (such as gold, silver, bronze and iron), whereas the American Indians used 'worlds' or 'suns.' Other cultures, such as the Sumerians, Egyptians, Persians, Aztecs, and the Norse, all had similar references but different wording. Since India is the only nation which has retained a reference to the Great Year in their culture, we will proceed with their terminology. I will give you time to become familiar with the holographic image." He and Sirona stood up and walked about talking quietly to each other.

When Myttrwn returned, Andrew commented, "You know, this reminds me of an Old Testament Biblical passage, I believe it is Daniel 2:31-45, which talks about an image with a head of fine gold. I don't recall the details but I do remember the feet being part iron and clay. That fascinated me as a boy. So, is this is what it meant?"

"Ah, you see, there have been references to the Great Year right in your own literature," replied Myttrwn, delighted that they were making the connection.

Angi puzzled, asked, "But why is this important considering that most of us are not capable of surviving one zodiacal time period, let alone thousands of years?" At that moment she realized that there were two exceptions in the room; Sirona and Myttrwn.

Myttrwn turned to Angi and replied, "Because Angi, when humanity loses such knowledge, it becomes disconnected with the stars, and is in danger of losing its way in time. Humanity is currently on the brink of losing its sense of origin and its future."

Morgan, mulling over the information, added, "Is that what the Mayan 2012 prophecy was all about? They referred to 2012 as an awakening to a New Time ....is that 'time' the same as the '*coming times*?"

"They have much in common," replied Myttrwn, "but before venturing down that road, I'd like to address Andrew's earlier question as to what causes the Great Year."

"The earth's solar system revolves in a twenty-four thousand year cycle around a companion star. Your astronomers are beginning to suspect there is a dark dwarf star possessing no real luminosity of its own. As your solar system circles this star, the electromagnetic field of the star causes subtle changes in human consciousness; in the descending twelve thousand years, mankind loses elements of its consciousness, knowledge and awareness and regains it again in the ascending twelve thousand years. As mankind's consciousness changes, so do civilizations and human development."

"So, if I am reading this holographic image correctly," observed Bryce, "in 1700 CE our earth emerged from this Dark Age which you are calling the Kali Yuga. Is that correct?"

"Yes, the ascending Kali Yuga, occurred between 500 CE to 1700 CE. Since 1700, you have been in a transition period, from the Kali Yuga to the Dwapara Yuga," replied Myttrwn.

"I am assuming that your planet is further along this ascending arc so what would be the viewpoint of your people towards us?" asked Dylan trying to anticipate what to expect. "Do we appear primitive........barbaric.......dim-witted or what......?"

"Dylan, our students learn about the Great Year of every planet and what features to expect when we travel to these planets or when their people visit us. Their feelings towards you may be cautious as they may expect you to be more emotional or unpredictable."

Looking around, Dylan responded, "Well, that's good to know, although I'm not sure how we can ameliorate their concerns."

Vette, following the discussion, spoke up, "In summary, what you are saying is that the '*coming times*' is the earth's entrance into the Dwapara Yuga following this three hundred year transition."

"Yes, Vette, that is the answer to Wolfram's question but we have more to discuss on this matter. At this time perhaps we should take a break. When we return we will focus on the two Yugas closest to your time; the Kali and the Dwapara." And with another verbal command the holographic images disappeared.

Unknown to them, while they were deep in conversation, carts of food had arrived and two long tables set up for lunch. Drapes were pulled back to reveal an inner courtyard like the ones in the House of Learning. Fresh air and sunlight burst into the room.

As they headed for the food, Vette whispered to Angi, "This journey is an ever-ending kaleidoscope of wonder. While my understanding of our world keeps getting reprogrammed, I can't wait to hear more."

"Vette, if the flight of the medallion is any sign, my upcoming training sessions should be mind boggling. This still hasn't improved my apprehension over this medallion."

During lunch, the air bristled with chatter as members shared their views about the session, most steering clear of their thoughts on Myttrwn. Once the meal was over, Sirona signaled Myttrwn was ready and everyone returned to their seats. In anticipation, they waited as Myttrwn magically recreated their holographic teaching tool.

Without hesitation, he began. "Let's discuss the Kali Yuga, descending from 701 BCE to 499 CE, and ascending from 500 CE to 1700 CE. During that time all world cultures deteriorated, losing much of their previous knowledge, including the knowledge of most cycles. At its lowest point, mankind was living a life of ignorance as few could read or write. The written word was preserved by a small number of individuals and occasionally some religious organizations, if at all. The destruction of knowledge was rampant. From about 330 BCE onward, different conquering armies or groups destroyed the libraries of the Persians, Chinese, Egyptians, Phoenicians, Greeks, Romans, Druids, South American Indians, Europeans, and many others. This does not include the losses due to fire, floods or other disasters. The loss diminished humanity's knowledge of its past as well as its future. It was a time of conquest and subjugation by force."

"I expect the lives of its people were fairly crude?" asked Angi.

"Indeed, Angi, life was hard and pleasures were sensory such as eating, drinking and sex. Disease, misfortune and famine were commonplace. Slaves were treated as property and human sacrifice existed. Healing, if available at all, was mainly for the elite and even at the time of the Greeks, pretty much materialistic and physical, many people not living long enough to care. It is only when humanity moved away from the Kali Yuga that your lifespan began to approach one hundred years and human stature began to change from about five feet to six feet and more. Have you noticed, your children are getting taller? During these Dark Ages religious understanding was rigid, materialistic and ritualistic. Rival religions were abhorred, attacked and adherents forced to convert or be slain."

"Well that hasn't changed, we're still fighting religious wars," replied Bryce. "Just look at the chaos in the Middle East and elsewhere."

"That's an important point Bryce, as it indicates that even after three centuries humanity is still dragging along a lot of Kali Yuga baggage which eventually needs to be jettisoned." Myttrwn stopped at this point before moving on. Now let's look at the Dwapara Yuga.

"Since September 1699 CE, humanity has been in the Dwapara Yuga. As the light increased and the consciousness of humanity improved, there has been a growing feeling of the unity of people, energy and nature. In this Yuga the life span, and the intellectual and spiritual powers of mankind have been advancing. By the end of this Yuga at 4100 CE your life span may reach two hundred and your children will be even taller."

The height of humanity's future children reminded the team of the students back at the House of Learning.

Morgan thought to himself, "Is that what was meant by giants in the old texts? Were these the remnant of the descending Dwarapa Yuga?"

Myttrwn continued, "The changes in this ascending Dwapara Yuga will be amazing. Knowledge will rapidly expand, and instant communications and space travel will become realities. In this energy age, mankind will understand matter as different rates of vibrational energy, atoms as points of scintillating light, and that there are no physical structures at all, the reality you think you know is an illusion."

This prompted Morgan to add, "Wasn't that what Einstein said, a world class scientist on Earth of the last century? I think it went something like, *'Reality is merely an illusion albeit a persistent one.'*"

"That was indeed a Dwapara Yuga wise man," replied Myttrwn. "This shift in consciousness means that people will be seeking greater meaning in their lives, more empowerment and have a desire to improve the world."

"How will learning and healing change?" asked Angi.

"Learning and healing will become more individualistic and healing will focus on making the individual healthy. As it existed during the descending Dwapara Yuga, healing through rays, colour, and sound will return along with the use of anti-gravity, sunlight, and magnetic fields. Spiritual practices will allow the individual to have direct experience of higher consciousness, and control his or her inner energies. The unity of all religions will become a reality."

"I'm pleased the Dwapara Yuga seems to hold much promise, but are there any negatives?" asked Andrew.

"In the short term, there could be increased world conflicts, pollution, famine and cataclysms. You have already had a lot of that in the past three centuries. In addition, change may come so quickly it may threaten conventional and historical facets of life, something you are already experiencing. However, your current technology has reached a point of overload with serious security issues. The over emphasis on material and technological gadgets and the need for endless stimuli is reducing the meaning and purpose of many lives. These will have to be addressed."

Wolfram, pondering the Yuga information, asked, "If what you have been saying is true, then why is there so little evidence of this glorious past? The current academic theory is that we've progressed in a straight line from a primitive state to modern man."

"Ah, I was waiting for that question. The evidence is there but unrecognizable."

"Is that because we have either ignored it or we don't understand it?" asked Morgan.

"A bit of both, Morgan," said Myttrwn. "Most people prefer to stick to the reality they know, and are not interested in cyclical repeating patterns. In addition, how does a world like yours identify with small communities of spiritually enlightened individuals living simply on the earth? Or how do you study a culture which regards the society greater than the individual, and where individuals are measured by their degree of enlightenment? Your scientific community lacks a spiritual understanding of life so their left-brain thinking cannot translate a right-brain style of symbolic communication from the past."

"Fair enough, but do you have any examples?" asked Wolfram.

Myttrwn knew they were struggling and obliged. "There are many, but to name a few; the Irish round towers or the multi-layered pagodas in the Far East were originally designed to collect and channel electromagnetic waves to serve as energy conductors. Their purpose was to help plants grow and make people feel better. Other legends and myths in your world refer to '*singing to the stones*', a practice whereby sound vibrations were employed to move gigantic stones by alternating the effects of gravity. In addition, certain metals and crystals were used to focus energy, which was the reason why kings and queens sat or meditated on thrones made of precious metals and inlaid gemstones. In the Amazon basin there still exists an Indian Black Earth or Terra Preta do Indio, a self-renewing soil which grows several crops each year and never needs fertilizer. You are also familiar with ancient huge stone buildings and structures, canals and underground water systems which cannot be copied or explained. And, of course, this medallion which Angi wears. I could go on but these will suffice."

"Myttrwn, we are aware of other ancient anomalies but the reasons remained a mystery until know," said Andrew. "I wonder if you might explain another phenomenon to us, does everyone on your planet have the ability to perform magic?"

"Andrew, magic was a way of life in the descending Dwapara Yuga, and it will return in the ascending Dwapara Yuga. Unfortunately, as the Kali Yuga progressed, magicians resorted to black magic and tricks which resulted in magic being branded by religious organizations as idolatrous, evil and demonic. You live in a magical world designed for your spiritual growth. Each one of you has the ability to become a magician..........you are already moving in that direction."

The team looked at each other in dismay, but said nothing.

As Myttrwn and Sirona rose to end the session, Myttrwn added, "Tomorrow we will meet again. Angi, Sirona will set up a time for the three of us to begin your medallion training. Corb here will escort you back to your abode. In time you will know your own way." And they were gone.

The team gathered to follow Corb, his seven foot stature and white uniform, an easy beacon.

THE SERPENT'S SONG

Chapter 2

The House of Learning & Plaza

From the House of Learning second level balcony, Zolar silently watched Corb lead the group of twelve across the plaza. A potted bush partially camouflaged his presence. The plaza was expansive and their progress slow as they stopped periodically to chat. Only an occasional word drifted towards Zolar for him to ascertain what they were talking about. Students scurried around them as they rushed to their next classes.

Zolar was as tall as Sirona, a man approaching middle age, who had taken eons to advance through the ranks to his elevated position as Head of the House of Learning with a position on the Council of Elders. His attire was a simple white suit with a blue vest, the only ornament being a golden serpent badge with a pearl backing designating his membership on the Council. Just like Myttrwn he had a matching gold serpent ring on his left middle finger. His physical appearance of a sallow complexion, brown piercing eyes, heavy eyebrows and graying hair hanging to his neck gave him a somber appearance.

Zolar was struggling with conflicting thoughts about his guests. He had voiced his objection to their arrival several times, his words still etched in his memory. "Our standing policy is to restrict visitors from any planet until they had distanced themselves from their Kali Yuga," he declared to the Council members. "The fundamental reasons are well known. Most carry too much negative and aggressive baggage which hampers their relationships with more advanced societies. In addition, their unpredictability and emotionalism create too many unwanted problems." Zolar, a stickler for rules, was respected for his defense of the principles which governed their kingdom. As a member of the Council of Elders he had the right to voice his opinion whether or not it agreed with that of the Queen. This was such an occasion.

As he continued his observation, he recalled his most recent comments at the Council with regard to the medallion, "We need to wait until Gaia has moved further into its Dwapara Yuga. That has been our policy. Why change now?" But the Council didn't agree with him. He then remembered with anguish the final outcome of the discussions. Since the medallion was created on Earth and had miraculously survived over two thousand years through wars, disasters and vast movements of people, it belonged there. Sirona and Myttrwn would be directed to manage the project. Zolar continued in his thoughts, "I had no argument with the medallion's miraculous survival. It was the necessity of inviting the earthlings to Tir na nOg with which I disagreed. Why now? Why twelve?" Not having more power on the Council weighed heavily on Zolar. Centuries ago his once powerful family had lost much of its status due to a freak intergalactic event leaving him the sole member in a powerful position within the kingdom.

Zolar continued with his thoughts as he struggled with the issue, "Myttrwn began talking about this cursed medallion the moment Sirona made contact with the people of Gaia. He informed us that the medallion was created by a handful of Sacred Science practitioners in Egypt at the end of Gaia's descending Dwapara Yuga. While we all were sympathetic with the reasons for creating the medallion, descending Dwapara Yuga technology was still far too sophisticated for the people of Gaia at their present stage of evolution. And, as far as I was concerned, no amount of training would compensate for this huge gap in enlightenment and knowledge, whatever Myttrwn and Sirona said. I argued that Sirona could just as easily have maneuvered this woman on Gaia to open the Serpent's Gate from their side and have it closed from ours. But this idea was also rejected."

Assessing the group from Gaia as they moved across the plaza he lamented, "Can anything positive come out of this exchange? They have nothing to teach us and our ways and technology are too advanced for them to understand." Looking at Angi he went on, "There she is, the recipient of the medallion. She's a puzzle. Surely it was her DNA which qualified her to wear that magnificent medallion. It is a miracle her genetic material wasn't totally contaminated after centuries on Gaia when humanity's life span decreased. Was it fate or careful genetic manipulation? From what little I know, arranged marriages did occur on Earth but mainly with the elite and restricted to certain societies and groups. There's no indication she is connected to any royal line. And yet, she does have some of the features of our own women; the white blond hair, green eyes and she is the tallest of the females in her group. Could the genetic pattern remain so strong with the mixing of cultures?"

For a few moments he watched as Angi laughed with her colleagues. He was perplexed. Part of him wanted to know her more and the other part wanted to reject her outright. Bending towards rejection he continued his assessment, "Without Sirona's help and Myttrwn's mentoring that young woman might have killed herself and others in her amateurish handling of the medallion. I am uneasy with her having such power. The ramifications are enormous." Then a thought entered his mind, "But maybe.........just maybe, there's another possibility. Could she be just the courier of this medallion and someone in our kingdom will take charge of it? That would make sense. But who? May be I could argue that it would be prudent for us to retain this technology for Gaia until Gaia was at a more enlightened stage. That strategy would be in full agreement with our laws. I will bring this up at the next Council meeting." Feeling that the issue might have a practical solution, he relaxed and turned his attention to the rest of the team.

"Wolfram, is the tallest of the males in the group. Rumor has it that he was injured somehow and healed by Angi. I wonder if it was a serious injury."

"The red-haired one, Morgan, seems more emotional and sensitive than Wolfram. Yet, the others seem to respect his historical knowledge of their planet."

"Vette, is like the jumping Goro which lives in our desert. She's wiry, perpetually alert and ready to pounce."

"As for the two elders, Andrew and Bryce, they have maturity of age and are familiar with being in charge. They indicate there are other older members of their group back on Gaia. It would be interesting to compare these elders with our own."

Then his focus turned to the six individuals who kept looking around while concentrating on the conversation. "Imagine bringing your own security team to an alien planet when they must have known we were more advanced. May be they had no idea what to expect. Anyway, their inquisitiveness must be watched."

He remained behind the potted bush until the group entered the House of Learning.

With the remote possibility that the medallion might be stored in Tir na nOg for Gaia's use in the future, Zolar's apprehension had been temporarily allayed. Yet, he had little assurance his idea would be accepted by the Council. Restless, he also knew his next steps had to be carefully measured as his thoughts shifted to another matter before leaving the balcony, "So far, my credentials and pedigree have passed all tests for being a proper suitor for Sirona. I must not jeopardize that."

House of Learning

Returning to their dining area Angi hesitated and turning to the team said, "Let's unwind, it has been a long day," as she glanced at her watch. "There's time before our next meal."

"I agree," replied Wolfram as he made his way to one of the tables. "Today reminded me of my university days. To tell you the truth, I couldn't hold up my side of any debate on the topic of the Great Year. Imagine trying to dent the current thinking of our scientists regarding the evolution of mankind. Morgan, I'm counting on you, what do you think?" By this point the rest had joined Wolfram and Angi around one table.

"While I share your misgivings," replied Morgan, "I have to admit it answers a lot of those frustrating, bewildering questions and anomalies of past civilizations. Mark my word, I couldn't carry on a lengthy debate on the topic either. I know Myttrwn has only skimmed the surface. There are layers of information we will never get to on this trip. Nevertheless, he is opening some fascinating doors to a treasure trove of universal knowledge. It is like talking to an ancient. Just think of the questions I could ask about our history."

"Well, my head feels like mush," replied Vette. "Since we've started on this quest I've had my entire world view not only shattered but I keep encountering magical events which defy understanding. Look at Myttrwn, he zapped those holographic images in and out with verbal commands. By any chance did you note that the commands he used for the medallion were in a different, untranslatable, language to the one he used with the holograph?"

Everyone nodded, with Andrew adding, "Remember Myttrwn said that magic was common at the time of the descending Dwapara Yuga. This means, if we accept the Great Year concept, then humanity has lost its magical capabilities during our Dark Ages. In time I expect we will learn that all this so-called magic is nothing more than advanced science governed by specific laws. We already know that our modern technology seems like magic to primitive societies. It is the same thing. I was pleased to hear that we, this team, are already becoming magicians. Now I believe Angi is well on the way, but it is good to hear we all have potential." Andrew smiled to himself for he rather liked the idea of becoming a magician.

Bryce, who had been listening, was on a different tack, "Do you think, Andrew, there might be something in our ancient texts that would identify Myttrwn, I expect by a different name? I suppose it is too far back. But if he lived on earth he would have been a well-known leader and certainly his height would be noted." Bryce, struggling with the Great Year concept, was hoping an earthly historic link might help.

Andrew hesitated before replying, "Oh, to have my old computer, then I could look up some things or even contact a few old acquaintances. Perhaps, old friend, this nagging question will have to wait until we get home. In the meantime, Myttrwn did mention other signs were left for our time. Let's see if he'll identify some more."

Wolfram, still not satisfied that his question had been addressed, asked again, "But basically, does the Great Year concept make sense to you? We've heard from Morgan, how about the rest of you?"

Angi sensing Wolfram's frustration, responded, "It fits into some of our familiar cyclic patterns such as the time of day and the seasons. As Morgan mentioned, such thinking is familiar to some aboriginal societies. And while astronomy is not my forte, the concept that mankind goes through stages of enlightenment is far more appealing to me than our evolution from monkeys. I realize this is heresy to those who worship Darwin. But let's face it Darwin only popped up in the 1800s. Surely there must be room to discuss some other possibility."

"Oh Angi, ...Oh Angi...........you are skating on dangerous ice," came Morgan's mocking reply. "In academia, kingdoms have been built on Darwin's theory. While, in principle, you are right, there should be an openness to other possibilities, the chances of that happening are zero to none. I wish it were otherwise."

Continuing to seek input, Wolfram reiterated, "Well forget our academic world for the moment..............is everyone comfortable with the Great Year concept? Do you actually accept the premise that we are just stumbling out of a long Dark Age?"

Andrew came to his rescue and replied, "Wolfram, you are expressing, I believe, our common struggle with this material. Today Myttrwn introduced a challenge to our comfortable world view. He did not ask us to believe anything, he just shared the information knowing we would need time to compare this with our current theories. Let's take our time with this. More sessions lie ahead and Myttrwn seems receptive to questions. How about that?"

"Agreed," came the verbal comments from some and nods from others.

Not wanting the discussion to end Vette jumped in, "OK, then let's move on. What was your initial assessment of Myttrwn? Who wants to start?"

Wolfram volunteered. "His height, which must be over seven feet, seems average for this place. Even with his white hair, he looks and acts more like a spry fifty year old or even younger. So, let's focus on his age. It is mind boggling to me that he may be more than two thousand years old, and that's a guesstimate. Because we're assuming that he had to be a well-educated adult when the medallion was created. But he could have been hundreds of year's old even then, we have no idea. Morgan, when the ancient records talk about 'immortals' is there any possibility they could have been referring to someone like Myttrwn? Myttrwn did say others were sometimes granted such longevity. Of course this begs the question, granted by whom. But let's table who might be the 'others' and who is doing the granting for now and stick to Myttrwn."

Before Morgan had time to respond Angi interjected, "If we accept his comment that there are individuals and spirits chosen to watch over certain cosmic transitions, how many are there?"

"Oh this is so tantalizing," came Morgan's enthusiastic reply. "My head is bursting with possibilities. Angi, the number of 'others' could be a few or many, we have no way of knowing. I agree with Wolfram, let's leave these vagaries for now. But irrespective of this unknown selection process, one cannot rule out the fact that people live longer on this planet. Look at Sirona. In addition, Myttrwn said that by the end of the Dwapara Yuga, admittedly well into our future, we on earth could live to two hundred. But that's a far cry from thousands."

Andrew added, "I believe Sirona when she says he is her ancestor. So, for the present I am willing to accept his longevity. Not saying I understand it, but I have no alternative. Personally, I am fascinated at his agility and clarity of mind if he's truly that old. Imagine what our media would do with that gem if they found out his age. Pray that never happens." Hesitating for a moment as an afterthought he concluded, "You would certainly have to pace yourself if you expected to live hundreds of years...........let alone thousands." The thought hung unchallenged by everyone as each one thought of the possibilities.

"So, do I take it that we all agree, Myttrwn is unique? He's taller, older, more knowledgeable and certainly more talented than anyone we've ever met. I'm still left with more questions than answers, but that's what makes this so delightful," came Angi's thumbnail summary.

Before anyone had a chance to comment further, Morgan added, "And I believe he can read minds."

Startled, Vette asked, "Morgan, what gave you that impression?"

"Did you notice when he first arrived, with one glance he knew our names and I expect he knows more about us than we know ourselves. There's scientific proof that telepathy is possible. The Russians have been working on this for decades," responded Morgan, looking around to see how this was registering with the others.

"Wow. I wonder what life on earth would be like if everyone were telepathic," came Vette's response.

"It would definitely stymie politicians, sales people and the media, and countless others," came Dylan's quick reaction.

Angi, thinking for a moment, spoke up, "Now that you mention it, Morgan, have you noticed how quietly these students move about? At first I thought they were highly disciplined, which could also be a factor. But there is minimum chatter in both Houses. It never dawned on me to think of telepathy. Perhaps talking is not their first line of communication."

"If that's the case, then having us as guests must be taxing for them," came Bryce's thoughtful observation. "This reminds me of my childhood in Wales. Now the Welsh are known to be talkative, and family gatherings could be boisterous. I can remember as a boy my parents' exhaustion after the Christmas visit of three elderly relatives who were exceptionally talkative. So, if our hosts are mainly telepathic, then our chatter must be exhausting for them." Looking towards Andrew, "We need to keep this in mind as the days progress."

"That's a good point, Bryce. We're also a group of twelve, which might be overwhelming for them as well. It may be the reason why Myttrwn has taken us on as he and Sirona have had previous earthly contact."

However, the thought that they might be living in an environment where their every thought could be read by their hosts brought the group discussion to an abrupt silence as each member began to contemplate the ramifications.

Dylan interrupted the silence, "Now if this telepathy is real, I will need time to get my head around what it may mean to our safety."

Andrew, sensing the anxiety, interjected a word of calm, "Perhaps we're jumping to conclusions when it may only be Myttrwn with such a skill. The students may be highly disciplined. I recall my days in private British schools where discipline was strict and talking discouraged. Let's keep an open mind and not create problems where none exist."

"And what are we going to do if it is true?" came Dylan's abrupt question.

"Then we will face that when it comes," came Andrew's equally abrupt reply as he silently signaled Dylan to cease. Thinking to himself he added, "If confirmed, I will need a long chat with Sirona and even Myttrwn. If they can read our minds, then we are definitely at a disadvantage. Fine with friends, deadly with enemies."

As the group began to depart, Dylan added, "By the way, as we crossed the plaza today I saw Zolar standing on the second level balcony. He was behind a plant. He's a strange one."

Trying again to redirect Dylan, Andrew replied, with a slight edge to his voice, "Dylan, we are his guests and this is his House. I would also be curious if twelve strangers suddenly arrived on my doorstep. So far everything has gone smoothly. I will again remind everyone we are under the protection of the Royal Family. This is our first week in a new world. We are bound to run into questions and unknowns." This assurance seemed to register but their discussions had generated some new concerns.

&

The Houses of Life & Learning

Within days Sirona had reassigned the team; Wolfram and Dylan were off with the emergency planes, Andrew and Bryce to the library/archives, Morgan, Vette and the others to participate in different class activities, Joel on food, and Angi to begin her medallion training program. Variety made for boisterous evenings as each shared snippets of their new-found experiences. Sirona had stipulated the assignments could be rotated, except for the activities of Joel and Angi.

On his first sojourn Wolfram had much to report. "What is most amazing is that those emergency planes are operated by the pilot's thoughts. Manual controls exist but are rarely used. Corb, my pilot, took me on an emergency call regarding a boy injured while climbing. He maintained a running dialogue between the accident site and home base during the entire trip. The boy and his troupe were easily located. Do you remember those two clear capsules on either side of those vehicles? Well, Corb and I gently placed the injured boy into one of these capsules. Corb attached leads to the boy's body and informed me that the readouts were being simultaneously registered on the plane's panel and at the House of Life. He described the unit as a transport healing chamber, which meant that the healing process had commenced at the accident site. Apparently, they have no heavy reliance on surgery or drugs in their healing process. I will be fascinated at your take on this Angi."

"Did you see what happened when you reached the House of Life?" asked Angi.

"No, I just took Corb's word for it. Outside parties are not allowed access with a recently injured patient."

Then it was Dylan's turn. "Remember all that testing when we arrived? I expect some of it was to obtain a healthy portrait of our DNA and chakras. Apparently, this portrait is used to initiate any healing process should it be needed. Likely Corb already had this boy's portrait in his scanner before he left or could retrieve it quickly. I've heard of fingerprinting but this is in another galaxy. Otherwise my experience was similar to Wolfram's. My pilot, Rao and I picked-up a very ill male elder. He was also placed in the capsule and when we arrived at the House of Life I was convinced his condition had already improved."

Morgan's input from the classes presented a different perspective. "In all my years in education I have never experienced such concentration and discipline in a class of students. These students spend long hours in meditation, complex calisthenics, and learning about the Sacred Science. While we separate the sciences into specialities, sub-specialities and super-sub-specialities, here it is all one. Every student is expected to know how all sciences operate in a world they regard as One. I would love to learn more about this concept, perhaps we can ask Myttrwn. In addition, disciplining their thoughts seems to be an essential key to their advancement. After Wolfram's comments I now realize that this is connected to their technology. Have you ever wondered what it would mean in our world if clarity of thought was essential to operating our technology?"

"Imagine trying to enforce that concept on Earth," came the verbal slip from Wolfram.

Morgan didn't pursue this further but noted his colleagues were toying with the ramifications of his question.

"Morgan, do you think the students spend more time in their studies than we do?" asked Andrew, trying to understand how the students could master so many sciences.

"That's hard to judge, Andrew. I don't know how many years they have studied before reaching the House of Learning. They may be able to absorb more because they are more enlightened, use telepathy, perhaps have other skills we do not possess at this stage in our development, and perhaps they have more time. It is a puzzle. They are definitely bright, and so polite. In addition, while they are relaxed in their individuality, the main emphasis is on the welfare of their society as a whole. I have no way of knowing whether this concept is prevalent just in this school or whether it exists throughout the kingdom. There's so much I'd like to know before we leave," and with that he conceded the discussions to Andrew and Bryce.

Andrew and Bryce had an entirely different report. Andrew did the main speaking. "Since my Gaelic reading skills are somewhat limited it takes time for me to get through any of their documents. However, the vastness of their library and archives is indescribable, there are centuries of information. The head of the library showed us how to access any document. This resulted in us finding documents which were more than a holographic image. As you turned the pages of a book or document they became alive, and these were their ancient records. Current information is mainly digital or whatever they call it and even more sophisticated. Now that we know how to retrieve the information Bryce and I plan on spending more time in understanding their history. This may be slow work. Anyone interested in archival research is more than welcome to come along."

There were no takers. Everyone knew the two best candidates were already involved and would report back.

Nightly reports and questions soon found the team up late. The more they discovered the more they were impressed with Tir na nOg.

In the meantime Joel had been busy working with a member of Myttrwn's lab on addressing the food issues. Within days he and his friend Danu appeared at an evening meal with a small device and a box-like container with mugs and other items.

Joel took the lead after introducing Danu to the team. "Danu and I hope your daily protein ration has improved. To tell you the truth it is not easy to describe our meat products. However, creating protein this way avoids the animal issues we experience at home and the nutritional values can be more precisely programmed. It would be an answer to our world hunger, but that's another topic. When we contact home base we should ask if the next team can bring along a few samples. Myttrwn will give instructions as to how these should be transported."

Wolfram was first to speak, "I can't speak for the rest of the team, but I must commend you on your results. Our protein has definitely improved. I was willing to adapt, but am pleased with your latest products."

"Great job, Guys!" came a chorus of voices.

Joel, enjoying the spotlight, turned to the small container which had been placed on a serving table. There was no evidence of any outside wires or connections. He then asked Angi to come forward. "Angi I want you to take this mug, another item we created with their replicators, and place it into this grove at the front and in a clear voice ask for 'coffee', 'herbal tea' or 'regular tea', whichever you prefer."

Angi did as requested, saying clearly, "Regular tea."

From a small spout poured a piping hot cup of tea, the first the team had encountered since their arrival.

Joel continued. "Angi, if you would like some milk or a sweetener these are available in these gel capsules; the cream is computer generated and the sweetener is honey." Smiling he announced, "Perhaps everyone would like to test our creation."

Without hesitation members rose and each tried one brand or another. Some used the gel capsules.

"Hey, this is really good," came Andrew's first response. "You and Danu must be congratulated. It is nice to get a hot cup of tea."

Joel and Danu bathed in the praises, pleased with another success. Trying to give the team a bit more information he went on. "There is much I cannot explain. All you need to know is that this small device is capable of creating the fluid, selecting the beverage, and heating it using what they call their free universal energy. Danu did the programming. If you have any questions then please chat with Danu, the expert."

"So, now Joel how about the Pizza?" asked Vette. "Any luck there?"

"Actually Vette I'm in a bit of a fix. I am not a baker. While I can work with Danu to create the ingredients or their facsimile, I do not know how to make Pizza dough or crust. Anyone here with baking experience?"

No one responded.

Not willing to give up, Joel made a second plea, "Well, has anyone ever worked in a pizza joint?"

Still no takers. Almost ready to give up, he hesitated when Vette began to speak. "Actually, Joel, I use to do a lot of baking as a young girl. Bread and pastry were specialities of my Acadian people. I haven't done any baking in years but I'm willing to help."

"Vette, you've saved the day," came Joel's happy response. "You'll know ten times more than me. I will see if Sirona can reassign you to work with Danu and me."

Angi then piped up, "The Acadians on my Island have a reputation for creating the finest bread and desserts. I will fully support Vette in this endeavour."

And so it came to pass that with Danu's computer skills and Joel and Vette's input the team soon were savouring a variety of breads. The smell of bread baking enticing others to join them in testing the new-found delights.

Watching the interplay between the groups pleased Sirona and Myttrwn, with Sirona commenting to Myttrwn back at the House of Life, "This food interchange has been a real benefit. Our group is fascinated with the hot drinks and breads. It is good to have this sharing." With a wry grin, she added, "I expect you have already sampled the items?"

"Indeed I have," replied Myttrwn with a smile, "after all it is my duty to check everything that goes on in my lab." Then as an afterthought he added, "I had almost forgotten the delicious taste of fresh baked bread. I must look up that ancient Egyptian bread recipe for Vette."

Angi's training sessions with Myttrwn and Sirona would be the most demanding of assignments. As agreed, Sirona had set up a schedule which she hoped would give Angi time to adapt. What she had not anticipated was Angi's sudden reluctance to even proceed.

House of Life

Angi was troubled as she walked along with Sirona to her first training session with Myttrwn. It was one thing to be working with Sirona, but Myttrwn's tutorship had elevated the stakes. She decided it was time to convey her worries to Sirona.

"You know Sirona, everything has happened so fast I am still trying to adjust to this new life. Just months ago I hardly gave this medallion a second glance. Now I'm about to begin my apprenticeship with Myttrwn. Yet, I'm still unclear as to why this medallion is so important and what I'm supposed to do with it when I get back home."

"I see," came Sirona's only response.

The limitation in Sirona's reaction was maddening, Angi needed more. So, she tried again. "Sirona, my life's plan was fairly practical. I saw myself working in hospitals caring for people, someday getting married and eventually having children. I did not expect anything extraordinary. This medallion and its mysterious powers is a conundrum for me. I am also aware that you and Myttrwn have an entirely different perspective on what this is all about. I need you to share this with me." Still getting no response she stopped in the plaza and became more strident, as she knew once in front of Myttrwn she might lose her nerve.

"Sirona, I need your help. What are your expectations of me? I went along with the earlier stages of this venture in fear I would be attached to an unstable piece of ancient technology that could kill me. My curiosity overcame me when I stepped through the Serpent's Gate. It has only been with your help that I have managed not to harm myself or others in working with this technology. But we are about to enter a new phase. I have the right to be better informed as to what this all means. I'm not even sure I want the role, whatever it is. Have you ever thought I might not accept being the medallion's permanent companion," her voice punctuating the last words.

Sirona stared down at Angi. She had listened and suddenly realized the enormity of the burden they had placed on her. With little explanation, Angi had been hijacked from her familiar world into a foreign, complex one and asked to completely change her understanding of the universe. Because of the urgency of the circumstances, they had not provided her with much insight as to the importance of the medallion or her future role. Her genetic inheritance had allowed her to wear the medallion, but now she needed to understand what it meant. Thinking quickly she thought to herself, "I need to remember these earthlings do not have our telepathic and intuitive abilities. I have been assuming too much. Angi has every right to be upset and anxious. I must communicate her concerns telepathically to Myttrwn when we reach his lab. Angi's training may take more time than I thought." Sensing Angi's need for a verbal response she said, "That's a fair point Angi, you deserve and will receive more information on the medallion and what lies ahead. You have the right to decide whether you want to assume this responsibility or not. I want to assure you that you will be given every support and guidance. You will not be alone. In addition we will be working with your colleagues so they too will assume a greater role. Is that any help at this point?"

"Some," came Angi's reply, almost in a whisper. "I will likely feel better after we get through this first session," trying to comfort herself. She had gone along with the whole venture up to a point, but deep down she knew the road ahead was going to be more demanding. And in her frustration she thought, "Right now I feel like a child with a dangerous toy, a feeling I detest."

Upon entering the House of Life, they took a fast elevator to the top level where Myttrwn had his lab. As they exited the elevator they were confronted by an overwhelming display of technical gadgets, instruments, robots, holographic screens with blinking lights and data all operated by a number of attendants dressed in blue and white uniforms. The lab attendants' concentration was so intense that no one but Myttrwn looked up when they entered. Myttrwn walked towards them with a warm smile. En route he received Sirona's message about Angi's anxiety.

With no outward indication, he greeted them with, "Welcome to my lab, Angi. In time I will give you a guided tour. But today I thought we might spend time getting acquainted with a medallion similar to yours. Yours is not the only one of its kind. These medallions are just unique creations." His gentle manner and diversion relaxed Angi and peaked her curiosity.

"That would be great," replied Angi. Remembering Morgan's telepathic comment, she knew that Sirona had somehow communicated her concerns. Then, she thought to herself, "Wait till I tell the others, there are positives to this telepathy. Obviously, a great deal can be communicated quickly. What a time saver."

Myttrwn, signaled Sirona and Angi to accompany him into another section of the lab, his personal quarters. Upon entering, a verbal command brought down a watery-like screen over the entrance silencing the outer noise and providing privacy. "Angi, let's sit around this table while I summon a holographic presentation on the creation of a similar medallion. You will see how the gemstones are selected, and how they and the medallion are programmed." Angi took the middle bench of three in front of a white circular table. Myttrwn's verbal command initiated the program.

In the center of the table appeared a miniature 3D holographic image of two individuals in white uniforms beginning a discussion on completing the final steps of a high-tech medallion. The translation device in Angi's ear helped her understand what they were saying, except for certain technical words and commands. On a workbench in front of the two men sat a gold medallion devoid of its gemstones. While similar, it differed from Angi's in that a large serpent dominated the center. Angi knew her medallion had symbolic serpents etched on both sides of an oval design.

The two men took time in selecting which gemstones to use as they calculated the energetic power of each stone with a hand-held device. The stones were similar to her own medallion; an emerald, ruby, diamond, amethyst, sapphire, amber, topaz and others which she did not recognize.

Once the gemstones had been selected, the attendants discussed the cleansing of the stones, assuring themselves that each stone had been properly washed in sea water for twenty-four hours, rinsed with pure water, allowed to be energized by the sun, and placed in a large crystal cluster for charging. Assured of the purity, one of the men, took the gemstones, placed them in what appeared to be some kind of machine, punched in a code, turned a dial three times, and waited. This prompted Angi to ask "What are they doing?"

Myttrwn sitting on her right, responded, "They are programming the gemstones to the third level. That's the usual level of most medallions of this kind. This particular medallion is to be worn by a healer, a practitioner of the Sacred Science. It means that he or she will have the capability of carrying out feats of what you refer to as magic up to level three. The medallion can be programmed to a higher level but that is unusual."

"Will you be able to tell me what the gemstones of my medallion were programmed to do?" asked Angi.

"Yes, that is what you and I will be doing after this presentation. I will put your medallion into a similar device which will give us a complete reading of what was programmed into the gemstones and the entire medallion."

"But I thought you were there when it was created?" asked Angi.

"That is true Angi, but that was a long time ago. I also think you would like your own record as to what your medallion was created to do," replied Myttrwn.

"Yes, that would be appreciated," replied Angi, and she thought, "Another plus for telepathy."

"But before we do that let's watch the rest of the program," encouraged Myttrwn.

Next they watched as the two men introduced two methods for the insertion and removal of the gemstones. One method used verbal commands, which Angi found difficult to understand. The second, was familiar. The gemstones were placed next to the medallion which caused an electric arc to rise from a central stone, retrieve each gemstone, and insert it precisely into its correct socket. Removing the gemstones occurred by pressing a minute leaver at the back of the medallion near the central gemstone. At that moment she thought to herself, "My medallion, created on Earth thousands of years ago, was following a well-known formula. I wonder how many medallions have ever been created and how each wearer is selected. Perhaps, like me, it is all by the individual's DNA. So many questions." Then she asked, "Myttrwn, are there special commands for medallions or does each medallion have its own?"

"Tomorrow, I will be discussing word energy with the whole group, so for today I will just say that we use special word combinations to activate some of our technology. It is knowledge of such commands which, if known, would give your scientists a vast new understanding of the past."

As Angi watched, the two attendants next proceeded to chant over the medallion which lasted a few minutes. Angi was curious and asked, "Why are they chanting?"

"Our Sacred Science requires that we acknowledge the all-pervasive power of the Law of One in everything we do. The closest comparison I can give you is prayer in your world."

Angi thought to herself, "It is sad that we have mostly wiped away any reference to a higher power in our health system. Later, I must ask Myttrwn to explain what he means by the Law of One. Sirona used the same phrase when we first met."

Next the attendants began testing the medallion. Each function, initiated by a verbal command, resulted in a visible reaction; objects levitated, light increased and decreased in other objects, a mist appeared out of nowhere, and a broken gemstone was repaired. No sooner had the thought entered her mind, "Is this magic or real science?" when Myttrwn spoke.

"Angi, this is the initial testing of any medallion which may be similar to the testing of any newly manufactured item in your world. The computer stipulates whether the medallion has met the technical criteria, which it did. Next an item of this sophistication will be given an operational test with the intended wearer. In this case, such operational testing would involve all three levels, if possible."

"Myttrwn, I've noticed the snake symbol keeps popping up everywhere in your kingdom, can you tell me what it means?" asked Angi.

"The snake symbol is universal and represents the world of energy vibrations which are transmitted by sound. This was a global symbol at the time of the descending Dwapara Yuga. Ancient societies like Egypt already knew how matter was formed, the vibration of energy, cosmic strings (which they called the 'movement of threads'), waves and particles, knowledge of harmonic laws, and even quantum mechanics. You will soon discover that ancient mathematics is similar to what you have been using in your modern computers. In essence, your scientists are rediscovering what was already known before the Kali Yuga."

"Why is such symbolism so prevalent?" asked Angi, still pursuing the topic.

"Such symbolism was designed to evoke an idea or concept in its entirety. It was used to bypass the intellect and go directly to the intelligence of the heart. The sacredness of the symbol was an adjunct to our Sacred Science and during your Kali Yuga was transmitted through mythology. Such symbolism reinforced the wealth of connections and correlations up and down the hierarchies which pervade every sphere of physical, mental and spiritual life. By ignoring mythology your scientists have lost an immense understanding of ancient scientific knowledge."

As the holographic program came to a conclusion, Angi turned to Myttrwn. "Now can we test my medallion?"

"Absolutely, come over here and I will place it in this machine," said Myttrwn. "This time you can remove the medallion yourself."

Angi undid the clasp and passed the medallion over to Myttrwn who on another verbal command activated the computer program. Within seconds the lights ceased flashing and data appeared on a white panel above the machine. Another command from Myttrwn elicited a written report in English. Myttrwn passed the single sheet to Angi. "So what does it say, Angi?"

Angi started to read aloud the contents of the report, "It states that the origin of the medallion is unknown as it was not created on Tir na nOg. The type of gold used in the medallion can be found on Gaia near what is now known as Africa. If measured in Earth years the medallion is well over two thousand years old. It has been programmed to the seventh level, making it an extraordinary device even by Tir na nOg standards. Because of its complexity, the device should only be worn by an advanced practitioner of the Sacred Science, one well-versed in how to manipulate all seven levels and combinations of powers built into the device. Then it goes on to comment on the gemstones. The gemstones are from Tir na nOg, and are of the highest quality. After so many years there has been relatively little damage." Putting the sheet down on the table Angi turned to Myttrwn and added, "Thank you, Myttrwn. It helps to know more about my medallion but it also points out one glaring problem. I am not an advanced practitioner of your Sacred Science. In addition, it is a bit intimidating to learn that this medallion is programmed four levels above most medallions. What does that mean?"

Myttrwn cautiously selected his words, "Angi, we knew that with the closure of the Serpent's Gate and the earth descending into the Kali Yuga that many of the old training programs would be lost. While I am pleased the Earth has advanced as far as it has at this time in its evolution, it is still not able to understand a device of this complexity. You had to come here to get this training. After so many centuries it is a miracle that the medallion survived intact and your DNA was sufficient for it not to kill you. Truthfully, we did not expect a young woman like yourself to appear as the wearer. But your youthfulness is a positive. It is good you are apprehensive and frightened by the powers of this device. Training you to use the medallion to the seventh level will be my honour. It will take time but I know you can do it. Sirona and I want you to succeed. It is our role to help you." Then he thought to himself, "Seven.........the ancient number of the serpent. I had forgotten that detail. It was chosen to remind us that the creators of this magnificent device were practitioners of the Sacred Science. There was to be no question of its authenticity when tested."

Having obtained the information she sought, Angi wanted to share her feelings with Sirona and Myttrwn. "I feel like I'm standing on a precipice, uncertain of the next step. I never envisioned myself in such circumstances. I trust both of you and know you want me to succeed. I must also believe that myself. I need time to think this over. If it is any consolation, one part of me wants to proceed while the other wants to run."

Cautious, and not wanting to push her, Myttrwn responded, "That's fine Angi. Give yourself time," being fully aware of the scarcity of time. "Could I ask that you not discuss this with your group as this must be your own decision? Please meditate on this. Be assured Sirona and I will be available if you wish further information."

Prior to leaving, Sirona communicated telepathically to Myttrwn, "This is what Angi did when I first started working with her. She will come around. She needs time. Intuitively she knows if she accepts, this will dominate the rest of her life. I must also talk to you about the seventh level of this medallion. I've never encountered one before."

Angi walked back to the House of Learning alone, struggling with her thoughts. "Well, I got my wish. I have more information. I'm not sure if it helped. But if I proceed it is going to take an immense amount of training to control this powerful device. Will I live long enough to reach level seven? I owe it to Myttrwn and Sirona to get back to them in twenty-four hours. Time is of the essence."

That evening, Angi retired early to wrestle with her decision.

House of Learning, Angi's Suite

Angi filled the evening with bouts of meditation, sitting quietly or pacing. At one point, she lamented, "Oh, Gran, I miss your wise council. How often I heard you say, 'Angi, why don't you sleep on it, an answer will come in the morning.'" Heartened by the thought, she added, "You know, that is just what I will do!"

Restless, Angi tossed and turned, her subconscious refusing to let her relax. Having dozed off, a familiar dream upset what little sleep she would have. Again, she found herself in a pitch black room wanting to reach a raised dais in the distance. Straining, she could make out a dimly-lit altar. Hesitating, she stepped forth only to encounter the same menacing presence with flaming eyes that landed on her chest causing her to fall backwards.

Fear and helplessness lingered upon wakening. "A second round of that damnable dream. Let's hope a third never turns up." She got out of bed, pushed her feet into cloth slippers, and headed towards the balcony. "I will use my in-house therapy of fresh air, silence, and scenery to settle my nerves." Looking at the distant moons she estimated it was about four in the morning. Finding her favourite reclining chair, she sat down, comforting herself by wrapping her arms around her legs. Alone, with her eyes closed, she was unaware a familiar guest had arrived, until she spoke.

"You are dealing with a weighty decision this morning, Angi?" came Adawee's gentle greeting.

Angi looked up to find her feathery friend, the Snowy Owl, sitting on a branch of a potted tree near her chair, the yellow cat-like eyes staring at her. Her first thought was, "Apparently, others can read minds. I wonder if it is a common trait." Then responding to her guest's greeting, she replied, "Adawee, it is good to see you again. You are right. I need to make a major decision, one that could affect my entire life. I know you can't intercede, but if there is anything you can contribute I would be most grateful." Then a thought entered her mind, "I'm now asking an owl for advice. This journey grows in weirdness."

Sympathetic to Angi's dilemma, Adawee replied, "Maybe chatting about other things may help you find the answer."

"Definitely, a digression is what I need," replied Angi, grateful for Adawee's suggestion. "Let's begin."

Adawee repositioned herself on the branch and commenced. "Angi, do you believe people possess a basic wisdom, or are some people better than others?"

"I don't believe I've ever thought about this before," replied Angi, taking time before commenting further. "I guess I believe there is a basic human wisdom, but some may need leadership before using it."

"Then, do you think there is a basic goodness in people?"

"As a child I was taught that there was goodness in everyone. But as I grew older doubts set in. For instance, what goodness is there in those who abuse others, physically or mentally? Our world is just recognizing the destructiveness of physical abuse. It has yet to come to terms with the lingering wounds of mental abuse. These are but a few."

"Then your childhood views have changed, goodness is not prevalent," was Adawee's assessment of Angi's comments.

"Perhaps that was a bit rash. I would like to believe there is goodness in people. I do not want to give up on humanity no matter how much negativity inundates our lives. I expect a great deal of world chaos is because people don't care enough about themselves and others and far too many cannot forgive."

"Angi, all worlds struggle with this at some time in their evolution. That is why we introduce meditation very early into the lives of our children. Meditation helps them to renounce small-mindedness, personal territory and ego. It opens their minds to higher principles and instructs them to be honest and genuine."

"My daily meditation certainly helps me. Unfortunately, meditation is not promoted in our schools, instead, sadly, we seem to elevate the ego which inflates selfishness."

"On the topic of honesty, Angi, do you regard honesty and the willingness to share ones thoughts and feelings with others a sign of strength or weakness?"

"I personally regard honesty and openness as a sign of strength," came Angi's immediate reply. "Truthfulness ranks high in my books. I struggle with those who habitually lie. In fact as nurses we were taught lying is an early symptom of mental illness. Yet, in my world there are individuals who pride themselves on how well they can lie and get away with it. I can still be hoodwinked by a seasoned liar."

"Hoodwinked?...............You have a delightful use of words," came Adawee's reply as if struggling for meaning. Then she replied, "Ah, I understand. You are right, Angi, chronic liars are destructive. They eventually reach a point of believing their own lies and cannot see truth in any situation. Following on from this, what is your opinion of people who manipulate others?"

Hesitating for a few seconds, Angi replied, "I have encountered a variety of manipulative behaviours, some in my professional life. There is a range; some good and most not so good. I can understand a parent's role in maneuvering a child through his or her formative years to follow the right path in life. However, this gentle manipulation needs to be curtailed when the child grows up. Some parents do not know when to switch off such behaviour. But the real culprits are those who, because of their own insecurities and warped egos, feel compelled to dominate others in every relationship. Actually, it is just another form of abuse. Fortunately, I have also met individuals who have little desire to manipulate others. These are the peacemakers."

"Do you think that greater discipline would reduce the abuse in your world?" came Adawee's next pointed question.

"That's a tough one. In recent decades when discipline got linked to physical abuse, all forms of discipline were shunned. Lost was the understanding that a society is damaged when action and intellect are undisciplined and unsynchronized. It is no wonder we are facing an epidemic of bullying. Without discipline, it will only get worse. For me, discipline is connected with how one becomes a more gentle and genuine human being by overcoming selfishness. Until discipline becomes natural we may never reach enlightenment. Does that answer your question?" came Angi's thoughtful reply.

"You are doing just fine, Angi. Actually, the greater the self-discipline the more joyous life becomes. Those who have learned self-control know the way to real happiness. Is there anything else you would like to add?" for Adawee was not only learning a great deal about Angi, she was also gaining insight into her world with each reply.

"I can only comment on the portion of world that I know. It bothers me that our minds are being daily inundated with sensation and violent news. So many people crave positive energy. This daily diet of negative input is creating a society where pleasure has been cheapened, joy reduced, and happiness tied to money and the acquisition of material things. At the same time, mental illness and addictions are soaring as more and more people feel alienated, lonely and lost. With science replacing religion, people have nothing to live for, nothing to look forward to after they die and even ethics and morality are losing their place in our society. That's not a pretty picture, is it? Myttrwn says we are moving into the Dwapara Yuga and greater enlightenment. You would be hard pressed to see enlightenment in the midst of the picture I've just painted."

"Your description tells me that there is a lot of Kali Yuga still prevalent in your society even after its transition phase. You are right, more positive energy is needed."

"While I have given you a somewhat gloomy picture, I too must provide some balance. In the midst of all of this mess there are those who are the light bearers, who show tremendous kindness and caring for others. These are the angels that help preserve our world. Myttrwn says that such kindness will increase in the days ahead which gives me hope."

"Let's move to a different topic, Angi. What do you regard as sacred?"

"That's a huge topic. Let me see. I was brought up in a Christian community that taught that the sacred was all around me, and particularly in my church and community. In recent years, my views have changed by meeting others of different religions, and realizing our young people, who mostly shun organized religions, are focused on the environment. The sacred for me has shifted beyond buildings and single communities to the world at large. Everything is mysterious and sacred. Did that answer your question?"

"It did, Angi, in your own delightful way," was Adawee's reply. "The universe is sacred and every situation has the potential for sacredness. When gentleness, decency and truthfulness, become common then your world will flourish." With time running out, Adawee shifted to another topic and asked Angi, "What is your understanding of reincarnation and karma?"

"This too has changed," was Angi's quick reply. "As a child I was taught that reincarnation did not exist. Lately, I'm not so sure. When I first met Sirona she informed me that I was immortal. That was a surprise. This statement forced me to reconsider reincarnation. But I am a neophyte on these two topics. Perhaps this time I will turn the tables and ask you if you can give me some insight into these topics. Is that permitted?"

"Indeed it is," replied Adawee, as she shifted her position on the branch. "Angi, you are the creator of your own Hero's Journey. Seventy-five percent of your life has been predetermined by your own past lives. With each lifetime you have twenty-five percent to work on. If you do not change the twenty-five percent in a lifetime, then your past lives take control of your life. You can chose to do nothing, take an evil path or decide to grow. There is no point in blaming others, stumbling blocks exist to facilitate your decision making. As you now know, life is an illusion in which you get numerous opportunities to act. Basically, you control your own destiny."

"In other words, reincarnation keeps happening because I still haven't learned something or there are dents in my karma that need attention," replied Angi, after carefully following what Adawee had said.

"I don't believe I've ever heard it stated so succinctly," replied Adawee, "but you have captured the essence. If you aim for greater enlightenment, then you can reduce your return trips. The more you develop your mind the more divine you become."

"So, it is my choice to grow or retreat?" came Angi's almost enthusiastic reply.

"It is all in your hands, Angi," came Adawee's words of encouragement. "You control your destiny. As you will learn, the past and the future are illusions, this moment is critical."

"Adawee, thank you, this has been a timely discussion. Now, is it OK for me to tell my friends about these chats?"

"A little while yet, Angi. We need to meet again."

"Very well," replied Angi, reluctantly.

Then sensing Adawee's visit was about to end, Angi was determined to see how she departed. With no warning, Angi stared as Adawee evaporated in a mist.

"There is no end of surprises," thought Angi. "I expect she's another holographic image, just like Sirona when we first met." Feeling rejuvenated, she walked nimbly towards her suite. She now knew what to do.

Chapter 3

The House of Life

The twelve walked briskly across the plaza to the House of Life heading straight for the lecture room with the fourteen armchairs arranged in a circle. No sooner had they arrived than Sirona and Myttrwn appeared.

With little introduction Myttrwn got underway saying, "Today, I will take a few questions on the Yugas as I want to devote our full time to the topic of '*energy*,' a dominant feature of the Dwapara Yuga. Later I will make arrangements for a general discussion on all topics. Is that acceptable?"

Nods gave general consent.

Morgan was the first to speak, "Myttrwn, I don't have a question on the Yugas, but I wonder if you could elaborate on the Law of One?"

"Certainly, Morgan", replied Myttrwn, "The Law of One is a pivotal philosophy and moral code of our kingdom. To us there is one universal mind to which everyone and everything is connected. Everyone is a holographic reflection of this one universal mind. Distinctions of separateness which mankind insist on creating are unthinkable to us. Therefore, for us One represents all the qualities of the universe; male and female, odd and even, beginning and ending, active and passive, above and below, and much more. We represent this principle by the serpent biting its tail, the Uroboros. This symbol of wisdom identifies the seamless, eternal state of oneness. While the serpent is popular in our world and once was in yours, others, like the Egyptians and Mesopotamians used the Shen Ring and the Celts the torc or neck-ring to symbolize the same oneness."

Myttrwn continued, "The Law, in the Law of One, is a moral code attached to this philosophy which focuses on the relationship of the individual to the divine. It stipulates that if the universal mind is in everyone and everything, then all actions must acknowledge this principle. Under this law, each individual is expected to live a moral life, spending time in search of his or her own spiritual enlightenment, and demonstrate by their actions that they adhere to the Law of One."

Andrew was pressed to ask, "As I understand it, Myttrwn, you have no religious organizations as we understand them. Does that mean individuals can seek their own spiritual guide?"

Understanding Andrew's thoughts, Myttrwn responded, "Andrew, the Law of One is a way of life, not a religion. While individuals usually have one spiritual guide throughout their adult life, sometimes this may change for various reasons."

"In keeping with your Law of One, does it mean your strategies and technologies must have both a spiritual and scientific base?" asked Wolfram.

"That's correct, Wolfram. But in my recent observation of your world a critical dichotomy is appearing. Your scientific achievements are advancing rapidly while your spiritual life seems to be shriveling. This is dangerous."

"In what way is it dangerous?" asked Andrew.

"This lack of balance can destroy a civilization," came Myttrwn's reply as he, for the first time, showed genuine concern for the Earth but did not elaborate further.

Continuing the questioning, Wolfram asked, "In technology which has priority, the state or the individual?" realizing the power of the individual back home.

"Society as a whole has priority, the individual comes second," came Myttrwn's immediate reply. "Technology needs to benefit the greatest good. The individual is provided with a great deal of free services on the basis he or she gives back a certain degree of service to their community."

"Does the individual have any choice in the service?" asked Vette.

"This is negotiable, Vette. Sometimes the community makes the change or the Council of Elders asks the individual to serve the kingdom as a whole." Noting the time Myttrwn asked, "Perhaps we could leave any further questions on this to another day as we must allow sufficient time for today's topic."

With hardly a break in rhythm Myttrwn shifted the discussion. "As I mentioned before, the universe, ours and yours, is composed of energy which exists in waves. While this unified world of energy appears to have discrete objects, you are actually only seeing reflections of the real phenomenon. Objects appear separate because things vibrate at different wavelengths. The physical reality you think you are seeing is based on your own perception."

"If that is so, then how come we see the same thing?" came Vette's question, who was struggling with this new revelation.

Expecting the question, Myttrwn replied, "Vette, individuals have been programmed from childhood to accept a certain reality. While people share a global physical reality there may be slight differences between cultures. Nevertheless, the reality created by your five senses is limited as it can only grasp a small percentage of signals. Anything which does not perfectly fit your preconceived reality is filtered out. Your single dimension does not want, nor does it recognize, the multiple dimensions which exist all around you. For example, if you do not accept Extra Sensory Perception, then anything on that topic is deleted. As such, different people end up with slightly different realities. It is nothing more than their brain turning energy into a personal reality, a reality they favour and usually will fight to retain."

Suddenly remembering an example from her previous job, Vette replied, "I suppose that's why people at the scene of an accident often give widely different interpretations of events." Then she added, as if repetition would instill the idea, "So, if I understand what you are saying, this body, which seems solid, is nothing more than energy."

Myttrwn responded, "That's right, Vette, you are made up of layers of energy, which may be described as complex bundles of frozen light or frozen energy."

"Now that's something to contemplate..........I am frozen energy," came Morgan's response, voicing the struggle being experienced by the team.

"Morgan, perhaps you would prefer being called a body of light. The cells of your body actually emit pulses of ultraviolet light. These weak cellular light pulses are part of a light-based communication system that helps to coordinate the actions of your cells. Your DNA stores light as energy. When you are under stress, illness or have sudden outbursts of anger or aggression, you throw off light. The darkness of your light energy will one day be used to diagnose illness and prescribe treatment. But I am getting ahead of myself. To help us with this topic, let's carry out a few simple experiments."

Before proceeding, he added, "I am going to provide you with a small dish of frozen water crystals. I would ask that you do not touch the dish or crystals until our experiments are over." With that, his verbal command brought forth a floating laptop desk for each member containing a glass dish of white crystals sitting securely at its center. An invisible force maintained the frozen state of the crystals while a subtle light source created shades of blue, pink and yellow colours on the tips of the crystals."

Angi's quick observation to Vette was, "What exquisite crystals, just like the ones on a first snowfall."

"Yeh" replied Vette, "It reminds me of home."

Myttrwn ignoring the comments continued, "Just before we begin I would like to comment briefly on water. Water, two parts hydrogen and one part oxygen, is everywhere. It is in you and throughout your world. It is even in the air you breathe. For that reason, prior to your present materialistic age, water was considered holy and used for sacred rituals, drinking or bathing. Today, your waterways have become dumping grounds which will reap dire consequences if unchanged. I'm sure you have detected our drinking water is crystal clear and filled with energy. That was once typical in your world, but no more. Basically, whatever impacts water effects everything."

Remembering her recent trip to Ireland, Angi thought out loud, "The Celts used to have, and some still recognize, sacred wells."

Myttrwn did not respond but pressed on, "You will see that healthy water, which I've used, when frozen, creates symmetrical hexagon crystals. I do not have a sample but polluted water cannot do this, instead it creates a chaotic pattern or, in some instances, is unable to form any pattern. Now let's begin."

While he spoke the group stared at their crystals wondering what role these would have in the upcoming experiments.

"First we will test sound on crystals. Please watch your crystal's reaction to what you refer to as classical music."

The group stared at the crystals while the music filled the room. The crystals shifted slightly to create a unique hexagonal pattern.

Angi was pressed to ask, "Myttrwn, would the crystals form a different pattern with another piece of classical music?"

"Let's see," replied Myttrwn as a different piece of classical music filled the room.

The group watched as the crystals formed a different, but consistently beautiful pattern.

Myttrwn continued the experiment, "Next, I will play a segment of what is labeled in your world 'heavy metal music.'"

When this music filled the room the crystals reacted, unable to form any pattern, and eventually dissolved into a scrambled mess.

"I can almost feel the crystals struggling to do something but the noise is too overpowering," came Andrew's observation.

"If we accept that everything is alive, then Andrew, you are witnessing how garish music affects crystals. Sound is a travelling longitudinal energy wave. Each musical note corresponds to a particular frequency which is measured in hertz (Hz) in your world. Music, a universal language, adapts to the needs of the brain. These two examples demonstrate how different types of music affect the energy system in these crystals. Remember, your cell membranes are liquid crystals and there are other crystals in your body. They will react like this to sound."

"This is the reason classical music is said to benefit animals and plants. So, other than classical music, how would we know what sounds are beneficial?" asked Wolfram.

"The miracle note of the universe exists at 528 Hz. This sound is linked to the heart of everything as well as to the emotion of love. Calming sounds like chanting, laughing, your ordinary voice and nature have all been designed to function at 528 Hz. It is also the frequency needed to repair your DNA. Music tuned to 528 Hz, like the classical music I just played, can bring much healing. As you have now witnessed, music can be spiritually uplifting or degrading."

"You mean that the music people listen to can be making them sick. Now that's a real eye-opener," said Morgan. Turning to the others he added, "Imagine the uproar if we told people their choice in music could be more polluting than their environmental worries. This, of course, opens the whole topic of noise pollution."

"That is something we will discuss further when we delve into a later topic on healing," came Myttrwn's reply. "Know that the study of sound and its effects on humanity will become the greatest benefit to mankind in the years ahead. Eventually you will discover that sound can even nullify the power of gravitation which will open a new power source for your world. There are remnants of the effects of sound on people found in your communities where rituals still involve drums, singing and chanting. Unfortunately, during the Kali Yuga much of the scientific background to sound energy has been lost. But let's move on."

"The spoken word also has energy. You will recall a phrase in one of your ancient books, which I will now quote, '*In the beginning was the Word, and the Word was with God, and the Word was God.*' Words are powerful. The utterance of certain letters or words has been recited by spiritual and mystery schools in your world as a means of exciting certain nervous centers."

"Is that the purpose of mantras?" asked Vette.

"Mantras are precise and specialized tools created by those with the awareness and ability to use them to create some spiritual insight or healing. Mantras are one example of the power of words. Now let's see the effect of words on your crystals."

"First, I will bring in the calming voice of a woman describing a scenic tour of a European coastline."

The group once again watched as the crystals formed a different but pleasant symmetrical hexagon pattern in response to the sound and words.

Before anyone could comment, the next sample, a bombastic news broadcast reporting on killings and disasters, locally and internationally, filled the room. Immediately, the crystals scattered, struggled, and eventually formed a chaotic pattern.

"Now that's impressive," came Bryce's response. "I'm not surprised. I always thought our twenty-four hour news broadcasts of sensations and calamities were damaging our brain. Isn't it amazing, the very media which demands ongoing input into our lives could be their own, and our, worst enemy."

"Just a minute," came Dylan's swift reaction. "Are you inferring that the communication of news is bad for us? The alternative would be that we are kept in the dark and live in danger of the unexpected."

"Let's say some balance, more positive news, might be helpful," came Andrew's input, squelching the potential of an argument. "Surely, having a steady diet of fear and calamities can't be doing us any good."

Myttrwn interceded, "Very good. This experiment was to show you that words can improve your energy or sap your light. Fear stifles your ability to move forward. Just think, if the crystals respond to a relatively normal media broadcast, what do you think is happening when words are accompanied by outbursts of anger or hate?"

"And just think of the consequences of film and video games," replied Angi. "Most of these are filled with violence, noise and aggression. If you thought changing music preferences might be difficult, imagine trying to alter the film and video game world."

"While grappling with these money making empires could be definitely daunting, Angi, what about the everyday word pollution which occurs in gossip sessions, cocktail parties or through today's technology," came Morgan's reflective input. "It is no wonder certain individuals crave solitude. Wouldn't it be ironic if the current generation reaches a point of word overload and at sixty become hermits?" Everyone laughed.

"In addition, Myttrwn, we are also aware of the power of words which you use to create these magical teaching props. But I expect that is at another level all together," came Andrew's pointed input.

"Indeed, Andrew. In time, we will address this form of word power. But right now time is passing and I would like to do one more experiment, this time with your thoughts. I want you to think, but not vocalize, the words 'I love you' over your crystal dish."

The group did as instructed and watched as the crystals responded by forming another symmetrical pattern in response to the positive thought.

Quickly Myttrwn added, "Now I want you to do the same thought process but this time use the phrase 'I despise you' and say it with feeling."

The group again watched a similar reaction to the rock music and the negative news broadcast as the crystals struggled to create a pattern in response to the negative thought.

Myttrwn followed up with, "As you can see, thoughts can also produce an electrical disturbance, positive or negative. Thoughts and emotions are vibrational energy waves. Emotions hold the vibrational pattern in the liquid crystals which exist in your body. For this reason, positive feelings such as caring and love can affect not only your immediate surroundings but the world at large. Sometime in your distant future, at the time of the Treta Yuga, mankind will comprehend that everything is made up of ideas and thoughts.

As a result mankind will be able to more effectively manipulate and control such energy."

"Wow, this is an awakening. I had no idea thoughts had such power," came Angi's reaction. "Our culture has taught us that negative thoughts don't matter. As long as you refrain from any overt action no harm is done. This test demonstrates that those who harbour or promote resentment, hate, or anger, are destroying the world even if they say they are not involved in any outward conflict. The question is how to redirect people to understand that their own thoughts are causing such damage."

"OK, if the global mess we are experiencing on Earth can be attributed to the thoughts of people, how can we change their thinking?" asked Wolfram. "That, to me, is an impossibility."

"We will discuss this later, Wolfram. But first individuals will need to understand the power of their thoughts on energy. Then they will need to start getting rid of the negativity in their world and redirect their thinking," replied Myttrwn, pleased that they were beginning to grasp the enormity of the problem.

"I'm curious," Morgan added, "Does telepathy eliminate unwanted thoughts?" He now suspected this ability was more prevalent than he had first thought.

"Actually, Morgan, it doesn't totally eliminate the problem. Some become skilled in blocking their thoughts."

Vette couldn't hold back, "But still, if thought pollution clung to people like a rash, people would probably make every effort to change. In our world, negative character traits such as meanness of spirit, unkindness, self-centeredness, avarice, and greed are sometimes difficult to spot. Perhaps one day people harbouring selfish thoughts and negative emotions would be considered unattractive even if physically beautiful. I expect telepathy would also enable us to see the impact of our thoughts and words on other people. Now that's scary."

"You will likely have much to think about after today," was Myttrwn's signal the session was winding down. "What I want you to understand from this exercise is that sound, words and thoughts can have positive or devastating effects on people. This is especially true now that you have entered the World Wide Web. But before closing I have one more point to add."

The group looked at each other wondering what to expect.

"You should also realize that your intentions also have energy. Intentions can have a measurable effect on physical objects. For example, if intentions can affect the chemistry of water at a great distance, what effect do you think intentions are having in your world? I will leave this for you to ponder."

"You know that fits into something I've read recently," said Morgan. "There is now evidence that a researcher can affect his or her own research. How can we be sure that the results being reported have not been influenced by the researcher? This could have major implications."

At that moment, a single command from Myttrwn caused the laptop desk and crystal dishes to disappear. As he stood to leave, he added with a smile, "As you discuss this further may it not pressure you into silence. Its purpose was to have you understand the powerful effects of positive music, words, thoughts and intentions on your life and the world around you. Understand, much of your negative thoughts on reality were instilled from childhood, fostered in your educational system and are being daily reinforced by your media. These negative energies can deplete your light and lead to illness. Your brain now must come to terms with a different reality. The underlying question is whether you are able or willing to change."

While the intent wasn't to create silence, the walk back to the House of Learning was mostly muted as each member struggled with Myttrwn's gentle introduction to an altered reality.

๖

House of Learning, Dining Area

As was their custom, the group headed to their dining area, picked up a refreshment, and selected a seat, not knowing what to say. Dylan was the first to speak.

"That session put the kibosh into a lot of things," came Dylan's frustrated response. "All I need now is a sound gauge to find music at the 528 Hz level, reduce my desire for news, and definitely cool my intentions and thoughts. In summary, to imitate those students we've been encountering. By the way, how do they get their news anyway? There are no television monitors that I can see."

Morgan had been waiting for the chance and responded, "Has it dawned on you that they are all telepathic? I first thought only Myttrwn and Sirona had the ability, but I've changed my mind. Being telepathic they have no need for news broadcasts they just know. I haven't yet figured out how that works in a learning situation."

"Wow, just think of the implications in our world when we become telepathic as Myttrwn's seems to infer." Glancing at the smiling faces Vette went on, "I know.......... I know.........it is centuries away. But it will definitely be a blow to the communication industry."

"I will have to think about that, Morgan," came Dylan's hesitant response. "If you are right, then we're at a decided disadvantage. If everyone can read our thoughts and we can't block them, then our actions are known before we make a move. Angi can you do anything with your medallion?"

"Sorry, Dylan, I can't," came Angi's reply, "I just learned what Sirona taught me was just enough to get us here in one piece. My time with Myttrwn has shown me that my medallion is not one of a kind, similar ones have been made. But I did learn that this medallion is programmed four levels above most medallions."

"Any idea what that means, Angi?" asked Wolfram.

"Not yet," came Angi's hesitant reply, "I'm still struggling with whether I even want to proceed. Whatever I decide it is for life."

Startled by her comment Wolfram reacted, "You mean you might not proceed with the training?"

Andrew, understanding the enormity of Angi's predicament, interjected, "Wolfram I expect this is a decision that Angi must make by herself."

Angi's glance at Andrew confirmed his suspicions.

Wolfram caught the signal and made no further comment on the topic.

But Morgan seized the opportunity saying, "Then let's get back to our discussion. In music, I expect that there is a range of positive sounds. We will need to explore this further with Myttrwn. I definitely need to know more."

Bryce waiting to comment added, "I'd like to talk about words. You know the impact of certain words is not so strange. Some computers and robots already respond to verbal commands. I admit, Myttrwn's magical demonstrations are definitely in another league. Yet, we must remember that we've fought a war over the impact of a charismatic speaker on his people. Words can be more dangerous than you think."

Wolfram listening, decided to make his contribution, "I must commend Dylan on his superb summary of today's session and I agree with Bryce. While I may have had my suspicions, I had no idea how powerful music, words, thoughts and intentions could be. Just imagine what this is doing to our world. I've also noted that while Myttrwn cleverly leads us into his Sacred Science, I have an uneasiness it is going to come at a price..........I don't suppose any of you can answer that one?"

Remembering the quiet inference from Myttrwn and Sirona that the entire group would have a future role, Wolfram's comment registered with Angi, and forced her to say, "Surely, Wolfram, Myttrwn can't expect a small group like us to make any major impact in our world. The majority of people in the Western nations would scream like mad about their God-given right to listen to, say and think whatever they want, irrespective of its effect on their own health or their environment. After all, no one to my knowledge has every suggested that any of this negative energy might be killing them."

Vette now entered the discussion, "But Angi, change is already happening. In the past decades there have been improvements in the environment, admittedly, the steps taken are minute and do not include the entire globe."

"But Vette, do you actually envision people changing their choice of music based on its negative impact to their health," came Angi's reply, denoting her own skepticism at such a change.

Morgan jumped in, "Not likely. But Vette may have a point. If people realized that certain sounds, words, and thoughts were causing serious illness then maybe, just maybe, they might change. Just look at the decline in smoking."

Angi couldn't resist, "Oh help. Morgan, you are about to step into the wild world of health prevention, something that has had little headway in decades. The reasons are obvious, there are too many people and industries who are currently making a fortune on illness."

Vette caught Angi's gist and added, "You are right, Angi, people fight when they sense any threat to their lucrative income, or am I being a bit cynical?"

Andrew could see the implications, and decided to wade in, "I must say this session has stimulated an amazing response from all of you. I agree with Wolfram, Myttrwn and Sirona have a game plan, but the details are still obscure. These sessions are leading us onward. Myttrwn is not a man to waste valuable time. Whether its destiny or fate that brought us here, we will be expected to do something. Let's wait and see."

"You know, after this session I just realized what Myttrwn was gently trying to say to us in his first session. Our world, viewed from their more enlightened position, must seem like an unpleasant, loud, noisy, rough, undisciplined, and backward neighbour, one best left alone for fear of contamination," came Dylan's assessment.

"That's a bit strong," came Morgan's defensive reply, "I'd like to believe our group is its best representative and that there is room for improvement."

"There, Dylan, always count on Morgan to see the positive side," came Wolfram's calming reply. "But let's agree we've been given something to think about. It is also helpful to see ourselves from someone else's perspective, it is supposed to help us grow."

Andrew concluded, "The challenge is for us to see how today's information fits into the broader picture. Maybe our next session will give us a glimpse of Myttrwn's plan."

With the easing of tension, the conversations took a lighter note. Yet, for most the effects from music, words, thoughts and intentions on their personal energy and health would remain, causing them to rethink certain choices.

ᘒ

The House of Life

Decision time. Angi walked purposely towards her appointment with Myttrwn and Sirona. She appreciated their restraint and was not surprised to find them both present when she arrived at Myttrwn's lab.

Myttrwn's calm greeting displayed interest but no pressure, "I expect Angi you have something to tell us."

"I have," came Angi response, knowing perfectly well that both Myttrwn and Sirona already knew what she was about to say from the moment she entered the lab. Determined, she reassured herself with, "I don't care if they know or not, I'm going to verbally state my position for the record." Then she said, "While I remain uneasy as to what may lie ahead, I will proceed with the training. Perhaps it will give me insight into why I am here."

Sirona smiled. Her assessment of Angi had been correct.

Devoid of emotion, Myttrwn's only reply was, "Very good, then let's get started. Today, Angi, we will work on the basics. The ultimate goal is that you will eventually be able to operate the medallion with your thoughts. Prior to your arrival, Sirona kept me informed on how you were progressing with the medallion. Now, for my own records I need to conduct a few tests."

But before commencing, Angi wanted answers to a few niggling questions, and asked, "Myttrwn, I was wondering if we will be covering all seven levels of the medallion during my first visit to your kingdom?" Thinking to herself she continued, "With no program prospectus I'm just going to ask questions."

Myttrwn read her thoughts and responded, "Depending on my assessment, we will likely have time for the first and maybe some of the second level training. After that, each time you visit our kingdom we will continue with the other levels. Know that levels four to seven may take more time as they are quite difficult."

"That's a relief," thought Angi, "I prefer bite size learning units." Not wanting to let go of the opportunity she pressed on, "I'm curious, how many people have a level seven medallion?"

In a flash Myttrwn realized Angi wanted to know how many she might encounter with similar powers and responded, "There are very few, Angi. As I said before, most medallion wearers operate at level three, and are usually senior elders who have come through a rigorous training program either in our kingdom or elsewhere in our universe. The few who have had a level seven medallion, were usually specially chosen spiritual leaders of a group of people either on the verge of a long period of evolutionary turmoil or entering a new stage of enlightenment. Your medallion has survived over two thousand years of the Kali Yuga guarded by different spiritually minded individuals. There are no other medallions of level three or higher on your planet. You are unique."

Weighing his remarks, Angi replied hesitantly, "So, I'm unique. That's not what I wanted to hear. From your comments I seem to be bereft of some major credentials. I'm not a senior elder, a spiritual leader nor do I have years of medallion or similar training or experience. Sirona indicated that the ancient Druid medallion wearers had twenty or more years of training and experience. As such, I would have had to start my training at birth. I expect the Dwapara Yuga is what is meant by a new stage of enlightenment, and my knowledge of that is abysmal. As I see it, there are some gaping holes in my qualifications which supports my misgivings as to why I was chosen in the first place. Nevertheless, I remain committed. I am counting on your wisdom, Myttrwn, to tell me if I qualify. This actually comforts me as I will know one way or another what lies ahead."

Myttrwn smiled and gave a quick glance at Sirona. His initial misgivings at training such a young woman with a medallion of such magnitude were slowly changing. The more he got to know Angi the more he was encouraged that Fate had chosen well. While she was the youngest medallion trainee he had known, her honesty and humility were positive signs. He also recalled Sirona's observation, when pushed Angi seemed to instantly know what to do. If true, he thought, then maybe he had in front of him a cosmic anomaly.

At that moment, with the wave of his hand, Myttrwn sealed off his private quarters to the rest of the lab. Then he gestured to the round table saying, "Come with me, Angi, I would like you to show me what you can do."

On the table sat three items; a cloth napkin, a small open box and a glass paperweight. "I would like you to raise each item separately to this level," as he gestured with his hand, "and then lower each one gently back to its original position on the table."

As requested, Angi, using her hand as a guide, raised each item in sequence about two feet above the table and lowered each one as gently as possible.

"Very good," said Myttrwn. "Now Angi, I want you to raise the box to the ceiling, then over to the left wall and back to the table."

This request, requiring greater concentration, caused Angi to close her eyes. The box rose straight to the ceiling, bumping the tiles. The next step was more difficult. In a jerky motion she moved the box to the wall and back to the table.

With no comment Myttrwn pressed on, "Now I am going to create a ball of mist above the table. I want you to move the mist in a wide circle around the room, and when you return to the table, I want you to reduce the ball in half. Is that clear?"

"I think so," replied Angi.

With a verbal command from Myttrwn a ball of white mist materialized and floated above the table.

Angi, remembering her time on the Isle of Iona in Scotland, slowly guided the ball of mist around the room and stopped when it returned to the table. Concentrating, she closed her eyes to envision a ball of mist halved. Then pressing her hand over the medallion she commanded silently, "I demand you decrease to half your size." Not sure what to expect, she opened her eyes to find, to her delight, the ball of mist had been halved. Smiling she turned to Myttrwn and Sirona, pleased at her achievement.

Myttrwn was more than pleased. He knew the last two tests were deliberately intended to be slightly out of Angi's reported range. He thought to himself, "This is a first. It is rare to have a beginner perform tests like this. She seems to act on instinct. I can't believe that after so many centuries and genetic mixing there could be any inherent abilities left. Other than Sirona, she's had no instructor. Yet, she did it. I will have to recheck her profile. The first tests confirmed her genetic qualifications to wear the medallion. Now I will need to check each gene and vibration..........there has to be something to explain this innate ability. This presents an intriguing dilemma. For the first time I will need to block my own thoughts until I am sure of my findings." Showing no sign of his reflections, Myttrwn continued, "Angi. I've learned from Sirona that you were also able to heal others. This we will test on another occasion. I have sufficient material to begin." With that he dissolved the mist.

Sirona knew what had happened and realized the implications. She too would have to begin blocking some thoughts regarding Angi, a first for her as well.

Myttrwn reached into a drawer of the table and brought out some sheets of paper saying, "Our next step is for you to familiarize yourself with your gemstones. I've prepared this printed material for you as you may prefer this form of reference for your studies. While we're discussing gemstones, Sirona will program this information into your phone for easy reference."

Angi reached into her pocket and passed her cell phone to Sirona.

"You will see on the first sheet that I have identified the nine gemstones along with a numbering system. From this day, Sirona and I will keep testing your memory on this material. If we give you a number, we will expect you to immediately identify the gemstone. If we give you the gemstone name, we will expect you to give us the number. Let's try this. If I say four what is your answer?"

Looking at the illustration Angi found four and answered, "Amber."

Sirona joined in, "And if I say Sapphire, your answer will be?"

Checking again, Angi replied, "Three."

"I want you to memorize this material," came Myttrwn's firm instructions.

"I will be ready," came Angi's immediate reply. In looking at the sheet, she was pressed to ask, "And can you tell me why there are nine gemstones? Does nine have any special meaning in your kingdom?" As she spoke she pulled out several printed sheets which she had taken from Earth saying, "I was curious about nine gemstones, so I did my own research. What I discovered was that nine turns up more frequently than I would have expected. It is a worldwide phenomenon which cannot be a coincidence. May I read off what I discovered?"

"Indeed, I'm impressed with your initiative," replied Myttrwn, glancing at Sirona. Angi's resourcefulness pleased him and he was equally curious as to what was still available in the Earth records.

Angi positioning herself on one of the benches in front of the round table. "To save time I will just read off the items making no comment on any details."

Noting the amount of information Angi was about to report, Sirona and Myttrwn pulled out the other two benches and waited.

In a steady voice, Angi proceeded, "In the Americas, the Hopi Indians have nine ceremonies and nine prophecies that they believe have already been fulfilled which, according to them, will usher in a day of purification. In South America, the Mayan Indians speak of the Ninth Lord of the Night and, at a time of great change, a return of the nine Night Lords. In Peru their ancient records speak of nine healing gates. The Kogi aboriginals of Columbia speak of nine levels of consciousness."

"In the east, the ancient Chinese had nine cauldrons of transformation in which brewed nine ingredients to create an elixir of immortality, they also had a ninth heaven, and in the royal palace the doors, windows, stairs and fixtures existed in multiples of nine or a number that contained nine. The Tibetans speak of nine transitional states or states of consciousness. In the mythological Tibetan kingdom of Shambhala there exists a palace of nine levels and the kingdom's ninth state of consciousness was said to be listed as the 'radiant mind of enlightenment.' In India there are nine forms of the goddess Shakti who is worshipped for nine days."

"In the Middle East the ancient Egyptians had several nine-god groups, they believed in nine levels of the cosmos, and they stated that nine represented spiritual and mental achievement. The Chaldeans believed the number nine to be sacred and kept it apart in their numerology. Kabbalistic

Jews drew nine sephiroth of spheres above the Earth. Enoch, in antediluvian texts, left mankind nine vaults of ancient knowledge. In later centuries, there were nine Templar Knights digging under Solomon's temple."

"In the west the Greeks talked about nine ethereal spheres around the earth. The Romans had nine priestesses who were healers and Roman baby boys went through a purification ceremony when they were nine days old. The Etruscans worshipped nine gods. In the northern region, the Norse also had nine gods. The Welsh had a cauldron tended by nine virgins. The Christians refer to nine choirs of angels around the throne of God."

"In summary, the number nine seems to be associated not only with the Underworld, the Overworld and altered states of consciousness, but also with precession, ancient calendars, and maidens. Nine is the number of the Great Goddess on Earth who is considered thrice sacred and represents perfection. And, not to be forgotten, there are nine months to a human pregnancy. I also found this rather interesting bit of information in numerology which identified the positive characteristics of the number nine. These are selflessness, fulfillment, completion, universality, universal understanding, interrelatedness, compassion, idealism, tolerance, forgiveness, generosity, benevolence, humanitarianism, and justice. It seems that the number nine was held in great esteem by many cultures, but its importance has diminished in our modern world. While interesting, does any of this have any bearing on my medallion?"

Myttrwn and Sirona looked at each other and smiled. Myttrwn spoke, "I must say, Angi, your research is impressive. I have little else to add except that the number nine has been an ancient, eternal number and a significant symbol in both our worlds. What is amazing is how firmly it has been retained in your world during the Kali Yuga. All I can add is that it is a number of compassion, divine will, and often associated with great profits. It is a symbol of change and transformation. Some say it may also be a warning or turning point. As I recall, the number and type of gemstones in your medallion were chosen with immense care. The creators of the medallion knew the future and had high expectations it would survive. Your question is appropriate at the beginning of your training. May I suggest you share this research with your colleagues. Now let's get more acquainted with your gemstones."

Sirona remained. She had made arrangements with Myttrwn to be present for Angi's training. She too wanted to know more about this exceptional medallion.

"Let us begin with a bit of background on crystals," was Myttrwn's opening remarks. "Advancing what you've already learned in my general sessions, you will understand that all matter is an expression of light and energy. Which means gemstones are alive, each with its own energy, some greater than others. In time you will learn that crystalline structures also respond to a wide spectrum of other energies including heat, light, pressure, sound, electricity, rays, and even thought waves. Some of these we will be discussing later when we cover the topic of healing."

Always intrigued by Myttrwn's wisdom, Angi responded, "So, my medallion gemstones are alive, and able to respond to different stimuli. I guess I should talk to them, occasionally."

Myttrwn replied, "That's a good idea, Angi, this medallion will, in time, become part of your entire being. But let me elaborate further. In designing your medallion with a specific number and type of gemstones the intent was to expand the powers of each gemstone in order to achieve a powerful synergistic effect. The two vibrating power horses of your medallion are the central blue stone which vibrates at fifty-five and the diamond at thirty-three. The rest of the gemstones vibrate in the single digit range. However, when you combine two gemstones for any purpose, just because they are in this multiple configuration, their energy output will be enhanced. For this reason, you will need to know the properties of each gemstone in both its singular capabilities and in combinations. The possible combinations and permutations of gemstone power in your medallion is impressive."

While he spoke a white screen appeared in front of the round table displaying a table listing the gemstones along with their properties.

"You can see from both the screen and your printed material that there is a great deal of information for you to memorize. Let's first concentrate on the two power horses. The center stone, which is known on Earth as a Larimar stone, is one of a number of beautiful stones from Atlantis. It is not only known for its extraordinary healing properties, it also helps in dissolving boundaries, and promoting wisdom, clarity, peace, and love. In combination, it can greatly expand any of the other gemstones. I will work with you on this."

Angi gasped, as she remembered Nat Zieglar, the Boston gemologist who also thought the center stone might be from Atlantis. Then she thought to herself, "Perhaps someday I will be able to tell Nat just how accurate he was in his assessment."

Myttrwn ignoring Angi's thought, continued, "The Diamond, the King of the Gemstones, symbolizes the sun. The diamond as a prism gives off a rainbow of colours under certain rays of light. Its properties are known to enhance harmony, spiritual awareness, love and confidence. This gemstone also enhances the other stones. Any questions so far, Angi?"

Scanning the list, she replied, "Not at this time. I definitely have some homework to do." Realizing the session was about to close she folded the sheets of paper, picked up her phone from Sirona, and said her farewells.

Relaxing in the group's common dining area at the House of Learning, she got a mug of tea and sat down to review her documents when she was joined by Wolfram, Andrew and Bryce.

"What have you there?" asked Wolfram, as they took their seats.

"Homework," came Angi's reply, "I have much to memorize."

"So you decided to proceed with the training after all. That's great. Can we help?" asked Wolfram.

"You could help me with a memory game Myttrwn has devised," came Angi's reply as she held out the top sheet.

"Sure, just tell us what you need," came Andrew's response.

From that date, Andrew managed to make copies of the material for each team member to help Angi remember the gemstones. Numbers and gemstone names could be heard being called to Angi by different members of the team at all hours of the day. It worked so well that in time Myttrwn and Sirona bowed out, delighted with the group's involvement in Angi's training.

ਇ

House of Learning, Wolfram's Suite

Wolfram was just about to retire when a knock came on his door. "Who is dropping by at this hour?" he said as he made his way to the door.

Opening it he found Andrew and Dylan; Andrew looking solemn and Dylan showing an evident edginess.

"What's up?" asked Wolfram, quickly realizing this wasn't a social call. Glancing at Dylan's hand he enquired, "Is that a slingshot you are holding, Dylan?"

"Yes, I'm skilled at loading a lot into a small bag when I travel," replied Dylan, showing no levity in his response.

Andrew remained silent.

"What can I do for you both?" Wolfram asked, still unsure of the purpose of their visit.

"Let's go out on your balcony," said Dylan, pushing into the suite and aiming straight for the balcony.

Outside, the three observed the double moons and the quiet evening scenery.

Dylan began to speak, "After Myttrwn's sessions I'm unsure if we're all seeing the same thing. But let's agree what is before us are two moons and the time is somewhere between eleven and midnight. Do you agree?" the question was aimed directly at Wolfram.

Still perplexed, Wolfram glanced at Andrew who continued to provide no assistance and responded, "OK, Dylan, let's agree that's what we're looking at. So what?"

Dylan took his slingshot and a small pebble from one of his pockets. He pulled the rubber as far back as he could and let go, the pebble sailing high into the night sky. Aided by the exterior building lighting, before the pebble went any distance a ripple appeared in what seemed to be a liquid barrier. "There, that's what I wanted you to see. I just demonstrated it to Andrew."

Perplexed Wolfram turned to Andrew, asking, "Have you any idea what this means?"

Before Andrew had time to answer, Dylan interrupted, "I have my suspicions. At night we're locked into a sophisticated jail, one that we didn't even recognize until now. Remember that shield Sirona created around the Hill of Tara. Well this is another version, but this one comes with scenery. The question is why."

Finally Andrew spoke up, "Calm down, Dylan. Did you ever think there might be a perfectly rational reason? Admittedly, I can't think of one right away. Let's talk to Sirona and Myttrwn in the morning. There's no point in waking up the entire kingdom at this point."

Having thought it over, Wolfram added, "Andrew, you have to admit it is sophisticated. I guess what fascinates me is that unless Dylan had his handy slingshot and a suspicious nature, we would never have known it existed. Should we let the others know right away?"

"Let's leave this until tomorrow," came Andrew's council. "While Wolfram and I hold off on any negative speculations, I want you, Dylan, to do what you are trained to do. Think of options."

Dylan's frustration was showing as he concluded, "Now you understand why I was so upset that they might be able to read our minds. Let's pray there's a reasonable explanation...............Until tomorrow then," and with that he and Andrew left.

After he closed the door Wolfram returned to the balcony. His long list of 'what ifs' had already begun.

Chapter 4

House of Life

The night shield was baffling. After some discussion, it was agreed they would wait and hear what Sirona and Myttrwn had to say. Little was said as they headed to their next session in the House of Life.

This time Sirona and Myttrwn were waiting, as if intuition had alerted them that something was amiss. The reserved behaviour of the group was a telltale sign. Before any words were spoken, Myttrwn spoke, "I believe you need an explanation as to why we created a force field around your quarters at night?"

Angi thought to herself, "Another bonus point for telepathy. I trust Sirona and Myttrwn but cannot imagine why they needed to use this shield."

Dylan, ignoring the reality that Myttrwn knew his thoughts as he entered the room, responded with an edge to his voice, "Yes Myttrwn, this was unexpected. Why is it necessary to lock us in at night...............or is that what the shield is all about?"

Calmly, Myttrwn conveyed telepathically to Sirona, "I knew their curiosity would discover the shield. We will now reveal the reason." and to the group replied, "Let's sit down while I explain."

Everyone took their seats, vaguely registering the increased number of chairs.

Myttrwn proceeded, "Your short visit presented a dilemma. Since our day is different than yours, we wanted to avoid disrupting your DNA while you were here. So we thought it best to recreate your normal day sequence. We only need four hours to your eight hours of sleep every night. Now that you've found the shield you have three options; we can leave it in place, or we can train you to use verbal commands to control your own suite screens so you can sleep at night, or cancel the night shield and let you adapt to our pattern. However, option two will leave your suite in darkness at night while your balcony will be in daylight. Whereas, option three could leave you with sleep deprivation and possible illness. The choice is yours."

Relieved, it was Andrew's turn to speak, "Myttrwn, on behalf of the team we appreciate such thoughtfulness in preparing for our arrival. I hope we can be as accommodating when the situation is reversed. However, now that we know the reason for the shield could you leave the matter with us and we will discuss the options. Be assured whatever we decide it will be unanimous. I will get back to you later today."

Dylan thought to himself, "Unknowns always create problems. I'm amazed at how negative I became. I guess it is habitual, too many times preparing for the worst. If I had known yesterday what I know today I might have gotten some sleep last night."

In the end, the group decided to leave the shield in place. They had become accustomed to the routine and understood the physical ramifications of disrupted sleep.

Myttrwn was anxious to get started and said, "If that settles this matter for now, I would like to proceed with our discussion on energy, our focus today will be on human energy. Shall we begin?"

Relaxed, knowing why the shield was needed, the group also wanted to get on with their lessons. Just then they noted the extra chairs but made no comment.

Myttrwn seated comfortably proceeded, "As you now know, you are made up of vibrating waves of energy or, if you prefer, complex bundles of frozen energy. Energy in humans may be referred to as *'human aura'* or as the *'Human Energy Field.'* So as not to complicate this too much I shall stick to basics. The human aura is described as having three distinct levels; the physical which consists of the physical, etheric, emotional and mental; the astral which is the bridge between the physical and spiritual; and the spiritual which has a number of gradations. Each successive layer of the aura is at a higher frequency or octave extending out from the skin, with the spiritual field being the furthest from the physical field. Your auric energy pattern contains your entire health profile. Expert auric readers can identify these layers by colour. All of these levels influence each other. Remember, everything is interconnected."

"What then are the Chakras?" asked Angi.

"The seven chakras function as intake channels to receive energy from the surrounding universe. This universal life energy field which you float in is called *'prana'* or *'ch'i.* Over the centuries you may have heard this universal energy referred to by other names such as yin and yang, vital energy, monads, magnetic fluid and odic fluid, but we shall stick to the first two. The seven chakras are located near the major nerve plexuses of the body. A dysfunction in any of these chakras reduces the supply of energy to an organ which weakens the immune system and usually results in illness. Each chakra has its own colour which appears like a rainbow of pulsating light. The chakras can be affected by your personality, emotions or your spiritual development. Any blockage in your emotional or spiritual maturation can affect the flow of energy in your chakras. That is why a bout of depression or anger may be followed by illness. This is another reason for my concern over the spiritual weakening in your world, as this can have a serious effect on your energy and lead to widespread illness. To help you understand human energy I will now get you to participate in a simple experiment." With a verbal command floating lap desks appeared in front of each individual.

Everyone was now accustomed to Myttrwn's classroom theatrics.

Myttrwn proceeded, "I want you to place your elbows on the desk. Then place your hands together like this as if in prayer. Next I want you to rub your hands gently up and down until your feel a slight heat sensation. Now as you gently pull your hands apart, I want you to feel your own energy. It is subtle, so keep trying."

Concentrating, moments passed. Then participants could be hear saying, "I can feel it."........"This is real."....... "Wow, we are actually made of energy." Once they discovered the energy, they kept moving their hands in and out to confirm the sensation. Then Morgan asked, "What energy level is this, Myttrwn?"

"Ah, that's a good question Morgan," came Myttrwn's quick response, pleased that the first step had been achieved. "What you are feeling is the etheric energy field, the one closest to your physical energy field. It extends about two inches beyond the physical body and pulses about fifteen to twenty cycles per minute."

"Do you have another test to help us see or feel the other energy layers?" asked Vette.

"That is a bit more complicated," replied Myttrwn. "However, because I want you to fully understand this human energy principle I have invited a number of guests to assist us." On cue the door opened and familiar individuals arrived, each carrying his or her own flashing device similar to the one used by Sirona. "I would like you to spread out into twos so you can work with the scanning devices to see your own aura and any others in the room."

As the group rearranged themselves into couples Myttrwn asked, "And can anyone tell me why I needed the assistance of these individuals to help us today?"

"I remember," replied Wolfram, "Your technology is programmed to the individual's DNA."

"That's right," came Myttrwn's reply with a smile. "Now, I will let you proceed."

As Sirona joined Angi she said, "You and I have done this before, but I will be glad to share this again if you want to see the aura of the others."

"I'd like that," came Angi's reply. And to the group, she added, "What you are about to see will be truly amazing?"

Myttrwn relaxed as he let the groups interact. He was delighted to see the growing relationships developing between the Gaia and Tir na nOg individuals as he alone knew these would be crucial in the future.

First, each individual examined his or her own aura, then broadened the scan to include the others in the room. Like Angi's previous experience back in Scotland, each team member was fascinated by his or her own energy profile and stunned at the brilliance of the light in the Tir na nOg members, particularly Sirona and Myttrwn. When the initial auric testing was over the first to ask the obvious question was Andrew, "Can you explain Myttrwn why the members of your kingdom have such a bright illumination? It is at least ten times greater than ours."

"Because Andrew, we are mandated to maintain our light energy at a certain level. This increased light keeps us healthy. Our method is simple but demanding. We achieve this through meditation, a rigorous physical fitness program and compliance to the Law of One. In our world any energy imbalance must be rebalanced to bring our body back into perfect health. We can check this ourselves and in most cases do our own rebalancing. In comparison, in your world, nothing is done until a disease has penetrated through all levels down to the physical. Instead of you being responsible for your own wellbeing you have delegated it to strangers. Each one of you are co-creators of your universe. By healing yourselves you will be able to heal the world around you. You have more power than you can ever imagine."

"Is that a reason for your longevity?" asked Bryce.

"It is one reason, Bryce. In time I hope to get you to understand that disease or surgery takes a frightful toll on the human body depleting your light and compromising your energy field. The more you prevent illness the healthier you'll be and the longer you'll live. As mentioned before, the Dwapara Yuga will also bring you increased longevity. In the not too distant future you will understand that the health of the soul is far more important than the body. Future healing methods will see the patient as a soul. Disease will be recognized as one of the ways to point the individual in the right direction. Illness is a symptom, a teacher, to remind you that you are divine. In our next session we will delve more deeply into healing."

"Amazing, that was what my grandmother use to say," said Angi. "Whenever I got ill she would tell me that my illness was a sign for me to either change something in my life or that life was about to change."

"Did your grandmother also mention that you are a divine star, with each star being both exquisite and unique? This *Core Star* or your divine essence is located just above your navel at the center of your body. This is the place where you are wise, loving and full of courage. It contains your innermost goodness and where your creative energies arise."

Vette chuckled, "Well, it wasn't a star but my mother often talked about a diamond. When I was a young girl she told me that my task in life was to keep polishing my diamond so I would be ready for heaven. I thought it was just an old Acadian method to keep children in line. Little did I realize that it represented some ancient knowledge of this world of energy."

"You see, as you begin to think on my words you will start remembering bits and pieces of wisdom tucked into your memory, passed down from one generation to the next without fully understanding why. Now you are beginning to know why."

"If these energetic layers exist then how come they don't turn up in any of our diagnostic tests?" asked Morgan.

"It is happening, Morgan. You must be familiar with such devices as the electroencephalograph (EEG), electrocardiograph (EKG) and a superconducting quantum interference device (SQUID) which is a highly sensitive magnetometer. Researchers in your world have also been busy using different devices to capture the aura, associating auric change with disease, detecting radiation from living tissue, developing methods to enhance bone growth, measuring the electrical frequency of healers hands, detecting left/right brain wave shifts in healers and discovering that healers exhibit a brain-wave pattern of 7.8-8 Hz during times of healing. Efforts are underway. In time you will develop devices like ours that instantly show your auric profile and how to treat any imbalance."

Bryce had held his comments and was pressed to ask, "But Myttrwn if one looks back on our world, we have come a long way in the past century in overcoming certain diseases, surely this is a positive."

"The wonders of your medical advances are commendable, but I'm sure you realize that more and more people seem to be unable to maintain their health. You are reaching the zenith of your disconnected understanding of life. I'm sure you've noticed that just as one disease gets treated, another pops up. This is because the cause of illness has not been addressed. Making it even more complex, this separateness of thinking is duplicated in your professional groups and treatment modalities, some working in conflict with each other. In essence this is the very opposite of our philosophy of One. Ah, you see, even I have slipped into my next topic. I will leave you now to carry out any further auric testing or chats with your colleagues. If you discover you are out of balance your colleague may make arrangements with our lab to rebalance your energies. With that Myttrwn dissolved the desks and rose to leave, without Sirona who had signaled she would be staying with Angi.

ఓ

The Palace

Zolar, dressed in his formal attire walked uphill towards the palace, the gold embroidery on his blue vest and serpent badge glittering in the morning sunlight. After much research his hopes were high that he would get a positive hearing at the Council of Elders. Familiar with the Council meetings, he had cleverly placed his item near the end of the day hoping weariness and disinterest would facilitate a favourable decision.

Hesitating near the top of the hill, he gazed out over a familiar vista thinking to himself, "Where else in the universe are there such well managed gardens, orchards and lush green fields? The sight restores my soul and confirms my family's right to be here. We have been part of this royal plaza for generations and once held immense power. And yet, as much as I cherish this place, I am, once again, about to jeopardise it by challenging the wishes of my Queen, Sirona and Myttrwn. But, my reasons are sound. Being more advanced, it is our duty.........no, our moral responsibility ....to protect the weaker members in the universe. We've done it before so why not now. What harm is there in waiting?" Confident, he strode past the entrance guards and entered the palace oblivious of the pink marble splendor and the ivory, gold and jade décor. He proceeded along the corridor to the right of the entrance, greeting and chatting with old colleagues.

The Council of Elders Chamber seated three hundred, the seats arranged in a semi-circle in front of the royal throne. The three hundred seats were divided into units of seventy-five separated by four wide aisles. The seats were so arranged that each individual had a clear view of the throne. The lush décor of royal purple, gold and marble gave the room grandeur while wide window-like spaces on two walls provided a steady stream of light and fresh air. A circular golden snake sculpture hung against the wall behind the throne seats which were themselves lavishly carved in gold with inlaid precious stones.

On average, one hundred members attended regular meetings, more were present on formal occasions. The Elders either represented specific regions of the kingdom or held prominent advisory positions to the Queen. Selection for such prestigious positions followed strict rules with no assurance of permanency. Each member proceeded to his or her designated seat which was fully equipped with the latest technology. Zolar's seat was in a front row nearest the throne.

The arresting sound of a loud gong heralded the arrival of the royal party consisting of the Queen, Sirona, Myttrwn, and three retainers. The powerful commanding presence of the Queen was a paradox to her apparent youthful appearance. As was her custom, her long platinum braid, wrapped around the top of her head was encircled with a filigree golden crown with a serpent at the front. Her flowing gown of ivory lace was complemented by a wide golden belt with ties flowing to the bottom of her gown. The only jewellery was a golden serpent badge and matching serpent ring. Looking straight ahead, she made her way to the royal throne which was on a raised dais.

The ruling family followed a strict code of service to their subjects and obedience to the Law of One. The Queen did not regard herself as being above her citizens, but ordained to serve their interests. She encouraged honest achievement, advancement by merit, and community structure. She oversaw the welfare of her kingdom and worked tirelessly to promote intergalactic peace and harmony. She was as interested in the evolution of Earth as her own, for she believed all existed as One.

The Royal princess, Sirona, was dressed in royal attire similar to her mother with a smaller crown and a royal purple belt and ties, plus a golden serpent badge and an identical ring to her mother's. Once her mother was seated, Sirona took her place beside her on an adjacent throne seat.

Myttrwn was also in formal attire, with a golden vest and serpent badge. Wearing no crown he took his designated seat a slight distance to the right of the Queen. His authority was not only due to his longevity and royal linage but also to his titles of Prince of the Exulted and Prince of the Worlds. Within the royal palace these titles often merged to become a simple phrase of "Someone Who Prepares the Way."

The discussions on various kingdom issues dragged on through the morning and well into the afternoon. As anticipated, towards the end of the day Zolar's item was announced and he was asked to make a presentation.

Standing at his seat, he began, "Your Majesty, I realize that we have discussed the matter of the medallion from Gaia several times. However, I now possess additional information which makes it imperative that we reassess this matter. I have recently learned that the medallion has been calibrated at level seven, far greater than any in our kingdom. I am aware that in our past spiritually advanced individuals did possess such a medallion. While Myttrwn and Sirona have assured us that they can train this female from Gaia on how to handle the medallion's powers, this new information brings that into question. Coming from this less evolved planet, I cannot imagine this is going to be possible within the time frame of this or even subsequent visits." As he spoke Zolar glanced at both Sirona and Myttrwn to see if there was any reaction. Observing none, he felt he was making progress.

Prior to the meeting, noting Zolar's item on the agenda, Sirona and Myttrwn had devised their own plan. Knowing that any communication between them would be picked up telepathically by all members of the Chamber, they controlled their thoughts waiting to hear what Zolar had to say.

Facing the Queen, Zolar proceeded, "I have carefully reviewed our kingdom's records as to the rules and regulations for intergalactic relations. You will see on your screens similar issues which have occurred over the generations. Certainly, there has been nothing on the scale of this medallion. What I am proposing is not extreme, in fact I feel it is both prudent and logical. Because of the scientific magnitude of this medallion I am recommending that we halt the medallion's return to Gaia at this time. Instead, for a short period we should assume custody of this item until Gaia advances further into its Dwapara Yuga. This way we shall avoid an intergalactic calamity due to the inexperience of this woman, for no matter how carefully we train and supervise the process, accidents can happen."

As he was speaking the Elders were reviewing his summary of prior events and some were nodding their heads. When Zolar stopped speaking a senior Elder spoke up, "If this medallion is truly at level seven as you say, then I feel I should revise my previous position on this matter. I have never heard of anyone with a level seven medallion. The ramifications and complications for this young woman are immense. Surely we need to show leadership in this matter as this is complex technology even for us at our advanced evolution. I think Zolar has presented a reasonable argument that for a short period of time we assume control of this item until we decide that Gaia is ready. Are there any others who share this view?"

At least a third of the members showed some agreement. Sirona and Myttrwn remained silent.

Buoyed up by their support, Zolar in a conciliatory mood went on, "I can see that I have some agreement on this matter. I now bow to Myttrwn and Sirona for their response.

Sirona and Myttrwn had agreed Myttrwn would speak first.

Myttrwn realized it was a matter of time before Zolar and others would discover the complexity of the medallion if not by telepathy then by the chatter within the two main buildings. He knew that Zolar, being a stickler for detail, would have found facts to support his argument, however remote. Yet, he had hoped the matter had been settled at their last meeting. Choosing his words carefully, he responded, "Yes, the medallion is at level seven. This was confirmed by my lab tests this past week. While Zolar appears to have a logical argument for us to become custodians of this complex medallion I cannot support this recommendation for the following reasons. One, this medallion was created on Gaia to be activated at this time as Gaia emerged into its Dwapara Yuga. It was not created for any other world or planet. Therefore, it belongs on Gaia. Two, Angi Talismann has the only genetic structure to wear this medallion. If we wait there may be no other earthling with the same chemistry. You all know the linkage of DNA to such technology. Before you ask, there is no guarantee that a child or grandchild of Angi's will have similar genetic markers nor can we demand she marry an individual of our choosing. There is no evidence of royal lineage nor is she a product of centuries of arranged marriages. Can you imagine the genetic probabilities that presents. Three, if we take control of this technology then we are depriving Gaia of this advantage at a time when it is vitally needed. We have no right to do this no matter how logical the argument. We would be breaking our own laws by treating this planet like a child irrespective of what we think of their present stage of evolution. They are not children but evolving spirits just like us. For all these reasons and more which I have stated numerous times, I believe it is our duty to train this individual however long it takes. I have committed myself to that task. Her Royal Highness, Sirona, has also agreed to assist me in this training. If necessary, I will gladly return to earth to more closely supervise Angi as she adjusts to this technology. It would be morally wrong for us to confiscate this item. I stand firm in my belief that we must train Angi and in so doing we will be assisting Gaia."

Sirona then stood to speak, "I will not repeat what Myttrwn has already stated. I have known Angi longer than anyone, and I can assure you that she has the temperament and the potential to handle this technology. Understandably, it is all new to her but she is progressing." Then looking straight at Zolar, she added with some emphasis, "We have no right to impede the evolution of Gaia. This technology was created to facilitate their evolution, not ours. We cannot interfere with this mandate." She had known Zolar all her life. Yet, while her mother had included him in a recent list of possible marriage candidates, she disliked his proud, stubborn, controlling and distrustful nature. His evident resistance to Angi and their project had further alienated him as a future consort.

The Queen, having listened carefully, finally spoke, "Understand, I do not take this matter lightly and appreciate Zolar's efforts to have us rethink the matter. Therefore, as Council members you have heard his argument. The decision is whether we should retain this medallion in our kingdom until Gaia is ready which could be centuries in their time or we follow our original plan to have Myttrwn and Sirona manage this matter. Now, will you please vote on this? Vote '*yes*' if you believe we should become the custodian of this medallion, or '*no*' if we should not."

The Elders pressed their electronic devices and the vote instantaneously registered on their screens. The decision was thirty-five to become custodians to sixty-five against.

The Queen concluded the matter with, "It has been decided. We shall proceed as previously agreed. However, I would like to add, in light of the complexity of this medallion, that Myttrwn be prepared to return to earth should it be warranted."

Myttrwn had expected such a directive and bowing to the Queen replied, "Yes, Your Majesty that will be done, if necessary." The thought of returning to Earth was beginning to intrigue him.

The meeting soon ended. Most members left to return to their home base. Zolar lingered to discuss the matter with a few Elders who had agreed with his stand. But they knew it was to no avail, the decision was settled.

Zolar walked back to the House of Learning in a gloomy, rejected mood. His efforts had been thwarted. Mumbling to himself he said, "Only a third listened, I expected more support.............I know I'm right.............It is wrong to give Gaia this advanced technology ....It is wrong! This is a sad day for our kingdom, a sad day for me, and a sad day for my family. I must now think of another means to redirect this matter. Whatever I do, I know in time I will be honoured for my courage."

℞

House of Life

Days melted away as the team busied themselves in their various pursuits. Myttrwn's different reality had introduced challenges for everyone. Knowing their next session with him would be on healing, they were already seated when Sirona and Myttrwn appeared.

Sirona gave Myttrwn a quick telepathic message as they walked towards their chairs, "Your students are eager, that's a good sign."

Myttrwn, responding in the same way, replied, "Yes, everything appears to be on track but my intuition is troubled and I don't know why."

Sirona noted this with concern.

Seated, Myttrwn looked around the circle and began, "Our topic today is a heavy one. Let's review once again the energetic world. At this point there are a number of ways you might consider in describing the reality which I have revealed to you. One is to see the universe as a vast sea of radiating energy, constantly moving and changing with everything interconnected. Or, you may see it as a dynamic web of inseparable energy patterns. A third possibility is to see yourself as a 3-dimensional being rooted in a holographic universe of infinite interconnected dimensions. Or, you may prefer to think of the universe as one gigantic thought. Whatever you prefer, let us agree that the universe is a realm of energy, which is constantly vibrating. Since all nature is a seamless web, then, as I have said before, those who insist that there are boundaries of separateness due to race, religion, colour, sex, or national and intergalactic divides, are delusional. Such separateness does not exist. Are there any questions so far?"

Wolfram was the first to speak, "Myttrwn, for my sake, can you tell me what a hologram is?"

Myttrwn could see that there were others needing the same explanation and responded, "A hologram is a 3-dimensional or free-standing image formed by the interference of light beams from a laser, or other coherent light source, in which every piece contains the whole. If we focus on yourself, Wolfram, it would mean that every cell in your body contains the pattern of your whole being."

"So, while we appear separate, we are all part of a holographic universe or as you say a single thought. Now that begs the question, a single thought of who, God?" came Bryce's introspective question.

"That is a huge topic Bryce which we will have to leave for another day. It will give your group something to chat about after this session," Myttrwn replied with a grin, fully aware of their robust discussions whenever they met.

Andrew, listening and wondering, asked, "A final question on holograms, if I may. If we are a hologram within a hologram, what happens to time and space?"

"In the deepest reality, Andrew, there is a superhologram in which the past, present and future all exist simultaneously. Space and time form a four-dimensional continuum which your scientists call 'space-time.' Thus, you cannot talk about space without time and vice versa. Time is not linear, nor is it absolute, it is relative. Time is nothing more than changes in the configuration of the universe with rules that govern such change."

Andrew continued, "Then if the past and future do not exist, the only reality must be the present."

"That is right, Andrew," replied Myttrwn. "Your concept of absolute time and space needs to be replaced with the idea of a universe that exists in one vast '*here*' where '*here*' represents all time and all space at a single instance. Some refer to this as the '*Eternal Moment*'. Light exists where space and time come into existence. I hope that helps for the present as we must press on."

Morgan couldn't hold back, "Wow, these sessions are pure gold. I've started a list of topics which we might discuss before we leave. If not, I will keep it for future visits." They had all agreed that numerous trips would be needed if they were to fully comprehend all of Myttrwn's information.

Myttrwn smiled, and began his scheduled topic, "Throughout the Kali Yuga a materialistic view of the human body dominated the healing process. To understand its parameters I will list some features which you may recognize. A materialistic approach to healing views the human body as a machine with distinct parts, disease is physical, knowledge comes only through the five senses, objective signs of illness supersede subjective ones, memory is just stored data, and nothing survives after death. Disease is mainly caused by some outside force and getting rid of symptoms is more important than dealing with the cause of the illness. Pills or surgery do not address the cause of illness. Treatments involve costly specialist interventions focused on the part for which there are symptoms and the patient is expected to obey whatever is prescribed. This gives overwhelming power to the physician and diagnostic system and establishes a pathological belief that illness is inevitable and must be feared. This outdated model lacks an appreciation of emotion, consciousness and the energy life force of the soul and spirit. The fact that many health workers have little interest in spiritual matters has complicated this even further. For many health workers it may be difficult to make a quantum leap to accept an energetic world but I expect you in this room to do just that," his words coming more as a command than a mere suggestion.

Angi felt compelled to respond, "But, Myttrwn we do have individuals in what is called alternative therapies which incorporate energy concepts in their therapies, the entire healing community is not materialistic."

"I know, Angi, but their numbers are few. Some of these alternate therapists will usher in the new era. With that in mind, let's leave the materialistic mindset as we view the human body through a different lens. From this point we shall be looking at the human body as a dynamic energy system of body, mind and spirit and yourselves as co-creators of the universe. Instead of delegating the responsibility for your health to others you should take personal responsibility for your own being. This will restore your power to create a new reality."

"If I accept the premise that I am energy, what does that really mean as far as my body is concerned?" asked Vette.

"A good question, Vette. If life and energy is in constant motion, then your body must also be in motion. You will discover that human life is far more resilient than you may have thought. Did you know that ninety-eight percent of all atoms in your body are replaced every year, your skin renews itself once a month, your skeleton every three months, and your stomach lining every five days? You literally create a whole new physical body every seven years." Myttrwn watched as this information registered.

Vette continued, "So, the body I had last year is not the same one I have now?"

"That is right, Vette. Now if you can accept that news, then I ask you what do you think happens if a treatment module changes little from month to month or year to year?"

Angi responded, "The effectiveness of the drug changes. That concept was mentioned in my nursing program. As nurses we knew that medications had different effects on individuals as they aged, or even changed in weight. Sadly, this knowledge must no longer prevail as recently I've found too many elderly in the Emergency Room on medications that had been previously contraindicated for their age group. But, Myttrwn, I believe you have extended this concept even further. If our entire energy system is mobile then there must be questions about what is really happening with medications and other treatment modalities formulated within an out-dated understanding of the human body."

Myttrwn, pleased with their quick grasp of the information, pressed on, "To give you a better understanding of what is happening, let us stop for a moment to examine what occurs at the cellular level. The cells in your body emit weak pulses of light or ultraviolet light, a light-based communication system which helps to coordinate the actions of the cells within each organ. The nucleus of the cell is not the brain of the cell, it is the membrane. The membrane of each cell is a liquid crystal semi-conductor, an information processor if you like. The cell receives information from your sub-conscious and writes your DNA code. You can reprogram your DNA code by broadcasting a different message to the universe. Cells are reprogrammable. To help you with this let me show you a recent lab experiment." Upon his verbal command a holographic image floated in front of each member of two containers of cell cultures.

As they watched Myttrwn provided commentary on what they were seeing, "You need to know that these cell cultures are in quartz dishes because ultraviolet light will pass through quartz and not glass. As you can see, the two cell cultures have been placed side by side, but are not touching. The image you are seeing has been enlarged so you can see what is about to happen. Now, watch as a small amount of poison is added to the left cell culture."

The group observed not one but both cell cultures reacted identically, a mirror image death. Looking around Wolfram said, "I didn't expect that. What happened?"

"What you have just witnessed is cellular communication from one container to the other even though there appears to be no visible connection. I could show you similar tests with the same reactions, some with the cell cultures at great distances from each other. If cells can communicate, what do you think happens when people are exposed to a sick environment like your hospitals?"

Angi responded, "This is fascinating. You know, some time ago I read a research paper that argued against placing people in intensive care units in our hospitals because it could be detrimental to their recovery. After all, it was argued, people in a debilitating condition were being placed in an environment where death was common. If cells receive messages, then maybe what this researcher was trying to say had some validity. As to the effect of hospitals on all people, I will have to think about that."

"Further to my questions on cellular communications, what do you think causes illness?" Myttrwn waited to see what the question would elicit.

Andrew reacted, "Well, previously, I would have said that I contracted some virus or through some known or unknown means acquired the disease. But now that we are into an energetic world I expect illness is the result of some energy imbalance to a specific organ. Am I getting close, Myttrwn?"

"Very good, Andrew. As you will recall from our previous session an imbalance can be caused by thoughts. It is said that ninety-nine point nine percent of all serious illness and disease is caused by unprocessed trauma and withheld anger. Emotions are vibrations which hold the vibrational pattern in the liquid crystals of your body. Illness can also be caused by unfulfilled longing, the deeper the longing the greater the illness. In addition, dysfunctional thinking patterns can actually worsen and perpetuate different forms of illness. As I've said before, it is important to avoid fear or negative thoughts. Those who focus on negative things in life attract likeminded people. If you continually focus upon past hurts and psychic wounds you never allow yourself to heal in the present. Having said that, I must stress that it is not the illness which should dominate your thinking. Illness is but a sign you are imbalanced and a teacher sent to remind you that you are divine. Only through inner healing will you be able to rebalance your energies. You must change yourself if you want to be healed. Assuming an outside treatment will do all the work is an antiquated concept."

It was Bryce's turn to ask, "Do you actually believe Myttrwn that in the Dwapara Yuga that the dominant treatment mode for disease on Gaia will shift to an energy format? That's a massive change. Those who have built their lucrative careers on the materialistic model will not take this kindly."

"Bryce, change is never easy, but it will happen," replied Myttrwn. "Energetic healing will be the next great advance in health care in your world. Interacting methods with the body's energy fields will become a part of accepted medical practice. You are seeing the beginning signs in the laying on of hands, therapeutic touch, aura balancing, polarity, acupuncture, and related energetic approaches which are ancient healing methods. In the next century the idea of using drugs or surgery to treat anyone will be considered barbaric in your own world. Instead the focus will be on manipulating human energy. The future holistic healing systems will diagnose and prescribe healing for the different energy bodies, including the physical. The patient will be seen as a soul on its journey back home to the true self, and disease will be seen as one of the ways to point the traveler in the right direction. In time, the health of the spirit, the soul, will become the first priority, the second will be the physical."

"So, how will we describe healing in this new paradigm?" asked Angi.

"Healing will be viewed as dissolving the veil between the spiritual and material worlds. It won't matter what the presenting complaint is, in opening the way, the person will heal themselves. Illness will be regarded as a time to gain insight, to focus on inner values, and to acquire love. For all life experiences, even physical illness, are potential learning experiences for the soul. It is only through such testing that you can learn the deeper meaning of life."

"What does all this mean for the healing practitioner?" asked Angi, wondering how different this will be from the world she left behind.

"To become a true energetic healer will be no easy task," replied Myttrwn, "for you will need spiritual as well as technical training. The healer must enrich their own energy system so as not to drain the energy from the person they are treating. The healer must align themselves with the cosmic forces, clear away negative feelings, keep their body healthy through exercise, proper nutrition, plenty of rest, and practice at least thirty to forty-five minutes of meditation daily. They must also understand that such energy must be used with integrity, honesty and love. Healing is to be a spiritual experience, one of personal evolution and a release of creativity. As the energy flowing through a healer increases, so does their power."

It was Morgan's turn to ask, "Why is meditation so important?"

"Meditation is key, Morgan, as it transcends the limits of the linear mind, facilitates connectivity, accesses higher vibrational sources of information, causes gradual changes in the subtle-energy anatomy of the human being over a long period of time, achieves enlightenment and greater coherence of brain wave activity between the left and right cerebral hemispheres, and is associated with greater creativity and flexibility of thought. In addition, many secrets withheld from the conscious mind may be discovered through meditation. For this reason, we begin meditation training in early childhood."

"If these are the expectations of an energetic healer then it is certainly a far cry from what is expected of our current health practitioners. Discipline, which may have existed in the past, has been replaced with a dominance of instant information intake and output and an overpowering pursuit of financial gain or power. The idea of healing being a spiritual experience died years ago," came Angi's disheartened assessment.

Wolfram responded, "That's a bit heavy Angi, surely there are those who still function from compassion and a desire to heal."

"Yes, Wolfram, there are individuals with high principles but this is not the majority. Too often the best and most caring practitioners burn out with overwhelming workloads and little support. When political, financial and non-healing decisions dominate the health system, spiritual matters soon get lost."

"I will let that one rest for now," was Wolfram's response knowing Angi knew her world far better than his few months as a patient. "Perhaps Myttrwn, you could tell us what makes a good energetic healer?"

"There are many features which your scientists are slowly discovering. For example the hands of a true energetic healer can emit very strong pulsating magnetic fields, about one thousand times stronger than normal human biomagnetic fields. Their brain waves are also synchronized with the oscillation of the planet's magnetic lines and have been registered at 7.8-8 Hz during the healing process. Also during the healing process the healer and the patient's right and left brain hemispheres become balanced. Well trained healing hands enhance immune functioning in both the healer and the patient, raises the hemoglobin level, accelerates wound healing, relieves pain and stress, promotes relaxation, lowers diastolic blood pressure, and reduces anxiety. The healer is expected to work as a power source of multiple-frequency outputs to allow energy shifts at several levels, simultaneously."

Morgan suddenly thought, "Am I wrong or are all your students in the House of Learning being trained as healers?"

"Under our prime directive of the Law of One, we train all our people in the understanding of how to heal themselves and those around them. On this base we add other training for their roles as adults. If everyone is so trained there is less of a drain on the whole kingdom. That is why this healing center has time and resources to devote to the exceptions or unexpected issues which can affect any society."

"So that is the reason why we are all together in this training?" asked Dylan, relieved to finally get an answer to a question that had been bugging him.

"It is. In time I will be more specific as to your future roles but as a beginning step you must all start from this basic premise of energy, healing and how to improve your own light. We will not have time today to talk about treatment methods, but these too we will discuss before you leave."

"I realize it has taken us time to grasp this concept of energy," said Angi, "and it may be a harder lesson for others on our planet as this is quite a divergence from what they believe is their reality."

"I expect so, Angi. Unfortunately, such change may come so fast that it may threaten the historical and conventional understanding of how things work. But on the plus side by harnessing electromagnetic energy that exists in the vacuum of space you will be able to return cells to their healthy state by literally turning back the clock on disease. The study of sound or acoustic physics and its effects will provide a vast new source of healing. Electromagnetic cures will be found to treat the most common diseases. Ultraviolet-rich light will be used to identify organisms and treatment modules with no harm to the patient. Debilitating diseases will be quickly and economically corrected. Damaged ecosystems will be brought back into their former pristine state with the return of flora, fauna, and rich soil and freshwater. Cures will be directed to the energy field to stop the disease from reaching the physical body. However, since energetic healing is still in its infancy, there may still be a need for conventional drugs and surgery for some time to come."

Morgan was itching to ask the final question of the day, "Before we close, can you tell us Myttrwn what is death?"

"I was wondering when that would turn up. Well, Morgan, because nothing in the cosmos is ever destroyed, all that lives is immortal. Therefore, you, as part of the cosmos are immortal. Death is nothing but the disintegration of your constituent parts so that you may be renewed. You retain your upper auric levels or energy bodies when you die, the lower ones are dissolved in the dying process. Or simpler, the body dies while your mind and spirit go on. Death is a transition, a rebirth into another plane of reality. When you die you move from a 3-dimensional earth-space to a place of higher vibration."

"Now that is something to ponder. If we accept that we are immortal, then what is our ultimate purpose?" asked Andrew.

"Your purpose is to develop a light body which is achieved by neutralizing your ego, disciplining your emotions and mind, and transforming any inner negativity within your subconscious mind. Negativity and rigid intellectual opinions take their toll on the human body and soul. As I said before, magic is your birthright, no more or less miraculous than your ability to compute the reality you want when you are dreaming. A convergence of the ancient and modern worlds is underway and you are in the van guard." Smiling, Myttrwn stood up saying, "I'm sure you have plenty to stretch your minds for today." With that Sirona and Myttrwn left the room.

Chapter 5

House of Learning

In the days that followed the team could be found deep in conversation about Myttrwn's information. Slowly an energetic universe was registering, but just when it seemed entrenched, old ideas re-emerged. Shifting realities was proving to be more daunting than first assumed.

Dylan and his team had renewed purpose in their role knowing they were now part of a much larger plan. It was not that they did not feel included before, but their position was more firmly cemented with Myttrwn's explanation for everyone being trained together.

One afternoon, returning from their usual activities, Angi, Vette, Andrew and Bryce joined Wolfram in their usual dining area. As they were about to sit down, Wolfram asked, "Have any of you seen Morgan. He was supposed to join me here half an hour ago."

"No, I haven't seen him all day," was Angi's reply.

"Me neither," came Vette's reply.

Andrew response was, "Bryce and I have been in the archives and we haven't seen any of you until now. But it is not like Morgan to be late."

As Andrew was completing his statement, Morgan appeared perspiring and breathless, "Sorry Wolfram, I got lost. But, believe me, it was fortuitous. I discovered the most incredible demonstration of Myttrwn's 528 sound theory you could ever imagine."

"Let's hear more," was Bryce's response, as he sipped his tea.

"It is impossible to describe this in words. You need to see this to believe it. Why don't you come with me before it disappears."

Andrew, seeing the excitement on Morgan's face asked, "Come on Morgan, give us some details and let us decide." Andrew was still not convinced that there was anything that would force him from his comfortable seat.

"Would you believe there are about sixty harpists playing down on the first level of this building? I'm not kidding, at least sixty, there could be more. I'm not up on harps but the sound they are producing is magical. Come on, it is a chance in a million."

Wolfram, knowing his friend stood up and turning to the others said, "When my old buddy latches onto a musical gem it is best we tag along. From past experience, I've always found it worthwhile. Just look at the glint in his eyes. He's definitely found something............Ok Morgan, let's go."

"I'm with you Wolfram," came Vette's reply as she stood up. "He's captured my interest."

The idea of sixty harpists entranced Angi and she was out of her seat following after Wolfram and Vette. Directing the others she said, "Let's go and see what has Morgan so excited."

"You want us old guys to tag along?" asked Bryce, still not convinced he wanted to go.

By this time Morgan was already leading in the direction he had just arrived, and replied loudly over his shoulder, "Yes, everyone, you need to see and hear this."

Trooping behind Morgan they made their way along a third floor inner court corridor heading towards the outermost section of the learning complex. There was little chatter as they descended a marble stairway to the second level. Still seeing nothing Vette asked, "How much further Morgan?"

"Hold on.......we're almost there," said Morgan with a mischievous grin.

At that moment they walked through a familiar tingling sensation of an invisible shield. As they stepped beyond the shield they were engulfed in an overwhelming wave of angelic music being played by harpists seated in rows in the lower inner court. The screening system prevented the music disturbing other school activities. The haunting sound of so many harps caught the team off guard. The melody was so unusual that it caused them to smile and their eyes to fill with tears of joy.

Now whispering, Vette response was, "My God, it is unbelievable. It is like we have stumbled into heaven. Have you any idea, Morgan, what this is?"

Before Morgan had a chance to reply, Wolfram said, "Morgan, I might have known you would discover such a musical marvel. But I concur with Vette, what do you think it is all about?"

Pleased at their reaction, Morgan whispered in reply, "As best as I can figure out they are practicing for some upcoming performance. The music so affected me that it immediately reminded me of Myttrwn's 528 sound and its healing properties."

Angi's concentrated on the harps. She saw that they were similar to her student harp back home; portable, about thirty-three inches tall and eighteen inches wide. She felt moved to add, "I now regret my dismissal of harp music as a therapeutic tool. How much more I might have achieved if I had known that my music was more than just entertainment."

Surprised by the revelation, Vette asked, "Angi, do you play the harp? Is it like the ones they are using down there?"

"Yes, as best as I can discern it is the same triangular-framed small harp. Vette. It is a long story. We will talk later," replied Angi, still straining to get a better view of the musicians. "You know, I've never heard so many harp players at one time. Maybe the enclosure has some special acoustics. The sound seems to draw you into another dimension." She was equally surprised by her own overpowering feeling of wanting to join the musicians but realized she did not know the enchanting melody.

Vette continued, "Angi what was the argument for therapeutic harp music?"

Angi turned to face her friend as she replied. "Actually Vette, it was a recent presentation at the hospital. Apparently, the small portable harp is preferred as a bedside instrument. Now that I remember, the argument for therapeutic harp music was quite impressive. It was described as augmenting pain management, relieving anxiety, accelerating healing, easing the birthing process, reducing blood pressure and aiding mental focus. Studies had shown that live music was better than recorded music because of the full spectrum of acoustic sound vibrations. All that certainly fits Myttrwn's revelations but there was no mention of 528."

Morgan, feeling prompted, added his input in a low-keyed voice, "Since recorded history the harp, or the closely related lyre, was familiar to a number of cultures; the Sumerians, Egyptians, East Indians, Greeks, Romans and, of course, the Celts. The oldest depiction of harps goes back to 4000 BCE in Egypt, 3000 BCE in Persia and, it is mentioned in the Old Testament especially in connection with King David. Pythagoras, an Ionian Greek philosopher and mathematician who lived between 570-495 BCE, wrote that 'music heals', and he used the lyre as a healing instrument developing theories about the effect of its pitch and mode on the human body. So what Myttrwn is saying is not unique. The Celtic or therapeutic harp, like the one you see below, has about twenty-five to fifty strings. Now here's a fascinating tidbit. It was said that the Tuatha de Danann were noted for their magical harp music for which there are numerous tales of the music eliciting joy, pain and enchantment. What we're hearing could qualify for all three. In the ancient texts harp music is referred to as '*the voice of the gods.*' In the Celtic world harpists were well trained and highly esteemed. However, at the time of Queen Elizabeth I in England, Irish harpists were severely restricted when the Crown considered travelling harpists to be political subversives and turned them into outlaws. I read recently that by the 1800s, and certainly in more recent years, harp music has undergone a revival."

Vette, listening carefully, responded, "Morgan, I had no idea the harp had such an illustrious history. Angi, I'm still fascinated, what areas of the health system do you think would do best with harp music?"

Angi thought for a few moments and replied, "As I recall, it is being proposed for nurseries, intensive care units especially for neonatal babies, operating rooms, cancer clinics, and hospices. Apparently, there is some interesting work being done on non-responsive and comatose patients and there is evidence it helps those with Multiple Sclerosis, Parkinson's disease and children with learning and behavioural disorders. Perhaps one day it will become a regular part of all health centers."

Speaking quietly, the team pressed against the railing to get the full effect of the music.

Morgan, whispering, continued, "In this magical kingdom it is hard to know if my diversion to this place was coincidental or planned. It certainly supports Myttrwn's class material. By the way can you see Sirona? She's sitting in that far corner. Maybe it is a rehearsal for some royal event."

No sooner had Morgan mentioned her name when Sirona looked up, smiled, and signaled the group to join her. The music continued.

As quiet as they could manage, the six eased their way down to the first level and around an inner courtyard to where Sirona was sitting. By the time they reached her, chairs had been assembled for them to enjoy the rest of the performance. With no comment they sat mesmerized as the musical program continued. The students smiled at their enthusiastic clapping of appreciation when the music stopped.

Knowing their thoughts Sirona replied, "The students are rehearsing for a special ceremony of the House of Learning later this month. Three times a year the House of Learning identifies those students ready for their initiation in the pyramid. For some time students have been working hard to ready themselves for this testing. Not all succeed on their first try. So, this music is not only to mark the importance of the occasion but to give their classmates encouragement. I never thought of this before, but do any of you have a musical background?"

"I play the harp," said Angi, "just like the one the students are playing. As a child I performed in community musical concerts but nothing of late."

"I play the violin and piano," replied Vette, "and have performed with my family at Acadian festivals and other community events when I was younger."

"I play the violin," said Morgan, "and have played it in a professional musical group at clubs in Boston."

"I play the electric guitar," said Wolfram, "and have played in the same musical group and clubs as Morgan."

"I play the violin and bagpipes," said Andrew, "mainly playing the bagpipes in the military. My violin playing has been for personal pleasure and I have participated in choral group singing when time permitted."

"I also play the violin," said Bryce, "and like all good Welshmen, enjoy singing."

"I had no idea you were so multitalented," replied Sirona. "Why don't I introduce you to our Music Director, Carola. Perhaps you can join her in preparing some musical piece before you leave. I'm not sure we have all of your instruments but that can be remedied." Sirona signaled the Director to join the group.

Before Carola arrived, Morgan whispered to Wolfram, "This is fantastic........If we can find a few more musicians in Dylan's group and maybe persuade a few of the harpists to join us, we could create a fantastic group of musicians. I will work on a catchy name."

Wolfram with a broad grin turned to Morgan and whispered back, "I know what you are thinking Morgan. But when do you think we will find practice time with our already jammed schedules? Never mind, I know you............you are already way down the road with a musical group performing for the Queen. Dream on old buddy."

Carola was as tall as Sirona but seemed older. Her curly blond hair hung freely to her shoulders, circling an oblong face with intense blue eyes. It was obvious Sirona had telepathically alerted her to the musical talent from Earth as her first greeting was, "Well, who plays the harp?"

"I do," replied Angi, "and, I believe, it is similar to the one your students have. However, my two harps are back home; a student one and a golden harp." Then she thought to herself, "If I am going to play again I will have to grow my fingernails."

The golden harp triggered Sirona to ask, "Angi can you describe this golden harp?"

"It is very old, about the same size as the student harps but with deeply engraved gold on the outer shaft of the harp with different gemstones at various points. The strings are of gold and silver. It was given to me by my harp teacher, Albert Aucoin, who in his parting comments said that I would need it 'to play to the Lords of Anu.' I have no idea what he meant by that statement, and still don't."

The description caused Sirona and Carola to quickly glance at each other. Sirona spoke, "Angi does your golden harp look anything like this?" At that moment Sirona, like Myttrwn, conjured up a holographic harp of exquisite beauty, one that seemed to precisely fit Angi's description.

"Mine had a slight dent on the lower back corner," said Angi who was startled at seeing Mr. Aucoin's harp floating in front of her.

Sirona turned the harp to show Angi and said, "Like this?"

"That is amazing," replied Angi, "it is identical. But mine is back in a Canadian bank vault." Confused she added, "I don't understand."

"We will chat later," said Sirona, and she thought to herself, "This is astounding."

For the first time since they met Sirona, the rest of the team witnessed a surprised look on her face when the golden harp was mentioned. They too wondered what it meant but were pulled back into a conversation with Carola.

To their relief Carola spoke English. Knowing their thoughts she said, "I was one of the extras chosen to learn English when the mission to Gaia was first mentioned. Now I know why. As for you Angi we will have no problem getting you a harp, it is the other instruments that may take some work. However, all is not lost, let me call Lud over." With that she must have somehow signaled the student for he appeared instantly. Carola continued, "Lud is our expert in creating musical instruments in our replicating machine. He knows a bit of English, so I will stay around if any translations are needed. We will have to move quickly. Can one or more of you remain today to describe a violin and electric guitar to Lud. If we can create the instruments and get some music we will be well on our way. Sirona, is there any possibility you might be able to obtain more detailed information from Gaia, if that's possible?"

"I will talk to Myttrwn and see what we can do," replied Sirona.

Turning back to the group she continued, "While we're working on the instruments I would like you to think of a musical piece that you all can play. I will arrange to give you some help with your practice sessions. How about that?" was Carola's matter-of-fact response. Like all musicians, she was intrigued with the prospect of playing different music.

"I will check if there are any more musicians in the rest of the team," was Morgan's quick response. "Right now Wolfram and I will stay behind and work with Lud."

The lively departing chatter indicated that the idea seemed to appeal to all of the musicians.

Sirona left the group to attend to other duties. As she walked towards the House of Life she thought to herself, "This I must share with Myttrwn at once, especially the possible discovery of the long lost *Harp of Dana*. Myttrwn was right in his earlier assessment, these people from Earth are resilient and amazing. After months of knowing them I am just discovering that most of them are also musicians. I wonder what else I have yet to learn."

House of Life

"Angi is a greater mystery than I first thought," was Myttrwn's response when informed of the possible where-a-bouts of the ancient, lost *Harp of Dana*. "Sirona, you know the prophecy. This harp was to appear around this time, but we were certain it would be in our kingdom. Let's reserve any judgement until we are certain it is truly the lost harp. If true, it certainly adds another wrinkle to this venture. Has Angi ever played this golden harp?"

"She informed me her harp teacher, an elderly man, gave her this gift when she was a young girl. On that one occasion she played a musical selection under his careful guidance. He must have thought her capable of playing such an exquisite instrument. Then, according to my brief discussion with Angi, the instrument, because of the gold and gemstones, was carefully stored away by her grandmother. There it remained as Angi embarked on a very different career than music."

"Did she tell you anything about this music teacher?" asked Myttrwn, searching for clues as to how an ancient treasure from their kingdom ended up on Gaia.

"The details are hazy. She said that this Albert Aucoin, a native of France, was a descendant of a group of Irish exiled to that country sometime in the 1600s. Over the centuries the Irish married into French society, some preserving their great love of harp music. Perhaps the Irish in the 1600s took the *Harp of Dana* with them for safe keeping. The connection with the Irish is fascinating don't you think? As I recall, one possibility was that the harp had been given to an Irish king."

"That's true, particularly if that king had been a gifted harpist. Yet, it will be difficult to trace the historic route of such a small item on Gaia during its Kali Yuga. But still, it is not by chance that a harp of this quality turns up in the hands of Angi who was also the inheritor of an ancient medallion. Mark my word, Sirona, these events are connected. By the way, where is the harp now?"

"According to Angi it is resting safely in a bank vault in her hometown, a small city on an island in a country called Canada." As she spoke she brought up a map of North America pointing out the location on the Atlantic coast.

"We must inform the Queen when she returns from her trip. But I have even more to tell you about our Angi."

"More...........I knew something was up, you have been locked away in your private lab for days."

"Sirona, you and I have had a number of training sessions with Angi. I'm certain you've noticed that I have been gently pushing her well beyond what she should be capable of performing at this early stage of her training. What has amazed me is that each time she seems to reach into some natural reservoir and, following my instructions, does precisely what is requested, however slowly or hesitantly. Under normal circumstances a student at this level should be unable to perform such tests. Yet, Angi continues to carry out increasingly complex maneuvers as if it is natural to her. Intrigued, I began to search for an answer to this anomaly if for no other reason than to revise my training program for her. After a number of extensive tests I think I may have found the answer."

Sirona had never seen Myttrwn like this, he was almost excited. Wanting to share in the discussion she added her own observation, "When I first met Angi, I was also surprised by her quick response to what I knew was a foreign science to her."

"Sirona, do you remember when this group arrived, I kept saying there was something odd about Angi's genetic profile? I originally dismissed it thinking it was just something unique to Angi. But with her ease in performing these tests I decided to bypass her DNA and examine her vibrational profile. There I made the most amazing discovery. It is a pattern that I have never encountered before, and that is saying something for me. I believe it is this feature which allows her to instinctively respond to my requests. Somehow, she has either been born with this preprogramming or acquired it through wearing the medallion. Considering the randomization of her family's history I must believe it is the medallion. But that concept gets immediately challenged as it has never turned up with any previous medallion wearer. As you are my witness, Angi seems oblivious of this or even her special status as the wearer of the medallion. However, the addition of this golden harp, if true, introduces another dimension. We may have stumbled into an entirely different scenario than the one we originally thought."

"Am I sensing that this new information may change this venture?" asked Sirona.

"If I'm right, it could definitely complicate the challenges that may lie ahead and could introduce a number of perplexing unknowns. Prepare yourself, we might be working with some lofty players. But first, to reassure me that my assumptions are on track, today I am going to push Angi even further. She's expected momentarily. I will need you to continue to be my witness."

Within minutes Angi emerged from the lab elevator. Smiling, she walked towards her two mentors with a cheery greeting, "It is a beautiful day and I am ready for my next lesson." Receiving only smiles, she continued. "I expect Sirona has informed you of my harp playing?" Intuitively, Angi registered a change in her two mentors but could not decipher its meaning. She had grown accustomed to their stoic personalities. Deep down she trusted them and knew she needed their help to master the medallion. Dismissing her intuitive feelings she readied herself for her training session.

"Yes, she has," replied Myttrwn, casually, "Perhaps we will find time at the end of today's lesson to chat about your harp music and this golden harp."

"Good, I'd like that," came Angi's response attaching little importance to the matter.

Myttrwn, as was his custom, began the session by explaining what the day's activities might include. "Today Angi, we will focus on two topics; time and levitation. Until now we've concentrated on some basic steps with regard to the properties of each gemstone and with a few gemstone combinations. So far, you have demonstrated skill in moving and changing small objects. Now we will progress to a different stage."

"Great, time has always fascinated me," replied Angi.

"Angi, you will recall that in our group session I said that time is an illusion. Again I repeat, there is neither past nor future but one eternal moment...........your eternal moment. So, if that is the case, then you should be able to alter time especially with the help of your medallion. You are simply working with a single program." Instantly, without stopping to take a breath, he conjured up a simple clock with large white numbers on a black background. Then he continued, "I'm providing you with this clock to help you see what is happening as you perform these experiments."

"That's helpful," was Angi's only comment.

"Let's begin," replied Myttrwn, accepting Angi's momentary uncertainty as her normal response to something new. "As before, Angi, I want you to focus on your medallion, this time concentrate on the two blue gemstones; the sapphire and the Stone of Atlantis."

Angi sat on one of the three stools at the small table in Myttrwn's private quarters. Following Myttrwn's instruction, she closed her eyes to visualize the gemstones and then, as before, combined the colours, this time into a single blue light which encircled her body. Ready, she awaited his next instructions.

In a monotone, Myttrwn continued. "Angi, it is now two o'clock. With your thoughts, I want you to move time fifteen minutes into the future. Concentrate Angi, visualize the minutes ticking away," came his encouraging words.

Momentarily, Angi fought her old linear thinking, something that always popped up to restrict her progress. Blocking these thoughts, she held her medallion, making a silent command to the cosmos, " *Time,* I want to move fifteen minutes into the future." She visualized the clock numbers changing 2:05.......2:10.......2:15. Still she waited before opening her eyes. To her delight the clock read 2:15. Her immediate reaction was, "Wow, I did it.........I actually shifted time with my thoughts. Wait till I tell the others."

Telepathically Myttrwn said to Sirona, "While Angi is supposedly at Level 1, she has just performed a Level 4 skill. To be sure, I will retest."

Calmly he continued, "Now, Angi, let's do a similar test. I want you to shift time one hour into the future so the clock will register 3:20. Follow the same pattern as you did with the fifteen minutes only concentrate more."

Angi had decided early in her training not to interrupt her training sessions with too many questions especially when Myttrwn was in the midst of a new skill. Following an identical path, and clutching her medallion, she clearly enunciated each word to herself, " *Time*, on my command, move ahead one hour to 3:20." Again she visualized the time moving swiftly forward. When she opened her eyes this time the clock registered 3:20. Pleased with her success she blurted out, "This is fantastic..........I've actually shifted time one hour. Myttrwn, does this time shift also affect the world around me? The room seems the same. I expect there is a great deal of scientific detail I have yet to learn. Nevertheless, I'm beginning to enjoy my new found abilities."

Telepathically, Myttrwn said to Sirona, "That settles it. Somehow she has some innate ability to master this medallion. She still needs guidance but at a very different level than I first contemplated. At this rate she could complete her training in one trip. This is truly amazing!" And to his student he said calmly, "Angi, you have done well today. While this is just two simple time experiments, later we will do more complex tests to strengthen this skill. And yes, I will, in time, be giving you in-depth scientific information to explain what you are doing. Now, let's move on. For the next test I need you to step free of all furniture as I want you to rise two feet above the floor and stay there for a count of ten before descending. To do this, you will need to combine all the gemstone colours in your medallion creating a rainbow, then, as before, command the cosmos to let you levitate. A cautionary note, Angi, do not break your concentration until you feel your feet firmly back on the floor. Do you have any questions?"

Angi thought it through and replied, "None that I can think of." She did note his cautionary advice for this was the first safety instruction. She expected there would be more as she advanced in her training.

"We have lots of time.........relax and concentrate." Realizing the test might take some time, Myttrwn signaled Sirona to be seated.

"As instructed, Angi, closed her eyes and proceeded to acknowledge each gemstone, bringing forth each colour, and combining the colours into a vibrating rainbow which encircled her body. Then she addressed the cosmos silently with, "I want to rise two feet in the air, no further, and remain there for a count of ten before descending." From the beginning, Myttrwn made it clear that each command had to be precisely enunciated.

Nothing happened.

Undaunted, Angi repeated her command, this time clutching her medallion and concentrating even harder. She waited.

Still nothing happened.

Not accepting defeat, she dug down, visualized herself rising from the floor, and repeated her command, this time with even greater emphasis. Within seconds she felt a lightness as she became weightless. She then felt her feet leave the floor. Buoyant, she ascended upward a short distance and abruptly stopped. Not breaking her concentration, she mentally counted to ten. As she reached ten, she felt a gradual return of gravity which forced her descent. Again she waited with her eyes closed.

Myttrwn winked at Sirona, and telepathically said, "There, I told you. She's now at Level 5. I've never seen anything like this. I'm tempted to extend these tests but will restrain the impulse. No further tests are needed. Any preliminary assumptions we might have held have just been shattered. I've a number of theories but these can wait."

Angi was not sure what she would find when she opened her eyes. But her successful completion of the test was evident by the smiles of her two mentors. Her response was filled with satisfaction, "There, how was that?"

Not wanting to exaggerate the situation, Myttrwn simply replied, "You are an excellent student, Angi. You successfully completed all three tests which is all I require for today. If you would like to see yourself levitating, come here and watch this recording."

Angi watched the short video with both fascination and joy at her own accomplishment. Her thoughts were racing, "Under Myttrwn's mentorship it all seems so easy. I expect it is the medallion. This video shows I'm definitely progressing even if Myttrwn is restrained in his praise. I still would like to have a written guide to these training sessions, at least I'd know where I was at this point ....But then I expect there's no need of such references as everyone here just 'knows'." For a moment, she had forgotten that Sirona and Myttrwn knew what she was thinking.

It was Myttrwn's style not to pander to students as he felt it interfered with their learning. But he sensed Angi's need and with all things connected to his protégé he would rethink his stoic stand. At this point, wanting to divert the conversation, he said, "This completes today's assignments so perhaps we have a little time to discuss your golden harp."

Angi was glad for the change for she found the training sessions sapped her energy. All she had for comparison was her previous professional studies and thought to herself, "I suppose, like any new learning, it is tiring until you become proficient." Relaxed, she turned to address Myttrwn's comment, "Oh, you mean Mr. Aucoin's harp, I never really considered it my harp. I only played it once as my grandmother thought it too valuable to even be used at special concerts. My memory is a bit sketchy but as I recall it is about the size of your student harp, with about thirty strings. It is an exquisitely engraved instrument in gold and silver. The engravings consist of a variety of animals, reptiles, and little creatures playing musical instruments flowing from the mouth of a dog's head at the top of the sounding board. The pillars are also carved but with Celtic interlacing patterns of leaves, flowers and fruit. The metal strings are of gold and silver. An array of colorful gemstones are inserted in various parts of the entire instrument. Oh I almost forgot, there's a small dent on the back lower edge of one pillar. It is very much like the one Sirona conjured up yesterday."

Both Myttrwn and Sirona realized Angi's description was amazingly similar to that of the lost *Harp of Dana*, right down to the dent. Yet, neither wanted to voice their suspicions without seeing the instrument for themselves. So Myttrwn's response was tempered, "To own such a valuable instrument your harp teacher must have been a highly respected harpist. Angi, perhaps one day you can show me your harp, I would certainly like to see it."

"I'd be delighted, whenever you visit my planet," said Angi, as her thoughts drifted to the past. "I should have shown Mr. Aucoin more gratitude for his exquisite gift. I'm sorry I know so little about the man except the snippets he shared with me as a child. A man of mystery." Myttrwn's request had awakened thoughts of home, a homeward journey that for Angi might already be in jeopardy.

House of Learning & the Palace

Time in Tir na nOg was slipping by with everyone getting more and more immersed in another world. At the end of each day they continued to gather in their dining area to share their new found learning and to discuss the ramifications to their lives and the future. At times, the sessions bubbled over with bouts of laughter punctuating the clamor. Sessions with Myttrwn continued to challenge their views on life and reality. The positive features of telepathy were acknowledged, the negative ones tucked away as worrying but out of their control. Angi was the only one unable to share much of her training, something the others had long accepted.

Morgan was making headway with Lud in replicating musical instruments. Once a violin was replicated, it was tested by Morgan and Vette who competed with each other in playing Acadian and Celtic tunes. It took several replications before they were both satisfied, finally instructing Lud to proceed with the number of violins needed. Morgan joyously announced that he had discovered two more violin players within Dylan's team; Rick and Flora, plus four of the student harpists had asked to join them bringing the musical group to twelve. Once a guitar was replicated along with special amplification, a practice schedule was set up.

The choice of music proved daunting in light of the possibilities, the limitation of practice time and the differences in musical abilities. In the end, Morgan and Vette favoured a light dance selection of Irish jigs like Keegan's Jig and Lannigan's Ball. Morgan worked with Carola to create the music, got it printed and distributed. It was agreed the harpists would open the musical program while Morgan and Vette would take the lead for the jigs. Carola insisted that it should remain as simple as possible, for she too understood the handicaps they were facing. Once a decision was finalized, one could hear musicians practicing throughout the day.

With their time fully booked it therefore came as an unwanted intrusion when Sirona announced that the Queen would like to meet them at an informal reception at the Palace. This, as Andrew would later point out, was an unexpected honour. Sirona provided no additional comments as to why, other than a personal wish of the Queen. Fortunately, Andrew and Bryce had given them pre-trip instruction on court etiquette, the details each member now tried desperately to recall.

What to wear to a formal event, should it occur, had been discussed, but their travel baggage presented limitations. Each one packed a wrinkle-free white, quality, blouse or shirt as per Andrew's instructions. Angi and Vette also decided, on their own, to wear light-weight slacks under their outer travel pants. These slacks were hung up alongside their blouse in readiness for such an event. Sirona arranged for whatever services they required to be properly dressed, all the time emphasizing, "This is not a formal occasion, so relax, the Queen knows you will be there in your travel clothes." As often as Sirona stated this in their forty-eight hour window of preparation, the others knew from Andrew that meeting royalty meant that you had to be in your best attire. Andrew and Bryce came into their own at this point with Andrew reiterating his rules right up to the moment they departed for the palace........Stand straight and silent, the standing or seating order will be set by the palace. Guard your thoughts, remember they have telepathy. The Queen always takes the lead. According to Sirona she will shake your hand, wait until she extends her hand. Address the Queen as 'Your Majesty.' Only speak when spoken to, stick to the Queen's topic, and don't introduce another one on your own. Don't ask questions. Stay in the reception line until the event is over or when the Queen leaves the room. Drink and eat in moderation should anything be offered, and, remember you will be representing your world.

Dressed in their finest, the day arrived. Vette whispered to Angi as they were about to leave their living quarters, "And I thought the RCMP was strict. Andrew gives me the feeling we're about to enter the temple of the gods."

Before Angi had a chance to answer, Morgan joined them saying, "You are!"

"Thanks Morgan, that really helped," was Vette's snappy reply.

"Come on guys," came Wolfram's steady voice, "it is important for us to meet the ruler of this world. Just think what it must be like to have this kind of responsibility for centuries that must take a tough constitution."

Andrew joining the four added, "Yes, this is one of those lifetime experiences that will be remembered with great joy in years to come. There are all too few of these occasions in one's life. Keep this in mind, why have we suddenly been given this invite? Perhaps we will find out today. I'm definitely looking forward to this," as he back-stepped to join Bryce.

To their surprise, as they exited the House of Learning, Corb was sitting in the plaza with a flying bus ready to transport them to the palace. "Sirona thought it best to give you a quick ride to the palace," he said as if this was a normal occurrence.

"How kind," said Angi, as she stepped into a luxurious cabin of wide windows and cream, leather-like, bucket seats and thought to herself, "I wonder if this is Sirona's own transport. She certainly wants us looking our best and relaxed. Andrew's right, something's afoot, but what?"

Landing near the front entrance, Corb escorted them to the main doors where the guards, dressed in purple and gold, were obviously expecting them and waved them through. As they entered the palace foyer, the group stood in awe.

The Palace, larger again than the House of Life, consisted of multiple rooms and halls with no clear directional guide as to what lay along the different corridors. Pink marble glistened in the sunlight, the twenty foot ceilings were held up by huge pillars of marble trimmed in gold. Doors in the distance had golden serpents deeply engraved on each panel with gemstones artistically arranged to capture the light. They had little time to appreciate the floor mosaics and statues along the way as Corb was obviously under strict orders to get the party to their destination on a precise time table. Through a wide opening along one wall one could see an oval theatre which Corb indicated was the principal stage for the enactment of royal rituals or special events. According to him, a much larger amphitheatre existed in the community near the water which accommodated huge crowds. He also pointed out that although the House of Learning had its own library, the Palace also had a library with materials on governance and details on the administration of the kingdom. Corb walked steadily, bypassing the corridor leading to the Council of Elders Chamber and directing the group along an identical corridor, one that led to the queen's principal reception rooms.

As they walked along Angi pointed out to Wolfram the gardens, fountains and waterways in the distance saying, "I've never encountered such a magnificent building," she whispered, "Nor could I have dreamed it."

A guard, in the same purple and gold uniform as those at the entrance, stood in front of the reception room door preventing their advancement. Corb gave a message in his own language, the others translating it as, "This is the party from Gaia who are expected by her majesty. My instructions are to escort them into the room where Sirona will be waiting."

The guard opened the door and, upon seeing Sirona, extended the opening to allow the party to enter. Corb stepped back and bid his farewells.

Sirona was dressed in her usual uniform but with one exception, she was now wearing a golden crown along with her golden serpent badge and ring. She had assumed her royal status to introduce her friends to her mother.

Smiling, Sirona welcomed them with, "Come right this way, I want you to stand in a semi-circle right here near the royal seat. Angi, could you take the first position, then Vette, followed by Wolfram, Morgan, Andrew and Bryce. Dylan, I will ask you to arrange your team in their official ranking order." Stepping back she made a few last minute adjustments, and then nodded to an attendant who was standing almost invisible near a side door.

While waiting, Angi looked around. The reception room was about fifty by seventy feet with a fourteen foot ceiling. The room was bathed in light from ceiling to floor with open window-like spaces along one wall, a gentle breeze maintaining a comfortable room temperature. The décor was simple elegance of pink marble with golden banners fluttering in the breeze. Seating was minimal; three large ivory and gold chairs in one alcove, with several long cushioned benches along an outer wall. "I expect people stand when in this room and likely do not stay long," was Angi's observation.

They waited about ten minutes until a gong announced the arrival of the Queen. Sirona had indicated that this would be a less formal gathering so Angi assumed the Queen's elegant attire fit that description but she did wear her official golden crown with the serpent in front along with the same serpent badge and ring as Sirona. Angi's thoughts were concentrated on Dana na Gig as she made her way towards them, "She's so young looking, taller than Sirona and has Myttrwn's all-seeing abilities. I think she's staring at me and those emerald eyes are mesmerizing ....oh help, Andrew said to watch our thoughts. Clamp down, my girl, you are in the presence of royalty."

The group noted that Sirona and Myttrwn walked a few paces behind the Queen; Myttrwn took one of the three seats near an alcove and played no role in the Queen's welcoming activities. Sirona remained standing. Once seated the Queen turned her attention to the group saying in Gaelic (fortunately they could translate her words), "My daughter, Sirona and Myttrwn have been keeping me updated on your activities here in my kingdom. They are most pleased with all that has transpired in such a short time. You have adapted well to a very different environment. I felt it was time for us to meet." She, like Myttrwn, then scanned the group making a personal note of each one in preparation for their meeting.

At that point Sirona stepped forward and began the introductions, "Your Majesty, it is my pleasure to introduce you to each one of the Gaia party." Her mother rose and accompanied Sirona to the beginning of the reception line. To their surprise, Queen Dana na Gig proceeded to speak to them in English, a language she had just learned with the help of her daughter.

"Your Majesty, this is Angi, the one with the medallion."

As the queen reached out her hand she greeted Angi with, "Welcome Angi, it is my understanding that you are a rather unique young woman. May I see for myself this fantastic medallion?"

"Yes, Your Majesty," replied Angi as she stepped forward. The medallion, with all its splendor of gemstones, was resting on her white blouse.

The queen took a few minutes to examine the medallion while taking special note of Angi, a move noted by Andrew.

"I hear you are making progress in your training program, I hope Sirona and Myttrwn have not been too difficult in their demands," she said staring straight into Angi's face.

"Yes, Your Majesty, I am feeling much more comfortable with my training and greatly appreciate all that Sirona and Myttrwn have done for me." And with a smile, she added, "And 'no,' they have not been too demanding at all."

"That's good to hear," replied the queen with a faint smile and added, "Perhaps, before you leave, we might chat again, I would like to know more about this medallion and its capabilities."

Even Sirona wasn't expecting that. Sirona and Myttrwn had briefed her mother upon her return to the Palace on their latest findings including the possibility of the location of the *Harp of Dana*. This intrigued the Queen who insisted she wanted to meet the group but her primary objective was to meet Angi.

Angi's only reply was, "Yes, that would be nice," and thought to herself, "I wish I was more eloquent in formal situations like this. I need more help from Andrew." Then as an afterthought she added, "The Queen seems to have a special interest in my medallion. Perhaps she's just showing interest."

The queen smiled, for Angi's comments and her presence had confirmed all that her daughter had conveyed about this young woman.

After Sirona's introduction to Vette the queen commented, "So, you are the young woman who has created the delicious breads. My whole palace is enchanted with this new taste. You will have to train one of my staff before you leave."

"I would be glad to do that, Your Majesty. Danu is becoming quite proficient already," was Vette's only comment.

With Wolfram she said, "I hear from Corb that you could be a very good pilot of our emergency planes. Continue with this training, I'm sure it will serve you well in the future."

"I have enjoyed this experience, Your Majesty, and thank Corb for his patience," was Wolfram's reply.

With Morgan she said, "So you are the one that is organizing a musical group. I hope that you will have time to give us a taste of your music before you leave."

Morgan was bursting to say more but heeded Andrew's instructions and only replied, "Yes, Your Majesty, because of our limited time we will only be able to do a simple presentation with the kind help of Carola, your Director of the Harp Program." He felt it best to warn her that they would give it their best but it would have limitations.

With Andrew and Bryce she took some time, saying, "I do hope you have been able to access some of our history and cultural background. This will help us know each other better. It is also a pleasure for us to meet senior members of your society. I'm sure your sage advice has been fortuitous for your younger colleagues." Andrew and Bryce were pleased with their first meeting with the Queen.

With each member of Dylan's team she had a personal comment to let them know that they were known individually to her and she appreciated their presence in the venture.

It was well passed the hour when the reception was officially over, the Queen leaving by the same door she entered. Just before her departure, she invited the group to come to an adjoining room for refreshments.

They waited a few minutes before accompanying Sirona and Myttrwn into the next room only to discover it was a patio set up with white table clothes, cushioned chairs, and golden utensils with gigantic large pots of scented flowers placed at key locations. Once seated, royal attendants brought platters of fruit, vegetables and sweets along with a white liquid which they poured into gold trimmed crystal glasses.

Sirona and Myttrwn joined the Queen at the head table while the group of twelve were directed to three tables of four. Angi, seated with Andrew, Wolfram and Joel, asked Andrew, seated opposite, "Do you think this is a wine or a sparkling fruit drink? It has, I believe, a taste of pear but also something I can't identify. It is light, slightly dry and it tingles."

"Angi, I have no idea what it is but, as I said before, enjoy but drink sparingly. We haven't had this before and when in royal company it might be quite powerful. I must say those sweets have caught my eye. I expect the sweetness is due to honey, but what a tantalizing taste. See, I too must be careful," as he winked at Angi. "By the way, I expect this audience with the Queen was because of your medallion. She was captivated by you, and, you may note, she indicated she would like another audience. I expect the next one will be with you alone. I'd love to know what Sirona and Myttrwn have been saying about us. This is when I'd like telepathy."

Angi, Wolfram and Joel laughed.

Joel had been silent as he savoured the different offerings. Finally he spoke, "You know this has been a mind blowing adventure for me and our security team. I've not only learned more about worlds I never even thought existed, but have been flabbergasted by what can be achieved with their replicators. Imagine what we could do with this technology back home. I have no idea how I could, or would be allowed to tell anyone of this trip. That will be a tough order."

"Joel, you are not the only one. I expect we shall just be able to chat about this with our own colleagues for some time to come," said Wolfram. "I'm glad to have had a chance to learn so much and would like to get more pilot training. But, I know we must return home. But there's always next time, right?"

Before anyone else had a chance to talk a group of senior harpists entered the room and provided a half hour of angelic music, the tunes reaching out to the very souls of the party. Angi sat in rapture admiring their skills and wondering if she was up to a harp performance before the Queen.

Time passed, and eventually the Queen rose to mark the end of the occasion. The group thanked Sirona and returned to Corb at the reception room door. While he was prepared to fly them back to their House of Learning, they said they would like to slowly walk down the hill giving them time to enjoy the scenery. Unperturbed, Corb guided them to the Palace entrance and waved them good bye. The rest of the journey downhill was filled with lively chatter as they shared their perceptions of the day.

Chapter 6

House of Learning, Angi's Suite

Buoyed up, they sat for some time sharing thoughts and debating the purpose of the Queen's invitation. Andrew was convinced it had everything to do with Angi, while others argued it was a courtesy to all royal guests midway in their time in Tir na nOg. The matter remained unresolved as they said their '*good nights.*'

Angi, surprised by her weariness, went straight to bed. Her dreams were filled with marble palaces, foreign dignitaries and a lavish meal with the glitter of gold everywhere. Somewhere towards dawn she was awakened by the feeling of a presence in her suite. Sitting up in bed she tried to discern any movement in the darkness. A gentle morning breeze ushered in a faint scent of jasmine. She waited, her instincts sharpened. Then a familiar voice broke the spell.

"Well, Angi Talismann, you've certainly been dining in grand style. What did you think of the Royal Palace?" was Adawee's introduction.

The warmth of her voice comforted Angi and she replied, "Oh, Adawee, what a spectacular place, it was like a dream. Actually, better than a dream. Living in such magnificence must do something to one's soul. But I expect it comes with immense responsibilities. The Queen was gracious and even spoke English, much to our delight. Imagine learning another language so quickly. That's going the extra mile." Then she remembered her Snowy Owl had done the same and added, "Just like you, Adawee. I'm so impressed with such kindness that I'm going to get Andrew to teach me Gaelic when I get home. However, I can assure you I will not be able to master this language overnight, but I will do it in time." At this point, Angi turned on a nightlight to see that Adawee was sitting on a thin bar near her bed and commented, "I suppose you didn't fly through the sensory barrier at the door, as, being a hologram, you can appear anywhere, right?"

"You are clever, Angi. I did not need the doorway. I thought, this time, I'd spare you the journey to the balcony. I'm pleased to see you intend to keep growing. Learning another language, for whatever reason, is good for your brain. Now if you are awake, I wonder if we might continue our chats, as you call them."

Growing used to Adawee's unscheduled visits she replied, "Sure, I'm awake. What's our topic this time?" Angi moved to a comfortable position in her bed and thought to herself, "Now's the time for some comfy pillows. Ah well, work with what you got." She rolled up an apparent blanket and moved to brace herself against the head of the bed.

Adawee, shifted her position to stare directly at Angi saying, "Tonight I'd like to discuss dreams."

Angi repeated the word.........'dreams' and thought for a few minutes before commenting. "Now that I think of it, I suppose I have two versions; one I learned from my grandmother, the other I acquired through my professional studies. They are similar but different. I will begin with my childhood version. My grandmother's first question each morning was, "Angi, did you dream?" She waited until I provided my best description. Sometimes she commented but other times she just nodded. Basically, she felt dreams were a window into a person's whole being; physically, mentally and spiritually. When she thought it necessary she would provide guidance. She was rarely wrong. She was especially concerned about identical dreams which repeated three times."

"Your grandmother was a wise woman," replied Adawee. "Go on, what did you discover about dreams in your professional world?"

"In my professional education we took several psychology courses, a few mentioned dreams. Basically, leading psychoanalysts held different views. The older ones thought dreams were disguised expressions of the unconscious and might be philosophical pronouncements, illusions, fantasies, irrational experiences or telepathic visions. However, current scholars regard dreams as simply a reflection of everyday life. In addition, interpretation of dreams was relegated to qualified professionals like psychologists and psychiatrists, those requiring payment for their services. Lowly nurses were not included. So, I expect, the majority of nurses ignore the topic."

"So, Angi, what would a nurse do if a patient insisted on talking about his or her dreams?"

"Well, if the nurse had time, a rarity these days in the health industry, she would listen. Medical doctors, except psychiatrists, had no interest in such topics so nothing would appear on the patient's record. Even if the nurse listened she would let the patient form his or her own opinion."

"What you are saying, unlike your grandmother, is that dreams are no longer an essential part of your lives, and, I expect, any spiritual connection has been lost."

"I guess that's one way of looking at it. Today we pride ourselves at being so sophisticated that we no longer need the interpretation of dreams. The health industry is there to address our physical needs and God, the devil, dreams, intuition, extrasensory perception, and/or spiritual development, has been rationalized out of existence for a good many. As such, I learned never to share my dreams with outsiders, including my nursing colleagues. If I described some of my weird dreams to my colleagues they might snicker thinking it a joke, or question my sanity. Certainly, most would not consider dreams a guidance system, psychological or spiritual."

Adawee, repositioned herself on the pole and continued, "Your grandmother was right, dreams are an inexhaustible source of valuable information. As your older scholars identified, dreams arise out of the unconscious, the messages being delivered in a symbolic language. Dream vocabulary is specific to each individual and simultaneous interpretations are possible. It is the dreamer who decides which one is the most valid. Dreams also need to be analysed as a series, a single dream may be just a peripheral aspect of the message. That would explain your grandmother's daily request about your dreams, she was assessing the whole picture. Some cultures with great understanding of the symbolic language in dreams use this to guide them in their psychological and spiritual development."

"Well perhaps I have not been entirely correct. Nurses working with the mentally ill may use dreams to interpret psychological problems in their patients. I would doubt there is any reference to a spiritual message."

"Then there is some use of dreams to aid in the healing of certain individuals but it is not a general practice, would that be your assessment?" asked Adawee."

"Yes, that would be the best description. It is a tool in diagnosing mental illness," replied Angi.

"How limiting, it speaks of a society which has discarded their built-in Divine guidance system. Can you explain why you are different?"

"I suppose I owe it all to my grandmother which allowed my right brain to develop but this right-brain ability often clashed with the left brain world in which I lived."

"Yes, it is wise to remain silent. Do you think there are others like yourself who share your understanding of dreams?"

"Oh, I expect there are. They would likely be found in what we refer to as the alternative health community. Unfortunately, such individuals are usually shunned by the scientific health community. But I'm heartened to hear that there will be greater right-left brain balance in the Dwarapa Yuga. But I sense you have some concern our present system is not too healthy, is that correct?"

"That is right, Angi. But since societies in transition tend to discard old religious or psychological practices in their struggle to adopt a new one, are

107

there any signs a new one is emerging, excluding your comment on the alternative health community?"

"Let me think,"..............There was a brief silence as Angi thought of Adawee's question, then she replied, "I expect some would argue a replacement tradition is well underway but at this point it appears to be a hodgepodge of materialistic and politically correct beliefs, symbols, and practices. Most focus on the physical, and the whole process fails to address the deep seated anxieties and problems of our modern life. Those disturbed by their dreams are mainly referred to left-brain practitioners which I mentioned earlier. It is a catch 22."

Adawee repeated the phrase, "A *catch 22*..........what does that mean Angi?"

"Oh, sorry, it is a way of saying these individuals get caught in a situation where there seems to be no escape because of conflicting conditions. Dreams, if analyzed at all, are seen as a minefield to diagnose mental illness not as a spiritual guidance system. Our focus is on illness to be treated with drugs as the answer to everything. But, Adawee, what happens to a people adrift with no understanding of this Divine gift?"

"If this inner truth is neglected it may reappear as some personalized demon which can be frightening to an individual. Rudderless, lost without an understanding of their own guidance system, the individual must face their own deep-seated psychological and spiritual issues alone. Angi, do you think this is intractable?" asked Adawee.

"Perhaps I tend to be a bit overdramatic. Let me rethink my answers," Angi remained silent for a few minutes before continuing. "For the past fifty years our western society has marched to a scientific left-brain drummer. The departure of our current elder population will spell a further demise of traditional religious organizations, where our previous spiritual guidance once dwelt. Admittedly, even in these organizations dreams were rarely discussed although frequently mentioned in our religious texts. This loss will exacerbate the problem. Equally, I see little change in the education of health care professionals. We have specialized everyone into tighter and tighter corners with little room for innovation." Then she added, "If I suggested a need for serial dream analysers I expect it would just become another specialty. Yet, there is a booming business in dream literature, internet information and those who are willing to translate your dreams but these exist outside the health community. Whether this is enough or the translations are of any quality remains a question. So, as I see it, overall change may require a crisis or a miracle. As for your question of how long can a society exist before something happens, I have no idea. Once again I bow to your wisdom."

"It may not be as bleak as you think, Angi. Psychic abilities are natural qualities of every soul. You have the ability to pick up thoughts, impressions, hunches and energy patterns of those around you. As you have learned from Myttrwn, every thought is an electro-magnetic beam of energy. The problem in your world is that this ability has been allowed to wither. So, I expect as your enlightenment grows there will be more and more people with psychic abilities who will demand change. Then, the symbolic language of dreams will be reawakened for everyone and used to not only diagnose psychological and spiritual problems but to guide each individual along his or her own heroic journey."

"You mean that we all have telepathic abilities?" asked Angi, somewhat surprised by Adawee's comments.

"Yes, in the years ahead these will become more astute. For that reason it is good your team has had this venture into our world, they will be able to communicate to your world that having everyone so gifted is not a negative, but a positive. Admittedly, for some it will be a threat. But before your psychic abilities can be enhanced your people will need greater self-control and emotional detachment, a hard call in a world where sensationalism and emotional overload are the norm."

Adawee, before you go, and since we've been talking about dreams. I wonder if you might help me with a recent dream I've been having. It has occurred twice and I dread a third occurrence, but expect it will come."

Caught off guard, Adawee replied, "Certainly, Angi, what is this dream of yours?"

"In my dream I'm in a semi-darkened room, a lighted, raised altar sits at the centre of this huge room. I sense that I need to make my way towards this altar but do not know why. When I step forward some kind of monster with burning eyes attacks me and I feel myself falling into a dark pit. At that moment, I wake up."

There was no response from Adawee for about five minutes, then she replied, "Your grandmother was right about a thrice-repeated dream, Angi. As you may know, intuition is just another dream form which, for some, may appear as gut feelings, forebodings, or premonitions. Your intuition is interpreting clues in your present environment unavailable to your five senses. My interpretation of your dream is that it is a warning. There is danger ahead for you, Angi. Be vigilant. Whatever transpires, remember, sometimes the darkest moment often holds the greatest treasure. You are not alone in your journey, rely on your companions, they are there for a reason. I can add little else at this point."

"Thank you, Adawee, You've confirmed my suspicions. You remind me of my grandmother who always insisted I work out my own life. I like that." Angi wasn't sure whether Adawee couldn't or wouldn't provide more detail.

"It is nice to know that I may be of some help, Angi," replied Adawee whose movements signaled her departure.

"I know our time is up. Thanks again for opening another door for me. I will not ask this time but will wait until you think it is OK to tell my friends about you. I have much to think about."

"Dream on, Angi. Listen to your own soul for you have gifts not yet available to most of your people." And with that Adawee evaporated leaving Angi with lingering thoughts on her own safety and concerns for her earthly homeland.

ଧ

House of Learning

After days of solo practice, Carola, the Director of the Harp School, set a date for the musical group to get together. The twelve gathered in the same place as their first encounter with the group of harpists; an internal open air court on the first level of the House of Learning.

Carola first segregated the musicians; Angi joining the four student harpists, while Wolfram, with his enhanced guitar, joined the six violinists. Satisfied each musician had sufficient space, she pointed out their first session's objective, "We will begin by having each group play their part and, when we are comfortable with that, we will pull the whole program together. As agreed, the program will open with the harps playing a jaunty number which will connect with the primary music of Keegan's Jig and Lannigan's Ball. Then everyone will proceed with the musical jig." Looking around she sensed the expectation and nervousness in the group, some with greater instrumental experience than others and, for the students, their first time playing unusual music from another planet. Not wishing to delay, she gave the signal to begin by tapping on the musical stand with her hand.

Angi realized the small harp provided by Carola was far superior to her student version left behind on Earth. Her homeland harp was a plain wooden one with catgut strings, whereas this one was resplendent with deeply engraved symbols of nature and the strings were foreign, a material that seemed to come alive when played. When practicing she was surprised by the volume produced with little effort. "No need for electronics here," she thought, "I wonder how they achieve so much sound." Angi was glad to be joining experienced harpists which inspired her own musical effort. The students were young, enthusiastic and enjoyed playing something unique. With a few starts and stops the harpists completed their segment to Carola's initial satisfaction.

Then she focused on the guitar and violins, instructing them, "When the harpists reach the last two bars of their segment I want you to enter gently, and then burst forth into the selected music. This will be unfamiliar to our audience." Then smiling she added, "I want them to be captivated by your music, so put your heart into this." Carola, enamored by the music and its future possibilities, provided steady guidance using the professional skills of Wolfram, Morgan and Vette to pull the group into a cohesive whole.

Angi looked at Andrew and Bryce who were obviously enchanted with their role and comfortable with their replicated violins. She had recently overheard them discussing the differences in the replicated instruments and their own violins back home, Andrew saying, "You know Bryce, this is remarkable. That young boy has created the quality of a Strad in mere days. While I hate to admit it, it is superior to my expensive instrument in Scotland. Just listen, there is warmth, richness and depth of sound which is impressive. I expect there is no need to have an electronic enhancement to this instrument. Incredible!" Then Angi focused on the other musicians.

"Morgan and Vette seem captivated by each other's musical expertise. They've discovered a mutual interest in something other than this venture. That's a good sign. Wolfram is a master at that guitar. It is obvious he and Morgan have had a long musical history. Look at the ease they give each other signals as they play. And just look at Flora and Rick, I bet Dylan never knew they had such skills. While initially I didn't think it possible, this musical idea is gaining momentum. But will we be ready for a performance for the Queen.........that's another question."

Lulled by her thoughts Angi wasn't ready when Carola turned and said, "Now, on the last bar of the violin and guitar piece, I want the harpists to join in." Annoyed that they were not ready she tapped her hand on the musical stand. The ending took several takes before Carola was satisfied.

"That's good for a first practice," said Carola, beginning to think it time to bring the session to a close. But she had hardly completed the sentence when two students, dressed in green uniforms, arrived carrying what looked like hand drums. Carola turned to greet the two saying, "Well, does this mean you would both like to join this musical challenge?"

"Yes," came the joint reply in Gaelic. "We've been listening to your practice and believe we could add something if given a chance." They turned with pleading eyes seeking the group's permission.

"As you know, it must be the decision of the group if you can participate." Then she turned to the group and proceeded to defend the students saying, "I can assure you Bran and Togu, while young, are enthusiastic and capable drummers. We have few like them in our musical school."

Morgan was the first to speak, "Could they play us a short piece so we might hear what their drums sound like?"

The students were glad to perform. Pulling forward two chairs, they began as if of one mind. Their drum routine rose and fell on a rhythmic pattern ending with a few notes from Keegan's Jig, to demonstrate their quick learning of the music from Gaia.

While their skill was impressive, Wolfram asked, "We hadn't planned on drums, can we add them to the program at this point?"

Defensively, Bran replied. "We won't need the printed music, we already know where we can come in."

"I am sure these two can manage," came Carola's reassuring comment. "Let's go through the program again and I will let Bran and Togu come in as they see fit." Her confidence reassured the group who settled back for another practice session.

The drummers played softly along with the harps and became more integrated with the violins and guitar. As the session ended there were smiles everywhere. No vote was needed, the two were added bringing the group to fourteen, an accepted Tir na nOg number of twice seven.

Deep down they knew their first practice session as a group had gone well. But Carola, being a stickler for perfection, wasn't about to let them off lightly. As they prepared to leave she said, "From this date, I want you here every evening at 5:30 your time, until the performance. We have only weeks to get this program perfected and, as my students will tell you, I accept no excuses unless,"............ she looked at Angi, "it is a royal command."

As they were preparing to leave Vette stood up and announced, "By the way, Joel, Danu and I thought this would be a great occasion for the testing of our latest food creation, a pizza. If everyone will come back to our dining area I believe the rest of the team will have everything ready. Please note that there will only be a taste as our pizza production is still somewhat limited."

Carola, having previously tasted the bread, was enthusiastic about tasting something different and replied, "Thank you, Vette that would be a welcome closure to the evening." Then turning to the students she added, "You can come along. Your instruments will be safe left here for now, but return and put them away as I have another musical group here in the morning."

The students were thrilled.

The rest of the group deposited their instruments in their suites before joining the party.

The smell of pizza filled the air. In the dining area Danu and Joel stood on duty next to four silver, round objects, hovering about two feet above the floor. Another boxlike cabinet sat next to one floating ball for the storage of additional pizza. Plates, utensils and napkins were carefully stacked on the serving table. Joel took command saying, "With Vette's baking know-how and Danu's replication skills we have created our first pizza. As you can imagine, we had to time this evening's get-together very carefully. These charming balls are ovens which Danu will be glad to describe to anyone who might be interested. For me, I know it works as we have tested this many times. So, before we proceeded in placing the first four pizzas in the ovens I needed a signal from Vette indicating you were heading this way. This she provided on her cell phone. The tantalizing smell of tomatoes and cheese which you are smelling means that the first pizzas are ready. With that he lifted the lid of the barbeque-like device to reveal a bubbling pizza. Our plan is to give everyone a slice. I ask the experienced pizza eaters to help new comers in the eating of pizza with or without utensils. We should have plenty." Taking a wide paddle he lifted the first pizza out onto a wooden cutting surface where Vette and Danu stood ready to slice the pie. It took no time for everyone to gather their plates ready for the tempting treat.

The dining area was filled with chatter, laughter and demonstrations as more pizzas were prepared and eaten. No one noticed Sirona entering until she asked, "I heard there is some special food offering this evening. Am I too late?"

Angi, stepped forward saying, "Sirona, how delightful." Then a quick glance and reassurance from Joel she continued, "Come and have a slice of pizza. It is the latest creation of Vette, Joel and Danu. While we know the tomatoes and cheese are replicated, I must say it certainly tastes like a homemade pizza." She escorted Sirona towards Vette who was already standing with a plate and a slice of piping hot pizza.

Then Andrew asked, "Should we give you a piece for Myttrwn?"

Before Sirona had a chance to speak Joel responded, "No need. As we experimented with this, Myttrwn not only enjoyed the tasting but also provided input to make improvements in both the cooking items and the pizza content. It was his expertise that helped create these floating ovens."

Smiling Sirona added, "It was Myttrwn who alerted me to your party. He insisted that I should taste this pizza." Using utensils she placed a small piece of pizza into her mouth and, after chewing and swallowing remarked, "My, Myttrwn was right, this is different and delicious. You keep surprising me. May it continue."

With the disappearance of the final piece of pizza, the assembly began to take their leave, a few sitting at the tables engaged in discussion of other matters. Sirona's second objective was to inform them that arrangements had been made to call home at dawn the next morning near the transport gate. She would arrive to escort the group.

As they retired each pondered what critical messages needed to be delivered and who was best at crisp delivery.

"Home," thought Angi, "it seems light-years since we left," her thoughts going back to those they said farewell to just months before.

༄

House of Life, Transport Room

At dawn, they met Sirona at the entrance of the House of Life where she escorted them through security and into the transport room deep underground. This was the first time they had seen the gate since their arrival. The area was alive with activity with individuals in white uniforms focused on their duties. Circling the gate area were a number of separate rooms equally endowed with complicated equipment.

Angi thought to herself, "It is much bigger than I remember. The huge circular gate seems alive with those flashing lights on its outer rim. There's a command center above us with individuals fully occupied with the operation of this complex device. It is also busier than I expected."

With that, Sirona maneuvered the group to one side to witness the arrival of one female and two males dressed in simple but elegant uniforms from some distant planet. The flowing energy screen at the center of the gate remained for seconds before evaporating after the three exited the gate.

"They definitely look official," thought Andrew. "The welcoming party are those two senior members of the Queens Council, dressed in formal attire. I expect it is a diplomatic meeting with the Queen, but not major enough to warrant her presence. It is likely routine. I wonder if, in the years to come, representatives from Earth will be welcomed in the same way. Apparently, such visits occurred in the past."

Then Sirona directed the group to a side room where Myttrwn was waiting. As always his stoic but welcoming manner relaxed them, "I hope everyone enjoyed the pizza yesterday." He glanced at Sirona and smiled. "I certainly did as the trio worked on this project." Myttrwn was enjoying his time with his Gaia friends. He looked forward to their endless questions and their surprises. But realizing the importance of the occasion he changed the topic, "Now for today's business. Using the, now opened, Serpent's Gate at Tara we have been able to link up with your World Wide Web for this call."

"That's great," said Andrew, "So, this will be like an Internet phone call?"

"Not quite, Andrew. Our two energy systems are very different so the connection may be brief. Remember this is our first communication in some time from this side of the Gate, outside of Sirona's holographic connection with Angi in regard to the medallion. We will give it a go this morning, as we have surmised this is the best time of day for clear communication. If it does not work we will try again or will think of something else."

"That sounds reasonable," replied Andrew, trusting in Myttrwn's abilities. "Since this might be a small window, do you think we should narrow down who should speak and precisely what should be communicated?"

"Would you like a few minutes to get your thoughts together?" asked Myttrwn. "But first, could you give my technician your home phone number along with any details regarding a call to your country?"

"Certainly," replied Andrew as he moved towards the technician. After a brief discussion, he returned to Myttrwn and asked, "Can we have a few minutes?"

"How about ten minutes. With the information you have given to my technician we will need to discuss the details of this matter," replied Myttrwn.

When Myttrwn and Sirona left, Andrew turned to the others asking, "OK if we have no more than a five minute window let's make a list of priorities to discuss with our home contacts. Any suggestions?"

"First, we should tell them we're all right," said Wolfram, thinking of his grandparents.

Remembering their earlier discussions, Angi added, "We need to get them to set up some kind of screening system so we're not returning with any unwelcome problems."

Then it was Dylan's turn, "We need to ask Matt if they have had any problems regarding our return to the Hill of Tara." Matt was Dylan's second in command, a trustworthy individual. "Also, I asked him to check the long range weather forecast for the end of October. So, if we have time, we could ask about that."

"Fine, that seems enough for this inaugural telephone call," replied Andrew. Then looking around he added, "It would be nice if everyone had a chance to chat but this doesn't seem possible. I've had some experience with poor communications from remote locations. Expect a gritty, muffled or broken connection, anything may happen. The key is that Matt hears our voice and gets the message we're OK. Next, let's decide who should take the lead; Angi, Dylan, or myself."

There was no hesitation, in unison they replied, "You Andrew."

"Very well. Here comes Myttrwn and Sirona."

"Are we ready?" asked Myttrwn, "I've arranged for everyone to hear the conversation."

"Yes," replied Andrew. "I will take the lead while the rest of the team listens in. We've identified the priorities. Now, let's see how this goes."

Myttrwn nodded to the technician standing in front of a large console with flashing lights. The technician proceeded, skillfully concentrating on the technology. Within seconds the sound of a familiar open phone line filled the room.

"Andrew, for the best reception I'd like you to stand over here," said Myttrwn.

Andrew moved closer to the technician's booth.

Next the room was filled with a dial tone, a slightly different sound than the usual Internet version.

On the third ring an individual with a soft Irish accent answered, "Hello, this is the Sinclair residence. Can I help you?"

Everyone smiled, it worked on the first try and the line was clear.

Andrew responded, "Hello Matt, it is Andrew and the travelling crew from Tara."

"Fantastic," was Matt's exuberant reply, "I won't even try to understand how you achieved this. I will get the others, they are all nearby. But knowing you may have little time on this historical call, go ahead. I've got you on the speaker phone."

Andrew responded, "Matt, your right, this may be brief. First, we're all here and everyone is fine. We have been royally treated and have learned much. Matt contact Ian Fraser and have him set up a screening process for our return. This is only a precaution. Just have your team at Tara. Dylan wants to know if there have been any problems with the Tara arrangements for our return."

"No, everything's under control. Is October 31st still your return date? If so, can you be more precise on the time?"

Sirona stepped closer to Andrew and whispered ...."about 4:30 in the morning of the 31st."

Andrew repeated the time, "Matt, about 4:30 in the morning. It'll be dark."

Some static began.........but the connection held.

"Gotcha 4:30 a.m. on the 31st." Concerned the line might die, Matt added, "The long range forecast looks cool with rain. I will keep a check and come with extras."

They could hear the commotion as the others piled into the room behind Matt.

Tyloar, Wolfram's grandfather pushed forward to ask, "How's my grandson, Wolfram?" Andrew beckoned Wolfram to come forward.

"Granddad I am fine, everyone is fine, it has been an amazing venture." At that point the static increased, the team watched as the technician tried feverishly to clear the line.

Andrew, realizing the situation, stepped in, "We would love to chat more but it is not possible. We will be home in no time with much to talk about.

Our best to you all. Signing off." And at that moment the line went dead.

"You did it," was Andrew's exclamation as he turned to face Myttrwn. "Thank you to both yourself and your technicians." Then he added, "I know that the ramifications of this historic call were only feasible through your expertise, Myttrwn. May this be the beginning of a fine relationship between Earth and your kingdom?" Turning to the team he wanted to share his thoughts, "It was good to contact home base. I don't know about you but it seems ages since we left the Hill of Tara, yet it has only been a couple of months. Much has changed since then." There were nods all around.

"I'm glad it worked the first time," said Myttrwn. "Yes, I also hope this is a fine beginning for all of us. Since I will be meeting with you later today, I will leave you with Sirona, as my technician and I review this morning's activities."

The team followed Sirona back through the transport room and out into the main lobby of the House of Life. Bidding her good bye at the entrance, they walked back to the House of Learning chatting happily about the call and the prospects of their homeward journey. Like all travelers, there comes a time when the appeal of home beckons.

Chapter 7

House of Life

After their mid-day meal they set off for the House of Life and another of Myttrwn's sessions. Over the weeks Myttrwn had generously given them open sessions where they could ply him with questions. Comfort with the new theories varied.

Myttrwn and Sirona were already present, chatting adamantly over something. They broke off when the group arrived.

"Oh, to have the gift of telepathy," thought Andrew. "I expect everything is not as rosy as it appears. It is hard to detect abnormalities when one is struggling with an alien language and culture, especially this one. Stability exists with Sirona and Myttrwn and their chosen associates, but it is hard to judge how extensive that is. Must talk to Bryce about this later today."

As Myttrwn surveyed his protégées he felt moved to say, "I'm pleased we've covered so much in such a short time. I'm aware some of you are grappling with my revelations. It takes time. Today, we may be in more familiar territory. Our focus will be on your divine journey in which you alone make the choices. For a moment let us once again envision a world of energy around you, one in which holographic images appear and keep changing, providing you with a stage for decision-making. Each lifetime you arrive like a seasoned actor receiving your script and costume for another role. You are aware you will be working on twenty-five percent of your divine image. Your choices can either improve the quality of this image or cause it to deteriorate."

Wolfram was pressed to ask, "I'm assuming, Myttrwn, this twenty-five percent is a cosmic formula. Who decides on the twenty-five percent? I don't suppose I could negotiate for thirty percent or more to clear my slate faster."

Myttrwn grinned, "Actually, Wolfram, it is a cosmic decision, one calculated after millions of years. It is commendable you want to achieve more, but the quality you achieve with the twenty-five percent may do the same thing."

"So, reincarnation means we still have work to do, is that right?" asked Vette.

"Yes, Vette, and you have a variety of paths to help you achieve the best results, if you use them correctly. That's what we're about to discuss," replied Myttrwn.

Genuinely interested, Vette continued, "I expect these paths were well known in the past, but may be less visible today?"

"Let's see," Myttrwn replied, pleased with their ongoing interest. "Today, we shall focus on two; one internal and the other external. Another path is your dreams which we will leave for a later session. The more important of the two is the internal path. Whether you know it or not, the greatest battle in life is the one between your soul and ego. Your soul keeps pulling you towards truth and light, whereas your ego, nourished by your five senses, keeps pulling you towards the materialistic world and darkness. The five senses you know well as sight, smell, hearing, taste and touch. Your hero's journey is to slay this internal enemy irrespective of the mesmerizing display of enchantments in your outer world. For at the end of your days you will be measured on the outcome of this internal struggle, not by how many trophies you acquired in the physical world. You alone must pull aside the veil of the unknown and step, with a gentle heart, devoid of ego, into the light. You cannot blame anyone else for your failure. If unsuccessful, further reincarnations will follow until you succeed."

"If the conquest of the ego is so important, why haven't our religious organizations concentrated more on this?" asked Wolfram.

Before Myttrwn could reply, Morgan interjected, "Perhaps it would be difficult for them to start preaching an anti-ego sermon when so many of them are caught up in the acquisition of materialistic wealth and power themselves. I expect that's the reason so many people have walked away from organized religion in western countries because it was barren of spiritual guidance. Sadly, too many people today find themselves isolated and alone facing insurmountable problems."

Myttrwn let the group talk on as they chewed on the topic.

Bryce entered the discussion, "Now that I think about my childhood religious classes I can recall references to virtues and vices, good and evil, truth and lies, the devil and Hell, but I do not recall much about ego bashing per say. And recently, even the devil and Hell have been scratched. Later, psychology courses said little about overcoming the ego. I wonder why?"

Myttrwn responded, "I've examined some of your religious texts and would have to concur, there is little direct reference to this major internal struggle except for one book called the Bhagavad Gita, a text from India, material preserved from ancient times."

Dylan, having listened to the discussion, felt compelled to ask, "But surely Myttrwn, you are not inferring that every one of us need to become some kind of spiritual hermit or yogi, removing ourselves from the world to carry out this internal battle. Most of us exist in a tangible world. So what do we do?"

"True, but even if you are in the physical world, your choices in life should provide you with a continuous process of self-discovery. Meditation may give you a means of achieving this internal enlightenment. You may have observed that every student in this kingdom is skilled at meditation. Through meditation you can slowly learn to control your senses. Self-control is essential to your psychological and spiritual growth."

"Fine, I am aware that certain team members do daily meditation. Perhaps before we leave you might give the rest of us some understanding of how to meditate. That's a beginning." But Dylan was not quite ready to accept meditation as the only path and asked, "You mentioned a second path?"

"The second path may be more familiar. Perhaps Morgan could give us a description of his understanding of mythology, a topic we shall now explore."

Surprised by Myttrwn's request, Morgan responded. "Oh, I'd be delighted," and putting on his professorial persona he proceeded, "Mythology refers to the collected myths or body of stories of a group of people which are used to define their fundamental views of the universe, nature, history, customs, traditions and taboos. It defines a community, giving them a sense of belonging, and explains their moral, psychological, social and spiritual practices. The main characters of such tales are often gods and goddesses, demigods, or supernatural humans. Before you ask, there is confusion over what constitutes a myth, a fable, legend or folktale. After centuries, especially when so many tales were transmitted verbally, the lines got blurred. In addition, as religions change, past myths sometimes get reinterpreted with the former characters demoted to subhuman forms such as elves and faeries. This has complicated the understanding of ancient myths."

"That's fine Morgan, but our current academics tend to have a very dim view of mythology. Am I right?" asked Andrew.

"Indeed," came Morgan's immediate response, "Their views vary, none positive. Some believe the ancients used myths to describe the acts of their self-created gods or goddesses, or to justify rituals or magic, or they are poetic fantasy using allegorical instructions to shape the individual. There are always the exceptions. A few actually thought myths reflected patterns in the mind or were possible expressions of a society's goals, fears, and dreams. But few academics waste their time on the topic as they believe it is not their job to define morality and see myths as contradictory to the technological world we currently live in. Yet, I've found a treasure trove of valuable information in myths."

"That's a fine review, Morgan, and your attitude to myths is commendable," replied Myttrwn, and turning to the group, he continued, "While your scientists have identified some aspects of myths they have failed to grasp one of its main purposes. Because a previous civilization does not speak the same language or use the same words to describe his or her world, it doesn't mean they do not have similar thoughts."

Morgan interjected, "I suppose our scientists might be compared to that old story of four blind men examining an elephant. Each, in examining only one aspect of the elephant, assumes his segment epitomized the entire animal."

"I'm not familiar with that particular tale but the principle is correct." Then looking around Myttrwn asked, "Having heard Morgan's comments, why would a modern society bother with myths, traditions or legends?"

Angi remembering her recent chat with Adawee, spoke up saying, "I believe we need myths and rituals to help us go through the psychological and spiritual stages in our lives, a practice which, sadly, we seem to be discarding in our modern world."

"Yes, Angi, rituals and traditions were and are designed to introduce the individual to the transitional stages in their lives and, through initiation and ceremony, help them assume increasing responsibilities and as they move towards maturity to gain increased self-control."

"Are we talking about such ceremonies as marriage and funerals?" asked Dylan.

"Exactly," replied Myttrwn, "At the end of each ceremony the individual is expected to let go of their previous life and move on into the rites, traditions, practices and responsibilities of a different way of living. Let's stop at this point and see how many ceremonies you have already experienced in your own lives. Andrew, as one of the senior members of the group, would you begin?"

"I'd be glad to," replied Andrew, "I expect age will make a difference in what is reported. In my case, belonging to one of a number of Christian religious organizations, I was christened as an infant marking my arrival into my family and community. As a young man I went through various education grades and eventually entered university where, I expect, graduation can be identified as a ceremonial step. In the military there were definite stages and ceremonies as you advanced up through the ranks. Different social organizations also had their own set of initiations and graded steps. Marriage was another ceremony in my life which was followed by the christening of our own three children. Deaths and funerals in one's family also change one's life," he deliberately avoided mentioning his wife's death. "I could list other less formal ceremonies but will leave it at that. I expect all these changed me in some way. I'm now left with my funeral, another formal ceremony."

"Let's hope that's a long way off," smiled Myttrwn."Now Bryce how about you?"

"My life mirrors Andrew's except my wife and I did not have children and she died a few years ago leaving me a widower, a definite transition for me. I also had a formal retirement party when I left my employment at sixty-five, a ceremony of sorts. I won't mention my funeral but, like Andrew, I see funerals as transition points in life as dear friends depart."

Myttrwn then looked at the rest of the group saying, "I expect that since the rest of you are younger your ceremonial list may be shorter. Would anyone like to begin?"

Angi took the lead, "I have similar ceremonies to Andrew's early list of being christened, and going through an educational system with graduation ceremonies from high school and later in acquiring my nursing degree. My parents were divorced when I was little, which is not so much a ceremony but a major change in one's life, especially if you are a child. As for funerals, I recently lost my grandmother which definitely was an unexpected transition for me which I am still experiencing."

As Angi stopped, Vette began, "I came from a traditional Acadian family with similar ceremonies as noted by Andrew, Bryce and Angi; christening and the educational route which was enhanced by the stages of my police training and graduation. When my only brother, also a police officer with the RCMP, was killed in the line of duty, I felt it was my obligation to enlist to honour our family tradition. My two other siblings were married with children. This definitely changed my life."

This was the first time the group heard of Vette's reason for becoming a police officer. As Vette concluded her comments, Wolfram proceeded.

"My list gets even shorter. My family did not participate in any formal religious organization so my ceremonial life begins and ends with education. Graduating from high school I went into police training where there were strict initiations and a graduation. Later, I graduated with a law degree from a local university. I'd like to add, when Angi healed my rather shattered leg through the aid of her medallion that was, I suppose, a ritual, one that definitely changed my life for the better." He glanced at Angi.

Myttrwn looked from Wolfram to Angi. This was his first report of a recipient of Angi's healing capabilities. But not wanting a diversion he turned to Morgan and asked, "How about you Morgan?"

"My situation is similar to Wolfram's. My ceremonies have been primarily through education; high school and two university degrees. I was also married, my wife died recently and this was my first family funeral." He stopped there not wanting to proceed.

Myttrwn understood and turning to the others asked, "Now for the rest of you, can you share your experience with ceremonies?"

The rest mainly identified education and their military training as their chief ceremonies.

Myttrwn, responded, "It is good you all have had some experience with a ceremony. Again I ask, why are ceremonies needed?"

Morgan spoke up, "That's a good question because in our western society many traditional ceremonies are being lost. Some rather odd fads have replaced certain events like marriage ceremonies, but these are not sustaining. And yet, I know that older societies held resolutely to their traditions and ceremonies as if their very survival depended on it. Myttrwn, why?"

Myttrwn liked Morgan's inquisitive mind, and replied, "You are right Morgan, ceremonies are needed, as Angi stated, to carry an individual through their psychological, social and spiritual stages so they can move on in life. As the individual progresses from one stage to another such as childhood to adulthood or adulthood to elder, they are expected to discard the old ways and assume new duties and responsibilities. The primary purpose of such initiations are to indelibly register this transition on the unconscious of the individual. Thus, a culture nurtured in a ceremonial life remains connected to a spiritual star, every phase of his or her existence is alive with symbolism. He or she knows precisely the pattern to be followed in life and is strengthened by each ceremony. That is the reason why older societies regarded their ceremonies as essential to their continuity with the past and the future."

Listening, Angi was compelled to ask, "But Myttrwn, our world is in the midst of a transition from the Kali Yuga to the Dwapara Yuga. Many no longer follow any organized religious tradition, which means children do not have an official ceremony when they are born or named, leaving the educational system as their only ceremonial source. Graduation provides a mediocre ceremonial transition and the depths of symbolism and messaging might be questioned. In addition, as more and more people live together without a marriage ceremony, this too must have some effect on our society. What happens when such ceremonies are weakened or ignored?"

"As I mentioned before, each one of you is part of a whole. Male or female, young or old, soldier or statesman, you cannot exist alone as you need to be part of a larger entity. Through your society or community, you receive your identity, your ideas, and your understanding of the world around you. If you cut yourself off from this in thought or deed you break your connection with the very source of your existence. Eventually, your timeless symbols start collapsing which could damage your psyche."

"What symptoms should we be looking for that might identify such a breakdown?" asked Andrew.

"One example might be as children do not have a decided ceremony of separation to move on into adulthood, you may find that there is an inability of the child to mature away from his or her parent, leaving a society stuck in a perpetual state of being unable to grow up or grow old."

Andrew was pressed to add, "This reminds me of a Bible passage I once read, possibly from Corinthians, which says, '*When I was a child, I spoke as a child, I understood as a child, I thought as a child; but when I became a man, I put away childish things.*' That's definitely clearer now."

"Wow," replied Angi, "I believe negative signs are already appearing. In our western society we have an overwhelming fear of aging which is being nurtured by a multi-million dollar industry ready to cater to every whim, most procedures and products providing only temporary relief."

"I have another perspective of this failed transition from childhood to adulthood," said Morgan. "In recent years we in the academic world are experiencing a very different influx of students due to their parents. The media has begun to describe the situation as over-parenting, intense parenting and helicopter parenting."

"Morgan, would you care to explain the meaning of these words?" asked Myttrwn.

Morgan proceeded, "They have slightly different meanings but overall it describes parents who are excessively involved in their child's life in the desperate desire to shield them from any difficulty. Symptoms of the hovering, demanding parent are incessantly complaining to teachers about their child's grades or any perceived discomfort, some being belligerent in their demands for special programs and services solely for their child irrespective of the cost. I've also heard of parents accompanying their grown children to college or university enrollment or job interviews, making demands for easier class or work schedules and more benefits. In other words, they are thwarting their child's growth. I suppose subconsciously they believe this may retard their own aging."

Telepathically to Sirona, Myttrwn said, "This is astonishing. What becomes of a society locked in a childish mentality when difficulties arise? Would the parents or elders be capable of providing leadership?"

Angi thinking through the comments asked, "Are you inferring Myttrwn that mythology with its symbols and ceremonies is some form of psychology?"

Myttrwn pleased that the group was understanding the material replied, "Yes Angi, the mythological stories with their powerful symbolism were intended to help individuals understand the psychological and spiritual dangers of life and how to overcome them. Each stage of development came with a precise set of rules and responsibilities and it was expected that each individual, after a period of training, would have the courage to move on in his or her divine journey. Infantile urges would be purged as the individual moved into adulthood."

Morgan could not resist and added, "This means that mythology has been misrepresented by our scientists who have described it as stories of primitive religions, biographies of lost gods and goddesses, superstition, misunderstood history or cosmology. Instead it is a series of symbolic triggers to awaken the individual to their unconscious. The mythological figures were not only symptoms of the unconscious they identified spiritual principles common to all human societies down through time."

"Very good Morgan, now you understand why past societies fought so bitterly to maintain their beliefs, for they knew it was essential to the survival of the soul of their community. Any destruction of their mythology would undermine their very existence."

"That's precisely what happened to our aboriginal societies," said Vette. "When their language and beliefs were destabilized, their society collapsed propelling individuals towards self-destruction through addictions, prostitution, and homelessness."

"With this new understanding, have you any thoughts on what may happen to your society as old traditions are discarded and not replaced by strong symbolic guideposts? Or perhaps a new tradition is already underway, one that will last for generations to enhance, enrich and magnify the human psyche of your society?"

"Well, if it is underway it is not apparent," replied Andrew. "I don't see anything of that quality forming at this point. What bothers me is that somehow we've severed the connection of the conscious and unconscious in our mad drive for sophisticated nothingness which is being played out in the dark and destructive dramas portrayed in our media. I do not see a replacement strong enough to provide the guidance of either primitive societies or even the world of my grandparents. Myttrwn, how can one stop this slide which seems well underway?"

"I do not believe it is as bleak as you may think. Certainly, the guideposts of the Kali Yuga are about to fall. But you are entering the Dwarapa Yuga, a time of increased enlightenment, and somewhere in your society at this very moment there are individuals and small groups thinking about this. They understand the truth. New symbols, ceremonies and traditions will be created, not like the old ones and, while similar, they will differ around your planet."

"If I can summarize," asked Angi, "for we have been discussing some very significant material today. We have been given two paths to help us grow; one internal and one external. The internal one is the most important yet the most difficult for many as it is the battle between the soul and the ego. For us to reach our divine state we need to get rid of our reliance on our ego which is being constantly fed by our five senses. The second path, more external, are the *'Rites of Passage'* ceremonies which have been proscribed by societies to aid individuals through the psychological and spiritual stages of their journey from birth to death. These too are intended to focus on the personal responsibilities the individual has towards his or her society, which is now global. So both the internal and external paths need to be strengthened if our society is to survive. What has yet to be addressed is by whom?"

"That's an excellent summary Angi, and a way to bring this session to a close. The 'whom' we will leave for another session. But first I need you to think about today's material as it relates to your own lives. It might be helpful to share your thoughts regarding past ceremonies. Oh, I almost forgot, speaking of ceremonies, the Queen would like you all to attend a student ceremony scheduled for tomorrow afternoon. These are routine events to recognize those students ready for their first, second or third initiation in the pyramid. Sirona will guide you to the theatre." With that he rose and he and Sirona left the room.

&

Plaza & House of Learning

As they entered the plaza Wolfram chuckled, saying, "Is it my imagination Dylan or did I hear you say that you might be interested in meditation? Have you been converted?"

"You heard me right, Wolfram," replied Dylan. "In the past weeks I have learned that Myttrwn is a highly revered member of this kingdom. Many are amazed that he has taken so much time to sit and share his thoughts with us considering our Kali Yuga baggage. In addition, I came to the conclusion that anyone who has existed for hundreds, no thousands, of our years must surely have learned a thing or two. He is grooming us for something, I'm certain of that. And if that's the case I want to learn as much as this pea-brain can take in. If meditation is something I should know, then so be it. I bet you never thought I'd be saying that, heh?"

"I'm impressed," replied Wolfram, "Actually Dylan, you have just enunciated some of my own thoughts. Myttrwn makes no attempt to force us to accept his teaching. He gives us small bite-sized pieces of information and lets us think about it. I'm surprised how much I've absorbed in such a short time. I wish I had professors of this ilk at university." Then turning to the rest of the group he added, "Now I'm not saying that I'm comfortable with all of it, but I'm not uncomfortable either, if that makes any sense."

"I agree with you Wolfram," replied Angi, "Myttrwn is a remarkable teacher. He does the same thing in my medallion training, small carefully planned steps. While I'd prefer more comment on how I'm doing, I'm aware he is gently pushing me onward. My problem is that I'm not quite sure where I'm at in his unwritten curriculum. All I can say is that I am growing more confident in what I'm doing, if that's any measure."

As tempting as it was, the group still had no idea what Angi was learning about her medallion. It was agreed they would wait until she was prepared to discuss it. They were pleased she was growing more comfortable with whatever was happening.

As they walked across the wide plaza, groups of students circled them in their haste to get to their next class or assignment.

Andrew joined the conversation, "The one think I've noted is that with each session with Myttrwn, you have all been exuberant in your thoughts about its meaning and were prepared with questions whenever Myttrwn provided a forum. I still think our chatter must be wearing, however much he encourages it. Just look at these students. I have no doubt they are conversing as they rush by, but this plaza is amazingly quiet except for us. Imagine what this could mean to our post-secondary campuses."

"Considering the time lines given by Myttrwn for the Dwarapa Yuga, I expect it will be our descendants who will witness such change," came Morgan's reply after considering Andrew's comment.

"But Wolfram and Dylan have raised a persistent point," interjected Vette. "If Myttrwn is such a revered member of this community, then why is he taking so much of his valuable time and energy with our training?"

Andrew responded, "That's a question which remains unanswered, Vette, and we are over half way through our time in this kingdom. I am aware he is training all of us as 'one'............ but the future objective remains unclear. Something must be revealed soon or we will be back home asking ourselves the same question."

"I wonder if Myttrwn is coming back with us?" asked Bryce.

"Now that's a novel idea," replied Andrew looking at his friend, "What made you think of that?"

"It is his interest in our world and what has been happening over the past two thousand years. I know he can check for himself with the opening of the Gate of Tara. But nonetheless, over the past weeks I have noted he has been asking a number of rather point blank questions whenever he is on a one-to-one basis, as if he is checking our perspective on certain issues. Take a note yourself and see what you think. At first, I dismissed it as his method of getting feedback so he can readjust his teaching material. But I don't think so."

"I will definitely consider this old friend and let you know," replied Andrew, beginning to ponder the ramification of his friend's statement.

This prompted Angi to remark, "Can you imagine the impact of Sirona and Myttrwn walking down any street in our world. Their height alone would attract attention and when they spoke it would be quite a revelation. But is the Earth ready for two or more of these highly advanced individuals. For me personally, I would be delighted with their presence. I know there is much I don't know of this advanced technology which I wear. Actually, I'm still unclear as to what all this means. Let's pray Myttrwn is going to reveal this before we leave. I agree, there has to be a reason for his instruction and attention and it is not just this medallion."

"Personally, I have grown fond of Myttrwn's stoic intelligence," replied Morgan, "I don't care if he can read my mind. I now know that telepathy has positive features. I'm not oblivious that there are likely individuals capable of manipulating this talent even in this Shangri-La. We have been pretty well isolated here on this hill, excluding those airplane flights a few of you have experienced. With the amount of new stuff we've already encountered I'm glad for the confinement. However, undaunted, I've made out a long list of items for future visits which I intend to make," he said with a chuckle.

They spent more time talking as they ate their evening meal. Tired, most went to bed early knowing the next day would be a busy one.

Angi was surprised at how weary she was and quickly fell into a deep slumber once her head hit the pillow. Sometime before dawn an old familiar dream reappeared for the third time with greater intensity. The lighted altar stood out in the pitch black room, the room's indeterminate size lost in the darkness. She strained to see if there were any visible features on either side as she stepped cautiously through some doorway into the darkness, but nothing appeared. And, as expected, within seconds the blinding, burning red eyes shot out from the darkness, followed instantly by a heavy weight landing on her chest which caused her to fall backwards. This time she felt the resistance of a rigid floor before she sank into oblivion. She woke up in a lather, fearful of what lay ahead and convinced of its certainty. Speaking into a semi-dark suite she asked, "I don't suppose you are there Adawee? I could use your comforting reassurance right now." Minutes passed with no response. Resigned she declared, "I guess I'm on my own. I dread my forward path but cannot stop it even if I wanted to. It is approaching rapidly so I best prepare. This is a time for meditation as sleep is impossible." She walked across the marble floor towards her favourite spot on the balcony with its recognizable scenery.

&

The Royal Theatre

The importance of the student ceremony registered the next morning as students appeared in their finest, ready for the afternoon at the Royal Theatre. The group from Gaia gathered for their mid-day meal in the same clothes worn for the Queen's reception. Uncertain of the time, they waited. On orders from Sirona, Corb appeared to say he would be flying them to the theatre, a short distance from the Palace.

Sirona's royal airplane sat waiting as they stepped onto the plaza. Students looked on at a distance as they boarded. The plane rose effortlessly into the air and headed towards the palace. This time Corb flew over the royal structure and headed in the direction of an outdoor theatre in the distance. He landed in an open field within walking distance. Disembarking, Corb escorted them to their appointed seats.

Morgan was ecstatic as they walked through the entrance and entered an open-air structure that took advantage of the sloping hillside.

As they sat down Corb said, "It will be awhile before the program begins. This theatre is typical of all our theatres but smaller. You are sitting in the royal section, the Queen, royal retinue and some of the Council Elders will be seated in front of you. When the ceremony is over, stay here, I will return to take you back to the House of Learning." With that he departed.

Morgan couldn't contain himself and blurted out, "Just look at this place. This is a functioning ancient Greek theatre only this one surpasses anything I've ever seen. Its marble sparkles in the sunlight. If you like I'd be glad to provide more details?"

"As if we could stop you," replied Wolfram with a chuckle, "Press on, it is best we get enlightened about ancient Greek theatres while we're here. Theatre design has never been my strong suit but Vette may have more to say."

Morgan turned, "Ah yes, Vette, you will love this with your theatrical background. Likely most of what I'm about to say will sound familiar."

"Theatre design wasn't my area of interest either when I was at university, so Morgan let's hear all about it," replied Vette.

Morgan took the cue and proceeded, "The Greek theater design was far superior to the Romans. Our word "theater" comes from Greek for *theatron*, which is the semi-circular, terraced rows of seats where the audience sit. You can see that stairs divide the sections into nine wedges. Actually, theatron comes from a Greek word meaning 'viewing ceremonies,' now isn't that a coincidence. As you can see, this whole structure has been cut out of a hillside. The seating wraps around that circular area down in the front. While colourful cushions have been provided for the elite, I find these marble seats quite comfortable." Moving so that he could have more space, he continued, "That large circular area is called the *Orchestra*, and is where the actors or speakers perform. The rectangular building towards the far side of the Orchestra is called the *Skene*, its marble structure, which looks like a temple, is where the actors change their masks and costumes. The entrance passage or ramp which we walked through is called the *Parodos*, or passageway. There are usually two; we entered the one closest to our seating area. Both the audience and the actors use the passageways to enter and exit the theatre."

"But Morgan, we're sitting near the top of this section, how will we hear anything?" asked Angi.

"That's the beauty of these theatres," replied Morgan, "Recently, we've discovered that the ancient Greeks knew a great deal about acoustic physics which they likely acquired from the Egyptians. You'll soon discover that a performer or speaker standing in that open-air circle below can be easily heard in the top rows. Research has shown that these structures were perfectly shaped to act as an acoustic filter, suppressing low-frequency sounds and allowing the performer's voice or music to rise uninhibited."

"Any idea Morgan what produces this effect?" asked Andrew, "Is it the stone structure itself?"

"I'm not sure," replied Morgan, "Perhaps we can ask Myttrwn the next time we meet."

The conversation eased when students appeared at the two passageways. According to Morgan the two sections closest to the entrance with easy access to the Orchestra would likely be for the House of Learning faculty on one side and the Royal retinue on the other. This was precisely what transpired as senior students in white walked past the first sections and took their seats, one group beside the faculty section and another beside the royal section. Next came the students in blue who filtered into the adjacent sections beside the senior students. These were followed by those in green, a larger number who occupied the three central sections. Novices in striped uniforms arrived last and were relegated to the upper rows of all sections, their numbers were even greater than the greens. The one exception were the harpists, in both green and blue uniforms, who took their places on seats assembled at the back of the Orchestra. Once all were in place, Zolar and the faculty of the House of Learning entered and assumed their respective places. The faculty were dressed in white a few resplendent with an embroidered serpent on the left upper shoulder of their gown, in colours of blue, crimson or gold. After another brief wait, the royal party arrived led by the Queen with Sirona, Myttrwn, other royal members and the Council of Elders in their respective order.

Angi whispered to Vette, "The faculty is much larger than I thought."

"And some of their uniforms are beautiful. Just look at Zolar," replied Vette in as quiet a voice as she could manage.

Wolfram leaned towards Morgan asking, "What do you think the faculty serpent colours mean?"

Morgan thought before replying, "I expect it is some kind of designation with gold the highest as their numbers are few. Actually, they remind me of my Boston University bunch."

In the front row of the House of Learning section sat Zolar, with his immediate advisors. As his dark eyes scanned the audience, he seemed surprised to see the group from Gaia. One of his aides whispered something into his ear.

"It appears Zolar was not informed of the Queen's last minute invite to us," thought Andrew to himself. "The news doesn't please him." Then he added, "He's an odd one. I'd like to be positive but I sense a malevolence in that man for which I have no evidence. Perhaps my years of foreign service has made me overly suspicious."

Once everyone was seated Zolar stepped onto the centre of the Orchestra in front of the harpists to assume the role of Master of Ceremonies. The Gaia group, aided by their translating devices, listened.

Zolar began in a commanding voice, "It is my esteemed pleasure to welcome Her Royal Highness, members of the royal family, Council Elders, faculty, students and visitors to this event. Today, we meet to recognize those individuals who have reached a point in their training where we feel they are ready for their testing in the Temple of Initiation. Names are presented for consideration and today I have chosen four. But first we will honour the occasion with our usual program of a prayer, speeches from two of our Elders, and then a musical composition from our harpists." The program identified, Zolar turned, bowed to the Queen and returned to his seat.

Wolfram said to the group, "Amazing, Morgan was right, every sound is perfect."

A faculty member wearing a golden serpent on his robe stepped to the center of the Orchestra. Everyone rose from their seats and waited. In a robust voice he prayed, "Today as we gather, let us remember our oath of allegiance to the Law of One. For all is One and the Absolute One is all. This we hold to be our guiding principle in our learning and service to our community, kingdom and universe." When finished everyone sat down. The speaker returned to his seat. .

The two Elders, long familiar with the ceremony, provided short but encouraging remarks. The first one, male, was philosophical. His remarks focused on the need for students to acquire inner meditation and steadfast sharpness of thought in order to achieve stability of mind. Enlightenment, in his words, was achieved through three paths; morality, concentration and wisdom. Morality to transform the mind into love and compassion, concentration to fix the mind on a single point at a time, and wisdom to understand life as an interconnected web within One.

The second speaker, female, took a different approach, speaking more to the individual student. She stressed that in their quest for divinity it was imperative that they constantly develop their minds. Aspects of this development included a rejection of small mindedness, the need to overcome selfishness, to cultivate a state of goodness by having no room or desire to manipulate situations, and to honour truth. For only when they had achieved these qualities would they awaken the sacred in the universe.

As the second speaker returned to her seat Morgan thought to himself, "I wonder why our academic events can't have such brief and enlightened speeches. These days we seem overinvolved with politics and economics. We've lost something. But with the closure of the speeches I can now enjoy the music. I'm about to hear the entire program." He sat back and closed his eyes.

As the second speaker returned to her seat, Carola, sitting near the harpists, rose. The students positioned their harps and upon her signal began their musical presentation. The music began softly like a leaf blown in the wind. Then it soared as musicians proceeded with a magical mixture of poignant melodies. Minutes evaporated as the audience floated along the waves of the angelic sound. When the music stopped a momentary hush fell as the audience struggled to regain reality. Appreciation came in a groundswell of clapping.

When the clapping eased, Zolar rose from his seat. The expectation of his announcement was palpable for many students had spent years preparing for this moment. But Zolar appeared nervous, hesitating, glancing up at the group from Gaia and then to the royal family.

Andrew noticed the nervousness and whispered, "I wonder what's up, Zolar isn't a man prone to nervousness?"

Then turning to the audience Zolar proceeded, "After much consideration, I have selected the following four candidates for the first level of initiation." Again he hesitated then, clearing his throat, he continued, "The candidates are Angi Talismann, Vette Gallant, Wolfram Stark and Morgan Mandelthrope."

Being unfamiliar with the language he stumbled on the surnames.

Dylan reacted, "What the hell, is he mad?"

"Am I hearing things?" asked Wolfram, "Did Zolar just mention our names as the four candidates? Is this some kind of joke?"

"Hold on," cautioned Andrew, "Let's see what transpires. I believe, Zolar has just stepped into a minefield..........wait.............."

Confused, everyone in the audience began looking from side to side. The Queen was in an animated conversation with Sirona and Myttrwn. When the Queen stood up the theatre went silent. In a crisp commanding voice she asked, "Zolar, would you repeat the names of your four candidates?"

Zolar obliged, this time louder, pronouncing the same names.

Sirona was out of her seat, her fury aimed at Zolar, "This is insane. You have no right to list our guests as initiation candidates. This is preposterous!"

The Queen, recognizing the disaster unfolding before her, beckoned her advisors. They talked briefly. Within seconds two guards appeared on both sides of Zolar, under orders from the Queen to escort him to his quarters and remain there. In an unprecedented move, the Queen stepped onto the Orchestra and spoke to the audience in a commanding voice, "This ceremony has now concluded. I ask you to please return to your respective quarters." The theatre emptied.

Sirona and Corb dashed up the steps to where the group sat, Sirona giving an abrupt command, "Corb I want you to take this group to the Queen's reception room at once." Turning she added, "I will come to you as soon as I can. Myttrwn and I will be meeting with the Queen and her advisors." And shaking her head she mumbled, "This is unprecedented."

Time passed as they waited in the Queen's reception room.

Andrew, wrestling with his thoughts openly remarked, "Surely this cannot be. You four are not prepared for such an initiation. Zolar knows that. So is this some stunt............. but I expect stunts are not part of this kingdom. I'm sure he has sealed his doom ....but why?"

Bryce, standing nearby, added, "My old friend, this is what we feared. Somehow we've ignited a power struggle likely between Zolar and Sirona and Myttrwn. The consequences of this could be immense. Is there no other option?"

"I never liked that damn cold fish anyway," blurted Vette, her frustration erupting. "We're being fed to the lions. I hate this feeling of helplessness."

"Impotent, is more like it," replied Morgan, "We're in a different world and no matter how positive our opinion, I have a sinking feeling we've entered a vortex for which there may be no easy exit."

"What about substitutes," argued Dylan, "I and my team could take the place of you four. We've faced lots of trials and might be better prepared."

"Your offer is noble Dylan but it is unlikely they will accept substitutes," replied Andrew. "Zolar was precise in who he wanted for this. Let's hold our fire until Sirona and Myttrwn get here." However confident his words, Andrew feared the worst.

The arrival of food signaled a quick decision wasn't eminent. As more time passed the outcome grew bleak.

When they finally appeared, the look on Sirona and Myttrwn faces signaled trouble. Sirona was the first to speak, "It has been decided. Myttrwn and I have three days to prepare the four of you for the initiation."

"Am I missing something?" asked Andrew growing irritated, "Why couldn't the Queen reject Zolar's decision?"

Myttrwn replied, "Andrew, in our kingdom, the Queen rules for the people and her mandate covers court administrative, diplomacy and the military. Each person appointed to a senior position like Zolar are given significant powers. Our selection of such individuals has been such that neither the Queen or King or Council has ever had to intercede. As you know, Zolar is in charge of the House of Learning. He alone decides who is to be selected for the initiations. Our society trusts these chosen leaders to operate under a very strict set of standards. For the first time, Zolar has chosen to ignore such rules with his decision today."

Andrew, unprepared to let it rest, continued, "But surely just because this is unique, why can't the Queen or Council overrule him. You just said he has defied your own rules."

Sirona interceded, "As Myttrwn was saying, our constitution doesn't allow this, which means this is a matter which will have to be re-examined but that takes time. Zolar had two objections about your presence; first he stated that you should not have been allowed entrance to the kingdom at your unrefined stage of development, and, second, he felt the level of technology in the medallion was far too advanced for your world at this time. He argued that we should take possession of the medallion until your world had reached a more appropriate Dwapara Yuga level. Of course, this would be in contradiction to the entire reason why the medallion was created in the first place."

"So, Zolar took the matter into his own hands," replied Andrew who was still fighting. "What does he expect to gain by insisting that four of our group go through this initiation? I thought your world was far more advanced. He's nothing more than a tyrant, a madman or both. Angi, Vette, Wolfram and Morgan are unprepared and the outcome is uncertain. Am I right?"

"What about substitutes?" asked Dylan, now more determined than ever to propose another option.

"Sorry, Dylan, it is not permitted," replied Sirona. Then looking at the stressful faces in front of her, she added, "You have no idea how much this displeases me. Myttrwn and I tried every argument to have this stopped but to no avail. Zolar has used all means at his disposal to support his position. His final ploy was to insist that by going through the initiation you will be more qualified to take this advanced technology back to Earth."

"Sure, if we survive," interjected Vette.

"Let's hear from the four on this," asked Andrew. "Angi what are your thoughts?"

Angi knew in her heart that this was fated. She also decided not to mention her dream. She replied, "This is definitely an unwelcomed turn of events. The unknowns are ample even with my medallion. But having it and whatever training I've already mastered, I'm willing to proceed. Bureaucratic decision making is something I recognize. I trust that Sirona and Myttrwn have done their best. So, there is no point in us beating this to death. Let's maximize whatever time we have."

Wolfram then replied, "Well, if Angi's prepared to proceed then so will I. I'm definitely uneasy about this diabolical plot. You have to agree, whatever Zolar says from this point is suspect. I would argue there's more to come. From this point I will assume my old police persona and be on guard. I am glad Vette's in this with us."

It was now Vette's turn, "I agree with Wolfram, this man can no longer be trusted. My gut feeling tells me we have been put into the hands of a madman whose stated reasons bear no resemblance to his true feelings. If truth is a priority here, then he just disqualified himself. I'd personally like to do him in, but that's not on the books. I am just glad it is the four of us."

Morgan, having been relatively silent, was pushed to say, "I'm caught in a bind. A fraction of me is dying to know what is in that pyramid, but the rest of me is screaming to cut and run. I will admit, I am not a risk taker. This trip for me was a gigantic leap. I will need the skills and training of my colleagues to survive. But I will vow to do my best at whatever is thrown at us. As a team we will make it."

"Very well," came Andrew's resigned reply, "You are all willing. But for the record, I want it known that I am extremely irritated over this entire mess. I do not like being side-swiped nor being left on the fringe. I have come to consider this team as my family and I will fight like mad to protect each one of them."

"Andrew, I too regard you as part of my family so Myttrwn and I will consider every angle. We have three days and have been given a free hand in this training. That took some negotiating. To do this, I want Angi, Vette, Wolfram and Morgan transferred to my quarters in the palace at once. We will begin tonight."

Andrew asked, "What can we do?"

You will return to the House of Learning. For the next three days you will continue your usual activities. Daily, I will report to you myself to fill you in on our progress. I regret that I cannot have you coming back and forth during the training, the four must be in isolation."

"Isolation, what for?" asked Andrew, the irritation of being shut out detectible in his reply.

"I know," replied Wolfram suddenly aware of the reason for secrecy if they were to outfox Zolar, "It is because of telepathy. It is to our advantage that no one gets wind of the preparations. Right Sirona?"

"Something like that," replied Sirona not wanting to discuss the matter. Then turning to Andrew she added, "Be assured, on the day of the initiation I will have the rest of you with Myttrwn and myself in the pyramid command center located on the same level as the transport gate. We will follow every step of their journey."

"Fine," answered Andrew, suddenly grasping Wolfram's statement. "But I insist on seeing the four the night before the initiation to wish them luck. Is that permitted?"

"Very well, that will be arranged, but just you Andrew," replied Sirona. The others seemed irked at being excluded.

Wanting to soften the situation Sirona added, "For your information the first initiation calls for three hours on each of six levels, with a brief spell on the seventh. This brings the total time to about twenty hours, less than one of your days."

"Twenty hours...........that's a hell of a long time under fire," replied Dylan.

Angi felt a cold chill creeping up her spine and thought, "So this is it. My dream is about to become reality." As she looked at her companions she noted that the darkness of her own thoughts was replicated in their faces.

The music had stopped.

THE SERPENT'S SONG

Chapter 8

The Palace, Sirona's Quarters

Sirona and Myttrwn wasted no time. A large reception room was transformed into a training centre, complete with a glasslike box the size and shape of two old-fashioned telephone booths. Sleeping arrangements consisted of two rooms across from the training centre, one for Angi and Vette, the other for Wolfram and Morgan. A few personal items had been transferred from their suites for the three days.

Vette and Angi were together in their bedroom. Vette, testing the makeshift bed, commented, "This reminds me of my rookie days in the RCMP; temporary and basic. But then again we won't be needing much. Angi, I expect Sirona is a tough taskmaster when the situation demands."

"She certainly is," replied Angi, remembering her early medallion training back in Scotland.

In a somber mood, Vette said, "Angi, I will only say this to you. Zolar and this initiation business makes my stomach churn. He's intelligent, cunning and capable of almost anything. I get prickly when my enemy controls a gigantic closed building which we're about to enter. This whole thing stinks and I can't do a damn thing about it."

"Vette, don't be fooled by my easy agreement. I have the same misgivings but I realized that it was pointless wasting time discussing something that was out of Sirona's and Myttrwn's control. It reminds me of my former life. There were times when I had to bite my tongue over some idiotic rule or policy, admittedly not as dire as this. And speaking of constitutions, Canada almost goes ballistic at any hint of changing our constitution. It would be our misfortune to encounter a 'first' in this kingdom."

"Yah, you are right, Angi. The RCMP was jam-packed with rules and regulations and some equally unwise policies. Whatever Sirona and Myttrwn can do to make this easier, I'm all for it. Let's find the others and get started."

Wolfram and Morgan were just exiting their room when Angi and Vette opened their door.

"I'm glad we're together," said Wolfram, "Combining our talents, especially Angi's medallion, should give us a fighting chance. Add that to whatever Sirona and Myttrwn have to offer, we should be fine."

"But that oversized phone booth looks menacing," came Morgan's input, nervous about so many mounting unknowns.

Opening the reception room door they found Sirona and Myttrwn sorting clothes on a long table.

"Come over here," beckoned Sirona, "We've decided you'll be wearing our field uniforms. The uniforms have been modified for you. I believe we have your sizes but I will need you to try on each item so we can be sure. Once you have collected your set, we will return to your bedrooms. I will go with the women and Myttrwn will go with the men. You will be training in these. It may take time to get used to the boots."

Angi thought as she touched the material, "It is light and smooth to the touch, I bet it is also loaded with sensors."

Sirona proceeded with an explanation of the items. "The uniform consists of a tunic, pants and boots. The long-sleeved blue tunic slips over your head and goes to your hips. The tightly rolled collar on the tunic contains a head covering suitable for all weather. The pale gray pants are loose fitting and are designed to fit into the boots which will come to just above your ankle. The foot coverings, designed to keep your feet cool and dry, make their own calculated adjustment as circumstances demand. At first, you'll feel a slight movement as your boots conform to your feet."

When the uniforms were collected they headed back to their bedrooms. Once dressed Angi and Vette discovered concealed pockets on the tunic and along the pant legs. Vette then asked, "How effective is this material against attack?"

"It will repel most items hurled at it like rocks, sand, or small weapons like knives," was Sirona's reply. "For combat missions we wear a different uniform. Now walk about the room. Tomorrow, I will be adding a belt with attachments. We will begin testing these suits tonight. Let's join the others."

As they entered the reception room Wolfram and Morgan were already present, dressed in identical attire.

Myttrwn walked towards the glasslike structure and said, "In the next three days, this chamber will be used not only to test your uniforms but to familiarize you with how it reacts to certain elements. This testing device allows only one occupant at a time. Wolfram, how about you starting the process?"

"Should I unravel whatever is in this collar before I enter?" asked Wolfram.

"That would help. Can I get the rest of you to do the same?" replied Myttrwn. Sirona assisted where necessary.

They watched Wolfram through the enclosure as Myttrwn went to a small outer panel and initiated the program. Wolfram endured five minute intervals of rain, snow, heat and wind. Emerging from the testing chamber, he exclaimed, "Wow that was something. This uniform came alive; parts tightened, then released and tightened again. The uniform was great, but Myttrwn, I need help with this headgear. I never got the hang of it."

"We can deal with that," said Myttrwn as he proceeded to check Wolfram's uniform for breaks or problems and asked, "How about your feet, Wolfram? Did they stay cool and dry?"

"Yes, the boots are fantastic. They're not only lightweight, but they kept readjusting on their own. In the snow I could sense some warming. My feet were never hot, cold or sweaty."

"Good," came Myttrwn's satisfied reply. Then turning to the others he said, "Now that you have witnessed what happened to Wolfram, I will proceed with the rest of you. Morgan, your next, then Angi and last Vette. Be aware, tonight we will stick to five minutes, and then we will add five more minutes each day for each element."

After a few minor uniform adjustments and a demonstration on how the headgear worked, the evening ended with Sirona saying, "That's all for tonight. We will begin at dawn tomorrow. I expect you to appear in these uniforms. On the third evening I will have them cleaned for your initiation. Tomorrow's schedule will include an explanation of the pyramid and an introduction to your belt and attachments. Angi will be spending time with Myttrwn regarding the medallion. We have much to cover and little time."

It was hard to sleep. The abrupt change of events had caught them off guard. Staring into the darkness, each wrestled with their own fears. While Myttrwn's comments had changed their view on death, its potential immediacy was an alarming concept.

Dawn arrived too quickly. Dressed in their newly acquired uniforms the four discovered food laid out on a table set up in one corner of the reception room. The entire wing of the Palace had been declared off limits by Sirona. Her hand-picked crew wheeled the food into an outer corridor and departed. Not wanting anyone to see the four candidates in kingdom uniforms, Sirona wheeled the food into the reception room herself.

Sirona, with the aid of a hologram, began the first day as she foretold, "As you can see by the cut away, the pyramid has seven chambers, seven being the serpent's symbolic number. The four of you will enter the pyramid through this doorway at its base. We will gather at dawn in front of this door on your initiation day."

"I see each chamber gets smaller as one advances," noted Vette.

"Yes, but the holographic program will give you the impression that the space is much bigger no matter which level you are on," replied Sirona.

"Is the holographic program specific to each Grade of Initiation?" asked Angi.

"Actually," replied Sirona, "the first four chambers of the pyramid have similar elements for all three grades, just like you experienced last night. But, the situation grows more intense as you advance from Grades One to Three. Chambers five and six will consist of one or more of the following; darkness, confusion, monsters or spirits, flashing lights, extreme sounds, snakes or some combination. The seventh chamber is different. In that chamber your path may be restricted by invisible barriers as you make your way towards a raised altar with, in your case, four golden crystals. Your objective is to retrieve these crystals."

"How much time can we expect to spend in each chamber?" asked Wolfram.

"Since you will be in a Grade One program, you can expect three hours in chambers one to six, the last one is usually less," replied Sirona.

"How long is it for Grades Two and Three?" asked Wolfram.

"Grade Two is five hours, and Grade Three is seven," replied Sirona.

"Who designs the holographic programs?" asked Morgan.

There was a hesitation before Sirona replied, "Zolar and his assistants create the programs."

"That's not what I wanted to hear," replied Angi, "How can we be sure he won't adulterate the Grade One program?"

In a forceful voice Myttrwn responded, "I will make sure. I will check your program the morning of the Initiation," trying not to betray his own uneasiness.

"That's comforting," replied Vette and thought to herself, "But I expect Zolar is clever enough to mask or bastardize such readings. This situation grows more dangerous by the minute."

It was Morgan's turn to comment, "As I understand it, in Grade One, the four of us should experience in the first four chambers something like the elements tested last night. The next two chambers will present other hazards. The seventh chamber is where we are expected to collect the crystals. Is that a capsulated version of what's before us?"

"That's right," replied Sirona. "Also, I would advise you to seek the highest ground in whatever chamber you are in as this will lead you to the next chamber. In the first four chambers, when the three hours are up, you will first hear a loud click before a gate swings open to the next chamber. But in chambers five and six you will need to answer a riddle before the gates open."

Wolfram gritted his teeth, and said, "Damn it, I'm lousy at riddles."

"Then leave that joy to us three," replied Morgan. "By the way, Sirona, what happens if we fail to answer the riddle?"

"You have three chances............if you do not succeed, the door will remain closed and we will have to rescue you. But, we will know this as we will be monitoring your every movement."

"That's reassuring as long as the technology works," replied Wolfram. Then he thought to himself, "Keep the negativity down, old boy, or you are going to spook the rest of the team."

"OK," said Morgan, "let me try again. In the Grade One initiation we will expect to go through four holographic programs in the first four chambers where we will encounter different elements such as rain, snow, heat and wind. In the next two chambers we should encounter different holographic programs and have to answer two riddles to open the gates. After about eighteen hours, we finally enter the seventh chamber where we must retrieve four crystals placed on an altar. Is that it?"

"That's it Morgan, except I must point out, the holographic programs will seem all too real and they will have built-in obstacles. These obstacles vary with each program," Sirona was hoping no one would ask about obstacle probabilities as it would absorb too much time. No one asked.

Then Vette interjected, "Am I missing something? What you have described seems relatively innocuous. So, why the special uniforms and advanced tools?"

It was Myttrwn's turn to speak, "Actually, Vette, the uniqueness of this particular situation warrants the extra caution. We too are concerned about the outcome. We should, under our laws, trust Zolar that he will do precisely as expected," Myttrwn hesitated before continuing. "But, just in case, Sirona and I want to be sure we have given you every possible advantage."

"That's alarming," thought Wolfram, "Myttrwn and Sirona are as apprehensive as I am. I best prepare for hell and be grateful for all the armament they can provide."

With a sigh Angi commented, "Well, it is good to have our joint suspicions out in the open, but there is no point in dwelling on this. Let's move on. Is there anything else we should know about the pyramid?"

Sirona, also eager to press on, replied, "Just that the exit door in the top chamber will open when you retrieve the crystals, it is part of the initiation program." With no further questions she directed them to the long table which had been replenished.

"Today I will introduce you to your belt and attachments. Once described, I want you to practice using them for the rest of the day." She began by passing around four silver-toned belts with a number of metal hooks, saying, "You will need only a small number of these hooks on this journey."

Each one examined the belt and felt the strength of the metal hooks.

Sirona continued, "On the first hook you will attach this cylinder," she passed an empty cylinder for them to examine. "This cylinder will contain a special liquid intended to provide you with sufficient water and nourishment for twenty-five hours. Take sips, as needed. I advise you,...........no, I command you,........ do not drink or eat anything presented to you in the pyramid."

The four examined the slim metal cylinder and under Sirona's instructions learned to open and close the firm clasp and attach and remove it from their belt hook. "Your cylinders will be filled on the third night by Myttrwn."

Next she picked up what appeared to be a set of goggles. She demonstrated their secure fitting and removal, saying, "These will be in this soft fabric case. From this point on, we will get you to wear these in the testing booth. Note, if you press the top of the goggles once, you can get distance and twice for night vision. A third press takes you back to normal." She watched as each one tested the goggles for themselves.

Pushing on, Sirona picked up a small round bag and emptied the contents on the table, saying, "Angi will be familiar with this item, it is a.........what do you call it?........Ah yes, a First Aid kit, only this is our version." She then proceeded to describe each item. The first was a flat metal object that fitted into the palm of her hand. "If you flick the switch upward it will provide a spray for germ protection of any wound, and pressing it downward gives you a spray to mend your uniform." Then she turned to the rest of the kit. "This is a tube of burn ointment. This single pad can expand to cover a wider surface if you stretch the corners. This raised corner if pressed will return it to its original size. Similarly, this silver square is a blanket. Press one corner for it to enlarge and the opposite for it to return to normal. This stick-like device expands by pulling at both ends to make a splint which can encase a leg. This cord is tough enough to support your entire body. This metal object can be transformed into a knife, boring tool, or utensil. This is fastening tape and finally, this flat item can become a cup."

"What do we do if anyone needs something for pain?" asked Angi.

"Ah yes, in this square package tucked into a side pocket of the bag, there are two tablets. I caution you that these are very powerful. Myttrwn assures me these have been modified to your bodies. Each one will give relief for twelve hours. Actually, I'm hoping none of these will be needed. Examine and practice using the items I've opened on the table. Keep your own kit intact." To avoid a mix-up, each one snapped their own kit to their belt.

Then continuing, Sirona waving a pair of gloves, said, "I'm adding a pair of gloves. They are suitable for all climates. Tuck a pair into one of your leg pockets. You can also use one of the uniform pockets to store your crystal when it is retrieved."

Next she brought out a bronze cross-like item with a loop at one end which she held in her hand, saying, "This is a vital implement on any field assignment. Myttrwn has reduced the number of applications and programmed it to respond to your language. Its smallness defies its many uses. We refer to this as our 'Aqk', you can use any term you wish. Let me show you how it works."

Before Sirona began Morgan whispered to Wolfram, "That looks like an Egyptian cross, we call it an 'Ankh'..........I wonder,..........." his comments ceased as Sirona began the demonstration.

Using different commands the Aqk became a short walking stick, a long walking stick, a throwing stick, and a weapon, a long stick with a bright light in its looped end, different types of lights, a metal umbrella, and a shield. Once the demonstration was over Sirona said, "Now I want you to space yourselves in this room and practice with your own Aqks. By early afternoon I want you to be able to do exactly as I have just demonstrated."

Giving themselves about ten feet distance they spent time with Sirona and Myttrwn mastering the Aqk. The afternoon of the first day was absorbed in the testing booth, more practice with the Aqk, getting familiar with the First Aid items, and Angi working with Myttrwn. For the first time the other three witnessed Angi's growing expertise with the medallion; her levitation, the ease of moving objects around the room and her quick response to Myttrwn's commands.

Exhausted at the end of the first day, they fell into bed and into a deep slumber.

The second day, after an early meal they waited wondering if it would be a repeat of day one. But to their surprise a large screen had appeared with Myttrwn standing guard preventing access to what lay behind it.

Sirona directed them to four chairs some distance from the screen. Myttrwn took charge. "This morning we are going to introduce you to your travelling companions. With that, on a verbal command, the screen evaporated to reveal four identical but different coloured dogs that sat motionless.

"Labs,"..........exclaimed Angi, "How marvelous. Are they real?"

"Labs," asked Wolfram, "What kind of dog is that?"

"Ah Wolfram, you are about to hear," replied Myttrwn with a slight grin. "In this kingdom we have a great respect for working dogs. When Sirona asked Angi about her preferred breed of dog, this was her answer. After some investigation, I would concur. To save time I will give you a short course. On an eastern island in the home country of Angi and Vette these unique

Labrador dogs were bred to assist the fishermen. I've chosen the female for her smaller size. As a working dog they are very intelligent, and quick at running and swimming. Webbing between their toes aids in swimming and may serve as snowshoes. Its interwoven coat is waterproof. Its jaws are powerful, and it is reported, they enjoy holding objects gently in their mouths. They have a steady temperament, love company, have a good work ethic and are relatively quiet, but they do bark. The only difference between these four and your back home variety is that these are bio-robots. I've used different colours for easy identification. Now, I would like you to silently think of a name for your dog. Sirona will ask each one of you to come forward, whisper that name to her. The secrecy is to avoid name duplication."

"Let's begin," said Sirona, "Angi come along." Whispering, Sirona said, "Angi, this cream coloured dog with the white paws is for you. What name have you chosen?"

"Skylar," whispered Angi.

"Fine," replied Sirona, "Now repeat that name three times into the dog's right ear."

Angi did as instructed and the dog came alive, wagging its tail in response.

"Angi, take Skylar back to your seat and wait. Command her to sit. She will obey you." As instructed Skylar sat beside Angi, waiting.

Next came Vette, who was directed to a coffee coloured dog with a splash of white over one eye and ear. She chose the name 'Rafie.' Wolfram's dog was black with a lightning white streak down its nose. He chose the name 'Dusky.' And finally Morgan's dog was fox red in colour with a white chest, the red colour almost matching his own hair. He chose the name 'Macky.' As he returned to his seat Morgan whispered to Wolfram, "I always wanted a dog."

Myttrwn continued, "For the rest of today I will be working with each one of you to get acquainted with your dog. You'll need to be a working partnership by tomorrow. Note that as a bio-robot these dogs neither eat nor drink, otherwise they will appear quite normal."

The dogs proved to be not only a welcome addition but their gentle disposition helped reduce the stress.

Day three found everyone in full training mode testing the uniforms and tools and getting better acquainted with their dogs.

At day's end, Sirona asked them to change back into their regular clothes as she would personally make sure their uniforms were ready for the next morning. She also wanted them out of uniform when Andrew arrived. Her instructions for Andrew's visit were precise, "You will make no mention of your training; uniforms, tools or dogs. I will escort Andrew to the men's bedroom where you four will be waiting. He will have fifteen minutes, no longer." She feared any more time might endanger their well-crafted plan.

At precisely five o'clock, Sirona ushered Andrew into the men's bedroom and left, trusting the group to follow her orders. Andrew's demeanor was both formal and warm-hearted. With a forced smile he greeted them with, "My, it is good to see you four. I expect Sirona and Myttrwn have been busy. I know they've done everything in their power to help you. My frustration, and that of the rest of our team, is that we can't do more. You are well and ready for tomorrow?"

"Yes," replied Wolfram, "We've been well cared for and are as prepared as we can be." Seeing the worried look on Andrew's face he wasn't about to say more.

"I needed to see you for myself," replied Andrew. "I know you can't reveal anything, I prefer it that way. Tomorrow is going to be a long day for all of us. I know you will make it, especially with Angi and her medallion. But try and reduce your risks, get through this as fast as you can. We will be following your progress and will celebrate when it is over." They had little time to discuss much more when the time ran out and Sirona returned. As Andrew was about to depart he turned and unexpectedly hugged each one, saying, "See you at dawn tomorrow morning.".......... When Sirona and Andrew departed the room went silent.

Angi finally spoke, "Months ago, I could never have imagined being part of such a unique family. Andrew has become like a father to us. He's deeply worried but like an old soldier stands stalwart before the battle."

"He reminds me of my father," replied Vette, "When we get home, wherever that is now, I must make arrangements for Andrew and my father to meet. They should get along splendidly."

Before Morgan could comment Sirona returned carrying a tray. "You will need a good night's sleep. You will be rising before dawn. Myttrwn would like you to drink this before retiring." Trusting Sirona and Myttrwn, they drank the amber potion.

They slept soundly and were surprised at how alert they felt the next morning.

In her familiar but commanding voice, Sirona woke them with, "Come, it is time, get into your uniforms. Myttrwn and I will do a last minute inspection. While you cannot eat, you can drink. I want you to take this greenish liquid prepared by Myttrwn. It is intended to boost your entire body. Myttrwn has transported the dogs to an alcove just inside the pyramid entrance. On the dogs collar you will find your Aqk and goggles, two items I do not want Zolar to know about. He will complain about the uniforms but my mother has already approved them. You will need to activate your dogs as we've practiced. I will not be able to say much at the pyramid site so I will say it now, "You are a remarkable foursome. I know you have the intelligence and ingenuity to get through this. With Angi's skills and our enhancements it should work. But I assure you, Myttrwn and I will be relieved when this is over."

Not knowing when they might have another chance, Angi replied, "On our behalf, Sirona, we want to thank you and Myttrwn for everything you've done for us. Your steady support and vast knowledge has transported us to another realm. We've been well prepared but will also breathe easier when this is over. So, let's get on with it."

Courageously, they followed Sirona and Myttrwn to their fate.

The Pyramid, Chamber 1

Corb flew them in Sirona's plane, landing within two hundred feet of the pyramid entrance on the plaza between the House of Life and the House of Learning. Sirona and Myttrwn's plan was deliberately timed to give Zolar little room to maneuver. Sirona and Myttrwn led the four candidates onto the plaza, everyone astounded at seeing them in kingdom uniforms. Wolfram, the last to embark, was stopped by Corb.

"Wolfram, all the best," said Corb. As he shook Wolfram's hand Corb transferred a metal object saying, "This might help. You know how it works. Slip it into one of those pockets."

Wolfram did as directed realizing that Corb's actions denoted a widening uneasiness over Zolar's antics.

Corb, not wanting Zolar to telepathically detect the object, advised, "Wolfram, in front of the pyramid, focus on the door. I must leave. When this is over, I and my crew will greet you at the top of the pyramid." Then glancing over the party gathered he added, "I can assure you it is unprecedented to have the Queen at these events." With that he turned to fly Sirona's plane back to the palace.

Assembled in front of the pyramid were the Queen, Sirona, Myttrwn, Zolar and his two guards, the four candidates and the rest of the Gaia team.

Zolar, still defiant, upon seeing the four, reacted saying, "They are not supposed to be in our kingdom uniforms, this is not permitted."

"I've approved the uniforms, Zolar," said the Queen in a commanding voice.

Unwilling to give up, Zolar then focused on the second negative, "Angi must give up her medallion."

"Cease," demanded the Queen, "Zolar, you are trying my patience. Angi will not give up her medallion. Get on with it, you have already exceeded your demands."

Zolar acquiesced. He didn't care, his plan was set. Convinced of his superior intelligence to that of Sirona or Myttrwn he thought, "My objective will be achieved. I know I am right. In time I will be honoured for my ingenuity." He led the four towards the open doorway saying loud enough for all to hear, "A Grade One Initiation calls for three hours in the first six chambers of the pyramid with less time in the seventh. You must exit the pyramid with one crystal each." At the entrance, making no effort to speak to them, he turned abruptly and strode back towards the Queen.

The two guards resumed their duty under the Queen's further orders, "Zolar, you will be escorted to your quarters where you will remain under guard until this initiation is over." There was little warmth in her remarks.

The four candidates turned, waved, and entered the pyramid. The huge entrance door slid shut leaving them in the silence of the pyramid. In the semi-darkness they spotted the dogs.

"There they are, our travelling companions," said Angi, "thanks to the genius of Myttrwn." They each went to their own dog, retrieved their Aqk and goggles and activated the bio-robots. The dogs came alive.

"Well, Morgan, you got your wish," said Wolfram, "We're about to learn firsthand what this pyramid is all about. Let's hope we live to tell the tale."

"Yes, indeed, we will definitely have a tale to tell," replied Angi, "Eighteen hours will pass quickly. I expect that open field ahead is the beginning of Chamber One."

After walking a half hour Vette said, "It is hard to believe this is a holographic program, it seems so real. This certainly appears natural with rambling bushes and a wagon path which leads to that high ground in the distance. Can you see it? It is almost too perfect with the sunlight dancing across the field and the gentle breeze bending the grasses. But I see clouds ahead."

"Yeh, I see the ridge and the clouds," replied Wolfram. "I estimate, if we maintain a steady walking pace we might reach that high ground in about an hour and a half."

The dogs scampered ahead chasing each other through the long grass, stopping periodically to ensure the four were close behind.

"Those clouds are moving rapidly," replied Angi. "Is it rain or wind?"

It didn't take long to find out. Within minutes a fine mist descended, soon turning into a drizzle which caused the dogs to draw back. The group pressed on.

As promised, prior to their departure, Sirona had indicated she would be contacting them through their ear translation devices. Her clear voice made the contact with, "We have you on our monitors. Tap on your ear pieces if you are receiving."

Doing as instructed she continued, "Good, I will not interrupt a lot but will keep in touch. Tap on your ear device if you need me. Off for now."

Angi thought to herself, "So far so good." But her intuition alarm bells were ringing as she added, "Why do I feel the second shoe is about to drop?"

An hour passed as they trudged on. The drizzle was replaced by rain, first a sprinkle, then a steady shower which forced them to adjust their goggles and head gear. Then the rain started accumulating in puddles along the wagon groves.

By the time they reached the second hour, the rain was running steadily down the path, their boots sticking in mud. But their destination was getting closer.

"Another hour of this rain and we could be wallowing in fairly heavy water," observed Wolfram. "Let's speed up. I'd like to get to that raised bit of land in the next half hour." And to himself he thought, "This lower ground could be trouble if that rain intensifies." The dogs, comfortable in the rain, stuck closer.

The rain began to come down in sheets reducing visibility. While their faces and hands were soaked, their uniform remained dry with no water entering their boots.

Within two hundred yards of their objective, out of nowhere, a wave of water rushed down the wagon path with such force that it caused Angi to stumble. Falling, the force of the water pulled her past her three companions. Wolfram reached out to grab her but she slipped out of his grip.

He yelled to the others, "Grab a bush,......... grab anything......... I'm after Angi." He pushed through the raging water keeping Angi in sight as she struggled to regain her footing. Out of the corner of his eye he saw Skylar race along the bank and into the water. With her powerful jaws she grabbed Angi's clothing and pulled her towards the side of the wagon path. Skylar had Angi up on the bank and was holding her firmly when Wolfram arrived.

As he reached her Wolfram exclaimed, "Angi are you all right? Your one member we can't afford to lose. Good old Skylar. Without her you may have been propelled back down the path for some distance."

Angi, pulling herself up, hugged the dog saying, "Skylar you are my heroine. I knew we needed these dogs." Then realizing her situation she added, "Wolfram, that was scary and we've just begun."

"Come Angi, this could get really treacherous if we don't get out of this gully." As they trudged back they found Morgan and Vette clinging fast to two bushes as the water rushed past.

"Come on," commanded Wolfram as he assisted them onto the bank. "Another blast of water like that one and we could be back at square one. Let's stay on the higher ground. It may be slower but safer."

The dogs, sensing danger, stayed near and walked along as they plied their way through the storm.

Reaching the raised piece of land they found a winding path to its summit and stood on the ledge watching the water rise in the valley below.

"The water's rising fast," said Vette,.............."What time is it?"

Morgan looked at his watch and replied, "We should be within ten minutes of the third hour. I wonder how the hell we're supposed to hear a click in this storm."

"Let's move towards that rock wall and wait," suggested Vette, already taking the lead. "Maybe we can hear the click easier back here." Finding a slight overhang in the rock they huddled and waited.

The third hour came and went.

Vette reacted, "I bet that bastard set this program for the max. Let's tap on our ear piece and see if Sirona has any wise words."

Sirona responded knowing the reason, "Yes, we've noted the third hour has passed and".................the connection went silent. Tapping the ear piece a number of times still produced no response.

Angi not wanting to believe the unbelievable, said, "Perhaps its temporary."

"Not likely. Let's face it," came Vette's angry reply, "In my suspicious mind this is when Zolar interposes his own program intended on leaving us stranded in this mausoleum. Prepare for the worst."

As the pounding rain bounced off the rock and poured over its edge, Wolfram responded, "As much as I'd like to disagree, Vette may be right. We're on our own until Sirona and Myttrwn can get through."

"Now we need Angi's magic," said Morgan, as the full impact of the danger began to register.

The House of Life, Monitoring Room

The pyramid monitoring room in the House of Life was filled with flashing panels and screens with Myttrwn giving orders to his six technicians who were monitoring the four initiation candidates. With Sirona's first communication with Angi, Vette, Wolfram and Morgan, everyone relaxed convinced what lay ahead was a long but routine day ending with the four candidates exiting the seventh chamber in about twenty hours.

Due to space limitations, Myttrwn had Andrew and Bryce join him and Sirona in the monitoring room while Dylan and the security team joined Corb in readiness for the retrieval of the four at the end of the day.

The atmosphere changed when communications ceased and the monitors faded. Thinking it a momentary transmission problem, Myttrwn reacted giving his technicians explicit directions to regain control. His apprehension increased when none of the usual diagnostic and corrective measures proved effective.

In a momentary pause, Andrew, interjected, "Myttrwn, what happened?"

After more rounds of technical problem solving, Myttrwn turned to Sirona, Andrew and Bryce, and, cautiously said, "I believe this is Zolar's handiwork. I knew he was clever, calculating and dangerous, which are unacceptable characteristics in our world, but even I didn't expect this. At worse, I thought, he would make the Grade One program as difficult as possible. What appears to have happened is that he deliberately altered the Grade One program to fail after running normally for over two hours lulling us into the belief that all was well. He's rigged it to disengage at this point so that his intended program would take over, possible one more advanced than Grade One. At the same time, he has managed to place a powerful screen over the entire pyramid blocking all communications."

"Can you get into the pyramid and rescue the four at this point?" asked Andrew.

"Not without blowing up all the gates which might further endanger them," replied Myttrwn.

"Then what you are telling me is that they are stranded in an advanced initiation program for which they are definitely ill prepared," said Andrew his voice rising. "Surely you must have encountered something similar before, maybe a candidate got lost, injured or was too ill to finish."

"Rarely," came Sirona's reply, "I can recall only once when we had to enter Chamber Seven for an older candidate, and then we were able to spring the exit door with the aid of Zolar and his crew."

"Well, get Zolar's crew in here," replied Andrew growing exasperated.

"That's underway," replied Myttrwn, "but I expect Zolar worked alone on this. If so, he's the only one that can break the code. The overall pyramid blockage presents a major problem as we're unable to access the pyramid at all."

"Well then get Zolar, and have him undo this mess," demanded Andrew.

"That's exactly what I intend to do," said Myttrwn as he pressed a button connecting him to the rescue team. "Corb, this is a Code Red order. Go at once to Zolar's quarters with an emergency plane and escort him with one of his guards to this monitoring station immediately."

Corb needed no explanation, the urgency in Myttrwn's command told him all he needed to know. His four friends were in danger. He dashed to the plane.

That done Myttrwn continued, "Now Andrew don't forget Angi's abilities, she knows how to speed up time so that they will not have to endure the length of time usually programmed for the higher grade testing."

"That's fine, Myttrwn, as long as Angi is OK, but what happens to the others if Angi is hurt and can't perform those functions?"

"Let's hope it doesn't come to that," replied Myttrwn, not wanting to show his own growing misgivings over the situation. He then turned to Sirona, "You must notify the Queen. Tell her we're monitoring the situation and will keep her posted."

Sirona left the room to speak to her mother.

An hour passed before a technician reported that he had four blimps on the monitor still moving about.

Myttrwn examined the monitor and declared, "That's the dogs, stay with them. At least we can follow their movements. I placed the strongest tracking devices in those robots. Let me know if there's any change. Keep working on the other programs."

"Dogs............what dogs?" asked Andrew.

Myttrwn then explained about the robotic dogs and their role, ending with, "There are strict rules regarding these initiations but no mention of robotic dogs. I had a prototype ready so created four identical dogs, the type Angi said she preferred. They are powerfully built and capable of many feats."

"Well, that's something," replied Andrew, still struggling to ascertain the dangers facing his team. He continued, "But Myttrwn, could the dogs be functioning even if Angi, Vette, Wolfram and Morgan are not?"

Myttrwn, sympathetic to Andrew's concerns, replied, "No, the dogs function on the commands of their masters, which in this instance are Angi, Vette, Wolfram and Morgan. If the dogs are moving about then I can assume the four are also on the move. Come here Andrew, you can see for yourself. But the timing now is in question. Zolar had no intension of keeping to the three hours, nor likely five, so we must consider seven hours per chamber. That means we're going to be here much longer than planned." And to himself he added, "I pray that is it, otherwise we will have no alternative but to send in a crew to rescue the four and mutilate the pyramid. Such action will be an anathema to the Council so I will have to make that decision with Sirona and bear the consequences. When Zolar gets here we will know for certain."

At that moment Myttrwn received an incoming call from Corb. Listening his demeanour changed, as he ordered Corb, "Take Zolar and his guard to my lab immediately. I will meet you at the first therapy unit."

When he turned his face was grim, "Corb has reported that Zolar has taken a powerful potion. He is unconscious. I will now leave here and take charge of Zolar's recovery. He's not going to die on me and escape his punishment. Sirona notify the Queen. I leave you in charge. We will keep in constant contact." Turning he gave his chief technician an order, "Proceed to link me up with your monitor, I want to follow what is happening with the dogs." With that he abruptly left the room.

Sirona, seeing the strained look on Andrew's face, replied, "I can assure you, Andrew, I'm prepared to blast our way through if need be."

The situation was grim as Andrew focused on the four green blips on the monitor, his only contact with his team who were locked in a pyramid programmed by an unconscious madman.

ß

Pyramid, Chamber 1 (cont)

Before responding to Morgan's request Angi asked, "Let's think this through. What happens if I skip past the fifth hour, in line with Vette's comment, and shift time within five minutes of the seventh hour? Are there any negative ramifications?"

"That's something we never thought to ask Sirona and Myttrwn," replied Morgan. "But, Angi's got a point. What if Zolar set the program for the fifth hour not the seventh, then we could find ourselves locked in this chamber with the water rising and no way out."

"True, we don't know this system well enough to predict the possibilities," replied Wolfram. "OK, as in this case, if nothing happens at the third hour, then we will have Angi first aim at five minutes to the fifth hour. If the gate still doesn't open, then she will proceed to five minutes to the seventh. Not wanting to put too fine a point on this, please keep in mind the rising water.........we haven't a lot of time." Then thinking to himself he added, "And we will be facing a more critical situation if both times are wrong."

"That's OK," replied Angi, "I prefer two bites rather than a four hour jump. If everyone's ready, here goes...............two, two hour time shifts."

"Just a minute Angi, let me take another look at the water," said Wolfram. He walked to the edge and looked down. Returning, he reported, "It is hard to judge but I would expect the water will be lapping at our feet by the seventh hour. For safety, let's stick firmly against this stone wall."

"What about the dogs?" asked Vette.

"I will hold onto Skylar and Dusky's collars so Angi can operate freely. Vette you and Morgan hold on to your dogs. Are we ready?"

Finally positioned, Wolfram gave the signal, "OK Angi, do your thing!"

Angi proceeded realizing this time the lives of her friends were in her care. Concentrating on the medallion's blue gemstones of the sapphire and the Stone of Atlantis she focused on the first time shift of five minutes to the fifth hour. Completing her task she checked her watch to be sure of the exact time. Confirmed she said, "We have five minutes."

The five minutes passed and when nothing happened she proceeded to the seventh hour.

At five minutes to the seventh hour, they again waited, watching the raging water splash over the edge of the ledge. Morgan ears picked up a sound. "That's it.........I heard a click..........listen," he said. At that moment the waters began to recede. A black gate miraculously appeared in the rock face and slid open.

"Quick," yelled Wolfram, "let's escape this prison. Great work Angi!"

They raced through the opening and stood at the entrance to Chamber Two. Within ten minutes the gate slid shut leaving a blank stone wall.

Morgan commented, "That answers our question about the gate. We now know there's a tiny window in which to scramble between the chambers. If we had miscalculated we would certainly have been locked in that first chamber. There's little room for error in this initiation program."

"Thank God for Angi's skills," said Vette. "Now that we know Zolor's plan, we might as well skip the fifth hour and go straight to the seventh."

"Wait a minute," came Angi's immediate reply, "We have no guarantee that's what he's done. He may have scrambled the timing just to confuse us. One gate might open at the third hour, another at the fifth and still another at the seventh. How can we be sure?"

"Good God, she's got a point," was Vette's response to the possibilities, "Now what?"

Waiting before replying, Wolfram stated, "If you can manage it Angi, perhaps we should follow an identical strategy for all chambers. We can't risk misjudging Zolar's evil intent."

"That's doable," replied Angi.

"So be it, then it is settled," replied Wolfram.

"Well before we dance into the next chamber can someone enlighten me as to whether we were in the last chamber three hours or seven, I'm confused," came Morgan's astute question.

"I'm equally uncertain," replied Wolfram, "Angi can you enlighten us?"

"That was one of my questions which Myttrwn has yet to answer. As best as I can judge, we spent seven hours in Chamber One. Remember Myttrwn's view that time was an illusion. So, if I've just manipulated the speed in which we've passed through time, then its seven hours. Does that make any sense?"

"It sounds logical to me," replied Morgan, "I will go with that until we get to chat with Myttrwn when we get out of this tomb."

Vette, doing some swift calculations, commented, "If that's the case, we need to recalibrate our pyramid timing. If each chamber is set at seven hours, then we're going to be in this pyramid for about forty-five hours, not twenty. If that's the case then we'd better be stringent with our cylinder fluid."

"But it could be less, depending on Zolar's plan for the other chambers," added Angi.

"Right, but I will be more content with the larger estimate and rejoice if it is less," replied Vette.

Suddenly realizing the ramification of Vette's statement, Wolfram responded, "Your right, Vette. Let's be careful with our supplies. We may have to spread them over a much longer time period than Sirona and Myttrwn planned."

The shock of their predicament was becoming obvious.

"We have few options but to gear down and press on. We know we are being manipulated by Zolar for his own ends, a feeling I detest," replied Angi. "Sirona and Myttrwn will eventually break through. In the meantime, if we're ready, let's see what our next test has for us."

House of Life, Monitoring Room

Everyone was riveted on the blinking movement of four dogs. At the seventh hour the chief technician announced, "They've entered Chamber Two."

"Well, that's progress," said Andrew looking at Sirona.

Exuding as much confidence under the circumstances, Sirona replied, "Yes, it means if they have conquered one chamber they can do the same with the others. We will stick to this monitoring while the technicians work at breaking Zolar's blockages." Silently, she kept repeating, "Angi, somehow make contact from your side. It might work. Zolar would not have considered that possibility."

After his initial examination, Myttrwn reported to Sirona, "Zolar's condition is critical but manageable. I am utilizing every available treatment but it will be slow as whatever he drank is potent. It is unlikely I will be able to get anything out of him before the forty-eight hours are up. I have yet to fully identify all the components he has swallowed. It is likely something of his own creation."

Myttrwn had brought Corb into his confidence and ordered him to prepare for a possible forced entry into the pyramid on short notice. Corb delivered this message to Dylan and his team, preparing them for the worst. Explosive materials were assembled along with several emergency planes placed on standby. Corb and Dylan worked out different strategies for the upcoming mission. Myttrwn kept Corb updated regarding any progress in the pyramid.

In the meantime, Andrew and Bryce relieved each other watching the monitors. They spoke little. Being old friends they did not need to verbally communicate the obvious. They were both troubled over the potential outcome and knew they had to stifle any misgivings or annoyance on their total dependence on outside sources for everything. Sirona and the technicians, sensing the anxiety of the two senior men, kept them updated on both the progress of the dogs and whatever technical breakthroughs they were achieving.

"As I estimate it," said Andrew, speaking to Bryce, "seven hours in six chambers plus a short time in the seventh, will take about forty-five or more hours, ... almost two of our days." Glancing at his watch he continued, "They have completed about nine hours........... It is going to be a long ordeal. I wish I could do more than sit here watching that damn monitor. But then again, it is better than nothing. They're moving, Angi does have her medallion, and there's the dogs. Thank God for such mercies. I best make some arrangements for us to rest." He walked over to Sirona.

Makeshift sleeping arrangement were quickly set up near the monitoring room. Sirona also made arrangements for food and refreshments to be delivered. Everyone waited, hoping for miracles and preparing for a disaster.

THE SERPENT'S SONG

Chapter 9

Pyramid, Chamber 2

From the driving rain of Chamber One, they entered a desolate scene of a rocky land outreach high above a winding river. An overgrown gray stone road followed the river, with a steep jagged cliff dropping perpendicular to the river on the right and an endless scene of scrub grass and low trees on the left. A steady breeze welcomed their arrival.

"This is different," said Vette as she walked ahead. "Even with the occasional sun glint the place is depressing. This seems to be the only road which leads first to that abandoned lookout building hanging precariously over the river. Then the road twists and turns up to the left towards what looks like a guard post in front of a deserted castle at the top of the hill. Morgan, this looks like it has been abandoned for some time. What do you think?"

"Yeh, it reminds me of my time in the United Kingdom or was it Europe? Anyway, this being a hologram it hardly matters," replied Morgan. "Those buildings are definitely deserted, unless for a lonesome ghost. Our objective has to be that castle, it is the highest point." Then as an afterthought he added, "I'd love to explore these old structures."

Smiling, Wolfram replied, "When we get out of this mess, Morgan, I will ask Myttrwn to drop you back in here for a second run. As for me, once is enough, thank you. As for ghosts, if we meet any I will direct them to you."

Angi chuckled, "You know, my grandmother was an expert on ghosts, but she's not available. I've had one ghost in my life, that wee boy in Scotland. That's enough for a spell. By the way, could we go back to the question of time? In Chamber One we must have walked for hours, but, as I recall, the exterior of this pyramid is not that large. Anyone with an explanation?"

Morgan was quick to respond, "Remember Myttrwn's sessions on our world view being an illusion. He insisted that the world around us, the world of time and space with its sensory interpretation is one aspect of truth. Our language and culture reinforces our current illusion of time and space. I expect these pyramid chambers are an illustration of that principle. They may work in combination with some sophisticated computer program, and we, somehow, do something to create these scenes. I bet their advanced students have the ability to pull this holographic or sensory veil to one side, likely with their thoughts, and walk directly to the next gate. Too bad we can't do likewise."

"You may be right, Morgan," replied Angi. "If that's so, then they would also avoid the physical tests which we will have to face. If I make it through this initiation I'm definitely going to push for more lessons from Myttrwn, no matter how many trips it takes. I would like to know how to bypass my five senses. Likely the world looks very different than the one I think exists."

"You are lucky you are not an ancient Egyptian," came Morgan's quick reply.

"Why?" asked Angi.

"They recorded three hundred and sixty senses. We identify only five. Some scholars argue that the three hundred and sixty senses could be altered states of consciousness but even that we can't duplicate in our modern world. You know, much of what I scoffed at over the years is now coming home to bite me. The more we deal with Myttrwn the more I realize that we in our so-called modern society are neophytes compared to our ancient ancestors. That concept would be a mighty hard pill for some to swallow."

"Morgan, your wealth of historic detail amazes me. But let's set aside that discussion for another time. Right now we must confront this reality." As Angi walked gingerly over some loose pebbles, she added, "Let's pray we're not facing snow or this road will become dangerous."

Vette walked back to join the group saying, "I just spotted an eagle soaring over the castle, but it likely means little. By the way, have you noticed the wind seems to be picking up, or is it my imagination?"

"I noticed the same thing," replied Wolfram. "Let's push on so we can get off this precipice before the wind really kicks up. It is not snow this round Angi, it is wind."

As they walked along the dogs, sticking to the high ground to the left of the path, ran on together sniffing the air.

"Speaking of learning things," said Wolfram, "We know little of these robotic companions. Look at them? They seem to be sniffing something or are they just sensing the wind. Myttrwn is a genius. These dogs look and act like normal dogs but I expect they are loaded with technology which Myttrwn hoped to test on this mission. That's fine with me. They are excellent buddies and give us a sense of security."

"I'm sure they've been programmed to each one of us. Look at how quickly Skylar came to my rescue. I swear they can read our thoughts," replied Angi.

"Now that's spooky," was Morgan's immediate reply, "It is bad enough that I think everyone in this kingdom can read my mind but now we have four dogs as well."

The wind strengthened as they progressed up the hill. The dogs eventually joined the four on the roadway out of the wind gusts. At the end of the first hour they had bypassed what remained of the lookout building and were well on their way towards the guard post.

Vette, taking a quick glance at the river below said, "This was certainly a secure location, but frightfully isolated. What would possess anyone to choose such a place?"

"Actually, if this was real, there might be other castles in the distance which they communicate with by fires or other means. As for the reasons, there are multiple possibilities," replied Morgan, "I can think of political and religious reasons for a start."

"Well it didn't work," replied Vette, "This place was destroyed a long time ago whatever the reason."

Fifteen minutes to the second hour they reached the guard post, another dilapidated structure with half a wall still intact. At this stage a dark gray cloud appeared forcing an increase in the wind which rushed around the stony outcrop lifting any loose dirt. Determined to reach the castle before the storm hit, they hurried past the crumbling structure. The path to the castle lay about three hundred feet behind the guard post.

"Let's stick closer together," advised Wolfram, "That gale is getting worse and we're exposed on this hill. But take a good look, that castle doesn't seem to have much to offer in protection. It looks pretty dilapidated from here with little remaining except that outer wall. It is sitting so high that the wind can attack from any direction. If we have five hours in this place with escalating winds we could be in trouble."

Pushing into the gale-force winds the small party slowly navigated the distance from the guard post to the castle, entering what appeared to be the remnant of the castle entrance. Once inside they were surprised by the enormous size of the structure, the remaining ramparts blocking out the diminishing light.

"This castle must have had several floors in its day," said Morgan, "Look over there, you can still see wooden beams and there's a broken stairway to the top of the structure. A rough guess, this structure could have housed hundreds of people. I wonder if any survived whatever happened. Anyway, that's not our concern. The biggest question is where a gate may be hidden in this mess."

"I'm amazed that so much of the wall seems intact considering the location of this edifice and the steady battering of the winds," said Angi. "How's our time?"

"We've been walking for about two hours," replied Wolfram. "So, if the gate opens in the third hour we better get cracking. As I see it, there's only two possibilities, the more intact wall to our left or the dilapidated one to the right. If we separate we can cover more ground. Angi and I could explore the one on the left while you, Vette, go with Morgan to the right. Be careful, that wind is brutal and this old structure doesn't seem too stable even with its huge walls."

"Fine, let's agree we will come together in half an hour at this very spot," said Vette, "With this wind it would be impossible to call out. While I might agree Wolfram that the gate is likely in the left wall, our dear Zolar may have just as easily planted it in the right to trick us. Come on Morgan, we've got work to do."

The half hour was almost up when Angi heard a dog barking. As she and Wolfram exited their area of the castle they saw Vette running towards them yelling, "Come quick Angi. Morgan's injured."

When they got to Morgan they found him lying to one side of a pile of fallen stones with a bleeding head wound and Macky standing guard.

"We separated for a moment when I heard Morgan yell out and then the dog started barking. When I got to him, Macky was pulling him away from more falling rocks. She hasn't left his side. His pulse is OK but that's quite a bang on his head."

Angi reached into her First Aid kit and pulled out the pad, stretching the corners and placing it over Morgan's head wound, saying, "The pad will prevent any dirt entering the wound from my hands. This could take time, the wound seems deep. Vette, keep a tag on the time." Then, concentrating on all the gemstones in her medallion Angi began repairing the wound from the inside out. She kept visualizing the healing process as each layer knitted and the bleeding eased. Finally, Morgan's opened his eyes mumbling, "What happened?"

"The wind must have dislodged those rocks causing one to come crashing down on your forehead," replied Angi. Then raising two fingers she asked, "Morgan now that you are conscious, how many fingers do you see?"

"Two, how many should I be seeing?" asked Morgan, still groggy.

"Two," answered Angi. "You've received a bad blow. Macky saved you from a worse fate. Do you have a headache?"

"Yes, now that you mention it," replied Morgan, trying to grasp his predicament.

"OK, stay there while I perform a few more minutes of healing," said Angi. Before beginning she again asked, "How's our time Vette?"

"We have twenty-five minutes to the third hour."

After minutes of further healing Angi asked again, "Morgan do you still have your headache? Do you hurt anywhere else?"

"The headache's gone. Thanks Angi. No, just my head. Now all I have to do is stand," came Morgan's response, growing stronger.

"Before you move, let me use Sirona's spray to protect the wound. I will replace this soiled pad with your own and use your headgear for more protection. Remember Morgan this wound will still be sensitive so it needs to be covered." She slipped the bloody pad into one of her leg pockets.

Morgan proceeded to get up.

Angi, watching his movements, advised, "Let Vette and I support you, Morgan, for the walk across the courtyard. Wolfram will lead the way. If the gate fails to open on the third hour I will give you another treatment. We need you well for the rest of this joyous trip."

Morgan, unstable, got to his feet with Vette and Angi's support. Once upright he said, "Thanks for the offer. I think I can navigate on my own. But stick close just in case I'm being too optimistic."

"Morgan, what about your Aqk?" suggested Wolfram. "You could make a walking stick to help you." He assisted Morgan getting the Aqk out of his belt and made sure he was ready to move on.

The group made their way across the courtyard to the larger outer wall. Wolfram led the way to the only surviving room in the entire castle, a side room with intact walls. When they reached the room Morgan, growing weary, sat down on a wooden log. Three dogs sat together, while Macky came and placed his head on Morgan's lap. The winds grew louder encircling the castle and breaking through every opening.

"We're within five minutes of the third hour," reported Vette.

Once again the third hour came and went.

"OK Angi, after you give Morgan another treatment, let's magically bounce to the fifth hour," said Vette. "This time I pray the gate opens on the fifth because that windstorm is intensifying and, I agree with Wolfram, this old building can't take much more punishment."

After treating Morgan, as before, Angi focusing on her medallion blue gemstones stated the precise time travel objective. Upon completion, she checked her watch to confirm the time.....five minutes to the fifth hour. They waited in silence.

"There..........I heard it," exclaimed Vette, "We're getting out of this chamber early." She no sooner finished speaking when an iron lattice gate materialized on the stone wall. Once it opened they scrambled into Chamber Three.

The technicians in the House of Life, monitoring the movement of the dogs, immediately reported their advancement.

ʁ

Pyramid, Chamber 3

At the entrance to Chamber Three Angi stopped and asked, "Let's take a sip of Myttrwn's cylinder fluid before we go on. We've burnt a lot of energy in the first two chambers. I'd also like to check Morgan's wound."

"Good idea," replied Wolfram.

Each one took their first sip of the fluid being careful not to overindulge as it had to sustain them for the duration.

Angi finding Morgan's wound intact, replaced the pad and secured his head gear. "No headache?" she asked.

"All's well on the noggin front," replied Morgan with a weak smile.

"We're ready to go," replied Angi.

"Well, there's no doubt this time," came Vette's comment after her first footsteps into Chamber Three, "We are into snow. It is already coming down."

The dogs, fascinated with their new environment, played and rolled in the white fluffy ground cover.

"If it is already snowing, let's get a bead on what constitutes high ground in this scenario," replied Wolfram, pressing ahead. Over his shoulder he added, "Best prepare for frigid. Put on your goggles, pull your headgear down tight, and put on your gloves."

Angi added, "Wolfram, we should also activate our Aqks to a long walking stick, deep snow can hide all sorts of problems."

"Gotcha," replied Wolfram as he stopped to do as directed.

Trudging along with their walking sticks through a silent screen of fallen snow, Wolfram asked, "It must be the snow. It is hard to see any distance in this weather, even with these goggles. I can't see anything beyond twenty to thirty feet and the visibility is deteriorating."

Vette responded, "I'm getting likewise, but within sight is a side path which leads across a frozen brook to a cave. Could that be it or does that seem too easy?"

"Watch that ice," advised Angi, seeing rushing water underneath the glasslike surface, "Let's use our walking stick to test its thickness."

"Yeh, you and Vette should be experts in ice and snow," said Wolfram.

"Oh here we go again," said Vette, "You Americans always think

Canadians spend their lives in snow and live in igloos."

"Woops, I've touched a nerve," said Wolfram with a chuckle, "Actually, since Morgan and I have always lived in cities where you just stay hibernated until the roads clear, I thought you might have some practical advice."

"Sorry, Wolfram," came Vette's swift apology, "I've had too many encounters with non-Canadians and their rather truncated view of our country."

"Vette that annoyance is inevitable," replied Angi placing her walking stick firmly on a section of ice as she applied her full weight. "This looks solid, but keep testing as you cross. It is about twenty-two feet to the other bank and ice is never even. Best we travel single file to reduce any weight concentration."

"I will go first," said Vette, "Then Morgan, followed by Angi and last Wolfram. Is everyone OK with that?"

"Agreed," came the reply, as they positioned themselves.

Vette and Morgan crossed without a problem. When it was Angi's turn she was half way across when she heard a crackling sound and called out, "Wolfram, take a different path, the ice may be weakening with our weight."

"OK," answered Wolfram as he gingerly stepped onto a patch further down. He was within three feet of the opposite bank when the ice gave way, and, with a yell, he broke through. The water was up to his chest as he floundered. Dusky, following Wolfram, managed to make it to the bank and hovered near the women.

"Hold still," yelled Angi, "Put the walking stick across the ice to give you balance. Come on Vette you and I will have to crawl out on the ice and rescue Wolfram."

Vette and Angi moved cautiously using their long poles as they approached Wolfram. "Grab the poles," yelled Angi, "Your gloves have gripping power even if wet."

Wolfram did as instructed and was amazed at the strength of the two woman as they pulled him out of the water. When he got to shore his wet uniform froze instantly.

"Let's get to the cave," said Angi to Vette.

Wolfram walked stiff legged behind them and made it to the nearest rocky seat just inside the entrance.

Right behind them came Dusky dragging Wolfram's Aqk. "Good girl. Come here," said Wolfram. Dusky dragged the Aqk and dropped it at Wolfram's feet. Then she manoeuvered her way to sit next to him to observe.

Angi moved into action, "OK Wolfram, I need to check your feet and legs that no water entered or you could end up with frostbitten toes." Using her hand to break the ice on his uniform, she gently pulled off one boot and felt his feet and legs with her hands. They were warm and dry. She examined the other foot and leg to discover the same. "Thank God for these uniforms," she said out loud, "Your feet and legs are fine." It was then she noticed the blood. "But you are bleeding." She checked his hands to find that in his struggle the ice had cut into his right wrist. She pulled off his glove, retrieved a pad from his First Aid kit and placing her hands firmly around the wound proceeded to heal it in layers from the inside to the outer skin. When this was completed she noticed his hands were gray, water had entered his gloves. Holding both hands in hers she applied extra warmth to improve circulation.

Wolfram watched and when the treatments were over he said with a grin, "Angi, if I had known it took a dip in an icy creek to get you to hold my hands I would have done it weeks ago. By the way, the gloves are already responding, just touch the inside and see how warm they are. The uniform is also heating up to get rid of the ice." He hardly finished the sentence when the thin layer of ice from his chest to his feet slipped to the ground.

Angi, pulled her hands away and looked into his face, saying, "Your jovial remarks mean you are obviously recovering from your icy dip. When we are through this misery we will chat again about warm hands." Before stepping away she helped him put on his boots and checked his uniform.

"Well, now that we're in the cave what are we up against?" asked Vette, acknowledging the end to their first crisis. "We will need to convert one of the Aqks into a light standard, the rest we can reassign to our belts."

The light showed that the cave was huge with long icicles hanging from the ceiling and a wide path leading into the interior.

"Oh great," replied Morgan, "how deep is this place anyway and where in this ice palace would someone hide a gate."

"Let's go back to basics," replied Angi, "Where is the highest point in this cave?"

Vette went to the head of the path to investigate. When she returned she announced, "There's a wide ledge in the distance, which must be the highest point. But to get there we have to pass through an icy, winding track which first descends before rising slightly to the ledge. I don't suppose these boots have cleats." She banged her boots on the ice. "No such luck. But they do have grip, I've tested it already. My suggestion is that we stick to the sides of the path where it is a bit uneven. Is everyone ready?"

"Vette we will need light for the descent and ascent but we cannot manage the walking stick and maneuver this icy stretch. Any suggestions?" asked Wolfram.

"Is there any chance someone here has some background in throwing to get this walking stick up on that ledge?" asked Vette.

Angi replied, "I use to throw javelins in my track and field days. I am out of practice and these uniforms are restrictive but I will give it a go." She calculate the distance and holding the walking stick like a javelin she threw it with all her strength. It landed a perfect distance to provide the necessary light.

"Fantastic Angi!" yelled Morgan.

Vette, with a wide grin, stated, "That's impressive............OK let's get on with it. What order should we use for this bobsled run?"

Wolfram responded, "Vette, let's stick to the same plan; you first, then Morgan, then Angi and I will take up the rear." Then he pronounced the final directives, "Go slow. No quick movements. Give each other lots of space."

Vette carefully calculating her descent, crouching down as she inched her way along the ice encrusted wall. At the bottom she called back, "It is your turn Morgan, follow the same route if you can."

Morgan took longer but made it without a mishap.

Angi, following Vette's instructions, took an identical path but slipped once before reaching the other two.

Wolfram, without the full use of his right hand, struggled on the descent and losing his step slid, landing at the feet of his companions.

Alarmed, Angi asked, "Wolfram, are you all right?"

"Other than my hurt pride, I'm fine," came Wolfram's abrupt reply. "I could not hold on to that last sliver of ice. I will do better on the ascent."

The four dogs stood watching at the top of the slide.

"What do you think they'll do?" asked Angi. "They look as if they are communicating with each other. Let's wait." First, the four tested the ice with their claws and in unison crawled on their bellies down the slippery slope. Upon joining the others they wagged their tails at their newly discovered skill.

"I bet they have already worked out the climb," stated Vette, "Those darling beasts can master anything."

"How's our time?" asked Angi.

"We are doing just fine," replied Morgan, "We have used up an hour and a half. My rough estimate is that even if it takes another hour for us to reach the ledge, we will still have a half hour before the third bell. And, may I remind you, so far Zolar hasn't used the third hour."

"I don't trust Zolar," said Vette, "So let's aim for the third hour. Everyone ready? We'll stick to the same order. Wolfram are you OK with that?"

"Yah, I'm fine, I'm well acquainted with the ice now."

Vette hugged one wall edging her way up the slippery path until she reached the ledge. As Morgan completed his run he had Vette to help him up onto the ledge. Angi, followed and had both Vette and Morgan to aid her. They watched as Wolfram struggled and when he reached them he had all three to pull him to safety.

They stood watching to see what the dogs would do. Again they worked in unison. Digging in their claws they inched their way up the icy slope and were pulled over the ledge by their designated owner. Exhausted by their efforts they found a smooth spot on the surface and lay down.

Exceeding the hour, the four candidates made their way towards a flat wall covered in ice at the back of the ledge.

"If there's a door behind that ice shield then we're in trouble," commented Morgan after patting the wall. "It must be a foot thick. Even if we could, it would take ages to melt this ice. Now what?"

They sat on raised bits of ice staring at the icy wall and trying to devise a quick solution.

Exasperated, Vette commented, "I will be damned if we are going to let Zolar win. Angi, can you perform some laser magic with that medallion of yours?"

"Not that I know," replied Angi, "Perhaps it is a later lesson of Myttrwn's."

'Laser'...............the word registered, and Wolfram replied, "If Angi can't, I can," as he reached into a pocket bringing out a small metal device he had forgotten about. "This is Corb's contribution to our journey, a simple lazar gun."

Amazed, Morgan asked, "Do you know how to use it? And Wolfram, not to rush you, but we're within fifteen minutes of the third hour."

"Yes, Corb taught me how to use it. However, I have no idea how the ice will react so please take the dogs and stand clear. I will work from the center."

The laser quickly cut through the ice, the blocks falling in a pile to reveal a beige stone wall.

As the third hour approached, Angi said to Wolfram. "You will have to stop or we will never hear the click, not that it has ever occurred on the third hour."

Wolfram, stopped, convinced it was temporary.

Instead, at the third hour Angi exclaimed, "My God, there it is. I heard the click."

"Angi's right," yelled Morgan. "Look, a gate has appeared on the wall. I will be glad for some warmth after three hours in this refrigerator. Don't forget your Aqk, Vette, we're moving on."

As they slipped into Chamber Four, the House of Life technicians in the monitoring room announced their progress, to the delight of those glued to the monitors.

&

The House of Life

In the House of Life monitoring station, no one had budged. Everyone kept glued to the monitoring screens mesmerized by four bright green dots which was their only contact with what was happening in the pyramid. Positive news finally began to relieve some anxiety. The technicians reported the four candidates had made it to Chamber Four and that they were making headway in dissolving Zolar's pyramid communication blockage. They could now bring up faint silhouettes of the four humans. Everyone now became transfixed on eight objects, four human and four dogs, as they continued to follow their progress through the pyramid.

Next, Myttrwn, who had been fully engaged in bringing Zolar out of his self-inflicted coma in his therapy centre, suddenly reappeared in the monitoring station saying to Sirona, "I've identified the components of his elixir and we are now detoxifying Zolar. This will take time but it is progress. He's being monitored by two of my best students. I'm also delighted to see our stalwart four are making progress. This means we can hold our fire until, and if, we see them falter. It is best we do not destroy the pyramid if it can be avoided." Then he emphasized to Andrew and Bryce, "Sirona and I have kept the Queen up-to-date on what is happening."

Andrew was pressed to add, "By the way, Myttrwn, have you noticed that the time in each chamber varies, not the strict seven hours we originally thought. But the exact conclusion of this initiation is at present unknown."

"Agreed," replied Myttrwn, "Zolar is using variation to confuse both the candidates and ourselves. My greatest concern is that he may have also revised the program to such an extent that the four are facing a variety of challenges, some quite advanced. But I have every confidence in their innate survival skills."

Tired and irritated, Andrew replied, "I'm not sure what you are basing that assurance on. Admittedly, they have Angi's medallion plus youth on their side, some innate skills and the dogs, but is that enough?" The ongoing stress was taking its toll on Andrew and Bryce. Earlier in the day they had tried taking a brief nap but gave up and returned to the monitoring room.

Sirona was pleased the four had reached Chamber Four but telepathically conveyed to Myttrwn, "If we see them falter, will we have enough time to rescue them? I know the Queen and the Council of Elders are stalling on any destruction of the pyramid, but deep down I know we're facing an inevitably tough decision."

Telepathically, Myttrwn replied, "Be assured, Sirona, Corb and his crew are set to act and you and I will make that decision. I believe the wrath of the Council will not be on us but Zolar who has dishonoured his position, shattered countless rules and will force a re-examination of his position and powers. I wish I could do more to help Andrew and Bryce. It will soon be over. Keep trying to contact Angi telepathically, it might work."

&

Pyramid, Chamber 4

"You've got your wish, Morgan, it looks like a desert ahead. We should be toasty real soon," replied Wolfram as he took the lead. "I guess we best leave on the goggles and head gear for protection against the sun. None of us has sunscreen. We will reconsider our Aqks once we get a bead on the terrain."

The four stepped into a scene of endless sand dunes to their left and in front of them with an eighteen foot high red rock blocking any view on their right. The sun, blasting down on the sand, was creating a heat haze which hovered in the distance. A wind, in bursts, lifted loose sand adding to the drifts. The setting was devoid of vegetation.

"I can't see anything on a raised level to the left or in front of us," replied Morgan, "So our only hope is behind this rock. By the looks of things we have about a half hour walk to find out. The rock stops in the distance."

"I agree," replied Wolfram, "Let's press on, it could be slow going in this sand."

The four dogs unencumbered, using their webbed feet to stay on top of the sand, scampered ahead, which gave their owners a pretested path.

Morgan's curiosity eventually pressed him to take the lead. First to reach the end of the rock he called back, "Wait till you see what I've found beyond the rock." Growing impatient he called out, "Hurry up, you won't believe this."

When the others joined him they looked in amazement. In the distance on a high rocky precipice stood a magnificent building partially covered in sand, the exposed white marble glistening under the blazing sun. There was no other structure in sight. Its architecture and grandeur spoke of wealth and nobility.

"That's definitely the highest point in this chamber," said Vette, "I expect we have about an hour's walk to get there," as she struck out in the direction of the edifice.

Within five hundred yards of the building they encountered a wide

170

sloping stone walkway with marble railings on both sides, much of which was covered by the drifting sand. Closer to the building they counted seven columns on either side of the edifice doorway, about thirty feet high from base to top.

Morgan, who had assumed the lead as they approached the building started commenting on what lay before them, "It looks unoccupied. Just look at the artistry along those walls. It is like nothing I have seen before. It is a bit Egyptian but that is a wild guess. The doors must be fifteen feet high and are made of metal, possibly copper or brass. Look at the workmanship on those doors. It is a magnificent structure, untouched by time. This had to be built for a powerful ruler, no minor official." As he walked up the main steps he said to Wolfram who was close by, "Let's look around the sides to see if there are any possible gate sites other than this main entrance."

Wolfram, taking two steps at a time, quickly joined Morgan.

Finding nothing Wolfram announced "It seems we have no alternative but to enter this building. Let's see if we can budge those huge doors."

Angi and Vette stood back admiring the beauty and grace of the structure while the dogs darted about the walkway and over the stairs.

"The structure seems unoccupied and there's no community in the vicinity, so this must have been chosen for security," said Vette, looking around. "A burial place may be. But the length and width of that walkway looks like it was meant for processions or spectacles. You know Angi, I'm beginning to sound like Morgan." She laughed.

"Hey you two, come on up here," yelled Wolfram. "We've managed to wedge this door open. I will find something to keep it ajar as those wind gusts might close it again. I do not think I would like to be entombed in this crypt or whatever it is, in case we need to exit."

To their surprise the interior was cool and possessed some form of invisible lighting which negated the need for their Aqk lights. Having squeezed through the outer doors, they faced another set of equally large double doors, positioned directly opposite the entrance, twenty feet across a corridor lined with sculptures. The structure seemed to contain just one major room. The second doors were covered in a soft fabric and opened easily to the touch. What greeted them was indescribable. The one hundred and twenty foot square marble enclosure glittered in gold and precious gemstones with purple drapery and several golden banners hanging from a twenty-five foot ceiling. A thick gold and purple carpet covered the steps leading up to a throne which sat against the middle of the far wall. The environment looked pristine, as if whoever had been there had just stepped out. The absence of people produced a poignant impression. The silence was broken only by the sound of water trickling down a walled waterfall on either side of the throne.

Wolfram chuckled saying, "Morgan is in his element. Just look at him."

Morgan, spellbound, walked ahead giving his professional opinion on what he was seeing, "Strange, I expected some kind of burial chamber. This is obviously a throne room. The golden gem-encrusted throne sits in front of that gigantic wall decoration of an engraved, golden snake on a purple background. The waterfall is a symbol of supreme wealth in a desert. Those pots on the seven steps leading up to the throne look like their filled with offerings of diamonds, sapphires, rubies and some gemstones I'm not familiar with. If one was materialistic this would be a heart wrenching treasure trove. But our objective is to escape this den of temptation. As you will also observe, the throne is the highest point within this room."

"Your right, Morgan," replied Wolfram, "I pray the gate isn't behind that serpent wall plaque. It must weigh a ton. But it seems to be the only possibility."

Unwilling to accept defeat, Vette began ascending the steps saying, "Let's take a closer look behind the throne, there may be some clue as to how that plaque rises." Suddenly, on reaching the second step a marble block by the throne opened releasing a short, powerful arrow which shot out and embedded itself into Vette's upper right leg. Vette cringed, grabbing her leg and began to fall. Rafie moved quickly and crouched trying to aid Vette's retreat down the steps and onto the floor. The wound was bleeding profusely.

Angi yelled to Wolfram, "Quick, retrieve the pad from Vette's kit. I've got to stop the bleeding."

Handing Angi the pad Wolfram asked, "Is there anything else I can do?"

"Yes, help me pull out this arrow. There's going to be tearing."

Vette winced as Wolfram rapidly dislodged the arrow. The arrow out, Angi went to work at healing the wound, the blood seeping through the pad as she worked. Soon the bleeding eased. After checking the wound a couple of times Angi was assured the jagged edges had knit properly leaving a pencil-like mark on Vette's leg. She then asked Vette, "How's the pain?"

"I can manage," came the whispered reply, "I've had worse in my line of work back home. Let me see if I can stand."

"No wait," replied Angi. "Wolfram, we've run out of pads. I need one for Vette. Any chance your wrist has mended by now? I will use the protective spray, then a silver sheet from our kit for safety and your pad for cushioning. Once I've completed all that can you help me get Vette up on her feet?"

"Sure, here's my relatively clean pad." And looking at his wrist he added, "I've practically nothing to show for my icy dip in the brook."

Angi proceeded to dress the wound and seal up Vette's ripped uniform. When completed Wolfram came to assist.

Vette tried nobly to stand but Angi, seeing the pain in her eyes and clinched jaw, asked, "How about we use one of Myttrwn's tablets?" She was now concerned the degree of pain might indicate the arrow had grazed the bone.

A few minutes after taking the tablet Vette replied, "Good old Myttrwn. That helped Angi. I think I can navigate now." Rafie moved closer. "I will activate my Aqk for a walking stick just like we did for Morgan."

"Why don't you rest Vette until we know what Wolfram and Morgan are going to do? We still have to get to that throne up there."

On cue Wolfram appeared, "Angi, I wonder if you can use your javelin throwing skill again. I'm thinking if you aim it in the direction of the throne it might release any other hidden weapons. But before we do that Morgan and I will activate our Aqk shields and we will get Vette and the dogs to a safe location. Then Angi, once you release the javelin I want you to hit the deck. Morgan and I will try to deflect any other arrows or hidden devices."

With everyone's agreement, they positioned themselves. Angi created a throwing stick from her Aqk and, pacing herself, she threw it in the direction as indicated by Wolfram, then dropped to the floor. Three more arrows were released which were diverted by the shields.

Seeing the arrows Morgan commented, "I expect, those arrows were intended as a first line of defense against any unexpected attack on whoever sat on that throne. I'm sure the first arrow would alert the guards who would immediately attack the individual. Now that we've released three more arrows no further missiles should appear .... of course, I might be wrong."

"Are you willing to risk your life on that assumption?" asked Wolfram, not convinced there weren't more defense mechanisms hidden near the throne.

"Sure, as long as I'm behind this shield," replied Morgan.

Still armed with their shields, the two cautiously approached the throne. Nothing happened.

"It is nice to be right on some things," said Morgan with a wide grin.

"How's our time?" asked Wolfram to no one in particular.

"We're within twenty minutes of the third hour," replied Angi. "We're cutting it a bit tight if Zolar has another third hour. Somehow I expect not."

"OK, Morgan, let's try and move this throne," said Wolfram, testing the item, "It is not going to be easy, it is solid."

As the two struggled to shift the throne Angi noted the third hour had come and gone with no sound other than the squeaking of the throne being moved. Once achieved, Angi and Vette joined their companions, Vette carefully maneuvering the few steps up to the throne with the aid of her walking stick.

"Vette, why don't you sit on the throne and raise your leg up on this," suggested Morgan, pulling a nearby pot of precious stones closer.

As Vette positioned herself she said holding a few gemstones, "Never in my life have I been so close to such wealth. Strange isn't it, I have no feeling for this stuff. I expect it is due to our time with Myttrwn. Deep down I am slowly understanding his concept of our world being a hologram, and grasping after such material possessions has little meaning."

Angi, taking the opportunity to wash her hands in the waterfall, replied, "I agree with you Vette. Myttrwn's wisdom is penetrating my unconscious and making me re-evaluate many things. When this is over let's philosophize more over a much deserved cup of tea back at our residence."

"Ok Angi, since we've skipped past the third hour, do your magic and fly us to the fifth hour," said Vette.

Angi did as requested focusing on the blue gemstones of her medallion. When they reached five minutes to the fifth hour they waited.

This time the click was heard by Morgan standing closest to the serpent plaque. "There it is. It will be sad to leave such splendour but we must move on."

Moments after the click the huge plaque rose effortlessly upward revealing a metal gate. As the gate swung open the eight proceeded through, Wolfram and Angi following Vette to make sure she was able to navigate after her injury. The dogs trailed behind.

At that very hour, the attendants in the monitoring room of the House of Life announced, with delight, the progress of the four candidates into Chamber Five.

&

Pyramid, Chamber 5

When the gate to Chamber Four closed the four found themselves in the dark. A gloom so penetrating that they could barely discern the individual standing next to them.

"Flick on your night vision," instructed Wolfram. "This is our world for the next few hours. And I thought the fog of Boston was thick, this definitely caps it."

The night vision feature of the goggles gave them some advantage but even this had its limitations for they were still unable to see any distance.

"Our critical dilemma," said Angi, "is with such restricted visibility detecting a rise of land or building will be almost impossible."

"Your right, Angi. This is going to be a problem. I believe the entrance is to our right where the dogs are headed," replied Wolfram. "You don't suppose the dogs have night vision as well, they're moving rather easily in this mush. Or do these dogs navigate on some other system?"

"Nothing surprises me about these dogs or Myttrwn's skills," replied Morgan, "The dogs likely have other built-in capabilities, we should use them as our lead."

"Good idea, right now I'd be grateful for any guidance. In this darkness let's keep close and resume talking." Then Wolfram added, "Vette are you OK?"

"I'm fine. I'm still using my walking stick and Myttrwn's medicine has relieved the pain," came Vette's response, speaking within feet of Wolfram.

Entering Chamber Five all they could discern about their environment was that they were on the ground floor of some elaborate building with possible rooms off in all directions. What little they could see with their goggles was that the building appeared deserted evidenced by the chaotic disarray of furniture and the layers of dust and cobwebs.

"Watch your step," yelled Wolfram as he stumbled over a fallen item on the floor, "It is the small stuff underfoot that is deadly. Let's stop and review our next move." He whistled for the dogs who appeared almost instantly.

"The dogs came from the right, should we go in that direction?" asked Morgan.

"The dogs are an option, but I'd like another, if possible," said Wolfram. "My concern in the intensity of this gloom is if we make a mistake it will be a nightmare backtracking. We could waste an awful lot of time."

Then unexpectedly a wee voice penetrated the darkness, "Can I help?"

Startled by the presence of anyone else in the pyramid but themselves, Angi asked, "Come here so we can see you?" The hair on the back of her neck began to bristle as the voice moved closer. The dogs, restive, assumed a guarded position in front of them.

Barely visible in their night vision goggles, walked a sickly child, a boy about six, his appealing eyes aimed straight for their heart. He was dressed in nondescript, worn-out clothes and walked with a shuffle.

"Do you live here?" asked Angi.

"Yes, this is my house," replied the expressionless child.

"Where has everyone gone?" asked Angi.

"I don't know," replied the child, reluctant to look at Angi.

"Where are your parents?" asked Angi.

"I don't know," replied the child, holding the same pose.

"What's your name?" asked Angi.

"Boyson," replied the child.

Morgan coughed, and elbowed Angi.

"What is it Morgan?" she asked, not wanting to interrupt her conversation with the child.

Whispering he replied, "Boyson is another name for poison. It may mean nothing or it could be trouble. Remember Sirona mentioned spirits.........this could be one of them."

Angi was not dismissive of her intuition or Morgan's warning but thought it wise to play along as, if this was a spirit, it might endanger their progress. Speaking quietly to the others she asked, "Should we ask the child for directions?"

"It is a lead," said Wolfram, "But I have a nagging feeling in my gut about this."

"So have I," came Vette's reply. "Twelve minutes.......... no more. Then we get rid of this waif and consider our own path. This child gives me the willies."

"Fine, twelve minutes," replied Angi, and turning to the child she said, "Boyson, can you help us find our way through this building?" asked Angi.

"Yeh, sure," came the reply," Follow me." Boyson, shuffling slowly, guided them down a long corridor and into a lit room where, to their surprise, was an extended table brimming with food and drink, as if set for invited guests. The room was also clean and devoid of cobwebs.

Morgan, stepping past Angi surveyed the feast and exclaimed, "Now that's what I need, some descent food. I can't remember when we ate last. The wine would hit the spot right now after all we've been through."

In the gloom the child's grin could not be discerned by the others. "It's all for you," said Boyson pointing to the table, "And there's more if you want."

As Morgan picked up a bunch of grapes Vette's walking stick came crashing down on his arm causing him to drop the fruit. "Vette, what the hell is wrong with you. We are famished. It has been hours since we ate last." Morgan moaned as he rubbed his arm.

Vette, yelled at Morgan, "Remember Sirona's command, not to eat or drink anything offered in this pyramid? You yourself said the boy's name could be trouble. I bet this food and drink are laced with poison. Zolar missed nothing.".............. Then turning she continued her rant saying, "Where's that conniving little brat, ghost or no ghost, he was here to destroy us."

As hard as they looked the boy could not be found. Following their rejection of refreshments, a high pitched laugh pierced the silence as if mocking them.

"Go to hell," came Vette's parting yelp. "We will not be lured into your diabolical plot."

"Whew, that was a close call," remarked Wolfram. "Stay alert. We will

S. Robertson

now have to weave our way back to the start. Thankfully it is not too far but we have lost time."

They had all been checking markers while following the boy so they were soon back at the beginning.

"Let's go with the dogs," suggested Morgan, "Them we know and trust."

And so the dogs were directed to find the gate, a first in their journey through the pyramid.

"I believe they are actually pleased to have been asked," said Morgan, "I'm new to dogs, do they have emotions?"

Vette had calmed down and now regretted the forcefulness of her action. "Sorry Morgan, I hope I didn't hurt you in preventing you from eating those grapes."

"I'm fine Vette. I should have remembered. If you hadn't hit me I might have been a goner. However, it still doesn't eliminate my hunger. Maybe when we get to where we're going we can take another sip of Myttrwn's brew."

"Morgan, to answer your question on dogs, my only experience is with police dogs who were trained to assist us in capturing criminals. Not that I had such a dog, but they were in our unit. They did show affection for their trainers, it was a very close bond. I expect we know far too little about our furry friends and especially these ones designed by Myttrwn." Angi, Vette and Morgan continued chatting about dogs as they continued following their guides.

Wolfram was not entirely sure following the dogs was wise but it was their only option. As they meandered through various corridors and rooms he tried to determine their direction by his own instincts. As they rounded a corner midway in their journey a loud piercing sound shattered the silence, assailing their ears, a sound that grew more penetrating and disorienting by the minute. Even the dogs started pawing their ears. "As much as I regret saying this, perhaps we should stop for a few minutes to consider some remedy for this," said Wolfram.

"I agree," replied Angi, "We need to cushion our ears. I'm getting nauseated. It is not like we can switch off this misery. I bet Zolar programmed an extra loud version of this just for us."

"Is there anything in these rooms we can use for padding against this onslaught?" asked Vette.

"There's padding in those benches over there," said Morgan, "Perhaps we can stuff it in our headgear."

"Good idea," replied Wolfram, taking the sharp device provided by Sirona to cut the pads. Each one assisted the other in padding their ears.

177

Once completed, Angi said, "Now, how can we help the dogs. There suffering."

"We will pad their ears as well," said Vette. "It is only for a short time until we clear this. We're experiencing one colossal demonstration of sound pollution. We should iPhone the environmentalists to come and protest." They all laughed, which relieved some of the tension.

Well padded, they moved on. The dogs eventually led them outside the building into an enclosed courtyard, the gloom following them. Once outside they removed the padding.

"This must be it," said Angi, "It is huge, so it will take time to find a gate."

"We're not stopping," replied Wolfram, "The dogs are still moving. See, they're starting up that far stairway. Let's keep them in sight."

At the top of the stairs they found themselves in a second enclosed courtyard, slightly smaller than the first with no exit or stairway.

"This must be it," said Wolfram, still uneasy about following the dogs fearing they might have reached a dead end.

All four dogs made their way to a far alcove where a sculptured snake was in evidence and sat down. In reaching the alcove the four were stunned to discover how large it was and that they were standing in front of a stone gate with no visible latches or hinges.

"Well, we have a gate, but is it the right one?" asked Morgan, sitting down on a bench near the sculpture.

"How's our time?" asked Vette.

"With all our coming and going, and ups and downs we've chewed up the time," said Angi. "We're within five minutes of the third hour. Let's stand around and see if anything happens on the third hour."

The third hour came and went.

Vette, joining Morgan was glad to get off her injured leg. "I suppose it is time for us to get Angi to bounce us onward."

"Fine, here goes," said Angi. At five minutes to the fifth hour they waited. But again nothing happened.

"So we're stuck here in this gloom to the seventh hour," said Wolfram. "Press on Angi. I will be glad to put this chamber behind us, it is creepy."

At five minutes to the seventh hour Wolfram, restless and moving close to the gate, heard a sound but this time there was no click but a metallic voice appeared saying, "To enter the next chamber you must answer a chosen question."

"Damn, I remember, this gate has a riddle to solve," said Wolfram. "OK you three it is all yours. We have three chances. I pray you are good at this as I do not want to be stuck in this darkened hell."

The voice then recited the riddle: "Voiceless it cries, wingless flutters, toothless bites, and mouthless mutters. What is it?"

After some thought Angi replied, "Snow."

Nothing happened.

"One down, two to go," replied Wolfram, wanting desperately to move on.

Silence fell as the three wrestled with the second reply. Then Morgan whispered to Angi and Vette, his proposed answer. They nodded their heads for him to reply.

In a loud voice Morgan replied, "Wind."

Within seconds they heard a familiar click and the gate swung open.

"Great work you guys," said Wolfram, "The riddle champs of Tir na nOg." And with a light step he took the lead into the next chamber.

Once again, their progress was noted in the House of Life. The four candidates had reached the sixth chamber.

THE SERPENT'S SONG

Chapter 10

Pyramid, Chamber 6

As the Chamber Five gate snapped shut behind them the four took time to sip Myttrwn's elixir to resuscitate their depleted energies.

"We're almost there," said Morgan, "Just this chamber and a short run in Chamber Seven and we're home and dry."

"Don't count your chickens too soon," warned Wolfram, "Zolar may have loaded his greatest surprise for the finale. I'm not dismissing our overall fortitude, but without the aid of Sirona, Myttrwn, Angi and the dogs this could have been a much sadder outcome, which is still not over. So, let's brace ourselves and take a look at what this chamber has to offer."

"I wonder why there's a closed door to the chamber entrance," asked Morgan walking towards it. Curious, he opened the door, and instantly slammed it shut.

"What is it Morgan?" asked Angi, noting the revulsion on his face.

"Oh God, the place is crawling.............I mean literally crawling with snakes. They're everywhere and may be inches thick over the entire floor. How in hell are we going to get through this? I have never seen so many snakes in my entire life."

"Snakes," replied Vette, "I am not going to look, I will take your word for it, Morgan. I detest crawly things. And a room full of snakes is about the vilest thing I can imagine."

"Let me take a look," said Angi, "May be there's an upper walkway or something which we can use to get above the snakes." She opened the door and took time surveying the chamber, several snakes almost escaping through the open door. Making sure the door was secure she returned to report, "There's nothing. We will be forced to wade through them. But on a positive note this time there's only one room as I can see the gate in a distant corner."

"Angi, how far is the gate from this entrance?" asked Wolfram.

"A rough guess, maybe four or five hundred feet," replied Angi.

"That's far enough," replied Vette, "And we'd have to endure this for at least three hours or more. Yuk..........that's downright gruesome."

"You know," said Wolfram, thinking through their situation, "As far as this initiation is concerned, even if we sit in this outer vestibule, we are still in Chamber Six. There's no one to argue the point. So, how about we stay put for a spell to reduce our contact time with these snakes. In the meantime, we might come up with some genius solution."

"I'm all for that," replied Morgan, "The shorter the time the better."

They slid down onto the floor and the dogs curled up together. Time passed as they discussed options to get through the chamber with minimal contact with the snakes but every solution seemed flawed.

It was well past the second hour when a thought came to Angi. "We've had no contact from Sirona since the beginning of this journey. Now that we are stuck here why don't I try contacting her from this side. What do you think?" Angi wasn't about to mention her dream to avoid upsetting her companions even more. But her suggestion was precisely that, just in case the dream was about to become reality.

"Good idea, but how?" asked Wolfram.

"Now I must tell you, I've never done this before as Myttrwn had just begun teaching me how to project myself into another space when we were hijacked for this initiation. What is supposed to happen is that I go into a deep meditation and try to make contact using Myttrwn's initial instructions. All I ask is that you don't touch me while I'm in this state. The dogs will stay quiet if we are quiet."

"Well, give it a try," said Vette, "We're going nowhere in finding a solution. We will continue to tax our brain while you are trying to communicate."

"Here goes," said Angi as she crossed her legs and placed her hands across her legs, palms up. She first surrounded her body in the multi-colours of the medallion gemstones. Then the prescribed breathing exercises helped her enter a peaceful zone where she silently gave a series of commands as directed by Myttrwn. Nothing happened except the steady, familiar universal hum recorded in her ears. Having learned to be patient, she waited continuing to mumble the commands as a mantra, over and over and over again. Oblivious of time, she tumbled deeper and deeper into a meditative state, waiting. Then, unexpectedly, a bright light emerged followed by a sense of weightlessness. Into view, as if in a dream, appeared the monitoring room of the House of Life with all its people and activities.

Myttrwn, sensing a change in energy, looked up and stated calmly, "Welcome, Angi, we've been worried about you."

The others were astonished at the ghost-like image of Angi standing in their midst straining to enunciate words. Finally she articulated, "Not much time..........we're in Chamber Six...........managing.........I had a dream...........

182

Chamber Seven had flashing red lights aimed at us.........could be trouble ....can't hold," and with those final words the image evaporated.

"Remarkable," was Myttrwn's first comment.

Andrew turned to Bryce and said, "Contact at last! I won't even try to understand how she did it. But it is a warning of trouble ahead. We have to act."

"That's it," said Sirona. "Myttrwn, she's talking about lasers. Zolar meant to kill them if they even made it to Chamber Seven. I will give Corb the order. We have no time to waste."

"I agree," replied Myttrwn, "We must prepare.........." he did not complete the sentence as his mind was racing ahead.

Sirona pressed an arm communication device connecting her to the waiting crew by the emergency planes, "Corb, this is Sirona, proceed at once to the pyramid. Use every means to breakdown the exit gate."

Angi took a few minutes to pull herself out of her meditative state. Smiling she looked around to see her friends and dogs silently waiting. Vette was first to speak.

"Did you get through?" asked Vette.

"Yes, but I couldn't hold the image," replied Angi, "They know where we are and that we're about to transverse Chamber Six. Everyone looks fine. I've no idea why communications ceased."

Wolfram noticed that Angi was pale and showing signs of exhaustion but held any comment, as he thought to himself, "These so-called magic acts are draining her and we still have two chambers to go. I will be glad when this damned initiation is over."

"I don't suppose you had time to ask Sirona and Myttrwn on how we might circumnavigate the snakes?" asked Vette.

"No, I didn't have a chance," replied Angi, "And by your question I expect you haven't thought of one either."

"Nothing.............we're stumped," replied Morgan, "If you want the truth, I'd be content at sitting here until someone decides to rescue us. But that's a chicken's approach. Actually, I want to complete this initiation just to stymie Zolar's well-planned attempt at getting rid of us."

Vette, inspired by Morgan's comments, responded, "You are right Morgan, I said it before and I will say it again, that damnable man is not going to win. Come on, we are bright people, there has to be a solution."

Just then a thought popped into Angi's mind which she voiced, "What about frost? If I can create a frost the snakes might go into a deep slumber."

"Hey, that might work," said Wolfram, pleased at a breakthrough, "Then we could use our shields and push our way through groggy snakes to get to the gate."

"Fine," replied Vette, "But how long will they stay that way?"

"I've no idea," replied Angi, "But it is the only option on the table right now."

"The time is marching on," said Morgan. "If we're going to go through this chamber we have to get on with it."

"What's our time?" asked Angi.

"We've got forty minutes to the third hour," replied Vette, "And please God let this one be at the third hour or Angi will have to be pumping out frost plus bouncing us onto the next hours."

"OK, let's get started," said Wolfram, "First, make sure you are fully protected, gloves, goggles, and tight headgear. Then we will create as large a shield as we can with our Aqks. We will let Angi's frost take hold before we move in and we will keep the dogs close as they may be upset with snakes."

"They may be upset with the snakes," replied Vette in a high pitched voice, "There're not the only ones. I'm praying this will be swift sailing as I do not want to spend one second extra in this cursed place."

And so they proceeded............Angi created a fog-like frost over the entire room leaving a white haze. Most of the snakes slowed and then stopped moving.

Before entering the doorway Wolfram stated, "Morgan and I will form a v-shaped pincer movement with our shields while you two use your shields on the wings. Stay in unison as we press forward. Signal if we need to stop. Right?"

"Right," came the united reply.

"Here goes," said Wolfram, hoping against hope that their plan would work.

In a plow-like manner with the dogs tucked close, they pushed the lazy snakes aside as they edged their way towards the gate on the opposite side of the room. But all snakes were not affected by the frost, and these presented a problem. The dogs growled and barked when snakes rose above the shields or dropped on them or someone's uniform. The four were not only pushing strenuously on their shields but also flipping the occasional snake away as they made their way towards the gate. Chamber Six held every conceivable variety of snake, large and small, fat and thin, and in a variety of colours. Reaching mid-way Wolfram signalled a stop.

"Angi the frost is only hitting the top layer of snakes. Any chance you could create a snowstorm or is that asking too much?" asked Wolfram.

"Sure, I will give it a go. If I cannot manage snow I will increase the frost," replied Angi.

Within minutes snow started falling as Wolfram signaled to push on. This change resulted in them thrusting aside both snow and drowsy snakes.

But finally, they reached the gate, five minutes to the third hour.

"Thanks, Angi, the snow worked," said Vette, "Honestly, I don't think I could have imagined a worse place............this is horrid. I know little about snakes but I suspect some of these are poisonous. Thanks heavens we had these uniforms."

Sweating, Morgan asked, "If any of you are good at praying now's the hour. Please beseech God that this gate is rigged for the third hour."

On the third hour, to their relief, another mechanical voice appeared saying, "To enter the next chamber you must answer a chosen question."

"Here we go again," said Wolfram, "Well, my riddle champions, listen and coax your brains into a quick answer, as this wiggly brood won't stay calm for long."

The voice then recited the riddle: "It may only be given, not taken or bought, what the sinner desires but the enlightened do not. What is it?"

Angi, Vette and Morgan struggled, various words whispered back and forth and rejected. Time was passing.

Restless, Wolfram commented, "Hey guys, I don't want to be difficult, but for God's sake have a go at it, you have three chances."

Vette was about to speak when Angi signaled she thought she had the answer. "Go ahead," replied Vette, "My reply would just waste a turn."

Angi in a loud voice said, "Forgiveness."

"Forgiveness," repeated Morgan and Vette...... "Are you sure?"

Their question was answered with a loud click as the gate started to open. At the same moment the snakes stopped moving as if overcome by some spell.

"Let's get the hell out of here," said Wolfram anxious to escape.

"Wait," said Angi. "We all agreed that this is when Zolar would have his last shot at us. So why don't you let me take the lead. I will place a shield around myself as an extra precaution."

Not entirely comfortable with the idea, Wolfram nevertheless conceded saying, "Fine, Angi you go ahead, I will follow you with Vette and Morgan coming behind. Let's get on with it, we're almost there."

Their advancement into Chamber Seven was recorded in the House of Life by the attendants in the monitoring room and conveyed to all present.

Pyramid, Chamber 7

Chamber Seven was an exact repeat of her dream with its pitch-black room and raised altar in the distance. Skylar ran ahead as Angi nervously stepped out anticipating the worst and thinking rapidly to herself, "It is imperative I take the lead as I possess the medallion and can create a protective shield. Perhaps if I absorb whatever Zolar has devised for us it will spare the others. This has been a fantastic journey and if it is to end here, so be it." With a deep breathe she momentarily turned to see her three companions standing at the entrance ready to advance into the chamber. Taking another step, a series of laser beams, aimed directly at Angi, shattered the darkness. Skylar, sensing the danger, jumped to protect her, the laser beam striking both as they tumbled onto the chamber floor.

Wolfram reacted, yelling, "We're under attack. Angi's been hit. Vette, you and Morgan stick to this wall and at its end crawl like hell towards that altar. I'm going after Angi."

Vette and Morgan did as instructed, the laser beams dancing all around them as they crawled furiously towards the altar, their only protection.

Wolfram, under laser fire, crawled towards Angi, Dusky trying to protect him. Reaching her, he shoved the dormant carcass of Skylar off, and with all his strength dragged Angi's lifeless body across the floor towards the altar, the laser beams tracking their movements, striking the floor inches from their bodies. Reaching the altar he felt for Angi's pulse. "It is awfully weak," he thought to himself, a chill entering his body. "Hold on Angi,........Just hold on.........It is over." He looked up to see Vette and Morgan huddled at the other side of the altar away from the pulsating laser attack.

Then suddenly a bright, flash explosion engulfed the chamber causing the exit gate to collapse. A group of uniformed individuals poured in, silhouetted against the first outside light they had seen since entering the pyramid. The laser gun fire ceased. In the midst of the confusion a hand reached up and collected four crystals.

Wolfram looked up to see Corb and Dylan racing towards him with a floating emergency cubicle, "Am I glad to see you two," said Wolfram, struggling to rise, "Angi's been hit."

"We know," replied Corb, "Get her into this cubicle and come with me."

Wolfram hesitated knowing the space limitation of the planes.

"Go...........go with Corb," ordered Dylan, "The rest of the crew and I will take care of the others. We will be right behind you. Sirona and Myttrwn are waiting."

"Come on, and take your dog," yelled Corb, "We all know about Myttrwn's latest creations."

They raced to the first plane, boarded, and Corb, speaking to Myttrwn in his own language, flew to the House of Life. Upon landing Corb and Wolfram sprinted through the corridor with the floating cubicle between them, heading towards the therapy centre where Sirona and Myttrwn stood waiting.

Hardly speaking, Sirona and Myttrwn rolled the cabinet into a single therapy unit, where Sirona quickly removed Angi's belt and placed her on a floating white slab. The unit was a sophisticated harmonic structure designed to capture the planet's normal energy grid for healing purposes. It was a symphony of light and sound, which Myttrwn had programmed to the human anatomy. Small flashing pieces of technology were placed at key points on Angi's body as Sirona and Myttrwn worked feverously in assessing her condition and preparing the therapy.

Sirona's only telepathic comment to Myttrwn was, "Look at the blood on her uniform. This was no ordinary initiation."

Once Angi was prepared, Sirona and Myttrwn exited the unit, and proceeded to initiate treatment from a hi-tech panel. Through a large glass window Corb and Wolfram watched as Angi floated in mid-air surrounded by a soft humming sound and pulsating light. At that point Myttrwn, turning to speak to Wolfram, noticed he was unsteady and beginning to fall.

"Get Wolfram into the next unit at once," ordered Myttrwn. His command bringing other attendants. "Put the other two in the following units, they're all needing therapy."

Within minutes, Dylan arrived with Vette in a floating cubicle. Morgan followed in another. The dogs were running beside the floating cubicles. On a separate cubicle came the remains of Skylar, which Myttrwn ordered transported to his personal lab. With a single verbal command, Myttrwn caused the three robotic dogs to take up positions outside their owner's unit and shut down.

After Sirona and Myttrwn made sure Wolfram, Vette and Morgan were stabilized they met with the rest of the Gaia team who were standing around anxious to hear the prognosis of their colleagues.

"How's Angi?" asked a worried Andrew, knowing she was the worst off.

"I will be honest with you," replied Myttrwn, "Although, Skylar tried to protect her, Angi still received a major blow from the laser and is in critical condition. I expect she was already exhausted from the effort of getting them through the pyramid, and was likely unable to achieve the protection needed. It may take days before I can tell you more. The other three have not only been grazed by a laser but they have also sustained some physical injury which Angi has healed; Vette a leg wound, Morgan a head wound, and Wolfram an injury to his wrist. It will take time to assess their mental state. Nevertheless, they should take less time to heal." Then looking at the anxious faces in front of him he added, "I expect any comment to have you return to your residence would be pointless."

"True," replied Andrew, "Bryce and I intend staying on and will keep watch until Vette, Wolfram and Morgan have recovered and there is more positive news on Angi. We will take shifts."

"We're sticking close as well," replied Dylan, "I'm uncomfortable with Zolar floating in that adjacent unit to Angi and we're still unsure if he was working with others. These four are not getting out of our protection again."

Myttrwn admired their loyalty and determination and telepathically said to Sirona, "So be it. Let's make the necessary arrangements. This could take days. I'm equally uncomfortable with Zolar in the same area but he's unconscious and will remain so until there's word of his trial." He had hardly finished speaking to Sirona when he heard a commotion along the corridor and went to investigate.

Walking towards him was the Queen and her retinue, she was saying to Myttrwn as she approached, "I'm here to find out for myself the condition of these four individuals. I hear that Angi has been badly injured."

"Yes, Your Majesty," replied Myttrwn, "They are all in our therapy units and are stable at this point. Angi is critical."

The Queen went to Angi's unit and stood for a few minutes before speaking, "Is that blood on her uniform?"

"Yes," replied Sirona, standing close to her mother, "Her companions encountered major injuries in the pyramid which she healed. All four were also hit by the laser attack."

"I see," replied the Queen in a voice that dripped of her displeasure. "Myttrwn, you informed me that you would have a detailed record of what happened in the pyramid. I wish to see it at once," demanded the Queen.

"Very well, Your Majesty," replied Myttrwn, "It will take me a few minutes to set up."

"I will wait," said the Queen, separating herself and Sirona to speak quietly about the situation. Her retinue moved to one side of the corridor and waited.

Myttrwn gave a verbal command to Dusky, Wolfram's dog, which instantly awakened and walked over to Myttrwn. "Come with me to my lab. Each dog was equipped with a camera. We can see one version from Dusky. Later I will combine the images for a more complete review."

"May we go as well?" asked Andrew.

"Yes, bring as many as you can spare but leave your security in place," suggested the Queen. "Myttrwn, make sure the rest of the Gaia members and any others in our kingdom have a viewing. I want as many as possible to understand what happened. There will be no secrets when Zolar is tried for this crime."

Myttrwn's attendants had arranged as many chairs as possible in his restricted lab for the viewing, some decided to stand.

On a wide screen they watched a silent portrayal of the journey the four had experienced in the pyramid, Myttrwn asking periodically if the Queen would like it speeded up so they would get the essence of the ordeal without sitting through the full amount of time. Nevertheless, hours passed. It ended with the chamber of snakes, the snow and finally Chamber Seven.

The Queen stood as if to leave and hesitated, turning to the gathered audience she said, "I would like to inform our Gaia guests that the pyramid in our culture is intended to test our students not to kill them. This is a horrendous demonstration of this important aspect in our lives. Before too many days pass, I will get Sirona and Myttrwn to explain to you the extremes to which Zolar has corrupted this process. We shall talk again." And on that she left the room.

Andrew and those able to attend the first showing were aghast at what they had seen, and impressed with the ingenuity and tenacity of their team. They returned to the treatment centre to relieve the others for the next viewing determined they would all see the combined images when they were available.

Andrew speaking to Bryce before he left for the viewing, said, "We shall be forever grateful to Sirona and Myttrwn and their swift preparation of Angi, Vette, Wolfram and Morgan. Without that this would surely have been a disaster. I'm not underestimating Angi's skills, they were essential. In addition, we were blessed by Myttrwn's genius in having these dogs wired to record what was happening. I would expect the dogs have been wired for much more. When you have viewed the material we will talk again."

By the end of the second day Vette, Wolfram, Morgan had been released from the therapy units and joined their colleagues waiting for Angi to recover. Curious, they also took time to see the viewing and provided additional comments on some of the details. Watching the event proved overwhelming at times as by then they realized Angi's contribution to their survival. While waiting, Sirona enlisted Vette to gather up the uniforms and belts and got the three back into their former attire. Myttrwn, also activated the dogs, realizing the bond established in their ordeal. This resulted at times in a rather crowded corridor of people and dogs.

The third day passed with little change in Angi's prognosis. It was evident that Myttrwn and Sirona were growing anxious over the slowness of her recovery.

Late the third night Andrew arrived for his shift to find Wolfram and Dusty still sitting in front of Angi's unit, the same place they had been hours before. "You still here?" asked Andrew. "Why not take a break. Get some rest. I will come and get you if there is any change."

"I will stick around," replied Wolfram. Waiting before his next comment, he said, "You know Andrew, I just learned that Angi knew the seventh chamber could be lethal and deliberately took the lead. I should have stopped her."

"Don't start blaming yourself, my boy," came Andrew's sound advice, realizing Wolfram's sense of guilt. "Angi did the right thing. After all, she had the medallion and thought she could provide enough protection to ward off whatever Zolar had devised. What she didn't realize is that Zolar had rigged it to kill you." He let that sink in before continuing, "By the way, when are you going to let her know how you feel about her?"

The question startled Wolfram, and he responded guardedly, "Ah Andrew, I'm ten years older than Angi. She needs a younger man."

"Well you won't be able to use that argument for long," replied Andrew.

"Why not?" asked Wolfram puzzled by Andrew's remark.

"Whatever our destiny, Myttrwn is about to ask you if you and the others will agree to be physically twenty-five years old, while Bryce and myself are to be fifty. On our behalf, the decision was easy. But as always you must make this choice yourself. Apparently we have a great deal of work ahead. You are going to spend a lot of time with Angi. Does that change your mind?"

Wolfram smiled and looked at Andrew saying, "If that's the case then Angi needs to recover as I definitely have something to say to her."

The conversation dwindled as they silently continued their vigil.

&

Angi's Therapy Unit

Alone, Angi found herself in a brightly lit venue with a loud humming sound in her ears. Walking about she felt no ground beneath her feet nor any atmosphere, everything seemed neutral.

"Am I dead?" she thought to herself, "Is this what it is like? According to Myttrwn we just enter another level of consciousness. Is this it?" Then sensing another presence she asked, "Is anyone here?"

Out of the mist came a familiar voice, "Well, Angi, you have had quite a journey through the pyramid," came Adawee's introductory comment as she landed on an invisible pole.

"Ah, Adawee, you are indeed magical. Am I dead?" asked Angi, glad to have company. The piercing eyes of the Snowy Owl stared down at her.

"You are not dead, Angi, but you have been badly injured," replied Adawee. "Sirona and Myttrwn have you in a light and sound cocoon which is gently restoring your damaged cells. You will recover but it will take time. This will give you and me a chance for another chat."

"I'm glad I haven't died," replied Angi, "I'd like to see my friends again. However, if you are here talking to me then you must be able to enter my unconscious which is mysterious indeed. I'd love to know how but will let it go for now. What topic would you like to discuss this time?"

"We will begin with your pyramid initiation. What did you think of it?" asked Adawee.

"This initiation was dropped on us out of the blue and in summary was extremely arduous," replied Angi. "I'm sure Zolar stacked the deck with the ultimate objective of eliminating us, but, fortunately with the aid of Sirona and Myttrwn, my medallion and Myttrwn's dogs we survived.................or I pray we all survived."

"Your friends are fine if that's worrying you. You were the most critically injured," replied Adawee.

"Adawee could you explain why we had to go through this grueling ordeal after all we're visitors not citizens of your kingdom?" asked Angi struggling with the '*why*' of the whole nightmare.

"Would you believe that this testing was necessary and ordained?" replied Adawee.

"Ordained........by who?" asked Angi.

"By Fate..........by Destiny..........by the gods..........it doesn't matter. You had to prove to our kingdom and your own that you were worthy of this medallion and the mission ahead," replied Adawee, waiting to see how Angi would react to such news.

"Prove what?" asked Angi, shocked that she had to prove anything or was unworthy of having the medallion. After all she thought to herself, "I have the genetic code to wear this, who else would they select?"

Adawee expected the question and replied, "Prove that you could dismiss your ego and be willing to sacrifice your own life for another, or that you were willing to commit yourself to a higher purpose, or that you were willing to think in a different way, or that in the suffering you would discover more about yourself. The truth of all heroic journeys, and everyone is on a heroic journey, is that you listen to your heart and not conduct your life according to some political, social or other dogma or agenda. Conquering fear gives each individual the courage to live. The ultimate aim in life is to acquire wisdom and to serve others, however you define 'others'. Early in your life, Angi, you chose to serve others, this was just a further test to determine the depth of that commitment."

"I see," said Angi. After some thought she asked, "How did I do?"

Adawee was growing used to Angi's point-blank questions and replied,

"You did just fine. On different levels you performed superbly. But it is not over yet, you have one final test which will occur in a few days."

"Oh help, not more tests," moaned Angi, "What is it this time?"

"You will know when it appears," said Adawee, "It is not my place to tell you ahead of time."

"I've become used to your ways, Adawee. You have rules to follow. So I will wait. But I'm not looking forward to any more tests." Wanting to change the topic she asked, "Let's return to the pyramid. Do I take it that this torture test was somehow prescribed? Was it by one individual or a group?"

"Not so much arranged by anyone, as it was required at this point in time to test you and your colleagues," replied Adawee.

"Was Zolar a conscious or unconscious pawn?" asked Angi.

"I expect if that is my only two choices, I would have to say an unconscious one," replied Adawee. "He was ready to act and the setting gave him the opportunity. Zolar is an individual who possesses an overinflated ego of his own importance, and this combined with his inability to forgive life's many wounds either to himself or others made him vulnerable. In his opinion he was doing a noble act by forcing you to endure the ultimate test of this kingdom. If you succeeded then he could stand virtuously before the Council of Elders and say that the medallion was in the right hands. Of course he assumed, being from Gaia, you would fail his well-orchestrated and impossible trials which would substantiate his poor opinion of your planet and in turn undermine Sirona and Myttrwn. It was a well-constructed trap to snare a number of individuals. He will be most distressed that it failed."

"That man is downright evil in my books," stated Angi venting her frustrations.

"Evil..........now that's a topic that needs some discussion. Angi, do you believe that evil can ever be eradicated?" asked Adawee, fluffing her feathers as she repositioned herself on the stand.

"That's a tough one," replied Angi, "Throughout our recorded history many have tried to eradicate what they considered evil. For example, one war ends and another begins. One disease is brought under control or eliminated and another pops up. We live in a world of immense suffering, some having it worse than others. As I said before, our media dishes out a daily litany of local, national and international tales of woe, the list seems endless. Such news aggravates anxiety and fear in people, some get so overwhelmed they disengage from life. To answer your question, no I don't feel evil can be eradicated at least not in my lifetime."

"Have you ever thought what your world would be like devoid of evil or darkness?" asked Adawee.

"You mean if we actually achieved peace on earth.........now that would be a miracle," said Angi trying to grapple with an inconceivable concept. "It would be nice to imagine we could have a month..........or even a year.......... with no wars, disasters or heart wrenching family issues but it is hard to picture."

"No health issues either.............what about that?" asked Adawee knowing this would be a familiar topic for Angi.

"What a fantastic idea," replied Angi.

"But what about all those people involved in such activities, would they be able to find other work?" asked Adawee, probing the economic implications of such a drastic shift.

Angi still grappling with the possibilities, relied, "Oh, I expect so. Mankind would use its energies on other issues like improving our environment and the lives of all people."

"That's a noble thought. But if there was less death from disease how could you feed, clothe and house all the people?" asked Adawee.

"We can't do that now so there would have to be greater population control which would aggravate a lot of people. But still, I think less illness would still be good," replied Angi unwilling to dismiss the benefit to mankind.

Pushing harder Adawee asked, "Is there any part of you that would allow both good and evil, light and dark, the opposites to exist side by side in your world, both intended to promote spiritual growth?"

"Are you trying to tell me, Adawee, that both good and evil are necessary? That misfortune and suffering are needed in our lives?" asked Angi, a thought foreign to her upbringing.

"Go on," suggested Adawee, not wanting to interrupt Angi's train of thought.

After a few minutes Angi proceeded, "I suppose, however remote, if we didn't have evil or darkness then we would be unable to appreciate goodness and light." A pause allowed another thought to enter her mind, "You know this reminds me of a discussion I once had with a gifted artist. He insisted that there would be no great paintings without shadows. And a playwright said a theatrical performance would be boring without shadowy characters. Yet, it sounds much more alarming when applied to real life. I was brought up to believe we had to fight and eliminate evil in our society, that peace was our objective."

"Don't misunderstand me, Angi, peace is an honourable objective but all societies have evil, sorrow and inequality. If you really want to succeed in life you need to know how to live in such societies by humbly passing through them. Your primary objective is to seek wisdom and love which cannot be acquired through material acts or goods. While life offers pain and suffering, compassion allows you to open doors to its spiritual treasures."

"Does this mean that any evil I've encountered in life is there for a reason?" asked Angi, "Adawee, you are not suggesting that suffering is good for me?"

"I think you already know the answer to that question, Angi," replied Adawee, pushing the topic a bit further. "You must admit, it is often in moments of greatest darkness or sorrow that you learn the most in life. Why is it that when people gather they dwell on their most negative memories?"

"Ah, I see. Because that is when they have encountered the best about themselves or those around them and some have received actual miracles under such circumstances. Just look at me, at my darkest hour of losing my grandmother and finding out I might die, this whole group of people appeared. They have become my new family."

"That is true, Angi. It is as if the cosmos receives a signal to join in the journey and comes bearing gifts such as the kindness of strangers or the opening of unexpected doors."

"I now know where this discussion is headed. You are leading me right back to Zolar aren't you?" asked Angi.

"I suppose so," replied Adawee, "What are your thoughts now on his role in your present ordeal?"

"If I have understood this conversation, Zolar was a willing pawn in my destiny. He was prepared to use his power and position to harm us just to nurture his ego. The risk was that he would substantiate his argument that we were unworthy of this medallion and whatever mission Sirona and Myttrwn was about to propose. He would succeed in holding back the Earth's advancement, and would have done it according to his interpretation of your kingdom's rules. He likely felt that in the end he would be richly rewarded for his actions. Of course, egotists never contemplate the alternative. If we succeeded then all his plans would have backfired."

"Very good, Angi, you are growing in wisdom. The cosmos wants you to succeed and in your dream world you are given the means to accomplish it. In the end you will be judged on how you perform during both the highs and the lows. Now remember there is one final test which will arise in the next few days," said Adawee, a signal she was about to depart.

"Very well, I will remember," replied Angi, not convinced she was up to any more trials. "But before you disappear, can you tell me when I can let my friends know about you. I was hoping this might happen before we entered the pyramid."

"Soon, Angi. I will appear in person to you and your friends. Then you will know who I am."

"Fine, ...I'm sorry you have to leave me here alone but understand, you likely have other duties," replied Angi, suddenly feeling drowsy.

"Rest, Angi. Let the therapy repair your body. It is always a pleasure talking with you." And with that she disappeared leaving Angi alone with her thoughts.

ࢭ

The Palace

A private meeting was initiated by the Queen with Sirona and Myttrwn to discuss the pyramid fiasco. They gathered in the Queen's residence, sitting around a small table overlooking an interior garden. The garden, designed with meticulous attention to grandeur and scent, filled the venue with an exotic perfume. On the Queen's orders, all servants had been dismissed to give them privacy.

The Queen began, "This scandalous situation has disgraced our kingdom. Zolar deliberately submitted our guests to an outrageous ordeal. My first mistake was accepting his word that it would be a basic initiation. I thought by agreeing to this it might silence any Council members resistant to our contact with Gaia. I was wrong. If it hadn't been for your quick action in providing them with special clothing and tools the outcome could have been disastrous irrespective of Angi's abilities. Have you anything further to add?"

Sirona understanding her mother's anguish, replied, "Perhaps we were all at fault and too dismissive of Zolar's motives. He certainly concealed his resentment over the post-plague demotion of his family's prestige centuries ago and his evident anti-Gaia stance. I thought it was his usual obsessive and rigid attitude to rules and resistance to change which orchestrated his actions. I now realize that his hatred and fanaticism ran far deeper than anyone could have imagined. Ignoring the decision of the Council, he took matters into his own hands and formulated a plan to murder our guests to prevent the medallion from ever being used. This will have far reaching diplomatic implications. Somehow he thought by killing himself he would escape punishment. Our screening methods certainly slipped up on this one."

Myttrwn, contemplating his reply, stepped in as Sirona finished, "You know I even mentioned the plague in my early talks with our Gaia guests fearing they might encounter some negativity outside the palace grounds. I never thought it would be smoldering right under our nose. This situation has highlighted several problems. First, Zolar was able to block his deepest thoughts for years which means that others may be doing the same thing. That is something I must think about as it pertains to our security. Second,

Zolar was able to reprogram the entire pyramid and create a lethal initiation program without a single whisper of suspicion. We must never let this happen again. My skilled technicians are presently stripping down his handiwork to reset the pyramid. I only hope that this has not frightened our students from considering their own initiation. My technicians are also making strides at unscrambling Zolar's communication blocks so we can prevent this in the future. This has definitely been a wakeup call for all of us."

Adding to Myttrwn's comments the Queen said, "We must also thoroughly review the role of Director of the House of Learning and the rules governing the school and initiation programs. In the meantime, Myttrwn, the Council and I would like you to assume temporary charge of the school until we've had time to make other arrangements."

"As you wish, Your Majesty," replied Myttrwn.

"Next, have you had time to explain to our Gaia guests that this was not our usual initiation process?" asked the Queen.

"Yes," replied Sirona, "Except for Angi who is still recovering."

"I will count on you Sirona to make sure she is fully informed as she has been the most damaged by this, a matter which greaves me greatly."

Sirona nodded.

"Now, how is Zolar?" asked the Queen, her voice raised at the mention of his name. "We must transfer him at once to more secure quarters pending his trial. He will remain under strict security and be checked frequently to prevent any possibility of him escaping the full weight of the law of this kingdom."

"I will attend to this at once," replied Sirona, "He will be moved to a palace security cell and remain under guard."

"Myttrwn, is he well enough to be moved?" asked the Queen.

"At present he's in a semi-conscious state but I can reverse that," replied Myttrwn. "I will work with Sirona to get him transferred. My only request is that I be able to see him on a regular basis to assess his mental and physical state. Once he learns of the failure of his plans he may fall into a deep depression and make another attempt on his life. He will surely know what lies ahead, a humiliating life for a proud man."

"Proud indeed," replied the Queen, displaying little sympathy, "If it wasn't for such pride he would not have resorted to such treachery. He not only considered himself above the law, he also believed he could defy a decision of his monarch and Council. Action like this leads to anarchy. The question is whether the four from Gaia will agree to face Zolar as is our custom. What do you think?"

Sirona thought before replying, "It may be a lot to ask. I'm not sure they will have recovered sufficiently to face him. Myttrwn, you have a better understanding of their condition, what do you think?"

"Don't underestimate them," was Myttrwn's immediate reply, "I definitely think they should be asked. If they agree, then may I suggest a smaller audience? The full Council might be a bit intimidating."

"Myttrwn, if you approach the four, I will press for a smaller audience," replied the Queen. "I would prefer they face Zolar in keeping with our laws, but I will accept whatever they decide. They have been through enough. Now let's move to a more pleasant topic. Myttrwn, I've been most impressed with your robotic dogs. Will you be able to repair Angi's dog?"

"I'm working on Skylar right now," replied Myttrwn, "The dog absorbed a major portion of the laser blast. What has surprised me is how much the dogs have bonded with these four. When I took the three dogs to download their recording information, the moment the procedure was over they were standing at the door wanting to return. Equally, the three from Gaia have insisted the dogs be with them at all times. Now I understand this may be a post-trauma reaction but, I may have quite a job disengaging them when it is time for the four to return to Earth."

"I'm sure you'll solve that," said the Queen with a smile. "So, you now have three records of the pyramid events?"

"Actually I have four, I was able to retrieve a lot more from Skylar than I expected," replied Myttrwn. "I will have that combined record for Your Majesty by the end of the day."

"This video record will be vital evidence at Zolar's trial," said the Queen, "As such, will you make sure a copy is stored in a secure location?"

"I've already attended to that," replied Myttrwn, fully aware that everyone was still unsure if Zolar had other accomplices.

The Queen then shifted the conversation asking, "Myttrwn how is Angi? I know cases vary but it has been days."

"She is recovering but slowly," replied Myttrwn, "I'm more assured of her recovery now than when she was first admitted. Exhausted, she was unable to establish a strong enough shield, so took a severe laser hit."

"I have reviewed her actions several times on that preliminary copy of the pyramid activities you gave me and was impressed with what she could do. Myttrwn, did Angi learn all this since her arrival in Tir na nOg?" asked the Queen.

"Your Majesty, that is the most astounding part of this and why I requested this meeting. As I previously mentioned to Sirona, my instructions seem to be tapping into some form of preprogramming within Angi. You watched her heal her companions, this is something I had not seen before but Sirona reported she did this prior to arriving in our kingdom. With regard to time shifting, we had just managed a one hour shift but you witnessed her doing double two hour shifts as if she had been doing it for years. The snow was never discussed. But the most astounding feature was her projection of her essence from within the pyramid into the monitoring room of the House of Life. I had just begun that discussion briefly mentioning the steps and commands, but we never performed the feat. Yet, she did it on her own."

"How is that possible?" asked the Queen.

"That is a mystery I cannot explain," replied Myttrwn

"That must be a first," smiled the Queen, "You mean to tell me in your vast years of life you have never encountered this before?"

"I have not," replied Myttrwn, "And at my age, this is an exciting conundrum. But I have more."

"Go on," replied the Queen, as she noted the smile on Sirona's face.

"Delving into this mystery I have made some intriguing discoveries. Let me first show you a comparison of Sirona's and Angi's DNA." With that he conjured up a screen displaying the comparison.

The Queen looked at the information for a few minutes before commenting, "This is not possible."

"I can assure Your Majesty, that these results have been tested many times with the same results. You will also note a comparison I have made with yourself and your two sons." More details appeared.

The Queen kept examining the data and finally asked, "How can that be? We've had no contact with that planet for generations. Is it possible the medallion changed her DNA?"

"To our knowledge there has been no contact with Gaia, and there is no evidence of genetic engineering or anything else. I have considered the medallion but realized her DNA had to be sufficient in the first place for her to even wear the item without dire consequences. But this is but the first mystery," said Myttrwn.

"There's more?" asked the Queen, already uneasy with the first revelation.

"I would like you to look at Angi's vibrational profile," asked Myttrwn bringing up more scientific data. "You will note the odd pattern here," as he pointed out the anomaly, "This has never appeared on any other profile I have ever examined. Let me show you a few familiar ones like mine, Sirona's and your two sons."

"None of them has this anomaly except Angi?" asked the Queen.

"None that I know of. And before you ask I have already checked the vibrational patterns of known medallion wearers in our kingdom. They too have no sign of this," replied Myttrwn.

"Are you telling me Myttrwn, that Angi, for some mysterious reason, possesses a DNA profile similar to our royal household and in addition also has this unusual vibrational profile? Are you also implying that it is this vibrational anomaly which gives her some innate ability at mastering the complex technology in her medallion?"

"That is my conclusion so far," replied Myttrwn, "But, Your Majesty, I advise caution. Because of the implications of this information I believe it should be held in the strictest secrecy. I am unsure as to what it means or what it may mean for our future relationship with Gaia. The remotest possibility is that Angi is some form of cosmic anomaly and that we have entered a more elevated arena than we first thought."

"Elevated..........you mean we may have slipped into the realm of the Seven Sages. We haven't had contact with them in centuries. Why now?" questioned the Queen.

"It is an assumption only, one which I cannot answer, except to say our relationship with Gaia may have greater significance than we thought," replied Myttrwn.

"Indeed..........I must discuss this further in private with Sirona and my sons," said the Queen, with a puzzled look on her face. "Myttrwn, you have presented a very complex set of issues for which there are no easy answers. I will need your expertise again. It would be easier if one of the Sages could appear to confirm your suspicions, but I suppose that's expecting the impossible. In the meantime, can you ask the four if they will face Zolar?"

"I am always at your service, Your Majesty, and I will discuss the matter with the four. But may I make one more suggestion," Myttrwn knew it had to be said.

"I thought you had given me sufficient for one day, but go ahead, what is it?" asked the Queen.

"We need to recognize the four in some way as, officially, they did complete the initiation and brought back the four crystals. I mention this because as their pyramid journey is being watched by others, it will become common knowledge that our guests from Gaia were forced to endure a far worse testing than we demand of our advanced students."

"I will think about it," replied the Queen understanding the diplomatic significance of Myttrwn's suggestion. "And what about the other Gaia members? Maybe we can do something on their last week with us."

"That would be a perfect occasion," replied Myttrwn, as he prepared to leave. He was well versed on the protocol of such meetings.

"Very well, we have much to think about and the days are drifting by. We will need to have more meetings on this. Myttrwn, keep me posted on Angi's condition. I will be relieved when she is out of therapy," was her parting comment.

"So will I," replied Myttrwn, leaving Sirona and her mother in an animated conversation over the anomalies and their implications to the royal family.

&

The House of Life & the Palace

Wolfram with his dog, Dusky, arrived at Angi's therapy unit to find it empty. He stared in disbelief, morbid thoughts clouding his mind. "Oh God, tell me it isn't so. She's just been moved...........But why?........Where?" Before he had time to conjure up any gruesome possibilities, Andrew appeared.

"I've been looking for you, my boy," said Andrew noting the grim expression on Wolfram's face, "Cheer up, its good news. She's just down the corridor. Myttrwn felt she was well enough to transfer to an ordinary bed. He's most insistent that she rest but we're all so delighted she's better that he's going to need a bugle to get our attention. Come on, let's join the others."

When Andrew and Wolfram arrived Angi was sitting up in bed surrounded by people and dogs. Pale but cheery she looked up to acknowledge their arrival by saying, "Wolfram my hero. I hear you gallantly dragged me, under laser fire, across the chamber to safety. My dearest thanks." She wanted to say more but would reserve it for later when she could speak to him alone.

"My pleasure," replied Wolfram, making a pretend bow. Jubilant that she was no longer floating silently in a closed unit, he watched as others chatted about trivial matters all seeking her attention.

Sirona and Myttrwn, having been in Myttrwn's lab, noted the boisterous activities at Angi's room. "Good news travels fast," said Sirona with a smile, "It is clear there has been a lot of worried people, including you and me."

Myttrwn, walking slowly behind her, responded, "They deserve a break, this will do a great deal to relieve their worries."

"It'll be difficult to get them to leave," said Sirona.

"I will rely on Angi," replied Myttrwn, "With her background she'll know the importance of rest and will find a gentle way to guide them."

As they reached the doorway, Sirona entered first, saying, "It is good to see our prized patient out of the light and sound unit. Myttrwn has informed me you will need extra rest before joining your colleagues back at the House of Learning."

"It is great to see you Sirona," said Angi, with a warm smile, "I was not sure I would make it. It was a fascinating experience being treated with light and sound while floating in mid-air. But first I must say that our survival in the pyramid had everything to do with you and Myttrwn. Thanks, seems such a small word at times like this. I hear there's a recording of our pyramid adventure. When I'm able I'd like to see it." Then looking around the room she added, "It is so good to know everyone came through this ordeal, but with one exception," and glancing at Myttrwn asked, "How is Skylar?"

"Ask her yourself," said Myttrwn as he released Skylar who dashed immediately to Angi's bedside.

Angi's face lit up as she hugged her dog, "Oh Skylar, my dear, dear Skylar......... It was your weight on my chest that I felt in my dream, totally unaware that you were trying to save me." Then looking up at Myttrwn she continued, "Myttrwn, I don't know what we would have done without your dogs. They served so many roles. Right from the start they were programmed to protect us. I can't believe they're robots. You are a fantastic magician."

Myttrwn, pleased by such appreciation, was surprised by his feeling of gladness at Angi's recovery, his thoughts eliciting an unexpected caution, "After so many centuries I almost forgot the joys of Gaia, but I must take care. I will be of little use if I allow my emotions to cloud my thinking. Right now I must convey the Queen's request." Unsure of their reaction he proceeded, "I have a question I need the four of you to ponder. It is a custom in this kingdom that the victim face his or her perpetrator prior to an official trial. While the Queen would like you to do this, there is some room to maneuver. Perhaps you would like time to think about it?"

Andrew was the first to react, "Myttrwn, you are asking them to face Zolar who tried to kill them not once but numerous times in that pyramid. Isn't that a bit steep? Angi is still recovering. But, it is their decision not mine, they must reply to the Queen."

"That's it," thought Angi. "Adawee's final test. But do I have the strength to face Zolar? I'm not sure. Right now I am weak and vulnerable. I will play for time and get stronger. I don't want to give Zolar the upper hand. If this is their custom, however difficult, I must comply." Before the others had a chance to respond Angi spoke, "I don't need more time. I will do it but I would like to be stronger before I face Zolar, if that's OK."

"If Angi's game, I will do it as well," said Vette, "Actually, I would like to have a few minutes to tell Zolar what I think of his diabolical plot against the innocent."

"I'm also in," said Wolfram, "Let's do it. It will bring closure to a negative piece of this trip. It is Angi's call as to when."

"If they are going, so am I," said Morgan, "We have walked through hell together and we will face Zolar together."

"In that case, include the rest of us," added Andrew, "From this point we're travelling as a mob, no more divide and conquer."

Pleased, Myttrwn responded, "That settles it. I will inform the Queen at once and the date will be conditional on Angi's recuperation. Just one point, I must ask that you not discuss your reply with anyone until the scheduled event, this must be your own thoughts."

"Agreed," came the reply from all four.

Myttrwn was impressed with their courage and willingness to participate in a custom of their kingdom, it would also endear them to the Council.

By this point all the excitement had drained Angi. She fell back on her pillow and closed her eyes.

"I guess that's our signal," said Myttrwn, gently waving his hand for everyone to exit and in a whisper said, "From this point I would ask that you come and go in small numbers with but one exception, Skylar can stay as long as she wants." Skylar hearing her name wagged her tail.

The Queen was gratified by their response and proceeded to make the necessary arrangements, holding the date and time open for Myttrwn to specify. During the interim, late one night Zolar was transferred to a Palace security unit. As the days passed Angi grew stronger, eventually taking walks along the corridor holding the arm of one or another of her Gaia friends. The dogs scampered about, sticking close to their masters. Dylan and his team continued guard duty still uncertain the danger was over.

By the time their face-to-face meeting with Zolar was announced, Angi had returned to her suite in the House of Learning. On the scheduled morning, Sirona's plane landed on the plaza to fly them to the Palace. Corb, once again their pilot, warmly greeted the four pyramid survivors as they entered the plane. Anxious, the entire group said little en route.

For the first time the group from Gaia was escorted into the Council of Elders Chamber, catching glimpses of its splendor as they walked to the front. As agreed, the Queen had assembled a smaller audience of Advisors and Elders to witness the event. On this occasion the Queen was already seated on the royal throne when they arrived. Sirona, Myttrwn, Angi, Vette, Wolfram and Morgan stood in a single line in the space between the throne and the front seats of the Chamber, where the rest of the Gaia team were sitting. Everyone waited.

At the sound of a gong, and under guard, Zolar was escorted into the Chamber to a position directly in front of the six standing individuals, in clear view of the Queen and Chamber members. Zolar was attired in a pale yellow uniform, with no visible restraints. His former appearance and manner had drastically changed. Standing with his head bowed, he seemed a broken man. Once in position, the two guards stepped back leaving Zolar exposed.

Sirona had agreed to lead the proceedings and spoke in a clear voice for all to hear, "According to the laws of Tir na nOg, the victim of any crime has the right to face his or her perpetrator before the official trial. Everyone here is well aware of what transpired in the pyramid involving our four guests from Gaia. They will now each have the opportunity to speak directly to Zolar, starting with Angi Talismann, followed by Vette Gallant, then Wolfram Stark and finally Morgan Mandelthrope. Zolar may respond to each individual if he so wishes." Then turning, she explained for the sake of those from Gaia, "Everyone gathered is either conversant in English or has been given an interpretative device. So, begin Angi when you are ready."

The previous night in a dream Angi had a visit from her grandmother who said, "Remember Angi, when life inflicts wounds as it will, be quick to forgive. Do not let anyone saddle you with guilt or hatred, for both will damage your soul. First, forgive yourself, then forgive the other person or persons. Carry no baggage. Walk on. Allow time to help you heal and grow from the experience." These words, indelibly etched in her heart, strengthened Angi's resolve.

Fully recovered, Angi stepped forward to face Zolar saying, "Zolar, I'm sorry my presence caused you such turmoil. I entered your kingdom in peace. Neither I nor any of my colleagues caused the plague that affected your family centuries ago. What you did not know was that our planet lost millions of its own people during this same catastrophe. After such global calamities people move on without wasting energy blaming any single person or group of people for such misery. During our stay in your kingdom you made no effort to communicate with us. In your mind we were the enemy. That was a tragic mistake. We survived your attempt on our lives with the help of Sirona and Myttrwn, the medallion and our own courage. Your own laws will judge you for this attempt on our lives. As for me, I seek nothing from you. I forgive you and honestly hope you find peace sometime in the future." With those words she stepped back.

Zolar raised his head slightly, looked at Angi, a sign of bewilderment etched on his face, but he said nothing.

The next to speak was Vette who stepped forward saying, "Zolar, I'm not as gentle or charitable as my friend Angi. I would honestly like to tell you precisely what I think, but will restrain myself. We meant you no harm yet you went to considerable effort to concoct a deadly plan to kill us not once but a number of times to satisfy your own egotistical, and I might say, psychotic imaginings. We too have family that would be most upset if we failed to return home. I am more upset over what you tried to do to my friends than for myself. We did not deserve any of this. I pray that you will be scrupulously judged by your own laws and face the full punishment you deserve. But, like Angi, I forgive you for I will be damned if I want to drag you along with me the rest of my life," and she stepped back.

Zolar again raised his head and looked at Vette as her forceful words had penetrated his stoic silence but he still said nothing.

Next came Wolfram who stepped forward and said, "Zolar, I am also more infuriated over your well planned plot to willfully kill my friends. You formed your own conclusions about us without making any effort in getting to know us. I do not believe for a moment that the kingdom's safety was uppermost in your thinking. No, it was your own ego nurtured by a smoldering hatred over lost privilege and wealth resulting from an ancient event which motivated your actions. You let this control your thoughts to the point that killing four people was, in your mind, fully justified. Basically, you used your senior position to try and execute us. It failed due to the intercession of Sirona and Myttrwn and Angi's growing expertise with her medallion. I learned years ago that retaliation is for suckers. I will not allow you to do any more damage to my life, so, like Angi and Vette, I too will forgive you. May the laws in your country exact its full punishment for your criminal behaviour," and he stepped back.

This time Zolar looked up at Wolfram, doubt dawning on his face. He seemed just about to speak but hesitated and lowered his head in silence.

Finally Morgan stepped forward saying, "Zolar I would like to thank you for giving me the opportunity of seeing inside your pyramid. It was something I thought about when I first glimpsed it upon our arrival. However, I regard your diabolical plot to kill us as both stupid and psychologically demented. We did nothing to warrant this. In your egotistical mind you created the problem and became the judge and executioner with no regard for anyone not even your own kingdom. I'm sure your actions will have diplomatic ramifications which will take years to unwind. For these crimes you must pay and your kingdom will execute their own laws. As for me, I join my friends and will forgive you hoping that, if your life is spared, you will eventually find peace," and Morgan stepped back.

Zolar looked up at Morgan, holding his gaze for a moment as if wanting to justify his actions, but resigned himself to silence.

Sirona and Myttrwn glanced at each other. The response from the four was more than they could have imagined. The four stood together and forgave their oppressor without any words of anger. Sirona closed the session with, "Zolar, you have been forgiven by your intended victims. This has been recorded and will be taken into account at your trial. In the meantime you will remain in prison until your official trial. Do you wish to make any final comment to the four?"

Zolar, for the last time, looked out on the Council of Elders, the place where he had known honour and prestige. At that moment a sickening feeling engulfed him as he realized, by his own volition, he had forfeited everything. There would be no rewards, the faces of former Elder colleagues registered disgust not honour. He shook his head indicating he would not comment and turning followed his guards out of the Chamber.

It had been a tense occasion and when Zolar left there was silence as everyone gathered their thoughts. Into this vacuum a Snowy Owl with rainbow feathers appeared landing on a metal bar near the Queen. Startled, the Queen's guards reacted as if to attack the owl only to find themselves paralyzed, unable to move.

"Adawee," exclaimed Angi, "You did come. Now I can introduce you to my friends."

"Adawee," whispered Morgan to Wolfram, "That's a Cherokee word for 'Guardian of Wisdom.' I wonder why Angi never mentioned a Snowy Owl. Angi never ceases to amaze. This should be interesting."

Adawee began speaking in a voice easily heard and understood by everyone in the Chamber, "I come in peace. I chose the owl costume for Angi so that we could have quiet chats together. The costume is from her world. I wanted to get to know this young woman with the miraculous medallion. In our chats I have learned a great deal about her and her world. I was the one who asked her not to say anything until it was time.......... That time has come."

At that moment the image of the Snowy Owl began to dissolve, being replaced first by a whirling rainbow ball which elongated into a glittering rainbow light out of which stepped a woman.

Angi for the first time came face to face with Adawee, a calming voice that she had grown fond of. Before her stood a slim woman, slightly taller than Sirona, of indiscriminate age. She had shoulder length, white hair, green eyes, a markedly calm expression, and was wearing a loose fitting, silk-like gown with no ornamentation.

Myttrwn, recognizing the woman, went to greet her as he was the only one in the Council of Elders Chamber who had met her before.

"It is good to see you again Myttrwn," said Adawee, "It has been a long time. I'm here today to inform you of our support for greater contact with Gaia. You shall learn much from each other. I can confirm that Angi and her colleagues have been well chosen. We will guide you in this venture for it has cosmic implications." Then realizing the impact her presence was having on the assembled audience she added, "I expect it might be helpful if you, Myttrwn, took a moment to inform everyone who I am, as most in this room I have never contacted or met in person."

"It is my honour," replied Myttrwn, in a slight bow. Then turning to the audience he said, "May I introduce you to Adawee, who is one of the Seven Sages of our universe. The Sages are highly enlightened and evolved individuals who exist mainly in spirit but, on rare occasions, appear in person.

The last time I met Adawee was five centuries ago when we in this kingdom were facing insurmountable difficulties."

"Thank you Myttrwn," replied Adawee, in a musical voice. "As on previous occasions, I shall provide everyone in the room with a firm mental memory of this day, to guide them in the future. As you work together resistance in both worlds must be expected as change is difficult, if not insurmountable, for some." Then turning she sought out her favourite, "Angi, you will need Myttrwn's guidance in mastering the medallion's powers for there are layers of complex and subtle energies to command. We shall continue to chat, but I will appear in this form from now on. Your initiation is over and now your true destiny is about to begin. But before I leave, I would like to meet everyone in the Chamber for all of you will become partners in this cosmic mission."

Adawee, with Myttrwn's help, walked about first speaking with the Queen, then Sirona and then each individual, addressing each by name and conveying an amazing depth of knowledge about their lives. Later they would say that in shaking her hand they received a powerful transfer of positive energy. No one was anxious to leave such an extraordinary event.

Before disappearing Adawee communicated telepathically to the Queen, Sirona and Myttrwn, saying, "The anomaly you have discovered in Angi's vibrational profile needs to be kept secret. It has a future purpose. Under Myttrwn's guidance Angi will become a gifted master of this medallion." With the visit completed Adawee evaporated in a rainbow mist.

The aura of the occasion lingered long after her departure, each person wanting to savour the moment. Eventually, individuals began to disperse, the group from Gaia anxious to pump Angi about her chats with one of the Seven Sages of the universe.

Andrew spoke quietly to Bryce as they walked towards their plane, "Today, any lingering doubts I may have had about this journey have been washed away. We have just encountered another dimension. I wonder how many there are."

"Endless," replied Bryce, struggling to grasp the day's events, "Just imagine the reaction on Earth as we try to explain this even to our 'special' societies. Do you think anyone will believe us?"

"Perhaps not," replied Andrew with a chuckle, "It reminds me of those adventurers in our past, trying to convince a home audience of the marvels of the New World. But we have one ace in the hole, we have Angi and that unbelievable medallion. You know Bryce, I am bursting with excitement and anxiety as to what lies ahead, and it fills me with incredible energy to live on."

Chapter 11

House of Learning

Their return to Earth was rapidly approaching. Respect for the Gaia team had escalated following the events of the Pyramid Initiation, and the arrival of one of the Seven Sages. They had survived an extraordinary pyramid ordeal and had forgiven their perpetrator, all in keeping with Tir na nOg practices. Adawee's arrival sealed their acceptance, they now belonged. Having Myttrwn in charge of both Houses also improved the situation.

While Sirona and Myttrwn negotiated a date for a departure celebration, Morgan took charge of re-establishing their music practice routine in conjunction with Carola who was still aiming for perfection. Their absorption in music was healing as they continued to work through the physical and mental after effects of recent events. Non-musical members returned to their previous activities as arranged by Sirona. Exceptions included Angi who was back with Myttrwn augmenting her medallion training and the four dogs who went everywhere with their owners, becoming celebrities within the royal hilltop compound. Evening gatherings were noisy as they sifted through their time in Tir na nOg and reset their minds for going home.

One evening as they sat around the dining table Dylan blurted out, "You know, I'm going to miss this place. I never thought I'd be saying that. After the first hiccups I've begun to understand and appreciate the Tir na nOg perspective on life and certainly respect their self-control. Admittedly, I'm still grappling with their telepathic abilities. Yet, I've also learned that even in this well ordered world there are individuals like Zolar who can become a danger to others. I expect there are others."

"That's something coming from you," replied Wolfram. "Dylan, you've been transformed. I also noted your keen interest in those small planes. I'm also impressed at how easily they perform. Can you imagine if we had planes that operated on the thoughts of pilots..........I must ask Corb if there were any accidents in the early days of piloting planes by thought control. It is fascinating to watch Corb operate such technology so efficiently. By the way he has informed me that he and possibly three others may be returning with us, has anyone else heard this rumor?"

"Yes, Myttrwn has hinted as much to me," came Andrew's reply, "Apparently the Hill of Tara gate is too exposed for easy transportation at this time. So, they are thinking of burying that gate in an underground tunnel. Such tunnels seem to exist all over our planet, which was news to me. They'll secure the main gate under the Hill of Tara while creating a temporary one under my castle in Scotland. I'm all for it but still have few details."

"I've come to trust and appreciate the care and learning provided by Myttrwn and will miss this when we get back to Earth," said Angi. "I'm trying to convince him to visit us which he seems to be willing to consider. Imagine the changes he'll encounter when he returns to Earth. I will let you know if he makes any positive comment on this."

Vette, patted Rafie, then changed the topic saying, "I know these darling dogs won't be coming home with us. I will miss Rafie. Maybe Myttrwn might allow them a visit at your castle in Scotland, Andrew. I know they'll be here when we visit, whenever that may be."

"Yah, the dogs," said Morgan looking sadly at Macky. "I will really feel bad leaving her here, I have never had a dog like this.............actually this is my first dog. It is amazing how much peace and security they bring. Why don't we ask Myttrwn about a visit?"

Andrew not wanting to take lightly their growing bond with the dogs replied, "We can ask but I'm sure they have to stay here. It would be quite a sensation if they were discovered on Earth. Robotic dogs like these would certainly stand out."

"I agree with Vette and Morgan," said Wolfram. "I'm really going to miss Dusky. She's been a great companion in recent days. I never thought I'd grow so close to an animal so quickly..........robotic or otherwise."

"Myttrwn truly knew what to create to protect us," said Angi patting Skylar. Then looking at Andrew she pleaded, "Can you try to convince Myttrwn, Andrew, that we might have the dogs visit us, if the time between trips is going to be lengthy."

"I will try, but understand, there are rules for such things," replied Andrew.

"Now that we're over this pyramid episode and being introduced to a Sage from another dimension, perhaps Angi might fill us in on her training status with Myttrwn. Angi, I was wondering what happens to your training when you return to Earth? If you don't have Myttrwn is there any danger your skills might atrophy?" asked Wolfram.

"That is a good point Wolfram, I will have to ask him," replied Angi. "It might be another incentive for his visit. I realize now there's years of work ahead no matter how positive Myttrwn seems to be about my progress. As Adawee stated, this advanced technology has layers and layers of subtle scientific programming which I will need to learn and manage. I suppose this begs the inevitable question, has anyone any idea what we are expected to do with all this information and my medallion, when we get back home. Have Sirona or Myttrwn said anything to you Andrew?"

"They've been very secretive," replied Andrew, "The few hints I've received are Myttrwn's insistence that we need to be physically younger because of the amount of work which, to me, speaks of decades. In addition, as mentioned before, my castle in Scotland is to become a new gateway, as there will be a lot of coming and going between our two planets. However, the main objective remains a mystery. You can be sure Myttrwn does not waste time or energy for no purpose, so whatever it is I expect we shall be kept busy for a long time."

"Knowing Myttrwn, he'll hold that card until the last minute, then will ask each one of us if we will personally volunteer for the role," said Wolfram with a grin. "I truly appreciate their constant insistence that each individual makes his or her own decision and not go through life like sheep. The one thing I've noticed is that life here while appearing tranquil is downright serious. Those young people in this House of Learning are fully committed to their studies and know precisely what service they will render to their community after graduating, or whatever they call it. Somehow, in our world, we have lost that sense of responsibility and service commitment to society unless it is tied to money."

"You are right Wolfram, we have been privileged at seeing a different way of life, and given an understanding that Earth is heading in a similar direction if we don't self-destruct first. All that is positive," replied Andrew.

"Maybe that's it," exclaimed Angi. "If the Earth is moving onward in its Dwapara Yuga, then perhaps we're going to have some role in assisting it along that path."

"That's a bit daunting," piped up Vette, "How are we going to achieve such a lofty goal being such a small group on a planet fraught with so much social and political upheaval?"

"That doesn't prevent us from trying," came Bryce's calm intercession, "Our past history has shown that it is often a single individual or a small group that does achieve the best results. I could list a number but you are all well acquainted with them. We may be small in number but with the help from Tir na nOg we could achieve quite a bit. Andrew and I have many contacts which, I know, will be willing to assist us. If we move carefully with a well thought out plan it may take time but it is better than doing nothing.

No one is asking for miracles, just a beginning...........like planting seeds in a garden."

"Well spoken, old friend," replied Andrew, "Before arriving in this fair kingdom we hardly knew each other. I admit, back on Earth we travelled together but that doesn't mean we were fully acquainted with one another. Here we've knitted as a group, perhaps even coming together as a family. Adawee insisted we were all chosen, and I believe her. We came together bearing different gifts, with Angi having the most because of her medallion. Let's keep an open mind and see what Sirona and Myttrwn have to say. Remember what Adawee said, this venture is important for both planets. So as we are sitting here pondering the next steps, I bet there's an equal discussion going on at the palace."

"Does anyone know what will happen to Zolar?" asked Wolfram, "Just interested in how this plays out on another planet."

Andrew immediately responded, "I've heard nothing specific except that Myttrwn hinted that at worst he might receive the ultimate punishment of death but expected, because of your forgiveness, he would be expelled to an outer inhospitable planet to spend the rest of his days, which for him could be considerable. His trial will not occur until well after we're gone. Bryce and I didn't have much time to delve into their laws, but what little we discovered is that such exile is a devastating sentence for anyone let alone someone who held such power and responsibility as Zolar. I've got little sympathy for the man as he planned your deaths in that pyramid. He'll have lots of time to ponder his actions."

"You know, Adawee said our pyramid initiation was ordained," came Angi's off-handed statement, remembering her prior discussion.

"Ordained, by who?" asked Vette. "Zolar.........or is that too obvious?"

"Actually, it was needed to prove we were rightly chosen for whatever role lies ahead," came Angi's philosophical reply. "Apparently, Zolar was a willing pawn to execute the trials."

The comment registered with Bryce who responded, "Now that's a fascinating theory and one that fits the stories of chosen heroes in our past. Remember those myths you once read? The heroes and heroines needed to be not only chosen but also tested ....that's one of the basic rules in mythology. Yes, now that I think of it this would fit that scenario perfectly. You had to be tested as you four will be leading this upcoming mission. The rest of us are your support team. Now all we have to find out is the purpose of the mission itself."

"By George, you are right on target, Bryce," replied an excited Andrew, "The pyramid testing was essential for these four. Their suffering is part of the process. Why didn't I see it? We've somehow stepped back in time to an era when such things were well understood even on Earth. In our modern world no one volunteers to be put through agony just to prove they are the rightful heir to a mysterious mission." And standing up he turned to the four who were sitting together saying, "May I take this opportunity to present to all of you our two heroines and two heroes for the journey ahead. Destiny has chosen them and we are fortunate to be their travelling companions. Admittedly, past myths had single heroes so having four must mean the task will be indeed challenging."

Surprised, and showing signs of embarrassment the four looked at each other not knowing what to say. Angi spoke first.

"That's very kind of you Andrew but I believe the title of heroine doesn't quite flash to mind for me. I admit I've had some mysterious happenings over the past few months, but still do not equate any of this to such a lofty conclusion."

"Believe me I don't feel much like a hero," came Wolfram's reaction, "Aren't heroes supposed to have some exceptional skills or something? My talents are quite meager."

"Heroine is not a word I'd use for me either," replied Vette, "Survivor might be a better handle. In fact, the whole idea sends shivers up my spine. Such a title comes with major responsibilities."

"Yah, I will go along with Vette's word of survivor," came Morgan's response. "As you were speaking Andrew some ancient heroes popped into my mind and in no way do I fit any such tales."

"Well, whether you believe it or not, to Bryce and I this whole adventure speaks of such," came Andrew's reply as he looked more intensely at them. "It matters little what the titles are, Bryce and I see the pattern, and it is there. Only time will tell how this unfolds. But mark my word you four, and the rest of us, have been chosen for something."

"We may get the first glimmer of this in the next few days," came Dylan's parting comment. "We've got a week before we depart. I shall carefully keep your comments in mind Andrew. As for me and my team, we will be delighted if we're all destined to spend the rest of our lives together whatever the mission."

The evening closed with each one retreating to his or her own suite their minds filled with unanswered questions and a mixture of thoughts about the future.

The House of Life

Wolfram sat with Dusky, waiting in the main concourse of the House of Life knowing Angi's training session with Myttrwn was about to end. Edgy, he was uncertain as to the outcome of his plan. Thinking to himself he pondered his strategy, "I've got a clear line on the elevator, I can't miss her. This is my best chance to talk to Angi before more time passes. I didn't expect to be so nervous. I'm just going to tell her how I feel...........Don't expect miracles, old boy, the age issue may not be the only problem." He had little time for further reflection when he spotted Angi and Skylar exiting the elevator. The speed of his response startled Dusky.

Angi, seeing Wolfram approaching, smiled saying, "I suppose you just happened to be in the building at this particular time of day?"

Not wanting to make light of the situation Wolfram replied honestly, "No, I've been sitting here waiting for you. I've been trying to get a chance to talk to you alone."

Sensing the determination in Wolfram's manner Angi replied, "Would you like to sit here in this busy thoroughfare or find a quiet spot somewhere outside?"

Wolfram loved Angi's directness and replied, "A quiet spot somewhere on the patio would be preferred."

"Then let's go," said Angi turning towards the exit. The dogs walked together in front of them, being admired by a group of students.

Finding a stone bench in a grassy alcove a distance from the main pathways of students and others, they sat down. The dogs sensing their mood, lay down.

Seizing the opportunity and not wanting to waste time with aimless conversation Wolfram began, "Angi I've hesitated saying much to you over the past months as we were rather focused on survival both on Earth and then here in Tir na nOg. I expect it was the journey through the pyramid that brought my feelings to a head. I was filled with guilt and heartache when you were almost killed in Chamber Seven. For a brief moment I thought I'd lost you. When you recovered I made my decision. Now, I'm not expecting you to respond but I wanted to let you know how I felt before our lives are again engulfed in another unexpected venture." Getting no reaction he pressed on, "Angi, I truly care about you and, if you agree, I would like to spend more time with you, just the two of us." In closing he thought to himself, "There, it has been said."

Angi could see he was struggling with his feelings and carefully replied, "Actually, Wolfram, I was wondering how I might tell you the same thing."

Stunned by her reply Wolfram blurted out, "You were thinking the same thing? That's incredible." All his misgivings started to melt away.

Angi continued, "Wolfram, these past few months have been the most extraordinary of my entire life. During this time I have come to rely on your steady, practical leadership and your compassion. I suspect your hesitation in making your feelings known earlier may have been clouded by some feeling about the difference in our age. But actually age means nothing to me and with Myttrwn's recent offer it will have no meaning at all. But in fairness, I also agree there has been little time for a personal life in the past months but we could make time when we get home. I'd like that."

Wolfram, exuberant, turned to Angi and replied, "So would I. Let's try for some time together even in the last few days in this enchanting kingdom. I could meet you here after your lessons. How about that?"

"Good, I'd like that, we could sit here and get to know each other better," said Angi, pleased the door had finally been opened.

"How long do you think we can keep this from the rest of the team?" asked Wolfram."

"Not long," replied Angi with a smile, "Our new family seems to know everything. Anyway I don't care. I've grown fond of you and I believe we deserve a chance at happiness. But I must tell you that you are going to be with a rather conservative nurse, one not prone to risk taking or emotional outbursts."

"Sure Angi," laughed Wolfram, "While that description may have once applied to a clone of Angi, it has little bearing on what I've witnessed over the last six months. I expect the full impact of your drastic evolution has not yet registered. Our universe has changed dramatically. You are now the sole proprietor of a magical medallion, an item of ancient complex technology which enables you to do unbelievable things. While you were hesitant at first, your skills have blossomed under the tutorage of Myttrwn. Besides that, you have been in conversation with spirits both on Earth and here in this kingdom. You are an amazing conundrum, a constant mystery, not only to myself but to the rest of our team if not this entire kingdom. To say you are unique would be an understatement of the highest order. But it is those features that endear me to you, where else would I find a treasure like you. But the world you left behind is no more, and the one we may be entering could be both exhilarating and fraught with problems. But whatever unfolds I want to share that with you. I'm sure none of us expect to return to our former lives, and I say that with a degree of sadness."

"Ah, I guess you are right, Wolfram," replied Angi with a sigh, "Somewhere in my deepest thoughts I wanted that old conservative life, it was comfortable and I knew the routines. You know, I really liked being a nurse and helping people. I expect that's gone no matter how hard I'd like it to be otherwise. I admit, I am still coming to terms regarding this medallion and all its so-called magic. I have difficulty envisioning myself as a magician or even a master of some ancient or futuristic technology. That's why I need you Wolfram, you can help me keep reality in check."

"Angi, I witnessed your caring during that pyramid ordeal and I do not think it is ending, it may just be getting restructured for a different assignment," relied Wolfram, trying to console both of them. "I'm glad you need me, that's a good start for believe me I need you. Life would be immensely empty without you. By the way some time ago I was thinking of our first meeting. That image of you popping into your grandmother's Bed and Breakfast living room from a morning run is forever etched on my brain, a tall girl with a beautiful blond braid and flushed cheeks. By the time we met again in Boston I was crippled and not expecting much in life. But you changed all that in Scotland when you healed my leg. That day I wanted to hug you but controlled the impulse. You have no idea how much that changed my life for I was able to once again think the unthinkable. I had a future, one I now would like to share with you."

"You first endeared yourself to me when I watched you struggle in the gym in Andrew's castle," said Angi, "You were so determined in strengthening every healthy muscle in your leg, a steeliness I admired. I am pleased that my initial medallion skills resulted in your disability being corrected. By the way, I hope Myttrwn when he recalibrates your age leaves that charming white streak in your hair, I rather like it."

"Then that will be one of my conditions before the process begins," replied Wolfram running his hand through his hair. "Myttrwn has always been most accommodating. Now this white streak will have a positive meaning when I see it each morning," as he relaxed with a broad grin.

"Also, Wolfram, I never thanked you properly for saving my life in Chamber Seven. Vette told me what you endured in getting my body away from the laser fire. That act proved to me you cared. I'm just glad you've finally verbalized it." Then shifting to a more serious tone she went on, "Wolfram you and I come from parents who went through a broken marriage even though our grandparents rescued us and gave us stability. Because of this I'd like to take our new relationship slowly if that's OK with you. As a child my parent's divorce left me with a great deal of sadness which was further complicated when I lost my mother a few years later. I've resolved much of this or I think I have. I've had boyfriends before but not a serious one. I regard you as a serious one."

"I like serious," replied Wolfram, grinning. "Angi, I'm so relieved I spoke up and am delighted with your reaction so you can take all the time you want. When we have a break back on Earth I'd like you to get to know my family.

My grandparents will be most insistent that we take over their antique business...........it will be hard for them to understand our new roles, ones which we have yet to discover. But basically they're good people, and will be glad there is a future for their grandson."

"I wish you had a chance to know my grandmother more," replied Angi, "She was a very special lady, but that's not possible," a feeling of sadness washed over her.

"I will get to know her through you, Angi, for I am sure she has made an indelible imprint on your whole being. Remember Myttrwn's session on positive thoughts, I'm sure it also applies to positive people," replied Wolfram, realizing Angi's loss was still raw being only months since her grandmother's death. Then a thought popped into his mind and he asked, "Angi is your father still alive?"

"I guess so," replied Angi startled by the question. "My paternal grandparents still live in New York. I've only been there once, a week before I began my university studies. My father went to California where, I think, he's been a medical doctor for some years. He's likely remarried and I may even have step siblings for all I know."

Wolfram proceeding cautiously not knowing how Angi felt about the situation, pressed on, "Would you like to meet him or them?"

"I never thought about it," replied Angi, with some hesitation. "He's my father, someone I haven't seen in twenty years but what memories I have are loving ones. It would be strange........but maybe," the thought lingering as she contemplated the possibility. "Would you help me?"

"I'd be glad to but we can talk about this again when we get back home," replied Wolfram, pleased to be able to help Angi. But the silence of twenty years registered as he thought to himself, "I wonder why her father never tried to contact his daughter in that length of time or did he rely on his parents to keep him informed. Strange."

"Have you thought about what we might say to Vette and Morgan?" asked Angi.

"Knowing them they'll likely know soon enough. Vette's so sharp she'll likely be asking questions when we get to this evening's meal." They both chuckled. Then Wolfram continued, "Actually, I think they're attracted to each other. Vette would be a good match for Morgan, he needs grounding at times. You know Angi both Vette and Morgan have become true friends over these months."

"Sometime I must tell you about the battle Vette and I had when we first met," said Angi with a grin.

"I can imagine you two clashing, your both strong willed," replied

215

Wolfram wondering what happened but also knowing they were now fast friends.

Angi continued, "But you are right, Vette and Morgan are the types of people I hope we have with us for a very long time. And what about the rest?"..........Angi stopped leaving the question unfinished.

"Let's cross each bridge when we come to it," said Wolfram, not caring. "Right now I would like to sit here and enjoy this moment." He was elated at the outcome. His future now had meaning. Then a sober thought entered his mind, "I'm not oblivious as to the complexities that may lie ahead. I pray that Angi's medallion doesn't keep attracting deadly admirers. But to hell with it, I will live with whatever comes..........I now have Angi. We can work this out together."

Angi sat contemplating the future as well, her thoughts racing," Thank God Wolfram finally said something, I was afraid he might leave it until we were back on Earth or never act. Isn't life amazing? I could never have expected this happening to me." In the joy of the moment she bent and kissed Wolfram on the cheek saying, "You have made this a truly memorable day for me."

"Me too," replied Wolfram, not wanting to add anything more to the occasion.

"Let's take a slow meandering route back to our residence," suggested Angi.

Wolfram took her hand as they headed to the House of Learning.

A figure stood at an upper window witnessing the blossoming of their relationship. Myttrwn smiled.

&

The House of Life

The day arrived. The team from Gaia were about to hear what lay ahead. Sirona had hinted at such the evening before when she announced they would be having a final session with Myttrwn the next day. As they made their familiar trek from the House of Learning to the House of Life they walked in silence lost in their own thoughts.

Sirona and Myttrwn were present when they arrived. They, like seasoned students, went directly to their familiar seats, silently noting the four extra chairs.

Myttrwn seemed relaxed as he began, "We've come a long way in three months, and I'm pleased with your achievement. But this is just a beginning.

This will be our last formal get together for this visit, but we shall have other meetings before you depart. Over the past months I have shared with you aspects of our kingdom so that you would understand where we were coming from. We have much to learn from each other. Angi has excelled in her training and at times has even amazed her teacher. But the medallion has many treasures yet to be revealed. An unexpected turn of events was Angi's contact with one of our Sages, Adawee. As highly evolved individuals, our Sages usually exist in a rainbow body, making it possible for them to slip between physical and spiritual worlds."

"That explains Adawee's rainbow feathers," stated Angi thinking out loud.

"Yes," replied Myttrwn, "And the spiraling rainbow lights when she appeared to us in the Council of Elders Chamber. Her arrival has heightened the importance of our venture. Such guidance is an unexpected gift and one that will bring both physical and spiritual blessings. It is most unusual to have one of our Sages appear in person, even if her initial contact with Angi was in the guise of a Snowy Owl. I expect Adawee will continue to contact Angi, both here and possibly on Earth." Then turning to Angi he added, "Angi, expect the unexpected."

"I understand," replied Angi, as she thought to herself, "Actually, the unexpected seems to be my normal these days."

Sensing the restlessness in the group Myttrwn continued, "I suppose you are anxious to know what lies ahead."

"Does it have anything to do with the Dwapara Yuga?" blurted out Morgan.

"Indeed it does, Morgan," replied Myttrwn, "What you may not know is that as the Earth leaves behind its Kali Yuga, it is also emerging from a form of quarantine, a designation which every planet endures when in its Kali Yuga."

"Quarantine.........Why a quarantine?" asked Andrew, surprised by the designation.

"Because, Andrew," replied Myttrwn turning towards him, "if you cannot live in harmony with each other on your own planet, you are a danger to the universe. At present, your world does not seem to know how to prevent or even effectively treat the disharmony which plagues so much of your planet. To remove the quarantine you will need to effectively address this problem."

"But Myttrwn, I've read in your history that you also had wars, and social and economic upheavals in the past," stated Bryce, recalling some of his archive research.

"You are right, Bryce, these occurred mainly in our own Kali Yuga," admitted Myttrwn. "At that time we too were blocked from returning to the universal family of planets until we corrected the situation."

A skeptical Dylan had to ask, "Are you telling us that local skirmishes never happen in your kingdom?"

"No, I'm not saying that, Dylan. When rogue states erupt into conflict we quarantine them just as you would any spreading disease. Once they correct their problem with or without outside help they are allowed to join the rest of our kingdom. Such exclusion is very unpleasant and most communities quickly learn prevention is far wiser. And before you ask, we do have individuals who flaunt the rules. This you have already experienced. There are strict laws in such cases. Like any disease, we know the debilitating effects of disharmony and strive to prevent its occurrence."

"Fascinating," thought Andrew and he was pressed to ask, "And Myttrwn you truly believe we are about to enter a more positive phase in our world?"

"Yes, but Andrew it will take time. Remember the Dwapara Yuga is scheduled to go on for thousands of years. You are at the entrance to this wonderful cycle," said Myttrwn. "It may seem impossible right now but I can assure you it is coming."

Slowly grasping the enormity of what Myttrwn was saying Angi asked, "Are you suggesting Myttrwn that our role is to somehow facilitate this transition. The healing of a patient is one thing, the healing of a planet is quite another matter."

"Ah Angi, as usual, you have intuitively grasped the objective. The objective is complex so we will have to piecemeal the task and will start with the people."

Andrew interjected, "Myttrwn, I am still unclear as to what this means for us. It is not that we're unwilling to do the impossible, but could you be a bit more specific."

Myttrwn could see the group was struggling and complied, "Let me elaborate. In our brief time together we have touched on a number of topics. The Dwapara Yuga is opening new doors for you to a physical universe of energy. The reality you thought existed has been redefined as a tightly packed form of energy or bodies of light which respond to vibrating energy and it exists all around you. This concept explains the interconnectedness of all things, or the Law of One as we identify it. Humanity and nature are One, what affects one affects the other. In concert with the Law of One, our students are instructed in the Sacred Science, a single body of scientific and spiritual thought. In your world all the sciences and anything spiritual seem to exist as separate entities a factor which restricts their effectiveness and reduces much of their understanding of ancient civilizations. In addition, the aim of our Sacred Science is the perfection of our existence not the aggrandisement of any one individual or group. Within its teachings there is an acceptance of cosmic mysticism, and an awareness that mystery and awe are part of our existence. We know that time and space can be altered something which four of your members have recently experienced. While our world differs from yours you have learned that we share a great deal in common. I do not expect your immediate acceptance of this information, just an awareness that another view is possible." Reading their thoughts he added, "You are still wondering where this is leading?"

"Having experienced Angi's skills in the pyramid, I have a personal awareness of your Sacred Science in action, but am still unclear as to what it means for us," said Wolfram. "I am willing to learn more if in the long run it helps to improve the welfare of our planet. I know this is going to take time but with your guidance we can do it," he stated with conviction.

"Time indeed," replied Myttrwn, "From this day forward I shall be pressing you to think in centuries not decades, and we shall measure success on a steady list of achievements, however small."

Vette had waited and decided it was time to say something, "Fair enough. All I can say is that I'm ready and will gladly follow whatever this team is commissioned to do. I like the idea of long term planning, it certainly beats the piecemeal version that currently reigns on our planet."

Myttrwn liked Vette's enthusiasm, loyalty and honesty which prompted him to say, "Let me again remind you as to what to expect in the Dwapara Yuga. In time, each one of you will not only be able to read minds telepathically but also read energy fields and know a person's past and present and the honesty of their statements."

"That is good news," replied Dylan, "We will then be on a level playing field. As for me, I'm still adjusting to the reality that everyone on this planet is telepathic. But then again, if everyone has the ability, I suppose you get used to it. I hope it comes on gradually so I can adapt. Myttrwn, I don't suppose you could narrow down the date of this transition?"

"I'm afraid not Dylan. But it will happen. As I said before, the signs of the Dwapara Yuga are already visible, your children are getting taller, your elders are growing older, you already have worldwide telecommunications and some are thinking of space travel."

"I sense we are still skirting the topic," replied Andrew, "What specifically do you see us doing in the coming months, Myttrwn?"

"Ah yes, the specifics," replied Myttrwn, catching Andrew's thoughts. "Well, first we will need to shift the gates. The Hill of Tara gate is too exposed and will need to be stored away for a spell while we erect a temporary gate beneath your castle in Scotland, Andrew." Almost on cue the door opened and Corb arrived with three companions, ones the team had already worked with, "And here is the field team who will return with you to address this. I believe you all know each other."

The four nodded to the group as they sat down in the vacant chairs.

Myttrwn continued, "Corb will be working with you in the next few days outlining his plans." Myttrwn sensed relief, a visible objective had finally appeared.

"That's good," replied Andrew, and he turned to ask, "Corb, have you any idea of how long this might take?"

"Depending on what we find, it should take about three to four months of your time," replied Corb confidently.

Andrew gasped, "That's incredible. I expected much longer."

Myttrwn looking into the future said, "When the gate in Scotland is operational, Sirona and I will come to your planet, this time for more detailed work." Myttrwn did not divulge the Queen's insistence that they oversee the project and continue with Angi's training.

Angi thought, "I knew he was thinking of coming to Earth. Great!"

This prompted Vette to ask, "Myttrwn, is there any chance our dogs can visit?"

With a broad grin, Myttrwn replied speaking to the whole group, "Have you noted that the four pyramid travellers now speak of 'our' dogs. I was hoping for bonding but the closeness of the robotic dogs and their owners is astonishing." Then turning to Vette he continued, "Andrew has already asked me about this Vette and I'm willing to consider it once we have the gate operational in Scotland. In the meantime your dogs will sit waiting and while they will not notice the lapse of time I'm sure you four will miss your companions."

"Yes we will," came Vette's reply speaking for the four, patting Rafie as she spoke.

"Can we explore some more specifics," asked Bryce following intently the discussions and looking forward to being useful when he returned to Earth.

"Very well," said Myttrwn, "In time we will need, with the help of yourself and Andrew to set up some type of organization which can operate legally within your laws. This I believe will be possible with the help of your many contacts.

"Yes," replied Bryce, "We have a great many individuals and groups who will be glad to assist us."

Myttrwn continued, "The services we will be considering must be rendered to humanity without cost and individuals must seek healing of their own free will. The curing of your people will include, but be not limited to, manipulating quantum energy to identify illness much earlier than is currently possible, creating light and sound treatment modules much like those you have already experienced, creating electrodynamic processes to return cells to their previously healthy state, protecting entire populations with electronic shields against communicable diseases, and restoring the planet's oceans, land and air. In addition, there will be periphery topics which we will be glad to share. The focus will be on creating a healthy and happy life for everyone."

"Any one of those topics could take a lifetime," replied Morgan recognizing the magnitude of what Myttrwn had so easily verbalized.

"Your right, Morgan. Our task will be to augment the Dwapara Yuga increased energy using our existing knowledge and expertise. I foresee years of fruitful engagement as we tackle these topics. I will be able to enhance your energies and decrease your aging, but even that has limits. It is good you are a group of twelve with more individuals waiting to join us back on Earth. You are awakening to a new era, one that will eventually bring peace, stability and economic justice to all. But having said that I do not expect it will happen without strife, for there are those who thrive on the negatives of the Kali Yuga, those who do not want peace, stability and a healthy population."

"I'm curious, Myttrwn, what does your planet get out of this?" asked Andrew.

Expecting the question, Myttrwn replied, "You may be unaware, but you have already brought us a great deal on your first visit to our kingdom. In the opening of the Gate of Tara you have neutralized a great deal of negative energy in both our planets. In addition to the delicious taste of bread, the courage of the four who survived a very difficult initiation, and your music, you have also engendered an energy which I have not seen in centuries. You have a unique way of addressing problems. In addition, there are other positives such as your musical orchestras which has instruments we have yet to play, and, I expect there are other unknowns to discover. This is not a one sided endeavour irrespective of what magical abilities you have witnessed in this kingdom."

"That is good to hear," replied Andrew, "This collaboration can help us evolve at a time when the Earth needs positive news."

"Your presence here has shown us that we can work together, and I hope you have found the same. We may be ahead of you in the grand cycle but that is good. In the great scheme of things the interconnectedness which I have referred to within your planet also applies to the universe, a future topic which we will explore at another time."

"And where does my medallion fit in," asked Angi, who was still unclear as to its purpose within this grand scheme.

"You will be leading the magical parade, Angi," replied a confident Myttrwn. "As you advance in the mastery of your medallion it will give comfort to your companions in their own magical abilities." And still sensing some uneasiness he continued, "I am aware you may not have enough details right now but I hope it is enough. Sirona and I will be working with you as we have done since you arrived in this kingdom. We will be available to answer your questions both here and back on Earth."

"With continued growth in this new venture and the guidance of both yourself and Sirona we will manage," said Andrew. "I have no doubt there will plenty of questions that's the hallmark of this team."

"In addition, Sirona and I are looking forward to your musical presentation in a couple of days. This will be a first for us. I hear Carola is working very hard with you for this presentation."

"Less than two more days of practice," thought Morgan to himself, "Are we going to be ready for a royal performance, we lost so much time in the pyramid and in the recovery period."

Myttrwn, just before bringing the session to a close telepathically shared a few thoughts with Sirona. "I'm going to miss this lively group. For the first time in ages I've been challenged not only with their constant questions but with training a student like Angi. It is good we're going to Earth, but what they do not know is our need to cope with so much verbal noise. We will have to schedule silent retreats." Myttrwn then said to the group, "Sirona and I will leave you now to talk with Corb and his team. I can assure you the future will be clarified once we're reassembled on Earth."

Wolfram had one more question, "By the way, Myttrwn when do you envision us returning to your kingdom?"

"Ah yes," replied Myttrwn, fully understanding Wolfram's question, "At the earliest, the next trip can't be programmed until Corb has set up the new gate in Scotland, and then you might want a different group to visit our kingdom. Is that any help?"

"It certainly is," replied a relieved Wolfram as he glanced at Angi.

Chapter 12

The Palace

Out of the blue Angi and Andrew were summoned to the Palace for a meeting with the Queen, no reason given. As they made their way up the hill they speculated on various possibilities but came to no conclusion. Accompanied by their Palace escort, they walked in relative silence to the Queen's private reception room.

Upon arrival they were greeted by Sirona, who was her usual friendly self but noncommittal as to the purpose of the meeting. Escorted into an open patio they discovered a long table with seven chairs. Myttrwn turned from speaking with the Queen giving them a warm welcoming nod. Sirona indicated which seats were reserved for them, and they, as was required, stood until the Queen was seated.

"We are expecting two more members to join us," said the Queen, "They should be along momentarily."

Within minutes two huge men entered the patio. Sirona rose to greet them. The taller of the two was more than seven feet in height, a powerfully built man with reddish hair and a somber expression. The shorter one by only inches had blond hair, a more athletic build and an outgoing demeanour.

"They must be family," thought Andrew as they hugged Sirona greeting her in Gaelic. Then bowing to the Queen they took the two empty seats waiting for them. "They must be Sirona's brothers, they match the description we have of their father."

To confirm his assumption Sirona turned to Angi and Andrew saying, "These are my two brothers." Pointing to the taller one, she continued, "This is Oengus Og my eldest brother and this is my second eldest, Bran Ai. Neither speak English so they will be using a translating device to understand our discussions. I will translate any of their comments."

In Gaelic, Sirona proceeded to introduce Angi and Andrew who, having learned from Sirona the basic Gaelic greetings of her kingdom, responded accordingly and reached out and shook the powerful hands of both men.

Sensing the importance of the occasion, Angi was left with her own thoughts, "Why just Andrew and me, why not the whole team? The Queen, Sirona and Myttrwn seem downright serious about something. In addition, the Queen wouldn't summon her two sons from other planets for anything trivial. But it is good to finally meet Sirona's brothers. They are certainly powerful individuals if size and presence mean anything. I wonder what's up. Have I done something to displease the Queen? That might explain why just Andrew and I were asked to attend. We're within days of leaving so I hope not. The suspense is unnerving."

Andrew's thoughts were on the same tack as he tried to fathom the purpose of the gathering, "It must be something of importance for the Queen to request her two sons to be present. Oh, if only I had their telepathic powers I would already know what this was about and eliminate the secrecy. Even Sirona and Myttrwn aren't revealing much."

The Queen, Sirona and Myttrwn knowing the thoughts of Angi and Andrew realized it was best to get on with the proceedings before speculation overcame reality.

"Because of the information which is about to be presented I am going to turn this meeting over to Myttrwn," said the Queen.

On that signal Myttrwn took charge saying, "Angi and Andrew, as you will recall when your group first arrived in this kingdom there was some delay in receiving clearance for you to move about. This slowness had a reason which we are about to reveal."

"Yes," replied Andrew, "I remember." He said little else wanting Myttrwn to proceed.

Myttrwn continued, "In our initial scanning of your DNA we discovered something odd in Angi's profile. Perhaps this would be easier to explain if you could see the data." With that he conjured up a large screen along a vacant wall which showed Angi's DNA results. "Now, I would like you to compare Angi's DNA with Sirona's." A second reading appeared below the first. And before anyone could respond, he added. "I would also like to add two more profiles, that of Sirona's two brothers."

Angi and Andrew stared at the information trying to make sense of what they were looking at.

Andrew spoke first, "Myttrwn I'm no expert in DNA data but am I seeing a similarity in all four DNAs?"

Angi, feeling an ache in her stomach, wanted to reject any such assumption, blurted out, "That's impossible." But as she re-examined the data she was forced to add, "But even if there are similarities, it is out of the question." Confused, she added, "I don't understand."

Andrew interceded, "I expect Myttrwn you have run numerous tests to confirm this?"

"Yes, Andrew," replied Myttrwn, "I can assure you I have run many tests and have discussed this at great length with the royal family members at this table. This was not a matter to be taken lightly."

Angi, feeling a cold shiver up her spine, pressed on, "But Myttrwn this can't be. You told us there has been no contact between our two planets in centuries. I come from fairly ordinary people with no evidence of royal or any other distinguished bloodline." She looked around the table trying to read the faces of how this information was being received by the royal family. Then a thought flashed into her mind, "Oh God, does this mean I can't return home? No, please God may it not be that."

The turmoil in Angi's mind registered with alarm in the minds of the Queen, Sirona and Myttrwn and prompted the Queen to respond, "Oh, my dear that is not the case." Then realizing Andrew was not telepathic, she explained, "Andrew, Angi thinks that this information may prevent her from going home. I wish to assure her that is not so. Angi we are here to share this information with you and chose Andrew, being one of your elders, to accompany you for this revelation. We just want to discuss the significance of this information."

Relieved, Angi asked, "Then Myttrwn can you explain how this can be. I'm completely lost."

"Angi, there are a number of signs which when pulled together, present an extraordinary message. Let me elaborate. First, you were the one chosen to wear this ancient medallion, having, as I told you before, a genetic pattern which prevented you from experiencing a grievous reaction. Next, you revealed that you may be in possession of the lost *Harp of Dana*, a great treasure from this kingdom. Our records indicate that it might turn up at this time. But, if true, it is not in our kingdom but on Earth, possibly a gift to an ancient Irish king who likely was an expert harp player. Somehow this reached you. Then, one of our Sages, Adawee, chose to appear to you, a great privilege in our kingdom. And finally I too discovered as your instructor that you possess an unfathomable inner ability in mastering the complexities of your medallion which I have yet to understand. These coupled with this DNA data told me that you are certainly an anomaly, one chosen at this time as a possible link between our two worlds. Such signs add great justification to our venture. In my extended life, I have discovered that on rare occasions we are gifted with such unexplainable symbols to let us know that we are not entirely in control. However astonishing this list of marvels, the cosmos is confirming that this is the time for our two worlds to proceed and you are its linchpin."

"But could these signs be just coincidental?" asked Angi.

"One might be a coincidence, two at the most, but not all," replied

Myttrwn, "The probabilities are just too great."

Andrew realizing the uniqueness of Myttrwn's list propelled him to ask, "Myttrwn, have you ever encountered anything like this before?

"Just once, some centuries ago," replied Myttrwn, "And at that time it was an older man." Myttrwn was hoping that Andrew wouldn't ask the next obvious question as to who this individual was or what he became. He was rescued by Angi's question.

"I suppose one might be pressed to ask, why me?" asked Angi.

Myttrwn was quick to reply, "That's a question you might ask Adawee when next you meet. The answer to this needs to come from a much higher source than myself."

Angi didn't wish to be impolite but had to ask, "Myttrwn, if my DNA is similar to this royal family, what does it mean for me?"

Sirona smiled, "It means that you and I are family Angi and for me that's a delightful revelation."

Sensing Angi's anxiety, Oengus Og felt it was his place to say something and signaled to Sirona for her help. Sirona translated his comments. "Angi, we don't understand how this has transpired, nor do we question Myttrwn's tests. They are simply true. So, accepting this reality I am pleased to welcome you into this family. We have taken considerable time to review and digest this information, but the signs are clear. We make no demands on you as we expect there will be plenty of work for you to do in the years to come. It is to our benefit to have a family member on Earth."

Then Sirona translated Bran Ai's comments. "I also welcome you, Angi." Then with a grin he added, "But I have a separate question. Where did you learn to master a throwing stick like you did in your pyramid journey which we have recently watched?"

Not expecting the question, Angi was glad for a diversion, "In my early education system I belonged to what we call a sports track team. There I learned to not only compete in running events against those of my own age but also to compete in throwing events such as a javelin, your throwing stick, as well as a shot, discus, hammer and weight."

"You are very good at this," replied Bran. "Perhaps when I learn more English we can talk again at greater length. I've also learned you play the harp. We shall be attending your performance tomorrow."

"I'm a bit rusty at harp playing right now and will do my best tomorrow. I like playing the harp but realize I must practice more."

Then it was time for the Queen to respond, saying, "Angi, I am pleased to welcome you into our family, having accepted the cosmic symbols as outlined by Myttrwn. You have shown yourself to be a responsible and capable representative of your planet. Adawee, one of our Sages, has also confirmed this. I am also delighted that you, Sirona and Myttrwn will be continuing your relationship as we create a long standing partnership between our two planets. I want to again make it clear that this information does not impede your travel between our planets, instead it greatly enhances it."

Andrew sat in amazement contemplating this latest revelation and thought to himself, "Angi never ceases to surprise me. I must acknowledge there are mysteries in this universe that have no easy explanation. This young woman, who I met just months ago, has gently opened doors to a fantastic world not only because of that medallion she wears, but now, somehow, by her genetic profile, both unexplained miracles. Myttrwn's statement yesterday *'expect the unexpected'* also applies to Angi herself. I could never have imagined this trip or any of its unexpected turns. I've been blessed tenfold." Then a thought compelled him to ask, "Myttrwn, if Angi and Sirona have similar DNA can Sirona also wear the medallion?"

Myttrwn had hoped this question would not arise but answered, trying not to reveal anything about Angi's vibrational profile, "I expect not," came his reply, "While they appear similar there are subtle differences." He gave Andrew a glance to indicate that it would be best to stop there.

"I see," said Andrew, receiving Myttrwn's non-verbal signal which caused him to wonder, "So there is more. I wonder why it is being held back. More mystery. I will not press it at this point, as Angi is already struggling with this DNA information." Instead, he changed the topic and asked, "Myttrwn, are there any restrictions in letting our team know about this DNA information?"

Myttrwn glanced at the Queen, who responded.

"I see no reason why not," replied the Queen. "I shall let it be known to our Council of Elders right after this meeting. We had to be sure of the facts and needed time for our family to discuss the implications. Myttrwn has a record of all the tests and will have this information available for our Elders. The kingdom will know by tomorrow morning."

The earlier unease had shifted to one of relaxed cheerfulness. More time was taken up with friendly chatter as the group got to savour this unexpected change in their lives. Angi was beginning to relax by the end of the meeting.

Once they returned to the House of Learning Andrew called the team together. They quickly assembled as they too were curious as to why Angi and Andrew had been summoned to a special meeting with the Queen.

Andrew first informed them that Sirona's two brothers would be in the audience at their presentation saying, "You can't miss them. They are both powerfully built men and will be sitting in the royal section of the theatre."

"Was that the only reason you were invited to the Palace?" asked Dylan.

"No, replied Andrew, "The main reason was about Angi." Then he divulged the details of the DNA data, the discussions and the outcome.

There was a moment of disbelief as the team absorbed the significance of the revelation.

Wolfram, the first to respond, said, "Angi, you are a treasure trove of mystery and it appears the cosmos agrees." Then turning to the group he added, "Let's take this opportunity to raise a toast to Angi, who is not only our inspiration for this wondrous venture but continues to open new vistas."

The team raised their mugs and glasses in a toast to Angi, all adding their own congratulatory comments on the raised status this information gave to their mission.

Wolfram sensing Angi's stress, took the earliest opening to whisk her away to a private spot where they could be alone.

"Oh Wolfram, I'm beginning to feel shell-shocked," came a moan from Angi. "Too many changes in too short a time. Just hold me before I scream."

"I'd be delighted," as he pulled her close and wrapped his strong arms around her. "As your shining knight I am honoured to be holding a true princess."

"Please, Wolfram, let's not go there," said Angi, in a whisper.

Wolfram gently spoke as he held her, "Angi, remember what I said to you before. Whatever unfolds we will face it together. Let this drift past. On a positive note this information will draw this kingdom and Earth closer together and that's good for all concerned." Wolfram continued to hold Angi knowing that life had just revealed another cosmic secret. Was there more to come?

$\wr$

The Royal Theatre

The morning of their musical program was spent in practice, Carola pulling out every musical director's trick to help them achieve their best performance. She had accomplished miracles given the brevity of practice time and the mixture of musical talent in the group. They left the practice in high spirits.

In the early afternoon they accompanied the harpists to the Royal Theatre, each carrying his or her own musical instrument. The day, like most days of their time in Tir na nOg, was clear with a gentle breeze, the sun dancing off the gold, silver and gemstones on some instruments. They walked up the hill chatting happily. The group from Gaia knew this would be their gift to the kingdom, a token of gratitude for all they had learned.

They were the first to arrive at the theatre and took their seats in the

Orchestra. Carola had arranged those performing the Gaia musical piece to be seated in the center of the musicians with the school harpists on either side. The performers sat and watched the audience proceed to their prescribed seats. The rest of their Gaia friends waved as they took their seats in a back row of the royal section.

Watching the activities Angi thought to herself, "It has been years since I've performed before an audience and this is certainly a more daunting event than any in my childhood. But we are ready, or as ready as we will ever be, thanks to Carola's efforts. She molded this program like someone composing a fine painting. All we have to do is to follow her directions and play our instruments to perfection, not a simple task. I wonder if this is what Mr. Aucoin meant when he said I would be playing my harp for the Lords of Anu.........I still do not know what that meant. Perhaps I will learn in time." Then her thoughts wandered, "Isn't it amazing, how quickly one adapts to another environment, and in this case, another world. It was good there were some similarities. Nevertheless, this is not Earth and the differences have pressed us to rethink some features of our own world. I shall miss the polite manners of these students and the wise and confident advice of Sirona and Myttrwn. I know we shall be together again but this has been a positive segment of my life. I am still uneasy about my raised status but, I will adapt...........eventually. Gran was right, life is full of mystery. I began this journey practically alone and within months have acquired two families, one on Earth and another in Tir na nOg. In addition, Wolfram and I have found each other, which has given me strength to face the future. All in all, it speaks of a wise and gentle hand guiding my journey. Now that's a topic I must take up with Adawee when next we meet. I realize there's a great deal of my invisible world that I know little about."

Two rows back sat Andrew, Morgan and Wolfram. As Wolfram watched the Royal retinue approach their seating section he commented in a whisper, "As you said Andrew, Sirona's two brothers definitely stand out, they are huge men. I wonder if we will get to meet them before we leave."

"Yeh," replied Morgan, following Wolfram in hushed tones, "Then we will have met the key members of the royal family. You know, Angi's change of status has raised some tantalizing questions."

"Morgan, tread gently," came a whispered command from Andrew, "We've entered rarified territory where the rules need to be clarified before blundering forth."

"I hear you, Andrew," replied Morgan, still whispering, "I will hold my inquisitiveness until a more suitable hour and, of course, after wise council from yourself," he added with a chuckle.

Andrew and Wolfram glanced at each other and smiled, Wolfram saying quietly to Andrew, "That'll be a first. But you never know Andrew, miracles do happen." Their chatting ceased when the audience settled down. As was the custom, the commencement of any theatre program was signaled when the royal party was seated.

At that moment, Carola, assuming the role of Master of Ceremonies, stood, tapped the lectern to silence the chatter of the performers and turned to speak to the audience. "Today, it is my pleasure to welcome Her Royal Highness, members of the royal family, and representatives of the Council of Elders, guests, and students and graduates of the House of Learning to a very special presentation." Then, completing the introduction she proceeded to give a few details of the program.

"This afternoon's program consists of two separate events; first there will be a musical performance followed by a special presentation by Her Royal Highness." Continuing she went on, "The musical segment will have two short pieces; first the harpists will be playing a composition which has not been heard in many years, one a few may recognize. This will be followed by a musical selection chosen by our Gaia guests. The type of music they will be playing is referred to as a jig. As I've been told, the jig is a common form of dance music performed in 6/8 time. Jigs can be fast and lively and performed by different instruments including the harp. The titles of the two selections are Keegan's Jig and Lannigan's Ball, which will be played as a single piece. I also wish to bring to your attention that we, for the first time, will be playing different musical instruments for this number, ones created through the assistance of our guests and our replication technology. These instruments will be left for us when our guests leave. I ask that you hold your applause until both musical pieces have been completed." Completing this brief description she bowed and turned to face the musicians.

In unison, the harpists began softly, the sound rising and falling as it soared up to the highest seats in the theatre. The haunting and uplifting melody tugged at the emotions pulling the audience along an intoxicating wave of scintillating music with hints of unthinkable treasures in some forgotten kingdom. The piece was short and ended abruptly leaving the listeners craving for more.

The audience waited silently in anticipation for the next musical offering.

As practiced, the Tir na nOg harpists supplied an entrance to the Gaia musical program, then faded as the Gaia musicians plus Bran and Togu on drums, launched into the two jigs. The lively music with odd instruments surprised the audience but soon they joined in, keeping time with their feet or fingers. The two young drummers, delighted at their newfound musical experience, wove a mesmerizing drum beat in and around the music of the violins, guitar and harps. When it ended the musicians smiled, pleased their performance went off without a hitch.

The audience was enchanted with the unusual musical treat and awarded all performers with a resounding round of applause.

Carola shone with happiness. Everything had gone as planned. She had opened an innovative musical door for the school. She had little time to relish her accomplishment because, knowing the next part of the program belonged to the Queen, she bowed and left the stage.

The clapping ceased when the Queen rose and walked down to the Orchestra with several members of her family and attendants. She opened the second part of the program with, "This musical performance is a fine example of all that is positive about our return to Gaia after many long years of silence. I would like to thank all our musicians for their effort especially our Gaia guests for providing us with the taste of their spirited dance music. We hope to hear more in the days and years ahead." Then turning to a more serious note she continued, "As you know, within days we shall be bidding farewell to our guests from Gaia. This inaugural visit has gone reasonably well." It was best to bypass the pyramid episode on such an occasion. She went on, "The transportation gates between our two worlds will be opening and we will be welcoming other selected groups in the future. I'm certain most of this inaugural group will be frequent visitors. We have already learned a lot from each other and hope to share more. As is our custom, when guests are leaving we present them with a small token of their time in our kingdom. On this occasion, it shall be slightly different. It is the decision of our Council of Elders and myself that we shall provide a Tir na nOg Badge to our guests to mark their first visit." Then speaking to the audience she added, "If you activate your viewers you will be able to see this presentation in more detail. I would now ask all our Gaia guests to come forward."

While the Gaia musicians laid down their instruments on their seats and stepped forward, their cohorts who had been sitting in the audience, rose and made their way down to the Orchestra. Sirona and Myttrwn began arranging the members in a semi-circle, positioning Angi, Vette, Wolfram and Morgan at the head of the line, followed by Andrew and Bryce and then the rest.

Two attendants with closed boxes positioned themselves to the left of the Queen in readiness for the ceremony.

There was silence as the Queen opened the first box which contained the first six metal badges, the serpent circles trimmed in gold glistening in the sunlight. The badges had identical serpent symbols with different precious stone backgrounds.

The Queen brought out the first badge and stepped towards Angi saying, "It is my pleasure, Angela Jenesis Talismann, known to us as Angi, to present to you this Royal Purple Tir na nOg Badge, as by now the kingdom is aware you have been accepted as a member of the royal family." Smiling, she said as she placed the badge on Angi's left shoulder, "Angi, this badge will henceforth recognize your royal status within our kingdom of planets."

Angi, taken aback by such an honour, noted the badge held fast without apparent pin or clasp. She shook the Queen's hand saying, "Thank you, Your Majesty, I am truly honoured." She couldn't think of anything more appropriate to say. It would now be difficult to dodge her raised status as she was in possession of a similar badge to that of Sirona and Myttrwn, a somewhat daunting attainment.

Then the Queen turned to the next three speaking first to the audience, "As you are aware these four individuals, including Angi, successfully completed a most arduous initiation in our pyramid, retrieving the crystals, as required. And for that we have decided the next three individuals should be awarded the blue Tir na nOg Badge." She then turned and taking out a serpent badge with a blue gemstone background saying, "Yvette Celine Gallant, known to us a Vette, I present to you our blue Tit na nOg Badge. This badge will give you the proper status you deserve in our kingdom of planets." Then after shaking Vette's hand she moved on to Wolfram saying, "Wolfram Maddison Stark, known to us as Wolfram, I present to you our blue Tir na nOg Badge. This badge will give you the proper status you deserve in our kingdom of planets." Following a few words and shaking Wolfram's hand she moved on to Morgan saying, "Morgan Hercule Mandelthrope, known to us as Morgan, I present to you our blue Tir na nOg Badge. This badge will give you the proper status you deserve in our kingdom of planets." Each one thanked the Queen as the badge was placed on their left shoulder. The three realized that they were now the proud recipients of a badge usually given to the more advanced students of the House of Learning.

As the Queen prepared to address the rest of the team members she again turned to the audience saying, "It was decided that we would create a special badge for distinguished visitors to our kingdom. You will note that this badge has an amber gemstone backing, a first for Tir na nOg." Then turning to the rest of the team she proceeded to give each one an amber Tir na nOg Badge saying to each one, "This badge will be recognized throughout our kingdom of planets and identify you as a special friend of the royal family."

As the Queen was proceeding with the dispensing of badges, the rest of the royal family, including Myttrwn, followed in procession shaking the hand of each recipient and chatting briefly. Sirona, translating for her two brothers, talked to each one as they made their way along the line. Later the Gaia team would share their amazement at how much the two brothers knew about each individual.

The presentation took time, all the while the audience sat in silence, conversing telepathically.

As the event was drawing to a close, a rainbow suddenly appeared over the theatre, created out of a cloudless sky. It lingered for a spell and then evolved into a huge bird in flight, after which the bird fluttered its wings and flew off.

The audience, looking up, pointed to the unexpected apparition knowing full well what it meant.

"That's Adawee," thought Angi, pleased that her exalted friend was part of this important ceremony, "She's blessing the occasion."

"Indeed she is," replied Myttrwn standing nearby having read Angi's thoughts. "As I said Angi, 'expect the unexpected.' The rainbow is Adawee's symbol. She is letting us know that she is watching over you and is indeed giving this ceremony her blessing."

The theatre emptied in its usual orderly fashion, the other musicians taking time to congratulate their fellow musicians over their achievement.

The Queen invited the Gaia team back to the Palace. The rest of the afternoon was filled with refreshments and further discussions on their visit, music, musical instruments and the future. The Gaia team would not have time to examine their badges until they were back at their residence. It was then the honour of the occasion fully registered. Within three months they had become part of the Tir na nOg kingdom, the ordeal with Zolar bringing them closer. As they examined the badges they were spellbound by the artistry and complexity. These were no ordinary badges but advanced technology which only Myttrwn could decipher.

"My guess," said Dylan with a grin, "Is that with these badges Myttrwn can now track us anywhere in the universe."

"Great," said Andrew, "We're going to need all the help we can get."

"I note that none of you have mentioned the unexpected arrival of the rainbow bird at the ceremony. I know it was Adawee, but I'm still struggling with that aspect of this venture," said Vette giving a pleading look at Angi.

Angi responded, "Vette, there are so many facets of this journey that defy understanding that I expect most of us are still wrestling with at least one, two or more. As for me, I've decided to handle each day, or each mystery, as it pops up because I know this is just the beginning. This has been a fantastic adventure, one that has given us new relationships, and an unbelievable future with lots of work. I will go with that for now."

"On that note, and it is a very positive note indeed, I will bid you good night," said Andrew. The others followed, weary after a long day of output and lofty events.

 R

The Houses of Life & Learning plus Return to Earth

Frustration mounted as each one tried, without success, to remove the Tir na nOg Badge from their clothing. In the end they had to get Myttrwn's help. Now that he was in charge of both Houses, he was often in their building. Once contacted he agreed to come to their morning meal.

With a wide grin he entered their eating area the next morning saying, "I hear you are having trouble disengaging from your badges. For a fleeting moment I forgot you weren't familiar with these items. Let me demonstrate how easy this is. Angi would you please come forth to help me."

Angi rose and went to stand next to Myttrwn.

"For the first time you will need to use your thoughts to operate this badge. It is simple but requires your full attention. Angi I want you to focus your thoughts on your badge, visualize yourself removing the badge from your blouse."

The moment Angi followed Myttrwn's instructions her badge released itself from her blouse and fell to the floor.

"That's it," said Myttrwn, "Now I'd like you all to do the same. And then I want you to reverse the process and re-establish the badge back onto your clothing. These badges are always worn on the left upper chest."

As instructed, a few taking several attempts, the team soon achieved the removing and reapplication of their metal badges.

Andrew took the opportunity to ask, "While you are here, Myttrwn, could you give us some information on these badges? They look more complicated than any badges we're familiar with on our planet."

"Ah yes, they are," replied Myttrwn. "These badges are advanced technology which I've simplified for now. The badge is programmed to your DNA so no one can use it but you."

"If that's the case, how did the Queen distribute these badges yesterday?" asked Wolfram.

"The badges are designed to allow the Queen this temporary transfer capability, but once it is attached to a recipient it becomes permanently linked to his or her DNA," replied Myttrwn, realizing he would not have time to address even the simple complexity of their badges before their departure.

"What happens if it gets lost?" asked Morgan.

"If it occurred in this kingdom I have a special device to find it," replied Myttrwn. "But if that occurs on your planet it would present a real problem." Then he thought of something, "But just a minute. Angi, I'd like to try an experiment. Would you go into your suite, wait five minutes and return?"

"Sure," replied Angi, and she left.

Once he was sure she was out of hearing range, Myttrwn turned to

Morgan and whispered, "Take your badge and place it at the back of that far counter."

Morgan did as instructed.

When Angi returned Myttrwn asked, "Angi,I want you to go into a deep but brief meditation and try to visualize Morgan's badge, which is now supposed to be lost. Tell me, if you can, where the badge is located?"

Angi did as directed and to her surprise Morgan's badge instantly came into view. When she emerged from her meditation she described the exact hiding place.

"There Morgan," replied Myttrwn, pleased that his idea worked so well, "You have your own tracking system in Angi. If, and I hope this is a rare occurrence, a badge is lost then ask Angi to locate it." And smiling he added, "Angi, you seem to have an endless supply of fascinating skills in addition to your medallion. More mysteries I've yet to fathom."

"Vette, then asked, "What happens if someone gets a hold of one of these badges and tries to dismantle it to learn how it operates?"

"In that case, Vette, the badge is programmed to recognize the intruder is not the owner and the system self-destructs. At that point you will need to contact me and I will have to create a new badge for you," replied Myttrwn.

Hearing this, Dylan was pressed to ask, "Myttrwn, how powerful are these devices?"

Myttrwn knowing Dylan's thoughts, replied, "I've programmed each one at its lowest level, Dylan, for your own safety. In time I will increase the capabilities but I must be sure you are ready. More training will be required. And to answer your earlier question, I could track you if I wanted to but I do not need to. I will explain more when I get to your planet. At this stage the badges are more decorative than operational. Does that quell your uneasiness for now?"

"Sure, just curious," replied Dylan, "And thanks for the tracking answer." He appreciated Myttrwn's skills, honesty and administrative carefulness, they would advance only when ready, a policy he respected. Then he thought to himself, "Likely this was a last minute decision of the Council after much argument. We're preparing to leave their planet so it would be impossible to get us trained in time. But it is tempting to speculate on what this tiny device can really do. Nothing is simple in this kingdom."

"While I'm here, I need to make sure you are ready for your physical readjustment scheduled for tomorrow," stated Myttrwn. It was agreed they would all receive the treatment, the majority to be at twenty-five years of age and the two elders at fifty. "I will meet you in my lab at nine o'clock your time tomorrow morning. I will start with the oldest and proceed to the youngest in your group. Expect an energy burst which might last for twenty-four hours. Angi, will you keep a check on the team and let me know if there are any untoward reactions. I expect none but one must always be careful." And on that note he left them discussing their upcoming transformation.

The next day was a skittish one for most as their bodies adjusted to the regained energy of being younger, a response which presented itself in different ways.

Returning from the House of Life Angi laughed as she watched Wolfram take spurts of running interrupted with dancing around her as they made their way across the plaza. "You are certainly cheerful," she said, pleased with his jovial behaviour. "Myttrwn's elixir has created some amazing outcomes. I guess I did not have the same reaction because of my small adjustment. I will just share your joy."

Wolfram walked back to join her with a giddy reply, "That's fine with me my Angi girl, you can share whatever you want," he said with a wink. "You know, I don't believe I've ever felt so light headed even after a good party. I should have leaped at this when we first arrived."

"Yes, even Andrew is skipping around like a teenager. While Bryce is fighting it he is still showing telltale signs of great happiness over his rejuvenation. I wonder when we get home if the others will notice any difference," said Angi, suddenly realizing their departure time was rapidly approaching.

Calming, Wolfram replied, "I'm sure my grandparents will be so glad that we've returned in one piece that it will take days before they notice anything," said Wolfram, getting onto Angi's wavelength. "And then I will tell them all about us and any questions regarding physical anomalies will completely disappear. For the first time in years they will realize the Stark and Harrison family lines may have a future, something that was dubious after my accident." Then thinking of his family he went on, "However, now that I think about it, taking a leap through a shimmering curtain into another world may not be to their liking. But you never know. My grandmother is the adventurous one and if she decides on doing it, Tyloar will be right behind her. He's all bluster and storm but when it comes to his family he'll do anything. It was that solidity that saved me as a boy. As for the others, I have no idea what they will do, but we will let them decide. Perhaps when the gate is anchored in Andrew's castle they'll feel different. Angi, just think of the tales we will have to tell in the weeks ahead."

"You know Wolfram," commented Angi, "we're not really saying goodbye to Tir na nOg. I expect we will be coming back and forth in the years ahead. I know I am going to have a million questions to ask Sirona and Myttrwn when I am back in Scotland. I realize there will be communications between us in the next three months but no time for my endless list of questions."

"Well, Angi, however the historical records of our planet describe this venture, for me it has been a momentous trip in more ways than one. Unfortunately, for all the obvious reasons we will have to remain silent on this to prevent unorthodox calamities. Not that Myttrwn and company could not neutralize any unwanted intrusions. We must walk cautiously from this point onward. Thank heavens we have Andrew and Bryce with all their senior experience and contacts, we will need this if this is to succeed."

"Are you packed yet, Wolfram?" asked Angi.

"Just about, not that there's much to pack, we travelled light. Oh, by the way, Myttrwn asked if I would leave behind my sneakers. I expect he sees them as a better replacement for their boots when visiting the Earth. Their replicators can create a pair in no time. I will be going home in the boots I wore in the pyramid."

"In that case, I will leave a pair of mine as well. Female sneakers are slightly different," replied Angi.

Laughing and chatting merrily they entered the House of Learning heading straight to their residence area to confer with their teammates on their exit plans.

The day finally arrived for their departure from Tir na nOg. Together they made their way to the Transportation Gate in the House of Life in their ordinary clothes each with a small travel bag. Sirona and Myttrwn were already waiting. Corb and his team entered shortly behind them dressed in identical clothes and carrying two bags each, one larger than the other.

Smiling, Corb responded to their unspoken question, "When you were enjoying yourselves in the pyramid, Myttrwn, who never misses an opportunity, had your clothes replicated so we would blend in when we travelled to your planet."

Morgan couldn't resist, "I suppose your second bag contains some kind of technology for the work on the gates?"

Remaining silent on specifics, Corb replied, "Yes, something like that."

Myttrwn interceded, "To accomplish the work in the timeframe set by Corb, we will need more advanced technology. Once the task is completed this technology will be returned to this kingdom. It is complex and may be shared at a later date." Then receiving Andrew's thoughts he added, "Be assured, Andrew, there will be no danger to your planet. Corb will explain more when you are back in Scotland."

Trusting Myttrwn and Corb, Andrew nodded his head. Corb had already provided much detail on what had to be accomplished at the Hill of Tara and Andrew's castle, engineering feats of immense intricacy.

The time of their leaving and arrival on Earth had been confirmed over a much improved communication link between Tir na nOg and Earth some days before. The weather was expected to be overcast and cool, being the end of October. It was agreed that a dawn arrival would be best.

Standing waiting, Bryce commented on the travel date, "Did you know that our return is set on a rather auspicious date? October thirty-first on our current calendar, is the time of the old Celtic festival of Samhain, often translated as 'summer's end'. It was a solemn and reverent time, filled with magic, and sometimes referred to as the Celtic New Year. It was a time when, it was said, the veil separating our world from the otherworld was temporarily opened. Some thought it was dangerous to be out on that night because it was the one night when the dead come out of their graves to dance with the fairies on the hills. In older times it was thought dead heroes came forth to help those in distress."

Morgan picked up saying, "It is perfect, Bryce, I like the Celtic connection. As I see it this is indeed a New Year in many ways. And the Gate of Tara, if seen by others, would definitely give many the feeling of a veil opening between worlds. I wonder if that was the origin of those ancient tales. But, these days it is unlikely that anyone seeing the Gate of Tara floating in the air will make the connection with Samhain. Few know much about ancient Celtic traditions."

"If they did see the Gate they will likely think it is some kind of elaborate Halloween stunt," said Vette. "As for me, I pray we arrive silently and unobserved. We'd have one gigantic headache if the media stumbled onto this."

"Not likely," replied Andrew, "It is fall and the weather is cool. Most Halloween events will be scheduled for later in the day and there are few tourists at this time of year, anyway that's what we're counting on."

"Nevertheless," intercepted Sirona, "We will have two of Corb's crew go ahead to secure the site with the same invisible shield as we used before."

Curious, Angi asked, "Are we travelling with escorts on our return trip?"

Sirona replied, "Yes, Angi, we have arranged the same escort service and, as before, I will be travelling with you." Upon saying that a group of familiar Tir na nOg individuals appeared in field uniforms ready for the transfer. They too wanted the experience of entering another planet.

As they were lining up to exit, the Queen and several of her chief Council Elders arrived. The Queen stated in a formal yet friendly manner, "I wanted to be here myself to bid you farewell. This has been an auspicious visit, and one that will not likely be excelled in some time. Perhaps one day I too will visit your planet with my sons. In the meantime I will be kept up-to-date by Sirona and Myttrwn. Please give our regards to your families and other colleagues whom we hope to meet in the future."

Each member of the team thanked the Queen and shook her hand as a last farewell to her kingdom.

Before entering the shimmering curtain of the Tir na nOg Gate, everyone also made sure to thank and shake the hand of their mentor, Myttrwn, knowing that his wise council would be with them for the rest of the journey.

The sequence of their entrance to the Gate was almost identical to their arrival, with Corb and his team leading the group and Sirona and Angi being the last in line.

As planned, they arrived at the Hill of Tara, to a cold blast of morning mist, a decided contrast from the sunshine of Tir na nOg. Their colleagues were waiting with warm jackets for everyone. The darkness was ameliorated by some light from the Serpent Gate of Tara and special devices provided by two of Corb's attendants. In the distance, barely visible in the morning mist they could see the lights of two buses for their transport to the Dublin airport. The Tir na nOg members took time to look around and get familiar with at least one site on Earth, although the mist was obstructing any distant view. Angi and Sirona's arrival marked the completion of the transport process.

Sirona standing next to Angi began her farewell, "Angi, I feel we've known each other for ages. I'm so glad we're now family. We will have much to share in the years ahead. I have lived to this age without a sister, this is a novel experience for me."

Angi turned and asked, still unsure of the protocol of such matters, "If we're family, is it permissible for me to give you a goodbye hug?"

"A hug," replied Sirona, searching through her vast memory bank, and smiling said. "Ah yes, that would be acceptable for a family member."

The two hugged each other, which came as a surprise to the other Tir na nOg members, and designated Earth as on a special relationship with their kingdom.

"We must leave now," said Sirona as a command to the Tir na nOg team.

Bidding their final farewells, they waved goodbye as Sirona and the Tir na nOg escorts entered the glistening curtain of the golden Serpent's Gate. And as before, to those standing on the hill, the gate suddenly evaporated taking the invisible protective shield with it.

Andrew made quick introductions of Corb and his crew to Dylan's backup team who were fascinated at the height of the four individuals. In the gray morning light, the small party made their way down the hill through the mist towards the waiting buses.

The next phase of their incredible adventure was about to begin.

ß

In the mist of the Hill of Tara

The spirits had waited, the gate activity alerting them that the three months had passed.

"Wake up, Wake up my fine young scholars," cried Imergin, the ancient Druid Seer. "Behold, they have returned. Just look at that magnificent Gate of Tara floating in space. Our waiting time is over." The spirit of Imergin and his students had been allowed to remain on earth for this momentous event.

The students stood admiring the Gate, watching the individuals exit, two-by-two.

Excited Imergin stated, "Take a look, they are all wearing Tir na nOg Badges. That is quite an achievement on a first visit. Oh, to be party to their stories. Something miraculous has happened. Look..........look..........at the female called Angi, she is wearing a Royal Badge. That is exceptional. She is now a member of the royal family. My sons, whatever doubts we may have had on their departure, they are returning with amazing credentials. The '*coming times*' now have their chosen candidates whether they know it or not."

"And what is our role?" asked an older student.

"We hang around my boy until the gods decide otherwise," replied Imergin. "I'm more than convinced that the call will now go forth to all former champions of wisdom, visible and invisible, to come to the rejuvenation party. We have all prayed for this day and it has finally arrived. There will be work for all, and mighty battles to be fought, for the Dwapara Yuga is about to blossom and we are going to aid the gardeners. All aspects of the Kali Yuga will be swept away. The candle of enlightenment has been lit, and it will grow stronger with each passing day. Come, we must prepare ourselves for the honour of the task before us."

The End

www.ingramcontent.com/pod-product-compliance
Lightning Source LLC
Chambersburg PA
CBHW080726020726
47503CB00010B/2809